"I think [...]
ag [...]

"Th-that's absurd. [...]
asked again.

"Call it curiosity. It's clear you are involved in some very dangerous dealings, and I can't help but wonder why. Lord Dudley is not a good choice of friends."

"Good God, he is *not* a friend," she croaked.

His hands moved up to frame her face. "Perhaps you need one."

Need. Her whole body was suddenly all aquiver. "Oh, I wish...I wish—"

A kiss feathered over her lips, lightly at first, but the sweet friction sparked a fierce flare of heat inside her. All sense—all sanity—seemed to go up in smoke.

Moaning against his mouth, Sophie clutched at his strong, sloping shoulders and let her body melt against his. Beneath the finespun layers of cloth, she could feel the chiseled contours of his muscles.

A rumbled laugh, a feral groan as their tongues touched and twined. Through the slitted eyeholes of his mask she saw a flash of green-gold fire...

Acclaim for the Lords of Midnight Series

Too Tempting to Resist

"Elliott provides readers with a treat to savor in this fun, sexy, delicious tale. With smart, sassy characters, a charming plot and an erotic bad boy/good girl duo, this fast-paced story will keep readers' attention."
—*RT Book Reviews*

"Nothing is more sensuous than a delicious meal, and Cara Elliott's food-inspired sex scenes are, quite literally, *Too Tempting to Resist*...likeable characters, a fast-moving plot, and unique, engaging sex scenes that are deliciously tempting."
—HeroesandHeartbreakers.com

"Haddan and Eliza's charming wit and banter will absolutely capture the reader from their first meeting...Haddan is the type of historical hero that women fantasize about...[It] can easily be read as a stand-alone, though most readers will want to rush out and find a copy of the first book to get more of Cara Elliott's Hellhounds. A real page-turner, readers will not be able to put this book down."

—RomRevToday.com

"Cara Elliott is the master of writing a breathtaking and romantic book built around an exciting, engrossing story of suspense and intrigue. I believe she is truly one of a kind in bringing all the pieces and characters to a fulfilling conclusion yet always leaving the reader begging for the next book."

—TheReadingReviewer.com

Too Wicked to Wed

"Elliott packs the first Lords of Midnight Regency romance with plenty of steamy sex and sly innuendo...As Alexa and Connor flee London to escape vengeful criminals, their mutual attraction sizzles beneath delightful banter. Regency fans will especially appreciate the authentic feel of the historical setting."

—*Publishers Weekly*

"A surprisingly resourceful heroine and a sinfully sexy hero, a compelling and danger-spiced plot, lushly sensual love scenes, and lively writing work together perfectly to get Elliott's new Regency-set Lords of Midnight series off to a delightfully entertaining start."

—*Booklist*

"The Lords of Midnight, all sexy and dangerous men, are introduced in this series starter. The romance, adventure, and sensuality readers expect from Elliott are here, along with an unforgettable hoyden heroine and an enigmatic hero. She takes them on a marvelous ride from gambling hells to ballrooms, country estates, and London's underworld."

—*RT Book Reviews*

"A very entertaining tale...Well-drawn characters, an interesting plot, and plenty of passion kept the pages turning. Alexa and Connor are worthy opponents and even more worthy partners as they try to unravel the mystery at the Wolf's Lair. Excellent and well rounded secondary characters, both friend and foe, make for a superb tale."

—RomRevRoday.com

"Filled with suspense and passion. The mystery is delivered wonderfully and will have you guessing up to the big reveal...hilarious and downright charming...The romance element will have the reader on the edge of their seat...The mental tennis match heightens the all too present romantic chemistry to the point that it seems to jump off the page...If *Too Wicked to Wed* is an example of what we are to expect, this will be a series loved by many!"

—FreshFiction.com

"I really enjoyed Cara Elliott's writing. She hooked me from the start...kept me glued to the pages...an incredibly sexy and romantic read...I would read more by Cara Elliott based on this novel. I look forward to reading the next installment of The Lords of Midnight series."

—TheSeasonforRomance.com

Praise for the Circle of Sin Trilogy

To Tempt a Rake

"From the first page of this sequel...Elliott sweeps her readers up in a scintillating and sexy romance."

—*Publishers Weekly*

To Sin with a Scoundrel

Too Dangerous
to Desire

Too Dangerous
to Desire

CARA ELLIOTT

FOREVER

NEW YORK   BOSTON

Copyright © 2012 by Andrea DaRif
Excerpt from *Too Wicked to Wed* copyright © 2011 by Andrea DaRif

Forever
Hachette Book Group
237 Park Avenue
New York, NY 10017
www.HachetteBookGroup.com

Printed in the United States of America

First Edition: November 2012
10 9 8 7 6 5 4 3 2 1

Forever is an imprint of Grand Central Publishing.
The Forever name and logo are trademarks of Hachette Book Group, Inc.

The Hachette Speakers Bureau provides a wide range of authors for speaking events. To find out more, go to www.hachettespeakersbureau.com or call (866) 376-6591.

The publisher is not responsible for websites (or their content) that are not owned by the publisher.

ATTENTION CORPORATIONS AND ORGANIZATIONS:

Most Hachette Book Group books are available at quantity discounts with bulk purchase for educational, business, or sales promotional use. For information, please call or write:

Special Markets Department, Hachette Book Group
237 Park Avenue, New York, NY 10017
Telephone: 1-800-222-6747 Fax: 1-800-477-5925

For my brother Cam
Despite all the mischief and mayhem
you got us into as kids,
I love you dearly.

Too Dangerous
to Desire

Prologue

The voice stirred a myriad of memories... *None of them good.*

Soft and sensuous as summer sunlight, it tickled around his head, a tantalizing whisper, wrapping his brain in a seductive swirl of honeyed heat and gold-kissed sweetness.

Another word floated through the half-open door and suddenly the sensations were like a serpent, trailing a sensuous slither over bare flesh, only to strike with diamond-bright fangs.

Oh yes, he knew that voice—and it was poison to his peace of mind.

And yet Cameron Daggett couldn't help edging a little closer to the shadowed portal and cocking an ear to listen.

He had only entered the building moments ago, and as he was one of the few people allowed to use the owner's private entrance, no one was yet aware of his arrival. Peering through the sliver of space, he could just make out the two figures standing in the smoky half-light of the corridor wall sconces. The oil flames were kept deliberately low—the regular patrons of the establishment preferred to come and go discreetly. However, as the whisper had warned, the flickers of gold-lapped light showed the pair paused in deep conversation were women. One of them was the familiar form of Sara Hawkins, the owner of The Wolf's Lair. And the other was...

"This is *highly* irregular, Miss Lawrance," said Sara in a low, taut murmur. "As a rule, I don't allow wives or sisters or others of our sex to intrude on the gentlemen who patronize this place. It's bad for business, if ye take my meaning. They expect discretion and privacy."

"I understand," replied the Voice from the Past.

No, he had not been mistaken. Cameron tried to draw a breath, but his lungs felt filled with lead. It *was* Sophie.

"Truly I do," went on Miss Sophie Lawrance. "And if it were not a matter of the utmost urgency, I would not dream of making such an irregular request. But the truth is... I am rather desperate."

Desperate? He knew that he shouldn't give a damn, and yet Cameron held himself very still, intent on hearing more.

"Yes, I can see that," said Sara, heaving a reluctant sigh. A pause hung for a moment in the gloom. "And so I will make a rare exception. Wait in there." She indicated a small side parlor. "I will fetch the gentleman. But I must ask ye to be quick—and fer God's sake, ye must be quiet as well. No tears, no shrieks, no gnashing of teeth, else I will have to ask the porter to remove ye from the premises."

"I will not make a scene," promised Sophie, her earnest whisper coiling and clutching at his thumping heart.

"And when ye are finished, ye must leave with all possible haste," added Sara. "Nothing personal, Miss, but the sooner ye are gone from here, the better."

Cameron's own inner voice of Self-Preservation shouted a similar warning. *Turn and run like the Devil. And don't look back.*

After all, he had long ago mastered the art of staying one step ahead of personal demons—not to speak of more mundane threats like bailiffs and Bow Street Runners.

And yet...

And yet, at this moment Cameron found himself incapable of listening to reason. Instead of retreating, he slipped into one of the secret passageways used by the staff and waited for Sara to return with the man Sophie sought.

Low voices. A door opening and closing. The click of Sara's heeled shoes as she returned to her private office.

Moving silently as a stalking panther, Cameron darted out of his hiding place and approached the parlor.

What reason, he wondered, had brought saintly Sophie Lawrance to one of London's most notorious dens of iniquity? Set deep in the dangerous slums of Southwark, The Wolf's Lair was a high-stakes gaming house and brothel that catered to rakehells and rogues who played fast and loose with the rules of Society.

And why, after all these years, should he care?

Because I am a god-benighted fool, thought Cameron with a shiver of self-loathing.

The door was shut tightly with the lock engaged. Drawing a thin shaft of steel from his boot, Cameron expertly eased the latch open. A touch of his gloved fingertips coaxed the paneled wood to shift just a fraction.

Sophie was heavily veiled, the dark mesh muffling

her already low whisper. Her companion was speaking in equally low tones, making it impossible to hear their words. However, he saw a small package change hands.

The gentleman let out a low brandy-fuzzed laugh as he tucked it into his pocket.

Sliding back into hiding, Cameron watched Sophie hurry away down the corridor, her indigo cloak skirling with the shadows, until she was swallowed in the darkness. A moment later, the gentleman emerged from the parlor, still chuckling softly. He turned for the gaming rooms, a flicker of lamplight catching the curl of his mouth and the slight swaying of his steps.

Cameron recognized him as Lord Dudley, a dissolute viscount with an appetite for reckless pleasures.

Dudley and Sophie? An odd couple, if ever there was one. The Sophie Lawrance he knew was anything but reckless. She was sensible—too damnably sensible to ever throw caution to the wind.

But people change, thought Cameron sardonically. He had only to look at himself—there wasn't the least resemblance between his present persona and the callow youth of...

Shaking off mordant memories, he followed Dudley into the card room. Timing his steps perfectly, he brushed by the viscount just as he started to sit down at one of the tables.

"Join us for a hand, Daggett?" called one of the other players.

"Not tonight," answered Cameron. "I've an assignation with an old friend."

The man leered. "A *lady* friend?"

"Pray tell, who?" chorused the man's cronies.

"Gentlemanly honor compels Daggett to remain silent on that question," pointed out the half-soused baronet who was shuffling the cards.

Smiling, Cameron inclined a mocking bow and sauntered away, Sophie's package now firmly tucked away in his pocket.

Luckily for me, I've never claimed to have any pretensions to honor.

Drawing in a great lungful of the chill night air, Sophie Lawrance forced herself to choke back the urge to retch.

Steady, steady. She couldn't falter now—she must ignore the sickening smells, the sordid encounter.

And yet, the bitter taste of bile rose again in her throat, and she felt the oozy ground beneath her feet begin to sway.

Breathe. She would not—*could not*—give in to fear. Predators pounced on any show of weakness, and this godforsaken slum was perhaps the most savage spot in all of England.

"Allow me to be of assistance." A hand suddenly gripped her arm to keep her upright and a snowy white handkerchief, scented with a pleasant tang of citrus and spice, fluttered in front of her veiled face.

Her first impulse was to scream and try to flee. But something about his light touch and calming voice held her in thrall.

"You appear to be in some distress."

"I...I..." Her stomach gave another little lurch. "I thank you, sir." Swallowing her pride, Sophie took the silk square from the shadowy stranger and held it close to her nose. Oddly enough, the fragrance seemed to calm the churning of her insides. She inhaled several slow, deep breaths, savoring the richly nuanced scent.

"Better?" he asked.

"Much." Now that her head had cleared, Sophie was eager to escape the dark, filth-strewn alley and the horrid nightmare of the evening. "A momentary indisposition, that is all." She shrugged off his hold and held out the handkerchief. "It has passed."

The stranger made no effort to take it back. "You had better keep it if you mean to wander around this neighborhood." The alley was dark, with only an intermittent wink of starlight penetrating through the clouds, so for the moment she had only a dim impression of his person. *Tall. Broad-shouldered. Strong hands, surprisingly gentle and warm.*

His voice, however, was coolly cynical. "Though I would recommend a more effective implement of protection if you mean to enter places like The Wolf's Lair. Say, a pistol or a knife. A lady's virtue won't last long without such a weapon." A pause, and then his voice turned even more sardonic. "But perhaps your intentions aren't virtuous."

"I—I assure you, sir," said Sophie tightly. "I am *not* in the habit of coming to . . . depraved places like this."

"Oh?" Skepticism shaded his voice. "Then what brings you here tonight, if not a craving for danger?"

"That, sir, is none of your business." Lifting her chin, she ventured a look at him, trying to make out some identifying feature. *Do I know you?* It was absurd, of course, but something felt hauntingly familiar about him . . .

However, the stranger had his hat pulled low, the wide brim shading his face. In the swirl of murky shadows,

Sophie could make out naught but the vague shapes of a straight nose, a sensual mouth. The only clearcut view was of long, raven-dark hair and the rakish glimmer of a gold earring.

Danger. His last word seemed a deliberately tickling, taunting challenge. Sophie sucked in her breath, suddenly aware of a strange prickling taking hold of her body, as if daggerpoints were dancing over every inch of her flesh. "In another few minutes I shall be safe from danger. That is..." Another glance at the earring. "...unless I've had the misfortune to cross paths with a pirate," she said, trying to mask her emotions by matching his cynical tone.

A smile curled on the corners of his mouth, half mocking, half...

Sophie couldn't put a name to the flicker of emotion. It was gone in the blink of the eye, so perhaps she had merely imagined it.

"A pirate?" he repeated, making her feel slightly absurd. Like a silly schoolgirl who swooned over novels of swashbuckling heroes rescuing damsels in distress. His voice then took on a sharper edge. "Isn't that just a romantic name for a ruthless cutthroat and a conniving thief?"

Sophie swallowed hard, feeling a shiver skate down her spine. "Who are you, sir?" she demanded.

"Why do you ask?" he countered. "Do you think we might be acquainted?" The question quivered for a moment in the chill night air. "Old friends, perhaps?"

"Impossible," she whispered. "I can't imagine that we move in the same worlds." Her dizziness seemed to have returned, and with a vengeance. Off-kilter, she found herself adding, "And yet you...you remind me of someone I once knew long, long ago."

"You speak of him as if he is dead." Without waiting for her to answer, he gave a strange laugh. "Perhaps I'm his ghost."

Sophie wondered whether he was drunk. *Or demented.* Inching back a step she looked around for the alleyway leading out to the street where her hackney was waiting.

"You want a name, Madam or Miss Whoever-You-Are?" he continued. "My two friends and I are called the Hellhounds." He let out a low, sarcastic bark. "I'm known as the Sleuth Hound as I have a nose for sniffing out trouble."

"I am surprised that you admit to such a beastly moniker," she replied slowly.

"I make no bones about what I am," he said softly. "What about you?" His head tilted down and then up, his unseen eyes leaving a trail of heat along her length. "Your manner of dress says you are a respectable country lady. But the fact that you are here, visiting a house of ill repute in the stews of Southwark, conveys an entirely different message."

She felt her cheeks grow hot beneath the gauzy veil. That he was right only fanned the flames. "You are impertinent, sir."

"No, I am observant." A pause. "More so than you think. Indeed, from what I've seen, I would say you are playing a very dangerous game. Have a care, for in dealing with those who frequent The Wolf's Lair, you are going up against the most ruthless men in London."

"Including you?" challenged Sophie, though her heart was pounding hard enough to crack a rib.

"Oh, I'm among the very worst of the lot."

"I must be going." Slipping past him, Sophie hurried toward the narrow gap between the ramshackle buildings.

But to her dismay, the Pirate moved along with her. "Allow me to see you to your vehicle. It isn't safe to walk through these alleys alone."

"You needn't bother." She flinched slightly at the sound of scrabbling claws somewhere close by. "I—I will take my chances."

"I think you have gambled enough for one evening," he drawled. "Besides, I'd be willing to wager that you wouldn't care to put your foot where you are about to step."

She stopped short, as a horribly foul odor assaulted her nose.

"Nasty, isn't it?" he murmured.

"I—"

His hands were suddenly around her waist, lifting her into his arms as if she were light as a feather. Beneath the folds of wool she was intimately aware of the lean, lithe flex of muscle.

Oh, what madness has taken hold of me?

Her wits were spinning and skittering topsy-turvy. How else to explain why the moment felt so hauntingly familiar? So achingly comforting.

Madness, she repeated to herself. The meeting with Lord Dudley ought to be reminder enough that youth and innocence were long gone. Only a fool yearned to reach back and recapture the past.

Fisting her fingers, Sophie tried to squirm free. "Please, put me down, sir!"

"As you wish." Her half boots hit the ground with a

soft squish. "We have passed through the worst. It's just a little farther to where the hired carriages wait. You will soon be back to the respectable part of the Town."

Slipping, sliding, Sophie hurried awkwardly toward the weak glimmer of oily light up ahead. The Pirate glided alongside her with a smooth, silent step.

Spotting her hackney parked at the near corner of the rough-cobbled square, she skirted around the snorting horse and quickly unlatched the door.

"Thank you. Though you need not have troubled yourself..." A gust of wind swirled over the stones, catching at her cloak and lifting the thin scrim of her veil just as she turned to take her leave.

"No trouble at all," replied the Pirate. He had moved close to help her climb up the iron rungs, and now their faces were but a hairsbreadth apart. "Indeed, I did warn you that I have a nose for trouble."

And a mouth for sin.

For suddenly his lips possessed hers in a swift, searing kiss.

It was over in an instant. He pulled back, so quickly that she was sure the glimmer of green eyes must have been only a figment of her heated imagination.

"Fie, sir! N-no gentleman—"

Her stammering protest was stilled by a rumbled laugh. *A pirate laugh, redolent with hints of hellfire dangers and storm-tossed seas.*

"Ah, but whoever said that I was a gentleman?"

Chapter One

$\mathcal{L}$ud, what a night." Sara looked up from her ledgers and blew out a harried sigh.

"That has a rather ominous ring to it." Cameron waited a moment, shoulder slouched against the shadowed door molding, before uncrossing his arms and entering her private office. "What's the trouble?"

Her face screwed into a pained grimace. "To begin with, Machrie and Frampton came to blows over politics at the faro table and I had to have Rufus toss them out—a great pity for my profits as they were losing heavily."

"You should simply have sent Maggie to take McTavish's place as the dealer," he replied, moving to the sideboard and pouring himself a drink from one of the cut glass decanters. "All conflict over Whig and Tory agendas would quickly have been forgotten—they both are easily distracted by voluptuous breasts."

"I shall remember that for the future." Another sigh. "And speaking of profits, you've chosen to tipple on my most expensive brandy."

"Isn't my company worth any price?" quipped Cameron, pouring her a measure of sherry and carrying it to the table.

Sara laughed. "Well, I confess that things have been awfully quiet here, what with the other two Hellhounds rusticating in the country."

Polite Society viewed Cameron and his friends Lord Killingworth and Lord Haddan as dangerous, devil-may-care gentlemen. An outraged matron had coined the moniker and it had stuck—mostly because the trio had encouraged the wild rumors that swirled through the drawing rooms regarding their exploits. In truth, the accounts were much exaggerated, but each of them took pains to encourage the gossip, as the innuendo helped deflect scrutiny from their personal, private secrets.

"Ain't it sweet to think of them living in conjugal bliss," continued Sara, her mouth quirking to a dreamy smile. "Who would have predicted we'd see not one, but *two* weddings within the last six months."

Cameron fluttered a hand in a faintly rude gesture. "Well, don't expect a third paw to be caught in the parson's mousetrap anytime soon."

"Don't ye believe in romance?" she demanded.

"My dear Sara, you may be assured that I haven't a romantic bone in my body." He drained the brandy in one long swallow and set it aside. Plucking the small package from his pocket he began untying the strings. "As for light fingers, that's an entirely different matter."

She snorted into her sherry. "Don't ye ever worry about Bow Street Runners?"

"Good God, those plodding oafs?" The knots unraveled, and the wrappings loosened. "If I can't stay several steps ahead of their hob-nailed pursuit I deserve to end my days in Newgate prison."

"I hope yer feet stay as light as yer fingers. I'd miss yer company."

"I'm exceedingly..." His words trailed off as the inner paper fell away, revealing a pair of teardrop-shaped pearl earrings. The settings were a classically simple design made of flame-kissed gold, each one highlighted by a faceted emerald. They were elegant, understated—and undeniably familiar.

His throat tightened. The jewelry had belonged to Sophie's mother, and was the one possession of any value that had been passed down to her eldest daughter.

Lost in a frown, Cameron continued to stare in mute consternation. He knew that for Sophie, the sentimental value of the earrings had always been worth far more than money. He couldn't imagine her ever parting with them willingly. This meant...

Trouble, hissed the most vociferous of his Inner Demons. *But that's no surprise—Sophie Lawrance has always been Trouble.*

Curious, Sara rose and came over to see what had silenced their bantering. "Oooo, ain't they nice." Lamplight dipped and danced over the perfectly matched pearls. Slanting a sidelong look at his expression, she hesitated and then added, "What? Decided ye don't like them?"

He slowly turned the earrings over in his palm, setting off a winking of dark and light sparks as the jewels caught the light from a nearby candle. They sparkled with an unusual smoky green color, just as he remembered them.

"Actually they're a good match for yer eyes," said Sara

appraisingly. "Why don't ye keep the pair fer yourself rather than sell them to a flash house?"

Cameron roused himself to speech. "I only have one pierced ear, and two would be rather *de trop*, even for me." He slowly closed his fingers around the earrings. The pearls were cool to the touch and yet they burned like hellfire against his flesh.

Don't, he told himself. *Don't stir up embers from the past.*

"Well, if they are for sale, maybe I'll consider buying them. I don't much care for flashy baubles, but those have a rare inner fire."

"I haven't decided." He began rewrapping the jewels. "Kindly pour me another drink. This one you may put on my account."

"Not that ye ever pay it." Sara huffed out an aggrieved sigh but picked up his empty glass and moved to the sideboard.

Muted clinking punctuated a papery whisper as Cameron slowly unfolded the note that had been tucked in with the earrings. There were only a few lines, lettered in Sophie's neat script. He read them over several times, and felt a pensive frown pull at his mouth. The message itself made little sense, but the tone was clear enough.

Something havey-cavey was afoot.

Which is all the more reason to run like the Devil, jeered the Inner Demon. *Sophie Lawrance chose to turn her back and walk away from you years ago. Whatever Trouble she is in, it's none of your concern.*

Shifting his stance on the carpet, Cameron told himself the Demon was right. It would be foolish to stray from his chosen path. He had taught himself to be a solitary, stalking predator—a hardbitten Hellhound who cared for naught but his own survival. Through bitter experience, he had learned how to outrun the past, moving swiftly and leaving only a quicksilver blur of shadows.

So yes, I should run like the Devil. I've come too far to stumble now.

Fisting the paper, Cameron shoved it back in his pocket.

"Here ye go. But the next time, yer getting cheap claret." Sara paused, drink in hand, and cocked an ear as the echo of an outraged shout drifted down from the gaming rooms. It was followed a moment later by the pelter of hurried footsteps in the corridor.

"Sorry te disturb ye, Miss Sara." Rufus, the big mulatto head porter, stuck his dark head through the doorway. "But Lord Dudley is cutting up something fierce." A flicker of his chocolate brown gaze was the only acknowledgment of Cameron's presence. "He claims someone stole a package of valuables from his pocket."

She swore. "I'll come sort him out. The pompous prig probably dropped it at one of his many other haunts." Her harried sigh ended with a word no gently bred lady would know. "Ye better go back and keep him from kicking the faro table to flinders. I'll be along in a tic."

"On second thought, never mind about the drink. Seeing as you are busy, I'll let myself out." Cameron turned up the collar of his coat as Rufus rushed away. "Dudley ought to be more careful with his possessions."

Sara gave him a fishy stare before pouring the brandy back into the decanter. "Aye, the stews are a dangerous place. Ye never know when a beast is going to leap out of the shadows and bite ye where it hurts."

"How true."

"Hmmph." The empty glass scuffed softly against the silver tray. "And yet, it seems a rather odd coincidence that an agitated young lady requested a clandestine meeting with Lord Dudley earlier this evening, and now he's had his pocket picked of a valuable."

Their eyes met.

"Life is full of serendipitous occurrences," said Cameron, maintaining a bland expression. "That's what makes it tolerably interesting."

Sara refused to be distracted by the quip. "I can't help but wonder..." Tapping a finger to her chin, she fixed him with a searching stare. "Ye had a very odd sort of look on yer face when ye were looking at the earrings. Call it what you will, but I had one of those argy-bargy feelings in my gut..."

"Female intuition?" he drawled.

"Aye. And it made me wonder whether for some *serendipitous* reason, you have decided to become the lady's knight in shining armor?"

"God perish the thought. You know me better than that."

"Ha!" she scoffed. "The truth is, I don't really know ye at all. Even to them who should know ye best, ye are a mystery, a...conundrum. Why, Haddan, one of yer closest friends, says that as far as he knows, ye emerged like a puff of smoke from some brass lamp in a fancy foreign fairy tale."

"*Poof.*" With a sardonic laugh, Cameron fluttered his hands, setting ghostly gray flickers scudding across the wainscoting.

"Who the devil are you?"

A nameless longing rose up in his throat. He turned away, masking his momentary weakness in the shadows. "I'm just a friend, Sara. Let's leave it at that. There are certain secrets that are best left buried in the past."

No wonder pirates are counted among the most dangerous creatures roaming the face of the Earth.

Sophie touched her plundered lips, her fingers blessedly cool against the still-burning flesh. *A kiss.* Dear Lord, it had been so long since she had been kissed that the sensation of liquid fire sizzling through her blood had left her feeling thoroughly singed.

In an instant, crimson flames and the smell of sulfurous brimstone would probably fill the carriage, she thought. To remind her that devilish desires were evil.

The carriage lurched as it turned off the bridge and headed for the more genteel surroundings of her uncle and aunt's neighborhood near Red Lion Square. "And yet," she murmured, daring to say it aloud, "for an instant I wished he would sweep me up and carry me away to sail the wild, wanton seas."

Clouds now hid the sliver of moon and the stars. Sophie was grateful, not only for the cover of darkness to creep into the scullery door unobserved, but also for the black panes of glass that swallowed any reflection of her wicked wishes. It was dangerous—and foolish—to long for what could never be.

After all, she was prim, prudent, practical Sophie Lawrance. The hard-edged words bounced against her brain as the wheels clattered over the cobblestones. She may once have indulged in a streak of wildness, but that was long, long ago. She couldn't afford to find danger alluring.

I must be the glue that holds my family together, Sophie thought to herself. Pressing the Pirate's scented handkerchief to her cheek, she blinked back tears. *No matter that my own heart was left cracked in a thousand little pieces when I made that long-ago decision to let Reason overrule Love.*

There had been no real choice. Her father had been too ill, and the young man had been too wild. Too volatile, too impetuous. And he had proved it by abandoning her without so much as a word of good-bye. Oh, that had hurt...

Rain began to patter against the hackney window, and for a moment she was tempted to give in to self-pity. But after a few watery sniffs, the spicy cologne seemed to seep and swirl through her limbs, giving her the strength to shake off such bleak thoughts. Leaning back, she squared her shoulders against the lumpy squabs.

The past was the past, and the present held a far more pressing problem. There *had* to be a way to keep Lord Dudley from destroying her family, and she vowed to herself that she would find it.

"I will *not* give in to despair." The words sounded very brave and defiant when said aloud. But as the minutes spun by and no brilliant idea came leaping to mind, they began to ring a bit hollow.

After all, how could she fight back? She was naught but a country clergyman's daughter. And he was...

A snake. A slithering serpent, a venomous viper— though that was maligning the reptiles.

An ugly description, but blackmail was an ugly, ugly business.

Her first acquaintance with the viscount had occurred

a little over six months ago at the local Assemblies near her home in Norfolk. He and his friend, the Honorable Frederick Morton, had been staying with the imperious Marquess of Wolcott, whose vast estate abutted her family's modest lands. And while the lord of the manor was far too high in the instep to ever rub shoulders with the country gentry, Dudley and Morton had come, though for the first hour they merely stared and did not join the dancing.

Then, strangely enough, Dudley had asked for her hand in a country gavotte, even though she had been sitting in her usual place with the other spinsters and matrons, keeping a watchful eye on the younger, high-spirited girls.

From the first touch of his hand, she had found him repellent. There was something cold-blooded about his smile, and his eyes had a reptilian flatness that sent shivers down her spine.

And her instincts had been right. Sophie felt her chest constrict. Oh yes, she had known he was evil—she just didn't guess *how* evil.

Dudley's blackmail notes had started a fortnight later. The demands had been small at first, and she had managed to cobble together payments by giving a few extra music lessons. However they had quickly escalated. Her jaw tightened. The earrings would buy a bit of respite. But after that, she had nothing left to offer. No more money, no more jewelry. No more excuses.

I'll think of something before then, thought Sophie, trying to put some force behind the assertion.

The hackney came to a jolting halt, saving her from further brooding. Drawing up the hood of her cloak, she slipped out the door and darted into the alleyway, praying that none of the neighbors would notice a flitting shadow stir the darker shades of night.

The carefully oiled scullery door opened with nary a squeak and Sophie quickly made her way up the back stairs to her bedchamber overlooking the tiny garden.

"Thank God for small favors," she muttered under her breath, shaking the mizzle from her cloak and hanging it inside the painted armoire. However, her relief at having her absence go undetected was punctured in the next instant by a whisper from the drapery-shrouded window seat.

"Where the devil have you been?"

Damnation. Swearing a silent oath, Sophie carefully removed her veiling and bonnet before turning around. "Don't say 'devil,' Georgie. It's not acceptable language for a proper young lady."

Georgiana retorted with a far worse word.

"You ought to be ashamed of yourself. You are a clergyman's daughter," scolded Sophie, mustering her sternest older-sister voice.

"So are you," pointed out Georgiana. "And I daresay that sneaking off for a secret midnight tryst in the Capital of Sin is a much more serious transgression than taking the Devil's name in vain."

"I may have to start keeping a closer eye on your reading material," replied Sophie tartly. "It appears that Lady Vere is right in warning me that horrid novels stimulate the wrong sort of thoughts in impressionable young females."

"You are trying to change the subject."

For all her tender years, Georgiana was sharp as a tack.

That fact was usually very welcome, but at the present moment it was proving decidedly uncomfortable.

Lighting a candle, Sophie carried it to her dressing table.

"If you weren't trysting, then what were you doing out at this hour?" pressed her sister.

The soft *ping* of hairpins dropping upon the wooden top seemed to amplify the ensuing silence.

"By the by," added Georgiana after waiting through several more *pings*. "It wouldn't be such a bad thing if you were trysting. You've spent most of your life shouldering all the responsibilities for our family. Once in a while, you ought to cut loose and kick up your heels, even if it means sneaking a few forbidden pleasures, before...before..."

"Before I turn into a dried-up old spinster?" Sophie gave a tight smile. "I'm on the shelf, Georgie, with my heels primly tucked under my skirts." Picking up a hairbrush, she set to work on her unruly curls. "My days of indulging in anything forbidden are far in the past."

"You make yourself sound as aged as Methuselah," grumbled her sister. "Twenty-seven is not so very old."

Despite her worries, Sophie let out a wry laugh. "That's exceedingly kind of you, for I know that to someone who is only seventeen, it must appear positively *ancient*."

"Not at all. You are quite well preserved. I only have to dust the cobwebs off you once or twice a week."

Their gazes met for a moment in the hazy glimmer of the looking glass before Sophie dropped her eyes.

"Please look at me," said Georgiana.

Sophie reluctantly turned around in her chair.

"You may still see me as a scrubby schoolgirl, but I'm not a child anymore." To emphasize the assertion, Georgiana rose from the window seat, the hazy moonlight outlining her slim, long-legged height and womanly curves. "In case you have forgotten, I'm engaged to be married."

Oh, be assured it has not slipped my mind. Lord Dudley's threats were a constant reminder of how her sister's future happiness depended on someone being brave and resourceful enough to fight back and find a way to beat him and his friend Morton, who, she had been told, was a partner in the blackmail scheme. *And that someone has to be me.*

"Anthony thinks me mature enough to share in his doubts as well as his dreams. I wish you would give me the same credit," went on Georgiana softly. "You have been acting oddly ever since we arrived here in London. And it's clear that something is amiss. Why won't you let me help?"

"I...I can't." Anthony Wilder, a cornet in the Blues regiment of the Horse Guards, was the son of a baron who possessed a large estate in Oxfordshire. His family felt the match was beneath him, but the young man had prevailed and won their reluctant consent. However, the slightest whiff of scandal would no doubt change that in a heartbeat. "Don't ask me why."

Georgiana scowled and her left brow angled up to a martial tilt.

It was the Be-Forewarned-This-Battle-Is-Just-Beginning look. And that it so rarely appeared caused another spasm of anxiety to clench at Sophie's chest. Normally the very paragon of sweet temper and good sense, Georgiana could be frightfully stubborn—not to speak of unselfishly brave—when her passions were aroused. If she knew of the blackmail threat, she would demand to join the fight to counter it, even if it meant sacrificing her own future.

And that must not—could not—be allowed to happen. Sophie knew that her best hope of seeing Georgiana happily married was to deal with the trouble quietly and discreetly on her own.

Her sister finally broke the silent clash of stares with a huffed grumble. "You are wearing that odious Don't-Argue-Because-I-Am-Your-Older-Sister-And-Know-Best look."

"I *am* your older sister, and in this case I *do* know best," replied Sophie. To soften the rebuff she added, "I promise that I will explain it when I can." It wasn't really a lie, merely a subterfuge. "But in the meantime, I am asking you to trust me."

The candle flame flickered as Georgiana released a long exhale. "Very well. For now, that is."

Yet another danger dodged, thought Sophie wryly. *If I were a cat, my nine lives would likely have been used up by this evening's adventures.*

"Did you enjoy Mrs. Hartwell's recital?" she asked quickly, grateful for a chance to move on to a safer subject. Georgiana was very fond of music and played the pianoforte with great skill.

"Yes, it was quite nice. Her daughter Marianne has a beautiful voice and we performed a number of duets, including a number of Aunt Hermione's favorite Scottish ballads."

"It sounds like it was a lovely evening," murmured Sophie.

"Perhaps next time you will not be struck with a beastly headache that requires the absolute peace and quiet of your darkened bedchamber," said her sister dryly.

"Georgie, you need not hammer home the point."

"Oh, very well. I shall cry *pax*." Georgiana was too good-natured to stay aggrieved for more than a fleeting moment. "But you must promise me that you won't cry off from the outing on Thursday evening. Uncle Edward has purchased tickets for all of us to attend a concert at Vauxhall Gardens."

"Vauxhall?" The place was a renowned pleasure garden, drawing people from all walks of life—which was part of its allure. They came dine, to mingle, to stroll, and to savor the aura of adventure that skirled through the dark leaves.

"Yes, isn't that exciting? We shall dine on the famous shaved ham in one of the special supper boxes while listening to Italian arias. And then, we shall have time to explore the pathways and pavilions before watching a display of fireworks light up the heavens!"

"How divine," said Sophie, trying to appear suitably enthusiastic.

"Don't you think it sounds wildly romantic?" Georgiana dropped her voice a notch. "Apparently, some of the ladies and gentlemen come masked, so that they may sneak away into the darkened shrubbery and engage in...illicit activities." Her pause was filled by a fluttery sigh. "Oh, how I wish Anthony were here in London, rather than galloping over the dismal hills of Dartmoor. I think it very shabby that his commanding officer did not grant him leave from the regimental maneuvers."

Sophie gave mental thanks to the colonel. She had

enough challenges without having to keep an eagle eye on two young lovebirds. "Patience is a virtue, my dear. The two of you will be together soon enough—and without having to risk scandal for a few stolen kisses."

Georgiana opened her mouth to protest.

"And besides, I highly doubt that Anthony would find shopping romantic." The main reason for their trip to London was to purchase Georgiana's wedding trousseau. "Think about it. Lace, gloves, muslins, mantua makers— the poor man would likely be bored to perdition."

"An excellent point."

"You see, older sisters can, on rare occasions, offer a small grain of wisdom."

"Oh, Sophie…" A fierce hug suddenly squeezed the air from her lungs. "You must think me a vain, selfish goose who cares for naught but her own pleasures. You have been so very good to me and Penelope, sacrificing your own happiness to be both sister and mother to us."

"Unhappy? How could I be unhappy with you two rattleheaded hoydens in my life?"

"Quite easily, I imagine." Georgiana gurgled a watery laugh through her sniffling. "We're a sore trial, I know. But I hope you know how dearly we love you."

"Of course I do." Sophie dabbed her sleeve to her sister's cheek. "Now dry your eyes and let's have no more tears. We are visiting a very fancy modiste first thing in the morning, and we don't want her to see you with a splotchy face."

"Right."

In truth, Sophie wasn't at all interested in fashion and fripperies, but she knew Georgiana, who had a good eye and excellent taste, enjoyed choosing fabrics and accessories. "And from there, we'll be going on to the Bond Street Bazaar, and Aunt Hermione's favorite warehouse for silks."

Her sister's expression turned dreamy. "I know the exact color that I want to find for your new gown. It's a deep sea shade, a hue somewhere between blue and green, aswirl with a hint of mystery."

"First of all, we are not spending any money on gowns for *me*." Their uncle, a prosperous banker in the City, had insisted on gifting Georgiana with a full trousseau. But despite his kind offer to provide her with some new clothes as well, Sophie did not mean to use a penny of his generosity on herself. "Because secondly, I would have no call to wear it."

"Ha! If you would stop dressing in grain sacks and hiding your beauty among all of the elderly matrons, you would have plenty of suitors falling at your feet."

"I don't need new gowns to attract a suitor. I have one," said Sophie dryly. "However I do not wish to marry Neddy the blacksmith. He is a very nice fellow, but I am quite certain that we would not make each other happy."

"I admit, the local choices leave something to be desired." Georgiana took a long moment to ponder the possibilities. "Perhaps you'll meet a tall, handsome stranger at Vauxhall Gardens."

Sophie inhaled a silent breath as the unwilling image of a rakish Pirate, gold earring gleaming against a tangle of sin-dark hair, invaded her thoughts.

"A gentleman of strength and substance," went on her sister, warming to the task. "Naturally, he must clever and charming. And willing to slay dragons on your behalf."

"Oh, naturally. However, I doubt that such a paragon

of perfection exists outside of a fairytale—except, of course, for Anthony."

"You can't be sure of that. After all, you haven't looked very hard."

Sophie closed her eyes for a fleeting instant. "I'm delighted that you found your knight in shining armor, Georgie. But not all of us are fated to be so lucky. If there are any reptiles that need slaying, I fear I shall have to sharpen my own sword."

Chapter Two

So, Sophie Lawrance was going to be spending tomorrow evening at Vauxhall Gardens.

After handing the street urchin a few coins, Cameron left Green Park and strolled thoughtfully along Piccadilly Street before turning left onto Bond Street. It had been a simple matter to track down her hired hackney and learn where she had been dropped last night. Over the years, he had woven an elaborate web of underworld informers throughout London. He used it mainly for his own business activities—he was, to put it bluntly, a thief, albeit a very discerning one who stole only the highest quality jewels and objets d'art from people who could afford to lose them. But on occasion, the network was useful for other purposes.

Indeed, he had learned a good many other details about Sophie's stay in Town. Servants were easily encouraged to gossip, especially as she and her sister were great favorites with everyone who worked at their aunt and uncle's residence.

A wedding. They were visiting London in order to shop

for a wedding. Not Sophie's—Cameron had experienced an inexplicable twinge of relief on learning that news. Though why that should matter was something he did not care to contemplate.

He paused to stare into one of the fancy store windows, watching the bustle of busy shoppers in the reflection of the glass. Word was, the three ladies would be stopping at a fashionable milliner located on the next corner. Curious, he loitered a little longer, pretending to adjust the folds of his cravat—which was, as usual, an exotic swath of patterned silk rather than the standard starched white length of linen.

An elderly matron with a trio of young ladies in tow frowned and gave him a wide berth. He caught the word "dangerous" as she huffed by. Turning he flashed a wink at the young ones, who had slowed to sneak a stare. Blushing furiously, they hurried to catch up with their chaperone.

Another example of my wicked, wicked ways, thought Cameron sardonically. *Did the silly chits think I was going to bare my fangs...* His sarcasm trailed off as a carriage pulled to a halt just ahead, and three ladies descended the steps.

He had no trouble recognizing Sophie's aunt. Hermione Hillhouse was perhaps a little grayer, a little stouter. However, her kindly smile was unchanged. She was followed by a tall, slender young lady with silky curls of guinea-gold peeking out from beneath the poke of her bonnet.

"Do have a care, Georgie," called Hermione. "The cobbles are uneven."

That was Georgiana?

Cameron recalled Sophie's younger sister as a pleasant, pudgy little child with a streak of mud always marring the tip of her nose. *But then, I daresay we all have changed since those long-ago days.*

Though not always for the better.

Sophie, however, was even more breathtakingly lovely than he remembered. Last night, the dark night and heavy veiling had obscured her face. Now, as she stepped down to the pavement, the afternoon sun painted every nuance of her profile with a softly gilded light.

She laughed at something her aunt said and Cameron felt his chest constrict.

Feeling a little light-headed, he picked his way through the crowd, the banal buzz of voices around him fading, fuzzing. The light seemed to blur, and suddenly the only thing in sharp focus was Sophie as she slowly turned and entered the shop.

The click of the door falling shut seemed to snap him out of the strange netherworld. Looking down, Cameron found to his disgust that he was leaning against the decorative railing of a shop displaying kidskin gloves in a staggering variety of colors.

Get hold of yourself, he warned in a silent snarl. How utterly embarrassing if anyone were see the supremely sardonic Hellhound reduced to a pathetic whimper.

He turned away from the array of soft pinks and purples, fully intending to hurry on to Jackson's Boxing Salon. There was no better refuge—amid the slap of leather and grunts of pain, he could pummel his emotions into submission by working up a sweat on the heavy punching bags.

But to his dismay, his feet rebelled against reason.

They slowed, and then stopped in front of an ornate arched window filled with beribboned bonnets and plumed turbans.

I will just pause for a moment, he vowed, peering over an ostrich feather for a clear view of shop's interior.

Georgiana was trying on a pert little confection of chip straw festooned with tiny red cherries. Sophie smiled and shook her head, prompting a remark from their aunt. Next came a more sedate creation, featuring shades of pale apricot and cream...

A frown flitted across Georgiana's face as she reached up to unsnag a ribbon from around her ear. "Why is that gentleman staring at us?"

"Where?" Sophie looked up from the patternbook.

"There. Right outside the window."

Shifting her stance, Sophie caught a glimpse of a dark shape moving away with muscled quickness. She hurried to the door, but a glance through its glass pane showed only the top of a high-crown beaver hat, fast melting away in the crowd.

"How odd," said Georgiana.

"Indeed," said Sophie, still looking out at the street. Even odder was the tickling sensation teasing at the nape of her neck. It was foolish to allow her imagination to run wild. There must be thousands of black hats in London with broad brims and grosgrain bands.

Yes, but how many of them are worn tugged down at a rakish angle?

Dismissing the question as too fanciful to deserve an answer, she returned to her study of ribbons.

"Oh, look," exclaimed Georgiana, lifting an elegantly

simple creation from its bandbox. "Wouldn't this look perfect with Sophie's new indigo gown?"

"Perfect!" echoed Hermione.

"Please, I don't need such extravagances." Sophie made a face, feeling guilty that her relative had ordered not one, but two new gowns for her, along with a lovely selection for her sister. "There is an old adage about trying to make a silk purse from a sow's ear. And besides, you have been far too generous as it is."

"Nonsense. You must indulge me, my dear. It is a great pleasure to shop with my nieces. I wish you would allow me to do so more often." Hermione was their late mother's sister, and she and her husband tactfully did their best to augment their father's meager earnings. They could afford it, but Sophie did not like to take advantage of their kindness.

"Thank you, but..." The bonnet was really very fetching. "But I have no need—"

"We'll take this," said Georgiana decisively, quickly handing it to the clerk behind the counter.

"And we will also take that darling Dutch bonnet to complement your new sprigged muslin walking dress," added Hermione. "Now, we must look for a military-style shako with a silk tassel to top off your riding habit..."

The carriage was bursting with boxes by the time the trio had finished their rounds of the Bond Street shops.

"What fun," said Hermione, fanning her cheeks. "Though I confess, sorting through all those fabrics and styles requires a great deal of energy. Shall we stop at Gunter's for refreshments?"

Georgiana, who was quite fond of the famous teashop's strawberry ice cream, quickly seconded the suggestion. "Shall we walk?" she added. "It's just a short stroll to Berkeley Square, and that way we can look at the shop windows."

Sophie fell in step with the others, but soon found her attention wandering from the fancy displays. *Why, oh why am I plagued by this strange notion of déjà vu?* she wondered, unable to keep from thinking of the Pirate, and the unsettling memories of the past. *One must never look back, only forward.* Ignoring yet another odd tickling at the back of her neck, she kept her eyes focused straight ahead.

Swoosh, swoosh, swoosh. Her skirts swirled around her ankles as she quickened her pace. And still, a sense of foreboding shadowed her steps.

The next window showcased a glittering array of rings and necklaces. The slanting sun deepened the jeweltone colors of the precious stones, flickers of ruby, emerald, and sapphire dancing through the clear glass.

Sophie spun around as a wink of gold cut across the reflection.

But once again, the man—the specter—darted away with maddening quickness. All she could make out was a fleeting flutter of brightly patterned silk.

"Are you feeling ill, Sophie?" Georgiana touched her sleeve in concern. "You look awfully pale."

"I'm just fatigued, that's all," she answered, rubbing at her eyes.

Her sister fixed her with a long look. "You haven't been getting enough sleep lately. It's early to bed for you tonight. Tomorrow's visit to Vauxhall Gardens promises to be an adventure."

"Adventure is the last thing I need in my life," muttered Sophie.

"Ha!" scoffed Georgiana. "Admit it—your life has been dreadfully dull for far too many years." She eyed the earthtone shade of Sophie's wool walking gown and crinkled her nose. "It's time to add a little color and spice to your drab routine."

Chapter Three

Color and spice. There was no denying that the vast Vauxhall pleasure gardens were a completely different world from the small town of Terrington. Sophie gazed at the central esplanade over the rim of her wine glass, fascinated by the parade of people filing in from the river landing. Shopgirls and tradesmen dressed in cheap calico and canvas were rubbing shoulders with aristocrats and ladybirds swathed in expensive silk and merino, the universal language of laughter and jests rising above the hodge-podge of dialects.

"Ooooo, this is so exciting." Georgiana leaned out over the railing of their supper box, determined not to miss a single detail of the surroundings. "I must describe everything to Anthony in my next letter."

Hermione smiled fondly. "I am sure that the two of you will come here together when you are married."

Her sister let out a fluttery sigh.

"Yes, and you will not have plot on how to steal a kiss in the bushes," said their uncle, a twinkle lighting his eyes. "A married couple is allowed to indulge in a peck or two."

"But doing something just a little naughty adds an extra edge of excitement."

Sophie raised a brow.

"Not that I have any experience in such things," added Georgiana hastily. "I—I have simply heard it said."

"Don't believe all you hear," murmured Sophie, as she held back a smile.

Her sister turned in her chair to hide the flush of color rising to her cheeks. After watching the ornate lanterns bordering the square blaze to life, she asked, "Might we take a walk through the gardens before the fireworks begin?"

"Come, Edward, the girls must not miss seeing the Oriental Pavilion," said Hermione, pushing aside her empty plate. "And of course, they are eager to explore the pathways."

"Very well." He rose and straightened his waistcoat. "We'll have a look at the buildings first, and then…" A wink "…move on to the shadowed walkways, where young ladies must guard against the temptation to stray down the path to Perdition."

Georgiana stifled a giggle.

"Oh, do stop your teasing and lead on, Edward," said their aunt. "I daresay our level-headed nieces are safe enough from Sin."

Sin.

Sophie tested the word on her tongue as she dutifully fell in step behind her uncle and Georgiana. It had a rather seductive sound, the soft hiss mimicking the ruffling of a summer breeze through meadow grasses. *Sin.* The whisper stirred a memory from somewhere deep inside her head—the fragrance of fresh mown hay, the texture of fescue against bare skin, the taste of sun-warmed kisses—

"Sophie?" Hermione cleared her throat. "Are you coming down with the sniffles?"

"No, no, I am quite well. I was simply woolgathering," she apologized. "There is so much to stimulate the senses."

"Uncle Edward is suggesting that we pass by the Pillared Saloon and then make our way to the statue of Handel in the Great South Walk," volunteered Georgiana. "From there we can turn into the gardens."

"That would be lovely." In truth, the sights were barely more than an amorphous blur. Her mind was elsewhere.

Sailing over an azure-blue sea with a laughing pirate at the helm of ship made of spun gold.

"Has the wine gone to your head?" asked her sister in an undertone, linking arms and leading her around one of the exotic columns.

She shook her head.

"It isn't like you to be so distracted. I wish you would tell me what's wrong."

Oh, where to begin? Dudley and Morton's threats, their father's retreat from reality, the dark specter haunting her peace of mind—despite all her hurried stitches, it felt as if her life were unraveling at the seams.

"Come along, girls, and stay close," called Hermione. "All jesting aside, we don't want to lose you. The gardens attract all sorts of unsavory characters who prowl the grounds after dark, looking for trouble."

Grateful for the interruption, Sophie quickly rejoined her aunt. For the few remaining hours of the evening, she would try to put aside her troubles and enjoy the devil-may-care spirit of Vauxhall.

"After all, she sighed under her breath. "My troubles will still be here come morning."

Cameron adjusted his silk mask and slipped out from the niche between the colonnading. His soft-soled leather boots skimmed noiselessly over the dew-dampened grass as he glided through the dense shrubbery. Laughter drifted up from the hidden benches, its rumble turning softly smoky in the flickering lantern light.

Sophie and her family were walking leisurely down the main path, their faces well illuminated by the blazing torchieres lining the way. She appeared amused, and yet her smile did not quite reach her eyes. Beneath the fire-tipped lashes hung a shading of delicate shadows.

Sadness? Perhaps pensive was a better choice of words, decided Cameron. Sophie had a tendency to let her head overrule her heart.

For a moment, he found himself thinking back to a time when they had shared their laughter, their hopes, their dreams, their kisses...their hearts.

Or maybe I am just flattering myself to think that her heart was ever mine.

They had been young. Too young—she had been sixteen and he had been just a year older—and he had been far too naïve. At that age, he had foolishly believed that love could conquer all...

A raucous laugh rang out from the nearby shadows, snapping him back to the present. There was still time to slink away. He was good at leaving no telltale tracks, no sign that he was anything more than a black-on-black shape flitting through the darkness.

Uncertainty warred within him, making him feel weak,

vulnerable. The fleeting reminder of his former self was uncomfortable—he wasn't much given to introspection. He had toiled damnably hard to live only in the present, trusting in only his own cleverness and his own mordant sense of humor for survival.

"And that won't change," he vowed softly. "It's only a momentary meeting." Two ships on two vastly different courses, passing briefly in the night.

Sophie's group paused at the entrance to the Dark Walk, an unlit pathway notorious as a trysting place for illicit lovers. After a short discussion, Edward gave in to Georgiana's pleas to venture just a few steps into its inky shadows. He offered her his arm and extended the other to Sophie, who edged back and insisted that her aunt take precedence.

"I'm not nearly as curious as Georgie. I've no need to venture into the unknown," she announced. "I'll wait for you here."

Hermione hesitated. "All alone?"

"Good heavens, it's nearly bright as day, and there are plenty of people close by." Sophie shooed them away. "I'm perfectly safe."

A breeze from the river shimmied through the overhanging leaves, and the low rustling seemed to spark the red-gold flames to swaying in a slow, sinuous dance.

Twining her shawl a little tighter around her shoulders, Sophie moved closer to the bushes, as if entranced by the shimmering patterns of light cast by the fire.

"That, my dear," intoned Cameron through his teeth, "is exactly the wrong thing to say when a predator is lurking nearby, just waiting for the right moment to pounce."

* * *

"Ssssssss."

Surely it was only her over-stimulated imagination that was turning the whisper of the wind into the flutter of her name. Sophie stepped back but then froze as it came again, this time a little louder.

"*Ssssssssophie*."

She peered left and right along the line of bushes. "Who's there?"

No answer, save for a faint chattering among the long-leaved rhododendrons.

"Be you demon or *djinn*, I refuse to be played for a fool." Drawing a deep breath, Sophie parted the greenery and pushed deeper into the thicket, determined to find the teasing, taunting voice. Perhaps it was the wine fueling her recklessness, but she was suddenly sick of being cautious, sick of being timid.

A hand gloved in black leather caught her wrist. "Brave girl."

Somehow she managed to swallow a scream.

"Brave," repeated the voice, "but foolish, despite your assertions to the contrary. I could be a mad murderer." His long, lithe limbs unfolding in a whisper of expensive wool, the Pirate—yes, it was her Pirate—rose from a crouch. "Or worse."

Sophie's first flare of fear died away as she recognized him—his touch, his scent, and something she couldn't quite put a name to. "What could be worse than death?" she asked, trying to match his note of cool cynicism.

"Ah, well, there are some who value their virtue above all things," he answered.

A lick of fire—or was it ice?—teased down her spine. "Is my virtue in mortal danger?"

His deep-throated chuckle stirred the leaves. "That depends."

"Are your answers always so cryptic?" she countered.

"I thought it was quite obvious what I meant. You were supposed to ask 'On what?'"

"Very well." She drew in another steadying breath. "On what?"

"On a number of things."

"Oh, fie! You are mocking me, sir, and I don't find it amusing." Sophie tried to pull away, but his grip kept her captured. "Let me go, you...you cutthroat pirate."

Releasing her wrist, he swept off his hat and inclined an ironic bow. "I prefer 'corsair.' It has a more elegant ring, don't you think?" The breeze ruffled his long hair and as he straightened, a few silky strands tangled around the gold ornament dangling from his earlobe.

It was, she saw, a tiny sword.

"And by the by," he added. "Allow me to point out that your lovely neck is quite unharmed."

Her freed hand flew to her throat, and once again he laughed.

She narrowed her eyes as a flicker of the faraway torchiere passed over his face, confirming her first impression of unremitting black. Hair, mask, coat—even his upswept shirtpoints were made of midnight silk. However, the wink of light also caught a spot of color.

Bond Street—the flash of pink beneath a gentleman's dark coat.

"You," she said tightly, pointing at his carelessly knotted cravat. "You have been following me, and I demand to know why."

"Have I?" He took a half-step closer and suddenly the

chill night air felt very warm. "Who knows, perhaps you have a legion of devoted swains dogging your steps."

"D-don't be absurd," stammered Sophie. "I'm a nobody. A simple country spinster with no connections, no money, and no beauty. I'm hardly the sort of woman to attract any attention."

"And yet I know your name, and all about your background, Miss Sophie Lawrance of Terrington, a small town on the Norfolk coast."

She swallowed hard.

"Does that frighten you?"

No, it intrigues me, though I can't explain why.

The Pirate seemed to take her silence as an invitation to come even closer. "No," he murmured, "I've noticed that for all your quiet ways, you don't frighten easily." His hands set on her shoulders and slowly drew inwards, until his thumbs were lightly touching the hollow of her throat.

Sophie felt her pulse skitter and kick up a notch. Her flesh began to throb against the butter-soft leather. "I could scream," she whispered.

"True. But I don't think you will." His mocking mouth was now but a hairsbreadth from hers. "I think you're hoping I'll kiss you again."

"Th-that's absurd."

"Why else wander down the Dark Walk, if not to indulge in your wildest desires?"

"I . . ." Sophie couldn't bring herself to go on. Lies and longings—both were sinfully wrong.

The Pirate seemed to read her thoughts. "Confused? Life rarely offers black-and-white answers, Sophie. It's mostly a muddle of shapeless grays. Only you can decide what form you want them to take."

"Why are you following me?" she asked again.

"Call it curiosity. It's clear you are involved in some very dangerous dealings, and as someone who is intimately acquainted with skullduggery, I can't help but wonder why. Lord Dudley is not a good choice of friends."

"Good God, he is *not* a friend," she croaked.

His hands moved up to frame her face. "Perhaps you need one."

Need. Her whole body was suddenly all aquiver. "Oh, I wish...I wish—"

A kiss feathered over her lips, lightly at first, but the sweet friction sparked a fierce flare of heat inside her. All sense—all sanity—seemed to go up in smoke.

Moaning against his mouth, Sophie clutched at his strong, sloping shoulders and let her body melt against his. Beneath the finespun layers of cloth, she could feel the chiseled contours of his muscles.

A rumbled laugh turned to a feral groan in the Pirate's throat as their tongues touched and twined. Through the slitted eyeholes of his mask she saw a flash of green-gold fire.

Dear God. Dear God. She felt herself drowning in the swirling depths. Desperately in need of something solid to cling to, she hitched her hips, forcing his legs apart. Her fingers tangled in his hair, drawing him down, down.

Without breaking their kiss, the Pirate spun her around, and suddenly his warm weight had her pinned against the trunk of a tree. Liquid heat spiraled to her core as the hard ridge of his arousal thrust against her belly.

Oh, this is wicked, thought Sophie, even as she opened

herself to his lush embrace. *Wicked.* How to explain the heady sweetness of his mouth, the mad surrender to primal lust? It must be a potent Pirate spell, a Corsair's concoction made of fire-kissed rum and demon desires.

The real Sophie Lawrance would never give in to temptation...

So I must be somebody else.

"Sophie...Sunbeam." The words were barely more than a sigh, yet they hit her with all the force of a physical slap. Only one person in the world had ever called her by such a pet name. A boy on the brink of manhood, bristling with uncontrollable passions.

Dear God, it couldn't be... Her head began to reel and her throat was suddenly dry as dust. She stared in mute shock for a long, dizzying moment before managing to make a sound.

"*Cameron?*"

"Ah, at last you've puzzled it out. I was beginning to think you had quite forgotten I ever existed."

"N-never," whispered Sophie.

He leaned back and regarded her in solemn silence.

Reaching up, she slowly untied the mask and let it fall away.

"Never say never." Cameron paused. "The truth is, the person you knew has changed beyond recognition."

"Never," she repeated. "I never forgot you. Even though we parted with harsh words that long-ago night. Even though you disappeared with nary a word of goodbye."

"I was angry, Sophie."

"I know." She sighed. "I know. I hurt you." *And you hurt me.*

He turned, and in the dappling of moonlight his sculp-tured features appeared cold and unyielding as polished marble.

Sophie pressed a palm to his cheek, needing to feel his warmth again. "I'm sorry."

His mouth quirked to a sardonic smile. "Don't be. It was all for the best. The blaze of youthful passion burned too hot. We would have destroyed each other."

As if echoing his words, a deep *bang* reverberated through the trees and a rocket shot skyward, painting the black velvet heavens with a luminous burst of color.

The sound reminded her that she dare not tarry here any longer. "Oh, Lord, I must be going." Sophie began tugging her disheveled clothing into place. "My uncle and aunt will be frantic with worry."

"Wait." Cameron took a small chamois pouch from his pocket. "You asked why I was following you—the reason is this." He unknotted the strings. "Give me your hand."

She hesitated and then did as he asked. "Cam—" Her breath caught in her throat as he gave a small shake and her heirloom pearl earrings dropped onto her palm.

Bang. The sky filled with a shower of brilliant green sparks. Feeling dazed, Sophie carefully closed her fingers around the jewels. A myriad of questions were exploding in her head.

Bang, bang, bang.

"Go now, before they send out a search party." He stepped back and turned up his collar.

"Please, you can't simply disappear!" she cried. "I must see you again. There are too many unanswered questions."

A tiny muscle twitched on his jaw. "Very well. Meet

me in Green Park tomorrow afternoon." He described the location. "At three."

She looked down at her fisted hand. "At three," she repeated. But when she looked up he was already gone.

"Oh, Cameron," she whispered, blinking back tears as she stared at the shifting shadows. Another bang rent the air, finally rousing her to action. Carefully tucking her treasure away, she pushed her way through the tangled branches and stumbled back to the main pathway.

"My dear Sophie! Thank God you are safe!" cried Edward. "We were so worried!"

"I'm so sorry," she apologized. "I didn't mean to alarm you. I wandered off the path, and lost my way."

Hermione clucked in sympathy. "It's my fault. I should have warned you that the maze of twisting pathways can be confusing. Many people become disoriented."

"No harm done," murmured Sophie, evading Georgiana's gimlet gaze. "Come, let us forget the matter, and not let it spoil our enjoyment of the fireworks."

"This way," said her uncle, offering his arm. "We shall have a better view from the South Promenade."

Bang, bang, bang. Sophie wasn't sure whether the thumping noise was the pyrotechnics overhead or her own pounding heart. Pasting on a dutiful smile, she looked up at the heavens and added her voice to the chorus of oohs and ahhs. But in truth, all she saw was the image etched in her mind's eye. *A lean, chiseled face. Harder, the features far more defined than she remembered.* Cameron had left Terrington a rebellious adolescent.

And now?

There were so many questions. If only some answers

would start coming to light. Beginning with how Cameron had come to have possession of her pearls.

More unsettled by the encounter with Sophie than he cared to admit, Cameron made his way to The Wolf's Lair, rather than return to his own solitary abode. Sara's friendly chatter—not to speak of her aged brandy— would be a welcome balm for the spirit.

In truth, he was badly in need of a drink.

Her company was undemanding, her private office a refuge, a place where his nerves could unwind. Quickening his steps he traversed the murky alleyway and slipped in through the back entrance.

"Well, well, well, we were wondering if you would turn up."

Cameron froze for an instant on hearing the Earl of Killingworth's low rumble, then casually tossed his hat on the sideboard. "What are you doing back in Town, Connor?" he asked. "Don't tell me that you are bored with life as a goat farmer. With a partner like Lady K, I'd have thought that pastoral pleasures would not lose their allure."

His friend—who was the former owner of the Lair— let out a bark of laughter. "Indeed not. I am quite content with my wife and my wool on the hoof, but one must occasionally attend to business in the city."

"Lady K's weaving business is going great guns," piped up a second voice from the shadows. A spark of flint and steel lit the lamp on the curio cabinet, illuminating the Marquess of Haddan's face.

Connor *and* Gryff? *Hell and damnation.* Cameron gave an inward wince. He was in no mood for meeting the two other Hellhounds. They, of all people, were the ones most likely to sense his fragile state of mind.

And they, of all people, were the ones he did not wish to see him so stripped of his defenses. So vulnerable.

"The *ton* is snapping up their woven Kashmir shawls faster than she and Connor can produce them," went on Gryff. Alexa Hendrie, a very clever young lady, had proved to be the perfect mate for the Irish Wolfhound, and together they were thriving in both love and business. "So he needs to purchase more looms." A cough. "As well as a few sundries to update the nursery at Linsley Close."

"Congratulations, Connor," muttered Cameron, pouring himself a large brandy. "And what, pray tell, brings you to Town?" he snapped at Gryff. "Last thing I heard, you were happily digging in the dirt of your country estate." Gryff was an expert on landscape design, and had just begun putting theory into practice at his ancestral estate.

"The gardens are blooming beautifully," said Gryff with a satisfied smile. He, too, had recently taken a bride. "However, our publisher needed me to check over a few last minute corrections on my essays before the book goes to press." His new wife Eliza was a remarkably talented botanical artist and together they had created a beautiful compendium on the classic estate gardens of England.

That married life appeared to agree so well with his friends only exacerbated Cameron's ugly mood. Raising his glass, he allowed a faint sneer to curl on his mouth. "Here's to hoping that my dear comrades-in-hellraising don't turn into total stick-in-the-muds."

Arching a brow, Connor glanced at Gryff. "Is it my

imagination, or does it seem to you that the Sleuth Hound has a thorn stuck in his paw?"

"I'd say it's lodged in a different portion of his anatomy," drawled Gryff. The lamplight played over his impish grin. "What's the trouble, Cam? Don't tell us your nose for trouble has landed you in the briars."

"Arse—both of you," he growled into his brandy. "Where the devil is Sara? I came here seeking entertaining conversation, and what do I find? That my fellow Hellhounds have become woefully domesticated. Weaving shawls, writing garden books..." He gave a mock shudder. "Good God, I suppose the next time I see you, you'll be wearing skirts."

The swish of ruched satin filled the sudden silence as Sara swept into the room. "What's all the barking about?" she asked, frowning at Cameron. "Ain't ye glad te see yer old friends?"

He responded with a very indelicate word.

"He's in a snarly mood," murmured Gryff. "Haven't a clue why."

Connor, whose temper was easily triggered, looked up, a quicksilver spark in his gray eyes. "Neither do I, but if he insults my manhood—or my wife—again, he'll be fishing his teeth out of his gullet."

"Come to think of it, he's been acting awfully odd ever since that veiled lady came here seeking an audience with Lord Dudley."

Much as he liked Sara, at that moment Cameron could have wrung her neck.

Gryff straightened from his slouch. "What lady?"

"Hmm, let me see...Leighton, Lightbourne...Lawrance. Aye, that was it. Miss Lawrance."

"And who, pray tell, is the mysterious Miss Lawrance?" Gryff's question was directed at him.

"Why ask me?" glowered Cameron. "Sara is the one who seems to know all the sordid details."

Without waiting for further invitation, Sara chimed in, "Well, I wish I could tell ye more, but the whole thing was all very havey-cavey. The young lady came in, claiming it was a matter of grave importance that she speak with Lord Dudley."

"Somehow, that scenario has a familiar ring to it," said Gryff. Both he and Connor had first encountered their future wives at The Wolf's Lair under similar circumstances.

The quip earned a reproving look from Connor.

"Oh, come." Gryff, always the most light-hearted of the trio, made a face. "Does no one else here possess a sense of humor?"

"Have a care, Haddan. Yer friends look ready to bite yer head off." Sara waggled a warning finger. "Now hold yer tongue and let me finish."

Gryff cocked a salute and refilled his glass. "You can't be miffed. Unlike Cam, I always pay my bill here."

"Oh, I always add his tab to yours, seeing as ye can well afford it." Sara smiled sweetly before going on. "Getting back to the young lady, she wasn't closeted with Dudley very long—a minute or two at the most. She left quickly, just as I had asked...and now here comes the strange part."

She paused for dramatic effect. "Dudley returned to the gaming rooms, looking like a cat with cream on his whiskers. Shortly afterward, Mr. Daggett arrives and plays a hand of cards at the same table, then he leaves to come visit me back here—and then all hell breaks loose. Dudley starts screaming that his pocket has been picked of a very valuable bit of jewelry. But when pressed, the viscount refuses to describe it."

"Interesting," murmured Connor.

"I don't see why," snapped Cameron. "Not every bauble that goes missing in London ends up in my hands. More's the pity, I might add."

Gryff set down his glass and steepled his fingers. "Something has gotten under your hide and is pricking a sensitive spot. My guess is it's a woman."

"Definitely a woman," concurred Connor. "And it's about bloody time your sharp-toothed sarcasm about love circles around and bites you where it hurts."

Gryff let out a low chortle.

Cameron felt a prickle of heat steal along his cheekbones. He was used to doing the most caustic needling, and it was damned uncomfortable to find himself the butt of their teasing.

"Ha, ha, very amusing," he replied. "Love has nothing to do with the matter. But seeing as you lapdogs can yap about nothing else, I think I shall seek more convivial company elsewhere." He started to reach for his hat, but a sudden thought made him hesitate.

Sophie was in trouble, and however much he loathed to reveal this chink in his worldly cynicism to his friends, he couldn't let pride stand in the way of the chance to help her. So, much as he wished to appear aloof and uncaring about anyone or anything, he forced himself to speak.

"By the by," he muttered, trying to sound casual. "What do you know about Dudley, Connor? Seeing as he's been a regular patron of the Lair for several years, you must be privy to his habits."

Gryff made a low sound in his throat, but Connor signaled him to silence. "What sort of habits do you mean?"

Cameron drew a deep breath. "Does he gamble beyond his means? Does he have any secret depravities…that sort of thing."

"In short, you wish to know whether he is a blackguard?"

Cameron nodded.

"Dudley is a thoroughly dirty dish," replied Connor. "As is his close crony Morton and their circle of friends. They are clever and conniving about twisting other people's weaknesses to their own advantage. They wouldn't dare diddle with the likes of us—they prefer more vulnerable targets. But that said, I wouldn't underestimate them. They are dangerous."

Dangerous. Cameron watched the play of shadows on the far wall. *How had Sophie become entangled with such men?*

"Thank you." He took up his hat.

"We are staying at my townhouse for another few days," said Gryff. "Come around tomorrow evening and sup with us."

"Perhaps," he replied absently, his thoughts still occupied with unsettling questions.

"It should go without saying, Cam," added Connor softly. "But if you need any help from us, you have only to ask."

Chapter Four

$\mathcal{I}$s there anything else you wish us to purchase for you?" Sophie poked her head into the morning room where her aunt was consulting with her housekeeper on the day's menus.

"No, the embroidery threads are all, my dear. Georgie has the color samples," replied Hermione. "You are sure that you girls don't mind doing your errands without me?"

"Oh, not at all," assured Sophie, who had deliberately mentioned that a visit to Hatchards book shop was among their plans. Hermione was not a very avid reader.

"I confess, I am a trifle fatigued from our outing, so I am just as happy to spend the day at home with my needlework." Hermione held up the waistcoat she was working on. "I am making great progress on my surprise for Edward's birthday."

"It's lovely." Sophie knotted her bonnet strings under her chin, relieved that she had overcome the first hurdle to her plans. "We shall see you later."

Her sister was another stumbling block, and one that would require a bit more fancy footwork to sidestep. But she would deal with that when the time came.

Georgiana, however, had her own ideas on the subject. As soon as the carriage started rolling toward Bond Street, she swiveled on the seat and set a hand on her hip. "*You* have a great deal of explaining to do."

Sophie angled her gaze out the window. "About what?"

"You know very well about what—last night, and your disappearance in the Dark Walk."

"I told you, I simply got lost in the shrubbery." A pause. "It was, well, dark."

"It was dark," repeated her sister. "Ha! And I suppose that you are also going to tell me that it was the rhododendron bush that left that little red love bite on your neck."

"Don't be absurd—plants don't have teeth." Sophie then quickly countered with a question of her own. "And pray tell, how would you know anything about love bites, and what they look like?"

Paper crackled as Georgiana hastily unfolded her shopping list. "I just remembered that Aunt Hermione asked me to get a pair of buttons in addition to her embroidery thread. We also need to stop by Madame LaForge's shop to pick up lace..."

The rest of the ride passed with no further mention of Vauxhall Gardens.

Thankfully, shopping for sundries kept her sister's attention happily engaged. Sophie did her best to keep up a cheerful chatter, but her own secret worries were far darker than the colorful ribbons and trimmings.

Given Dudley's escalating threats and Georgie's probing, she felt caught between a hammer and an anvil.

And then there was Cameron.

Cameron.

Feeling a telltale flush of heat color her face, Sophie twitched the folds of her shawl up a little higher. Dear God, the sight of him, the feel of him, and the taste of him had set her heart galloping with joy. Which was, she knew, a recklessly wrong reaction. There was still an untamed aura about him. A wild, impetuous streak that boded Trouble.

And yet, against all reason, her devilish, disobedient body still responded to his fiery charms.

"I made the right decision all those years ago," she whispered, hoping that saying the words aloud would give them credence.

"Did you say something?" Georgiana looked around a display of silk roses.

"I—I was just wondering whether you are ready to leave for Hatchards," replied Sophie.

"Yes, let me just have the clerk wrap my purchases."

A short walk brought them to the bookstore. "Are you looking for something in particular?" asked her sister as they passed through the entrance.

"Oh, I thought that I would browse among the section on gardening…" Sophie darted a quick look at the tall case clock opposite the central staircase. "A guide to growing roses would make a lovely gift for Papa."

"An excellent suggestion," said Georgiana. "I'll come along and help you look."

"Wouldn't you rather peruse the display of Ackermann's fashion plates upstairs?"

"No," came the decisive reply. "And look, the gardening alcove is deserted, which will allow us the perfect opportunity for a private sisterly chat."

Sophie repressed a harried sigh. It seemed that within the blink of an eye, her sweet, fluffy little kitten of a sister had grown into an independent-minded creature with newfound claws.

"Feel free to wax poetic about Anthony," said Sophie, pretending to peruse the nearest shelf. "You are always welcome to confide your feelings."

"Actually, I would rather talk about you, not me."

She pulled down a slim leatherbound volume and began leafing through the pages. "A boring subject, I fear. Aside from rescuing Mrs. Addison's pug from the pond last month, I've had precious little excitement in my life."

Georgiana slowly cocked her head and angled it side to side.

"What are you doing?" asked Sophie.

"Watching your nose grow longer and longer...you know, just like in that fairy tale you used to read to me and Penelope, warning of the consequences of telling lies." Another tilt. "By the by, that is a book on beekeeping, and you are reading it upside down."

Snapping the covers shut, Sophie shoved it back in its place.

"Honestly, if I didn't know you better, I would ask if you are having..." Georgiana dropped her voice a notch. "...an illicit affair."

"*Me*?" The word sounded perilously close to a squeak. Recovering her voice, she quickly added, "Good heavens, are you *mad*?"

"I know, I know, it's ridiculous. Ha, ha, ha."

"Ha, ha, ha," echoed Sophie weakly.

Her sister's tentative smile faded just as quickly. "But that doesn't alter the fact that you have been acting unlike yourself lately. Midnight forays, disheveled clothing, evasive answers." Georgiana fixed her with a searching stare. "And most of all, that guilty expression shadowing your eyes. Something is very wrong. Why won't you share it with me? Perhaps I can help."

God forbid. Once again, the thought of Georgiana involved in the sordid stink of blackmail sent a chill shuddering down Sophie's spine. Anthony's parents were already opposed to the love match. One whiff of scandal . . .

"No, no, it's something that I must deal with on my own." Sophie edged back and craned her neck for a look at the clock. Time was of the essence in more ways than one. In little more than a month, Anthony and his parents were coming to Terrington for the annual Hunt Ball. It was to be the formal start to the prenuptial celebrations, with the wedding to follow a week later. Somehow, she must keep Dudley and Morton's threats from destroying Georgiana's future.

"But don't worry," she added. "I hope to have it resolved soon."

Her sister scowled. "Your nose just grew another inch longer."

"That is *not* humorous." Turning to shield her face from further scrutiny, Sophie moved several paces down the stretch of shelving.

Silk rustled softly across the dusty floor as Georgiana stuck to her skirts like a cocklebur. "Neither is that odious You-Are-Too-Young-To-Understand tone. Damnation, I am *not* a child anymore, Sophie."

"Don't swear," she said automatically.

"Then don't provoke me."

"I…" Another peek at the clock. "I'm sorry, but may we argue about this later? I—I have to step outside."

"Where are you going?" demanded Georgiana.

"Never mind. It's just for a short while." Sophie hated to wheedle, but time was of the essence. "Please, Georgie. I am begging a favor of you—let me fly without further haranguing. It's terribly important."

Her sister's scowl softened. "Then it goes without saying that you can count on me."

"Thank you." Sophie heaved a sigh of relief. "I promise I won't be long." Gathering her skirts, she turned and hurried for the door.

Traversing Piccadilly as fast as she dared, Sophie darted through the entrance to Green Park and cut along the graveled footpath leading to the far side of the lawns. Just as Cameron had described, a secluded copse of chestnut trees stood beyond a fringe of bushes, their leafy shadows promising a modicum of privacy.

"Over here." The familiar voice floated out from behind the rough-barked trunks.

Sophie quickened her steps, an unwilling rush of excitement tingling through every fiber of her body.

Oh, surely it is wrong to respond like a shameless hussy—I am prim, practical Sophie Lawrance, she reminded herself. *Who always errs on the side of caution.*

But seeing as her life was already heading to Hell in a handcart, what did it matter if one more sin was scratched on her slate?

Peering through the shifting scrim of greens, Cameron saw Sophie lift her skirts and cross onto the grass. She moved with an unconscious grace, light and airy as the flutter of a butterfly's wing, and as he watched her approach he felt his heart begin to hammer against his ribs. *Memories, memories...* He shook his head, trying to banish the bedeviling past.

"Don't look back," he murmured, his gaze glued to the wisps of honey-gold curls dancing in the breeze. In a louder voice, he called again. "Over here."

She hesitated for instant before ducking beneath the branches. Her cheeks were slightly flushed, her breath a little ragged. "You came." A tremulous smile. "I thought perhaps last night was merely...a figment of my imagination, brought on by too much wine."

"You tasted of champagne," he murmured. *And an ethereal sweetness beyond words.*

Her color deepened. "I fear its effervescence affected my wits. I am not in the habit of...of..."

"Of kissing masked men in the bushes?" he suggested.

"Precisely. As you know, I am sober, sensible Sophie." The shade of regret in her voice might only have been a delusion of his own benighted brain.

Cameron inhaled deeply, the floral scent of her fragrance sending a sudden wave of intoxication bubbling through his blood.

Don't—oh, don't. Reason sought to make itself heard above its thrumming rush.

Too late. Something inside him snapped, unleashing a wild, primal longing that he had thought was long since tamed. "You are also sensual, sinful Sophie," he whispered, sweeping her into his arms. "Or have you forgotten those sun-dappled magical moments?"

"How could I ever forget?" Her hands skimmed along his jaw, her lips touched his cheek—hungrily, or so it seemed to him. "But sin has no place in my life anymore."

"No?" He teased his tongue along her mouth.

She choked back a moan. "No. My family depends on me." A sigh. "They need me. Now, as then."

"What of your own needs, Sophie?" Cameron let her body slowly slide down his. As her feet touched the ground, he took her face between his hands. "What of your own desires?"

"I..." The pulsepoint at her throat was skittering out of control.

"Don't tell me you have no desires," he whispered, licking the throbbing flesh.

The lush caress seemed to rattle her self-control. A sound—somewhere between a laugh and a sob—broke free as she slipped her hand inside his shirt and pressed it to his bare skin. "I—I can't deny it." Her palm touched the taut nub of his nipple, then suddenly pulled away. "But..."

Need speared through him, momentarily cutting through all the carefully crafted cynicism he had wrapped around his heart. Oh, how he missed her warmth and her laughter caressing his skin.

With a desperate growl, Cameron cupped her breasts, reveling in their soft, yielding ripeness beneath her corset. "God help me, but I want to rip away this cursed fabric..." His fingers hooked into the top of her bodice, sending her shawl slithering to the mossy ground. "And tear the laces free."

"Cam...Cam." Sophie shuddered and broke off his kiss. "Whatever my own desires, I can't give in to wild urges. It's too dangerous." She pulled back, blinking a beading of tears from her lashes.

"Ah, yes. Danger," he said evenly, forcing himself to regain a grip on his emotions. "That is, after all, what's brought us back together. I don't know how you've become involved with Lord Dudley, but be assured that he is dangerous."

"I know," she whispered. "I know."

He tipped up her chin. "I take it you have not willingly sought out his acquaintance?"

"Good God, no!" Her eyes squeezed shut for a moment. "But how in the world did you uncover the connection...and my mother's earrings?"

"I often pay a visit to The Wolf's Lair—not for the reasons you might think, I might add. The former owner is a friend. As is Sara, the current proprietor. I happened to observe your exchange with Dudley and saw the package change hands. Let us just say that curiosity is another one of my many failings. I picked his pocket—"

Her gasp interrupted his words. "You speak of danger! Good Lord, you ought not have taken such a terrible risk."

"Trust me, Sophie, danger and I are on intimate terms. You have no idea what terrible risks and terrible things I've done since we parted ways," replied Cameron.

The color drained from her face, leaving her pale as a wisp of smoke.

"But for the moment we are discussing Dudley. And as he is careless and I am clever, there was never a cause for concern," he went on. "However, I fear the same cannot be said for your contact with that viper. Now it's your turn for explanations."

Her heavy sigh stirred the surrounding leaves. "Around six months ago, Lord Dudley and his friend Mr.

Morton came to visit the…" A hint of hesitation. "…the Marquess of Wolcott."

Cameron stiffened at the mention of the name. *Wolcott. His most implacable enemy.*

"He sought me out at one of the local Assemblies." Her voice dropped to a taut whisper. "And threatened my family with public ruin if I did not pay his price."

A frown tugged at his mouth. "That makes no sense. Why blackmail an obscure country rector? Surely he must know that your father has naught but a very modest income."

"And alas, naught but badly wandering wits." Sophie bit her lip. "Papa's hold on reality has faded badly. Even if he wanted to answer Lord Dudley's questions, he couldn't."

"First of all, what information is he seeking?" asked Cameron.

Sophie averted her eyes. "It had something to do with a long-ago church document."

She still wasn't a very good liar. The hitch in her voice told him that she was holding something back. But for the moment he let it pass. "More importantly, what deep dark secret do Dudley and Morton hold over the Lawrance family? I can't imagine any of you engaged in the sort of skullduggery worthy of blackmail."

She forced a bleak smile. "Neither could I. But apparently a half-dozen years ago, my father signed some church documents that make it appear as if he embezzled money from the bishop's private charity. He was already becoming confused, and as the head of the household, I can assure you not an unearned penny came into our hands."

"Surely the bishop's secretary can vouch for his honesty."

"Unfortunately, Mr. Perkins died a year ago, and his replacement is a martinet who goes by the letter of the law. I do not look for any sympathy from that quarter."

"Do you know for certain that Dudley possesses these incriminating papers?" he asked after a moment of thought.

"Yes. He showed them to me. As I said, their meaning is open to interpretation. But a hint of public scandal, even if unproven, would likely ruin Georgiana's engagement." Her face pinched in worry. "If jilted, she'll likely be doomed to a life of spinsterhood in Terrington. And Penelope—she, too, would have little hope for the future. I can't let that happen."

"So you have been bribing Dudley and his friend to remain quiet?"

She gave a miserable nod. "Yes, I've been buying time."

"To do what?" asked Cameron softly.

"I—I don't know. I keep trying to think of something." She lifted her chin, resolve rather than tears shimmering in her eyes. *Strong, steady Sophie*—even as a slip of a girl, she had possessed the same quiet courage. "The demands have been escalating, and I fear that with the loss of my earrings, the next payment he asks for will be one I can't meet. And with the wedding fast approaching..." Her lashes flickered. "But somehow I will find a way to fight back."

Despite the seriousness of the subject, he nearly smiled. For all her claims of being a cautious soul, Sophie was not afraid to cut loose on occasion and raise holy hell. The two of them had shared a number of devil-may-care adventures as adolescents.

"I'm well aware of your mettle. But to fight—" began Cameron, only to fall silent at the sound of approaching footsteps.

"Oh, bloody hell," whispered Sophie as a figure shoved through the greenery.

Georgiana's eyes went wide with shock.

"I-it's not what you think," stammered Sophie, trying to wriggle out of Cameron's arms and straighten her clothing at the same time.

"Oh?"

"Truly. I can explain."

"Please do," said Georgiana, eyeing the disheveled state of Sophie's bodice. "This should be exceedingly interesting."

Cameron stepped back and calmly smoothed the wrinkles from his coat. "Nature truly works in wondrous ways. I would never have guessed that the plump little gosling I knew as Georgie-Porgie would turn into such a lovely swan." He smiled as her jaw went slack. "Allow me to congratulate you on your upcoming nuptials, Miss Georgiana."

"*Cameron*? Is that Cameron Fanning?

"In the flesh," he replied with a wink. "Though for various reasons, I now go by the surname of Daggett."

"Why, we all assumed you were dead!" blurted out her sister. "That is..." She swallowed hard as a rush of color turned her cheeks a vivid scarlet. "Sorry, that was horribly rude."

"Not at all," replied Cameron. "Any sensible person

would have come to the same conclusion. At your age, I was hellbent on breaking every rule in Creation, even if it led to my own destruction."

Georgiana regarded him with undisguised curiosity, taking in his broad shoulders, tapered waist, and long, muscled legs. "Well, it appears that you came through your rebellious youth unscathed."

"Life always leaves its mark, though some are more subtle than others," he murmured. Seeing her brow furrow, he added, "At some point you will understand what I mean."

Her puzzlement tightened to a scowl. "That is odiously condescending, Mr. Daggett."

"So it is," he agreed. "But that does not make it any less true."

"Speaking of truths..." Sophie cringed as her sister fixed her with a pointed look. "You were just about to explain to me why the two of you are trysting here in broad daylight."

"It's not a tryst," Sophie hastened to explain. "It's a..."

"A business meeting," finished Cameron smoothly. "Your sister is in need of someone to conduct a few discreet inquiries, and given my skills at moving through the dark shadows of Society, I offered to take on the job."

"Ha! I knew there was trouble!" exclaimed Georgiana.

"There is," conceded Sophie. "However, that is all I mean to say on the matter."

Cameron lifted a questioning brow. "You think that wise? In my experience, such refusals often do more harm than good. The person who is kept in the dark may feel compelled to take reckless action in order to discover the truth."

"If new information comes to light, I will reconsider the decision," replied Sophie. Cameron didn't yet know the full depths of Dudley and Morton's depravity, and she hadn't decided just how much of the tale to tell him. "But for now, that is all I will promise."

"Fair enough," he answered, earning an injured look from Georgiana.

"I thought you were on my side," she groused. "When I was little, you always stood up for me."

"Let there be one thing very clear between us, ladies." His smile turned sharply sardonic. "Don't look to me for noble idealism, for you will only be sadly disappointed. I serve just one interest—my own. If this strikes you as hard-hearted, so it is."

Georgiana bit her lip. "But you just said that you were going to help Sophie."

"No he didn't," intervened Sophie. "He said he was willing to accept a job. There is a big difference."

Her sister had no answer, save for an aggrieved sniff. "And what did I just interrupt? A business discussion of what payment he wishes to receive for his services?"

"That's *quite* enough, Georgie. You are acting like a child," snapped Sophie. "Please return to Hatchards. I will join you as soon as Mr. Daggett and I have finished discussing our transaction."

Tears beaded on Georgiana's lashes as she fisted her skirts. "Very well." Ducking under an overhanging branch, she brushed past Cameron. "But I, too, wish to make something clear. Hurt my sister again, and I shall have Anthony carve your liver into a thousand tiny pieces."

Cameron waited until she had stalked out of earshot. "Who is Anthony?"

"Her fiancé," answered Sophie. "He's very skilled with a cavalry saber."

"Ah." He fingered the pearl-studded ebony hoop in his ear. "Luckily, so am I."

"Does that mean you were a soldier?"

"I have been a great many things in my life, including a soldier." A pause. "And a fool."

"And what are you now? Your clothing is finely tailored..." She eyed his earring. "...and your baubles are expensive. So I assume you have come into some money." A horrible thought suddenly occurred to her. "Perhaps you have married an heiress?"

His expression remained inscrutable. "No, I earn my own keep," he said softly. "Though I daresay you would be shocked to know how." Dead leaves crackled beneath his boots as he shifted his stance. "I steal into the fancy mansions and country estates of the aristocracy and purloin their valuables. Mostly jewels, but occasionally I take paintings and other objets d'art."

"A thief?" she said softly, trying to read the undercurrents rippling in his eyes.

"Oh, I do have some scruples. I only take from those who can well afford the loss. But other than that, you are right to sound appalled. I am a hard-hearted bastard."

Sophie flinched at the word "bastard."

"Yes, a bastard," he repeated. "We both know the ugly truth of my heritage."

"You aren't," she whispered. "The truth is—"

He was quick to cut her off. "It doesn't matter what the truth is. I can't prove it, and who do you think Society will believe—me or my illustrious half brother?"

She looked away, knowing he didn't expect an answer.

Instead she asked a question of her own. "Is that why you have chosen to lead such a dishonorable life? To punish Society for being unfair to you?"

He let out a low laugh. "I've learned that honor exists only in storybooks. So, like a pirate, I live by my own rules. It has proven to be the perfect life for a devil-may-care fellow like me."

"I don't believe that," said Sophie.

"Ah, sorry to disillusion you, but it's true. I'm an un-repentant rogue." Cameron's smile held no warmth. "But regardless of what you think about my morality, I can help you."

She leaned down to pick up her shawl from the ground, using the moment to compose her conflicted emotions. "That was a clever faradiddle you told to Georgiana, but even if I wished to hire your services, I couldn't afford to pay you." She wound the silk around her shoulders, feeling suddenly chilled despite the sunlight filtering through the trees. "Th-thank you for returning my mother's ear-rings, I am grateful—truly grateful. However…"

Sophie hesitated, telling herself she was right to have rejected him all those years ago. By his own admission, he had turned into a man unworthy of admiration. "How-ever I think it best we leave it at that. I am returning home on the day after the morrow, and it's highly unlikely that our paths will cross again. But I am happy to know you are alive and well."

"Sophie, you would be wise to reconsider my offer," said Cameron. "I have made it not merely out of al-truism," he added quickly. "I have my own reasons for wanting to take a closer look at Dudley and his cronies."

She shook her head. Regardless of what sort of life he

had chosen for himself, she was loath to draw him into further danger. "You have already taken enough risks for me. I couldn't live with myself if you were suffer any consequences on my account."

A flash of teeth, an enigmatic smile. "I assure you, I am quite skilled at taking care of myself. If you were to ask my friends, they would tell you the same."

"Oh, Cameron, it would never work. We have both changed too much." Sophie touched her kiss-swollen lips. "Furthermore, I need to keep my wits about me, and I can't seem to think clearly around you."

"Perhaps you should trust your instincts."

Her throat tightened. It was oh-so tempting. Those broad shoulders had felt so solid, while her own were weakening.

"No," she whispered. "I can't take the chance."

Cameron turned slightly and appeared to be contemplating the dust motes dancing in the air. A breeze ruffled his hair, the long strands falling to hide his face.

"Good-bye then," he murmured, and before she could answer, he was gone, a black shadow flitting through the trees.

"Good-bye," replied Sophie to the empty space among the swaying leaves. A tear trickled down her cheek, but she quickly blotted it away. Only a fool would try to reach out and recapture the past. The Cameron she knew from long ago was naught but a phantom memory. The man he had become was a ruthless stranger. "Good-bye."

Chapter Five

Cameron paused for a moment in the doorway of the well-appointed library, inhaling the rich scent of beeswax, parchment, and age-worn leather. The lamplight cast a mellow glow over the carved bookcases and gilt-stamped bindings that filled the massive room, for despite his outward show of fun-loving frivolity, Gryff was a serious book collector whose lyrical essays on landscape design were earning kudos from experts in the field.

After another deep breath, Cameron entered the room.

His two friends were leaning over one of the work tables, paging through a folio of botanical watercolors. At the sound of his steps on the Oriental carpet, they both looked up.

"Are you thinking of growing roses as well as raising goats, Connor?" he drawled. "Never in my wildest dreams did I imagine the Wolfhound would become so...soft."

"These are Eliza's latest watercolors," said Gryff. "Which have been accepted for an exhibition at the Royal Academy." His new wife was fast garnering critical acclaim in the art world for her prodigious talents. "And it's me who is cultivating roses. The paintings show the new walled garden I've created next to her studio." He smiled. "In the language of flowers, roses signify love."

"No wonder their scent makes me ill," said Cameron, crossing to the sideboard and pouring himself a glass of brandy.

"It seems the Sleuth Hound still has a bloody thorn in his arse," said Connor, ignoring the earlier needling.

Gryff shrugged. "Considering all the foul holes he pokes around in, it's no wonder." To Cameron, he added, "If you've come merely to snarl and gnash your teeth, why not trot off elsewhere until whatever is ailing you has passed?"

Cameron quaffed a long swallow of his drink before replying. "Actually, I have come to ask a favor." The words did not come out easily. Early on, he had learned that the key to survival was to make himself impervious to emotion. Even to his fellow Hellhounds, he hated to show any chink in his cynicism.

"Ah." To his relief, Gryff did not reply with a barbed jest. Perching a hip on the table, his friend merely arched a brow. "Well, do go on."

After refilling his glass, Cameron looked to Connor. "Are your gaming skills still sharp?"

"You may think me a domesticated lapdog, but my teeth have not lost all their edge," replied the Wolfhound. In the past, he had kept The Wolf's Lair in business through his uncanny luck at cards. "I take you want some sheep fleeced?"

"In a manner of speaking." Cameron spun the glass in his fingers. "I was hoping you might consent to play a few hands with one, or perhaps two, of regular patrons at the Lair."

"Who?" asked Connor.

There was no avoiding the answer. "Dudley is my first choice. If he is not there, then Morton," he growled.

"Dudley—the fellow involved with the mysterious Miss Lawrance?"

As Cameron feared, Gryff pounced on the information, like a hungry dog scenting a meaty bone.

"Ha, ha, ha." A low chuckle followed the question. "It seems that despite all his protests to the contrary, the sardonic Sleuth Hound has finally been bitten by love."

"Love has *nothing* to do with it," muttered Cameron. "I have my own reasons for wanting to know more about what those two varlets are up to."

Gryff's laugh grew louder, but Connor's expression remained serious. "What is it that you have in mind?"

"I'd like you to win—and win big. According to my sources, their play is reckless and their debts are mounting."

Connor tapped his fingertips together. "That may not be easy. With all due modesty, my reputation makes most of the regulars at the Lair loath to risk playing against me."

"I'll take care of that," replied Cameron.

"And what shall I do with Dudley's promissory notes when I win them? Feed them to my goats?"

Cameron allowed a faint smile. "Hand them over to me."

"And then?" asked Gryff.

"And then, I shall make Dudley pay through the nose."

"What has he done to earn your ire?" pressed Gryff. "Aside from bullying your Miss Lawrance."

"I'd rather not reveal that quite yet." He turned to his other friend. "What say you, Wolf?"

"Very well." Connor raised his own glass in salute. "I must say, life in the country is idyllic, but the prospect of raising some hell with my fellow Hounds is rather appealing."

The soft knock on her bedchamber door was not unexpected. Sophie set aside her hairbrush and sighed into the looking glass. Georgiana had been grimly silent on the Green Park encounter throughout the carriage ride home and the evening's card party with her aunt's friends.

But she was under no illusion that the matter had been forgotten.

"Come in," she murmured, though in truth she wanted nothing more than to slip between the bedsheets and pull the coverlet over her head.

Not that quilted cotton would keep unsettling Pirate dreams at bay.

Georgiana padded across the rug and plopped down on the pillowed windowseat. With a small cough, she cleared her throat. "You are still in love with him, aren't you?"

"No." *Yes.* "No. Absolutely not."

A draft stirred through the draperies as her sister shifted and drew her knees to her chest.

"Cameron Fanning—or rather Daggett—was a youthful infatuation," Sophie continued. "But I came to realize that he was too wild, too impetuous for us to ever suit." *And now I know that I was right—so why does my heart refuse to listen to my head?*

"Is that why he went away?"

Sophie stared at her fogged reflection, wishing her

breath had blurred the look of longing in her eyes. Blinking back the sting of salt, she picked up the brush and resumed combing out her hair.

"You would have to ask him the reason," she answered. "We quarreled and exchanged some harsh words. Then he...he simply disappeared."

Wood creaked as her sister shifted again.

"It was all for the best," went on Sophie, echoing Cameron's assertion. *Perhaps saying it enough times would make it feel true.* "We would only have hurt each other. He was too passionate and I was too practical."

Silence, and then suddenly Georgiana's arms were around her, enfolding her in a fierce hug. "You're an awful liar, Sophie. Not to mention an overprotective mother hen at times." A sniff. "But I love you so very dearly."

"Oh, Georgie." Sophie felt her throat grow too tight for further speech.

"You don't need to hide your feelings from us," went on Georgiana. "Pen and I have seen you staring out at Highborn Hill when you think we aren't watching. We both recognize true love when we see it."

She choked back a watery laugh. "Good heavens, Penelope is only thirteen—what does she know of true love?"

"More than you think," answered Georgiana. "She's been secretly reading your collection of novels—including the naughty ones like *Tom Jones*."

"Oh, dear." Sophie grimaced. "Remind me to take a birch to her backside when we get home."

Her sister grinned. "We shall put the new ones under lock and key. I can't wait to start *Lady Avery's Awful Secret*."

"When did you purchase *that*?"

"While you were kissing Cameron Daggett in Green Park," replied her sister. "And speaking of the Devil, what are you going to do about Him?"

"Nothing," said Sophie. "He offered to help me, but I refused. So he left." She forced a smile. "At least this time he said good-bye."

"Is there a reason you refused him? It seemed to me that the two of you were getting along rather well."

"Too well. I can't deny that there is an attraction between us. But it's all wrong—he is too dangerous to desire," whispered Sophie. "My brain doesn't function properly when he is near. Like a magnet, he seems to exert some strange force that pulls my inner Compass of Reason all helter-pelter."

"Perhaps your compass needs to alter its course," said Georgiana quietly.

Sophie twined the sash of her wrapper around her fingers. "Anthony is like a bright, shining star in the Heavens, a steady guiding light that makes it easy for you to steer a straight line through turbulent seas. Cameron is far more mercurial." She drew in a ragged breath, thinking of his dark, sea-green eyes. "He is more like the flashes of lightning that flare in a raging storm."

"Storms can be dangerous," agreed her sister. A glimmer of mischief hung on her lashes. "But also exciting."

A laugh slipped from her lips. "Good Lord, do I have to curtail your reading habits, too? One wild romantic in the family is frightening enough."

Georgiana quirked a smile but then her mouth pursed in concern. "In all seriousness, Sophie, Anthony and I have discussed the future and, well, we both agree that you should not bear all of the burden of caring for the family, once we are married. Papa and Pen can come live with us, allowing you the freedom—"

"Let us discuss such momentous decisions after you are married," interrupted Sophie. *If you are married.* "At the moment, we must concentrate on all the myriad details of making your wedding perfect."

"Very well," conceded her sister. "But be assured that I mean to see you get a chance to follow your compass, no matter that it might lead through uncharted waters and storm-tossed seas."

"Right now, I'll settle for navigating through the rest of our shopping lists." Sophie gave Georgiana a last little hug and then waved her away. "Off to bed—you need your sleep. Tomorrow is our last day in Town and you've a busy day of fittings."

Her sister brushed a kiss to her cheek and turned for the door. However, in passing the dressing table, her gaze fell on the small porcelain dish next to the looking glass. "I didn't know you had brought Mama's earrings with you." She drew the dish out of the shadows. "Why didn't you wear them to Mrs. Griffin's soiree?"

"I—I forgot," murmured Sophie.

Georgiana arched a brow. "Well, no matter. They will look lovely with your new gown. The pale lace trim I chose will help bring out to their luster."

Candlelight played over the pearls.

"They are beautiful, aren't they? I'm so glad that you refused to consider selling them. Their worth cannot be measured in money."

"No, indeed." She rose. "Good night, Georgie. It's been a long day, and I am ready for sleep."

But when the door clicked shut, Sophie made no move for her bed. Instead, she returned to the table and picked up the earrings. For a long, long moment she held them in her palm, watching the flickering flames gild their silvery smoothness with flecks of gold. Then, on impulse, she fastened one in her left ear and returned the other to the dish.

Perhaps I should cast caution to the wind and become a pirate, too. I could sail away on a plundering ship, bound for the unknown, she mused, making a face in the looking glass as she tilted her head to and fro. Georgiana's comments had left her in a strange mood.

The earring danced in the hide-and-seek shadows, as if sensing her unsettled emotions.

"Perhaps Georgie is right and I've let my life become too staid. I wasn't always afraid to be daring. I took risks."

And I liked the thrum of excitement bubbling through my blood.

A needle of guilt pricked at her conscience. Her own past transgression was far more scandalous than her ailing father's unwitting mistake. It had happened one summer afternoon in the soft meadow grass of Highborn Hill. Mellowed by the warmth of the sun and a bottle of beer stolen from Lord Wolcott's cellar, she had shamelessly allowed Cameron to kiss her, to touch her...

Oh, she still had her maidenly virtue intact. But just barely.

Luck had been with her that day. If anyone had witnessed the interlude, her family's reputation would have been utterly ruined. Aware of how close she had come to

disaster, Sophie had redoubled her resolve to be strong
and sensible.

*Perhaps I'm not just afraid of Cameron, but I'm also
afraid of myself and my own dangerous urges.*

Sophie moved to the window and pressed her forehead
to the glass, letting the mist-damp night air cool her
heated skin. Skirls of feathery fog rose up from the small
walled garden. A nightingale trilled from somewhere in
the bushes, the soft song barely stirring the hazy stillness.

Closing her eyes, she felt her thoughts begin to drift off
in a slowly spinning swirl of images—a flash of lightning,
a storm-tossed sea crashing against a rocky shore...

Tap. Tap. Tap.

It took a moment for her to realize the sound was coming not from inside her head but from outside the glass.

Her lids flew open and she found herself face to face
with a leering smile. Above the gleaming teeth was a
black silk scarf, tied pirate-style around rain-tangled hair.
An earring—the spitting image of her own—gleamed
bright in the darkness.

Tap. Tap. Tap.

She blinked and opened her mouth to scream.

"Sophie, open the window," urged Cameron. "Before
we stir a up scandal."

Throwing open the casement, she stepped back to let
him slip into the room.

"Y-you're wet," she stammered.

"You're naked." His smile sent a frisson of heat tickling over her flesh. "Or nearly so."

"All the more reason why you shouldn't be in here."

He shook off his headcovering, sending a shower of
tiny droplets over the rug. "That's assuming I follow the

rules of Polite Society." A rumbling laugh, low as distant thunder. "But you know me better than that."

At the moment, Sophie wasn't thinking of rules, but how sinfully seductive his mouth looked with rain beaded along his lower lip.

"You're wet," she repeated and then, as if drawn by the fog-swirled force of some storm demon, she leaned in to blot them off with a gossamer kiss.

"You're naked," he murmured, and pulled her hard against him.

The dampness soaked through her wrapper, setting off hot and cold flares along the length of her body. Cameron was right—she *was* nearly naked. Distracted by the day's turmoils, she had undressed and simply thrown on a light wrapper, rather than seek the nightrail folded neatly within the armoire. And now the lawn cotton was molding to every intimate inch of skin.

Sophie clung to him for a heartbeat longer, savoring the sensation of hard chiseling of muscle against her softness before pushing him away.

"Y-you shouldn't be in here."

"You said that," replied Cameron. An unholy twinkle of amusement lit in his eyes. "But as I told you, I'm no gentleman. A gentleman would not invade your bed-chamber." His gaze slid down from her face. "And a gentleman would definitely not be staring at the tantalizing sight of your rosy nipples peeking through tissue-thin fabric."

She quickly crossed her arms over her chest, feeling...
Wicked. Wanton.

A rector's daughter should not feel a thrum of pleasure at seeing desire in a man's eyes.

Looking away, she snatched up a shawl, and wrapped it around her shoulders.

"It doesn't quite cover the intriguing 'V' between your thighs," said Cameron. "But I'll promise not to look."

Heat spiraled through her belly. A little angry with herself for letting his teasing stir up such unwanted reactions, Sophie gestured at the window. "You won't be looking because your eyes will be focused on finding handholds on the ivy vine. I am going to count to three…"

He curled a smirk. "And then?"

"And then I shall…I shall toss you out on your arse."

"Oh, that should be jolly interesting." Rather than retreat, he took a step closer. "There was a contessa in Italy who made the same threat. As I recall, we wrestled our way out to the balcony—a lovely little wrought iron nook overlooking the Tyrrhenian Sea—but once there, her strength began to ebb and we agreed to cease hostilities, so to speak."

"You are more incorrigible than ever," she snapped, her face flooding with color as she tried to not think of Cameron with his arms around a voluptuous Italian.

"And you," he said softly, "are more beautiful than ever."

The murmur raised gooseflesh along her arms. "I'm not." Tugging the shawl tighter, she told herself not to respond. Cameron was, by his own admission, an unrepentant rogue. "Georgie is the real beauty, while I am…just plain Sophie."

He said nothing but continue to stare at her through his dark lashes.

The dampness was now beading between her breasts and spreading down between her legs.

Clearing her head with a small shake, Sophie shifted again. "I don't understand..." Nothing was making sense—not his unexpected presence, not her fierce longing. "I'll ask yet again—why are you here?"

"Because last time you refused me, I disappeared from your life."

It suddenly hurt to breathe.

"You were right to do so, of course. Asking you to elope to Scotland was rash, reckless idea." Cameron flashed a self-mocking smile. "I was a penniless bastard, with no prospects, no future. It was supremely selfish of me to expect you to trust that I could take care of you."

"It wasn't that simple, Cam." Sophie didn't dare meet his gaze. "I couldn't leave my family. My sisters were so young, and Mama's death had changed Papa. He was already retreating into his own little world but her leaving us seemed to send him over the edge."

"Ah, yes." The hard edge of irony in his voice scraped against her heart. "Life never is simple."

"You could have said good-bye."

"Actually, I couldn't. I had no choice but to leave the area in a hurry, else end up on the gallows."

A gasp rose in her throat. "What do you mean?"

"Wolcott was intent on seeing me hang. You see, I had caught one of his houseguests beating a barmaid in back of The Golden Crown's stables. She was demanding the agreed-upon fee for her services and he did not wish to pay." His mouth thinned to a grim line. "So I relieved him of his purse and gave it to the girl, whereupon he raced back to Wolcott Manor and said that I had robbed him."

"Lord Wolcott believed his friend?"

"You need ask?" Cameron's voice was hard as stone.

"My half brother has always hated me. That his high-and-mighty father conceived a child with a mere nobody was a pollution of the precious family blood that His Lordship simply couldn't bear."

"Oh, Cam. I never knew about all that."

"Wolcott is very good at hiding all his dirty little family secrets," he replied. "He called me to the manor to confront me with the incident, and told me that he would see me hang for the crime of theft. So I knocked him down and stole a rather large sum from his desk on my way out the door. As you see, I wasted no time in choosing the path to perdition." A careless shrug. "The arrogant dastard must have been too proud to inform the local authorities, but be assured, he sent Bow Street Runners to track me down."

"You were hardly more than a boy. How did you survive?"

"By quickly learning to be tougher and smarter than the men pursuing me." Cameron brushed the curling strands of hair back from his brow. "But enough of the past, Sophie. I came to talk about the present."

She didn't dare meet his gaze.

"You can't deal with men like Dudley and Morton alone. You need my help."

"No, no, I can't let you get involved," she protested. "It's too dangerous for you. Those men are friends with the marquess, and Wolcott won't have forgotten his grudge."

A laugh, low and a little rough around the edges. "My dear Sophie, this will be child's play compared to some of the things I do. Bad as those men are, there was a band of Flemish criminals I knew several years ago who were far worse. They were known to lop off the limbs of anyone who trespassed on their territory. However, there was a particularly nice painting by Botticelli that I'd had my eye on, and I waited until a stormy night..." Cameron glanced at the window. "The castle walls were far higher than these, and the turreted roofs were treacherously steep. Luckily, I have a good sense of balance. My pursuers were not so fortunate."

He reached out a hand and slowly twined the fringe of her shawl around his fingers. "So you see, danger doesn't frighten me. It never has."

Her pulse began to pound as he drew her closer.

"What about you?" The question tickled against her cheek. "Admit it—deep down inside, you're not afraid of danger, either. Think of all our adventures, and the risks we took together."

"You give me too much credit for courage," she answered. "Those were youthful larks. For the most part, I'm prudent, cautious Sophie."

"So you say." Freeing his fingers from the silky threads, Cameron cupped her breast. "But I know better."

Dear God. Dear God.

He lowered his head, his breath hot on the damp fabric. "Yes, you've always been a paragon of common sense, a voice of calm reason who kept me from spinning out of control. But don't deny your own daring, your own passions."

She sucked in her breath as his tongue teased over her nipple. The friction of the finespun cotton made her flesh feel on fire.

"You have physical needs, physical desires." He licked again. And again. And again.

Her body clenched. "But it's wrong. It's wicked."

"This isn't wrong, it's oh-so right." His mouth closed over the jutting point and he gave a gentle nip.

A cry caught in her throat. "My aunt... my uncle..."

"Are asleep in a different part of the house."

"Cam—"

"Hush, sweeting. Don't talk, don't think, just feel."

Another throb of heat surged through her as he suckled her to a rigid arousal.

Dazed, dizzy, Sophie clutched at his broad shoulders to keep herself upright.

Lifting his head, Cameron let out a ragged sound, something between a laugh and a groan. "Do you remember that afternoon on Highborn Hill? The sunlight was warm as melted honey, the grass was bright as pure gold, and you let me unlock your passion with my touch?"

A liquid warmth pooled between her legs. Once, and only once, had she given in to burning desire. But that moment was imprinted on her body. Imprinted on her soul.

"Yes," she whispered, unsure whether the word was an answer or a plea. "Yes."

"Spread your legs, Sophie." He kissed her. "Please."

Her feet slid wide on the rug.

With a groan, Cameron found the opening of her wrapper and slipped his hand inside. His palm skimmed over her thatch of curls and then his fingers were dipping and delving through her feminine folds.

Sophie pressed her face against his shirt and bit down to keep from crying out.

"Sophie." He found her hidden pearl and his strokes quickened. "Sunbeam."

Wave after wave of pleasure pulsed through her body. She threw her head back, dimly aware of the dancing candle flame and drumming of rain against the windowglass.

Oh, was it possible to expire from ecstasy?

A rasping groan, echoing her own cresting, coiling tension.

She arched into his touch, and with a muffled cry came all undone.

Cameron held her close, waiting for her to come back to earth. His own breathing was a ragged rasp as he whispered, "Heaven help me, but my self-control—my sanity—is dancing on a razor's edge. I want nothing more than to bury myself in your sweet, sweet warmth. But for once in my life, I shall try to do the honorable thing."

He pulled back, and she felt that a part of herself had gone missing.

"Oh, Cam." She touched his sleeve. "You are honorable in all the ways that really matter."

"No." He caught her hand and pressed it hard against his rampant arousal. "I'm not."

She felt his heat pulsing against her palm.

"I haven't been a saint. Or a monk. I've made a life of stealing—money, jewels, artwork, not to speak of the pleasures offered by willing ladies."

Sophie didn't flinch. "You don't frighten me."

"I frighten myself."

They stood for a moment, still and silent, until he finally released his hold. "Forgive me—I didn't come here intending to paw over you like a ravening beast," he went on haltingly. "Some strange force seems to take hold of me. I don't know what to call it." He made a wry face. "Black magic, or perhaps the Devil's own madness."

Sophie could think of yet another explanation, but she didn't dare say it aloud.

"I had best be going," murmured Cameron, angling his face away from the candlelight. "Before the last shreds of my self-control turn to unholy fire and brimstone."

She watched him move to the casement, wanting to weep from how badly she wanted him to stay, despite his wild revelations.

A flitting of shadows. A swirl of chill air.

"But you haven't seen the last of me. For the moment, our interests are aligned in regard to Dudley and his friend Morton. So you aren't going to face them alone."

Chapter Six

A fresh pot of coffee, if you please," called Cameron to the footman as he strolled into the breakfast room of Gryff's elegant townhouse the following morning. "And bring a pinchpot of ground cinnamon instead of cream."

"Make yourself at home," drawled Gryff, looking up from his shirred eggs and gammon.

"I hope you're offering some decent food here," replied Cameron. "I'm famished." Picking up a plate from the sideboard, he proceeded to lift the covers of the four silver salvers. "Ugh. I expected more creativity from you. I'll think I'll put in an order for an omelet *à la grecque.*"

"You have exceedingly peculiar tastes," retorted his friend. "No one eats olives in eggs."

"I do."

"Then hire your own chef. Mine is French, and very temperamental." Gryff finished the last bite of his breakfast and pushed his plate aside. "I swear, if you upset him with odd requests and he gives notice, I'll roast your cods over the kitchen fire."

Connor chuckled as Gryff, still grumbling, picked up a

pencil and began reading the set of page proofs by his elbow. "Stubble your usual sarcasm, Cam. He's out of sorts this morning. His publisher has moved up the deadline for finishing the final editing of his essays."

Gryff muttered a few well-chosen epithets about printers under his breath.

"Oh, very well," said Cameron with a pained sigh. "I'll settle for toast and a very boring broiled kidney."

He took a seat at the table and devoured his food in silence. It had been a long and active night. Indeed, he had not yet been to bed. After leaving Sophie's chamber, he had made several other visits, the last one requiring a dash across a slippery stretch of slate roof tiles. Wincing, he set down his fork and rubbed at his bruised hand.

"Dare I ask what you've been up to?" asked Connor, eyeing the scraped knuckles.

"Just doing a little preliminary reconnoitering. I find that it's always worthwhile to know as much as possible about one's opponents." Cameron paused to pour a cup of the freshly delivered steaming coffee and gratefully gulped down several long swallows. "Ahhh, excellent— it's as black as the Devil's heart. Whatever else his faults, your chef does know how to roast his beans, Gryff."

His friend only grunted.

Turning back to Connor, he said, "I've learned that Dudley will be at the Lair this evening. He'll be alone, as his friend Morton is otherwise engaged. I trust that you haven't changed your mind?"

"On the contrary. I'm looking forward to it."

"As am I." He polished off another cup of the rich, aromatic brew and then rose.

"Where are you off to in such a rush?' asked Connor.

"Never mind."

"I hope it is to your own quarters to change your clothing." Paper crackled as Gryff turned to a fresh page. "There's a rip in the right leg of your trousers, and your boots are covered with green slime."

Cameron paused in front of the arched window and gave a mock bow. "Don't worry, come tonight I shall be sporting my usual sartorial splendor."

Connor squinted into the sunlight. "Speaking of which, is that a new earring?"

"Yes." He fingered the teardrop pearl. It was an exact replica of Sophie's heirloom that he had commissioned from an underworld jeweler, who was well skilled at making quick, accurate copies of fancy jewelry. "It has an interesting history to it—and no, don't ask, for I'm not going to divulge any of its secrets. Suffice it to say that I am counting on it being a good luck charm for this endeavor."

"Good luck charms?" A glint of steel flashed in Connor's gray eyes. "I'm the one playing cards, and no matter how good a friend you are, I'll be damned if I get my ear pierced."

"I wasn't overly pleased about taking a bullet in the leg for you," retorted Cameron. Rescuing the Wolfhound's bride from a clever enemy had required both fisticuffs and firearms. "But did you hear me howl?"

Connor shifted uncomfortably in his chair. "Oh, bloody hell..."

"However," he added, "your lovely wife might not approve, so I shall count on your skill, rather than luck."

"If I can't beat Dudley at cards, I'll eat your earring—

along with a platter of raw eggs and olives," growled Connor.

"Well, much as I'd like to see you forced to wolf down those items, I hope it won't come to that."

"It won't," said Gryff. "When has any of us failed to help a fellow Hellhound in need?"

Connor grimaced. "Actually, I can think of one instance…"

"Oh, stop your barking." Gryff dismissed the remark with a curt wave. "In the end, I more than made up for my carelessness."

"So you did."

"I shall leave the two of you to chew on each other," said Cameron. "But keep your teeth razor sharp for tonight's play at the Lair."

He made his way out to the street, but rather than head for his own out-of-the-way neighborhood on the eastern fringe of Mayfair, he continued on foot, crossing the square and turning down Duke Street.

Sleep. He, too, wished to be sharp for the upcoming evening. But before he sought a few hours of sleep, he couldn't help making one short stop.

"Damnation, how the Hounds would howl with laughter, seeing me act like a lovesick puppy," Cameron muttered. "God knows, I've shown them no mercy when I've sensed a soft spot on their hell-toughened hides."

His steps quickened over the cobbles. He hated feeling vulnerable. It was a damnable flaw, and he had learned long ago that in order to survive, he couldn't afford any show of weakness.

Sophie is a weakness, whispered the devil in his head.

No, Sophie isn't a weakness, he thought in silent answer. *She is...*

A beacon of pure, sweet light in my storm-clouded life.

A self-mocking sneer curled his lips. *Satan save me—I'm beginning to sound like a maudlin poet.*

Looking up, he saw a passing matron and her daughter hurriedly cross to the other side of the street.

It was no wonder. Given his wrinkled garments and stubbled jaw, he must appear a rather disreputable figure among all finery. *A dangerous pirate, stirring up trouble wherever I sail.*

Sunk in his brooding, Cameron stopped at the corner of Berkeley Square, uncertain of what to do. Stay or go—he knew which was the choice of a sentimental fool.

However, the decision was made for him.

"Mr. Daggett?"

Damnation. The shopping expedition must have run late.

"How lovely to run into you," continued Georgiana. "I am meeting Sophie and Aunt Hermione at Gunter's." Smiling, she shifted the hatbox in her hands. The maid by her side held several more. "Gorman and I had to wait for the milliner to add the finishing touches to these bonnets. We are leaving for home tomorrow at first light and wished to take them with us."

"I'm sure they are quite fetching," he murmured, eyeing the clusters of tiny pink cherries festooning her current headcovering. "Is Anthony fond of fruit?"

Georgiana laughed. "You are horrible—and always have been. I don't know what Sophie sees in you."

Neither do I.

"Nonetheless, won't you join us?" A mischievous twinkle sparked in her hazel eyes. "We are all going to order strawberry ices."

"I'm afraid that my reputation would suffer greatly if I were spotted at a tea shop eating ice cream at this hour of the day."

"On the contrary, I'm sure it would only add to your air of mystery." She shoved the box into his arms. "Besides, a gentleman is always supposed to offer assistance to a lady."

"But we both know that I have no pretensions to honor or chivalry," he murmured, falling in step beside her as the maid dropped back to follow them.

"I won't tell anyone," replied Georgiana.

He slanted a sidelong glance at her. "You know, you have grown from a pesky, playful child into a rather interesting young lady."

"Thank you," she said. "I think."

They crossed through the square's central garden and approached Gunter's. The day had turned quite warm, and a crowd was gathering around the shop's entrance, drawn by the cool promise of its rich treats.

"Oh, how lovely!" exclaimed Georgiana, waving to her sister and aunt. "They have managed to get one of the outdoor tables."

Heaving an inward sigh, Cameron reluctantly made his way through the swirl of pastel skirts. He had come here intending simply to observe Sophie from afar. But as he well knew, even the best-laid plan could go awry.

"I met an old friend on the way here, and he offered to help me with my boxes," said Georgiana to her aunt. "Surely you remember Sophie's friend, Cameron. He's the one who used to hurl rotten apples at your carriage, trying to knock the coachman's hat off his head."

"I no longer employ fruit as a weapon," he said, bowing over Hermione's hand.

"Ah. I am relieved to hear you are no longer dangerous, Mr...."

"Daggett," supplied Cameron smoothly.

Sophie coughed, and then looked up, her cheeks coloring slightly as she murmured a greeting.

"Please join us, Mr. Daggett," went on Hermione politely. "Would you care for some ice cream?"

"Thank you, but I just dined."

"Then you may have a cup of coffee while we eat our confections." Georgiana smiled sweetly. "I insist."

"Georgie, you are being impertinent. Mr. Daggett may have other, more pressing engagements," said Sophie. She still hadn't met his gaze.

"Do you, Mr. Daggett?"

"I..." Cameron caught sight of two gentlemen rounding the wrought iron fence. *Hell and damnation.* "As a matter of fact, I must run. I am already late—"

Too late.

"Well, fancy meeting you here, Daggett." Gryff tipped his hat to the ladies before adding, "I wouldn't have guessed that you have a secret craving for sweets."

"Actually, I was just leaving," answered Cameron gruffly.

Connor's flash of teeth had a predatory gleam. "Oh, come. We can't allow you to rush off with introducing us to your charming companions."

He had no choice but to comply.

Hermione looked a little flustered at being introduced

to an earl and a marquess. "W-would you gentlemen care to join us? Or am I transgressing some rule of protocol?"

"Have no fear, Killingworth and I do not stand on ceremony," said Gryff. "But alas, we have a previous engagement in the neighborhood."

Cameron had forgotten that Gryff's publisher was just several streets away. *A mental error—I will have to say sharper.*

"Perhaps some other time," went on his friend. "Do you live in London, Mrs. Hillhouse?"

"Yes, milord," answered Hermione. "But my nieces live in Norfolk."

"The village of Terrington, near the sea," volunteered Georgiana. "Sophie and Mr. Daggett were childhood friends."

Cameron had to quell the urge to pluck the faux cherries from her hat and stuff them down her throat.

"Indeed?" Connor's smile turned even more wolfish.

Gryff let out an evil chuckle. "I confess, I have often wondered if, like the one of the goddesses in Greek mythology, he simply emerged fully formed from Zeus's forehead."

"Or hatched from some devil-cursed dragon egg," added Connor.

"My goodness, Your Lordships certainly have very vivid imaginations, ha, ha, ha," said Hermione.

Cameron fixed them with a razored stare. "Yes, don't they?"

"Ha, ha, ha," echoed Georgiana. Spotting the package of typeset proofs under Gryff's arm, she craned her neck for a better look. "You don't perchance write novels, do you, Lord Haddan?"

"Sorry to disappoint you, but no."

"I adore the ones with clanging chains, gruesome dungeons, and dastardly villains. Though I do find it a little silly that the heroines always keep falling in a dead faint when confronted with danger." A pause. "My sister is far more intrepid. She never faints in perilous situations."

"Oh?" Gryff raised a brow.

"Georgie, you are being impertinent again," said Sophie in a tight whisper.

"I hope that you don't often find yourself in perilous situations, Miss Lawrance," said Gryff.

"My sister is the one with the vivid imagination, sir," answered Sophie. "I lead a very quiet life—"

"Ha! You and Cam were always embroiled in some exciting adventure. Remember the time you had to crawl through a bat-infested cave to rescue him. Both of you smelled like...bats for the next week."

"Eat your ice cream, Georgie," snapped Cameron as Connor swallowed a snort of laughter.

"It's more fun conversing with your friends."

Gryff moved a touch closer to Sophie's chair. "Refresh my memory, Miss Lawrance," he said casually. "Did Mr. Daggett leave Terrington to attend university? Or was it to..." He let his voice trail off.

Cameron cleared his throat, hoping she would pick up on the subtle appeal to keep quiet about his past.

"To see the world?" finished Sophie. "Mr. Daggett has always had an adventurous and independent spirit. Whatever he did, I am sure it was very interesting."

Oh, well done. Cameron snapped her a mental salute. Sophie was clever, careful, and loyal to a fault in protecting her friends. She could always be counted on in a pinch.

Which was why, come Hell or high water, he was going to rescue her from the sordid cesspool of Dudley and Morton's plotting.

But first, he needed to extract himself from this uncomfortable meeting without further ado. His friends had already learned far too much.

"Interesting as this conversation is, I must be going. And you—" he took hold of Gryff's sleeve "—are in danger of being late for your appointment as well. So let us be off."

Connor, who rarely bothered with such niceties, inclined a gentlemanly bow to the ladies. "It was a pleasure meeting you, ladies. I look forward to seeing you again."

"Daggett—I thought the name sounded familiar and now I know why." Hermione sighed as she watched the three men walk away. "Oh, to think I've met the Hellhounds, the three most notorious rakes in London."

"Rakes!" Georgiana's eyes widened.

Sophie choked on a spoonful of her strawberry ice.

"Oh, good heavens, yes. The newspapers are always full of gossip about those rogues and their scandalous exploits." Hermione pursed her lips in thought. "Though the stories seem to have quieted down. Perhaps that's because both the earl and the marquess were recently married."

"What of Mr. Daggett?" asked Georgiana after a tiny hesitation.

"I don't recall reading anything about his nuptials. "But then, I don't pay much attention to Society gossip," replied Hermione. "Not that there would be much mention of Mr. Daggett's personal life in the newspaper columns unless he is titled and wealthy."

"No, he is neither," said Sophie in a low voice.

"I wonder how he came to be friends with Lord Haddan and Lord Killingworth?" mused her aunt.

So do I.

"I can well imagine that there's a fascinating story to it," said Georgiana.

Sophie set down her spoon. "Your imagination—not to speak of your tongue—is becoming far too exuberant for a well-bred young lady. You must keep your passions in check, Georgie, else they may land you in the suds."

Her sister scowled but had the good sense not to argue.

Ha—who am I to talk about keeping passion in check? Praying that the telltale flush on her cheeks would not give her away, she dropped her gaze, feeling a little like a hypocrite.

Hermione fished a pair of spectacles out of her reticule and consulted her neatly penciled shopping list. "Oh, dear." She made a small clucking sound. "We have a few more stops to make than I realized, girls. If you are finished with your treats, we had best be off."

After the packages had been bundled into the waiting carriage, Sophie fell in step with their maid, happy to let Georgiana and her aunt take the lead and chatter away about the latest styles of shoe buckles.

Talk of fashion quickly faded to a faraway buzz as she contemplated the forbidden topic of rakes and rogues. Gently bred ladies were not supposed to know that such men existed.

Much less find them fascinating.

Sophie slowed her pace, letting the maid forge ahead

a step or two. So, Cameron's claim to being a hardbitten blade of the *ton* had some truth to it. The thought set her insides to turning a series of odd little flip-flops. Did that mean he kissed other women witless? Did he make their bodies thrum with sinful desires?

You witless widgeon, of course he does, she whispered to herself. The pleasures of London were there for the plucking. And he had made it clear that he had no scruples about grabbing what took his fancy.

"Including me," she added aloud.

"What was that?" Georgiana turned, her brow angling up in question.

"Er, you aren't including me in the plans to attend Mrs. Putney's musicale tonight, are you?"

"I thought you enjoyed her daughter's singing," said Hermione.

"I do, but if you don't mind, I'd rather retire early. It will be a long journey home and I'm feeling a little fatigued."

Georgiana shot her a fishy stare, one that promised a more thorough interrogation once they were alone.

"But of course, my dear," said Hermione, her guileless face wreathing in concern. "The city can be a little overwhelming."

"Yes, I shall be happy to return to the quiet of the country." Though with both Cameron and Lord Dudley to plague her thoughts, it was doubtful that she would find any peace of mind among the familiar surroundings of home.

Chapter Seven

Cameron lit a cheroot, using the flare of sparks to cover his quick survey of the hazed gaming room. He had deliberately chosen to arrive late, allowing no time for a private meeting with his friends before their plan was put into action. They had covered all the details during the short walk to Gryff's printer. Connor knew exactly what was expected of him.

And Cameron had every confidence that the Wolfhound would not fail.

Intuition, cold logic, nerves of steel—Connor had an uncanny ability to win at cards. He claimed it had nothing to do with Lady Luck, but rather with studying his opponents and understanding their weaknesses.

Drawing in a lungful of the sweat-damp, brandy-scented smoke, Cameron listened to the soft slap of pasteboard on the felted card tables, the sharp rattle of dice against scarred wood. He had no illusions that he would be spared scrutiny by Connor's steel-gray eyes. As for Gryff, he would likely be even more dogged in his determination to dig up the truth.

Damnation. Until now, he had managed to keep his

past well buried. But now that his friends had a clue to go on, they would sniff and claw until the truth came to light.

A *tap* touched his shoulder, interrupting his mordant thought. "Well, well." The low voice was edged with amusement. "I see your friend the Prodigal Wolf has returned for an evening."

Cameron looked around and nodded a curt greeting. The Honorable Caine Oswald was one of the few people whose cynicism matched his own.

"Come to devour the Town lambs, no doubt." Oswald cocked a brow. "Are you going to join the play at his table?"

Cameron shook his head. "Tonight I think I shall be content just to watch."

"A wise move." Oswald was a shrewd gamester himself. "Something about the Wolf's look tonight tells me his teeth are sharpened for the kill."

Straightening from his slouch, he gave a casual shrug. "Perhaps he's hungry to show all the new puppies here that old dogs can still be dangerous."

"Indeed." Oswald eyed him for a moment longer before turning to light a cheroot from one of the flickering candle sconces. "Rumor has it that the Hellhounds have become quite domesticated."

Cameron let out a soft laugh. "Don't believe everything that you hear."

"Oh, I'm far too skeptical for that. Else I might be quaking in my boots to be standing next you, Daggett." A flare of orange sparked in the shadows as Oswald inhaled a mouthful of pungent tobacco. "By the by, did you hear that the Duchess of Merton's gold snuff box was stolen from her country estate, along with a pair of diamond ear-rings?"

"You don't say?" Cameron signaled to one of the passing barmaids for a glass of brandy. "It's appalling how careless ladies can be with their baubles these days."

"Yes, isn't it? But then, the duchess is known for being a stickler for security, so no doubt she felt herself well guarded by the double locks and footmen that make Merton Manor a veritable fortress." A pale puff of smoke ghosted up toward the rafters. "Word is, the thief managed to scale one of the side towers and make his way across a razor-thin ledge and a series of steeply pitched slates to gain access to her private suite."

"As I said, don't believe everything you hear," murmured Cameron. "I've seen the manor. One would have to be rather mad to attempt such a stunt."

"Or rather daring." Oswald flicked a bit of ash from his cheroot. "The play at the Wolfhound's table looks to be turning interesting. Care to join me in taking a closer look?"

"Perhaps later."

"Suit yourself." The curl of a smile reveal a glimmer of teeth. "I sniff blood, and like any predator, I can't resist the scent."

As Oswald snaked through the tables, Cameron retreated deeper into the shadows to watch and wait. The evening appeared to be going exactly as planned.

"The same cannot be said for the rest of my life," muttered Cameron. "A voice, a mere whisper of breath and I'm stripped bare of all my richly threaded cynicism." A pinch of self-loathing pulled at his mouth. "I'm like that pathetic Emperor in the old parable, parading through the streets in imaginary finery, when in truth I'm naked as a new-born babe."

"Talking to yourself?" Gryff joined him in the alcove. "You're either drunk or delirious." A deliberate pause. "Or possessed by some other demon, perhaps?"

"Kindly stubble your sarcasm," he snapped. "I need to pay attention to the cardplay. Springing the trap calls for precise timing."

"Far be it for me to distract you," drawled Gryff. "You appear to have enough problems fighting off Cupid and his quiver of arrows."

"Arse." Cameron kept his gaze on the Wolfhound's table. The stakes appeared to be rising, for a crowd was beginning to gather.

Leaving off his needling, Gryff watched in silence for a few moments. "Ready?" he murmured. "It seems that we should be ready to make our move if Connor's luck holds and he wins this next hand."

Cameron flicked a mote of dust from his sleeve. "I'm counting on the Wolf and his wiles, not Lady Luck, whose favors are notoriously fickle."

"In a foul mood over women, are you?"

From across the room came the sound of a savage oath. Leaning back in his chair, Connor smiled and tugged at his left earlobe.

"Forget about my mood," said Cameron tersely. "That's our signal. You first. I'll follow."

Gryff circled around the faro tables, moving casually through the masculine fug of sweat, wine and bawdy jokes.

Connor looked up at his approach.

"Come, fold your cards, Wolf. We need to be off,"

said Gryff. "Have you forgotten that we have an engagement?"

"I'll meet up with you later," replied Connor.

Leaning low, Gryff whispered in his ear.

"Bloody hell and damnation." Adding a wordless growl, Connor reached and raked his winnings from the center of the table. "Gentlemen, you will have to excuse me."

"S-so soon?" Keeping to the shadows, Cameron had moved close enough to hear the note of alarm in Dudley's voice. "Am I not to have a chance to recoup my losses?"

"Not tonight," answered Connor flatly. He casually sorted through the promissory notes. "And as I am leaving Town on the day after tomorrow, I would ask that the losers kindly redeem their pledges by then. Send the money to Haddan's townhouse."

"I—I…" Dudley wet his lips as Connor's quicksilver eyes narrowed to a steel-edged stare. "I may need a few extra days, Killingworth."

"Indeed?" The Wolfhound curled a sneer. "Everyone who plays here at the Lair knows I don't extend credit. If you could not afford the stakes, you had no business sitting down to play at this table."

Cameron smiled to himself. His skills honed from years of practice, Connor had easily manipulated the man's pride into joining the game. And now, like a hapless rabbit, Dudley was trapped within the steely jaws of gentlemanly honor. To renege on a bet was to risk being shunned by Society.

The undulating flame of the wall sconce caught the sheen of sweat forming on Dudley's forehead. Cameron let the fear ooze up a moment longer before stepping out from the gloom.

"Ah, I heard you were in Town, Wolf." He cocked a sardonic salute to his friend. "I see you still enjoy feasting on lambs?"

Connor stretched a predatory smile. "A diet of goats becomes a trifle bland after a while."

"And it appears that the Wolf has not lost his craving for loin chops," sniggered Gryff. "Ha, ha, ha."

The other men at the table weakly echoed his laugh.

"Well, I'm glad to see your jaws have not lost their bite." Cameron plucked at his cuff. "If you recall, you owe me a rather hefty sum for that little bauble you bought for your bride. Seeing as you've a tidy sum sitting there, what say that we settle up?"

"As you wish." Expelling a bored yawn, Connor fingered through the gambling pledges. "Here, this one is for more than the amount." The scrap of pale paper bearing Dudley's signature fell to the tabletop with a whispery flutter. "I'm happy to pay extra for having you take over the tedium of dealing with the viscount regarding payment."

Cameron heaved a pained sigh. "You know that I much prefer ready blunt, but as a favor to a friend, I shall bite the bullet and take paper."

"I say, Daggett..." Dudley cleared his throat with a cough as Cameron picked up the note and tucked it inside his waistcoat pocket. "I'd be much obliged if you would give me some time to redeem my debt."

"Unlike you titled toffs, I do not have ancient family fortunes or estate assets to fall back on. I must earn my own keep," he murmured. "However, as I am currently plump in the pocket, I suppose that I can afford to be patient. You will, however, owe me interest on the loan."

"Of course, of course." Dudley blotted his brow.

Connor rose and without further word walked off with Gryff. A low murmur went round the table as the other men made ready to resume play. Cameron lingered for a moment before turning and slowly moving off toward the private parlors of the Lair.

"A moment, Daggett."

As he had hoped, Dudley followed him into the dimly lit corridor.

"I've heard that you are a savvy fellow when it comes to business dealings," went on the viscount. "As well as someone who is not overly fastidious about how those deals get done." A pause. "If you'll agree to hold off collecting until I am ready to pay, I promise that I shall make it very worth your while."

Interesting. The proposal added an unexpected twist to his plans and Cameron considered it carefully before replying. "An intriguing offer. But as you say, I'm careful when it comes to my money." He dropped his voice a notch. "I happen to know your funds are, shall we say, stretched at the moment—"

"H-how the devil do you know that?" interrupted Dudley.

"Oh, I have my sources. There is very little that goes on within the netherworld of the *ton* that I don't hear about." Cameron toyed with the fob on his watchchain, watching the viscount's fleshy face pinch with fear. "So, why should I think the situation will improve enough for you to pay me a handsome bonus?"

Dudley gave a furtive look up and down the dark passageway. "I can't reveal all the details, but I've a very good friend who expects to come into a great deal of money shortly. I'll be receiving a share of it."

"Why?"

A rumbled laugh. "Never mind. Suffice it to say it will be more than enough to make you happy."

"How long are we talking about?" asked Cameron.

"I can't say precisely," answered Dudley. "But if all goes well, it shouldn't be more than a month."

"Very well," replied Cameron slowly. "I'll take a gamble and agree to your terms."

"You won't regret it."

Ah, but I can't say the same for you, Lord Dudley.

Cameron inclined a mock bow. "I daresay I won't. I'm not in the habit of making deals that don't yield a worthwhile reward."

"Georgie, please, it's late and I'm in no mood for intimate sisterly chats." Sophie drew the coverlet up over her chin. "Go to bed."

"I will." Georgiana plunked herself down on the foot of the mattress and tucked her feet under her skirts. "In a moment."

She blew out a grumbled sigh. "Be advised that I don't intend to talk about It."

"You mean Him," murmured her sister with a mischievous smile. "I don't know why not. Aren't you the least bit curious as to how Cameron came to be one of the infamous Hellhounds?"

"No," she lied. "And even if I were, there is little point in chewing over the question. Neither of us has a clue as to how he's spent his life since leaving Terrington." That was not precisely true, but half-lies were becoming easier to utter. "So any discussion would merely be idle speculation."

"What's wrong with that?"

A pillow hit Georgiana in the chest with a feathery *thud*. Falling back, she dissolved in giggles. "Oh come, admit it! You're *dying* to know all the delicious details."

Sophie watched a finger of moonlight squiggle across the windowglass. It was gone in an instant, a quicksilver flicker drawing back into darkness.

"I mean, how did a penniless, runaway bast—er, boy come to have such powerful friends?" went on Georgiana.

"As I just said, there is really no point in trying to puzzle it out," she replied.

Ignoring Sophie's attempt to quash further talk of Cameron, Georgiana gazed up at the ceiling and let out a sigh. "My guess is that Cameron has traveled to the far corners of the globe. You have only to look at his earring to know that he experienced all sorts of exotic adventures." Another soft exhale. "By the by, do you think I could convince Anthony to get his ear pierced? He would look quite dashing with a gleaming gold hoop."

"If I were you, I wouldn't wax poetic over the allure of men with earrings," said Sophie dryly. "He might be more tempted to pierce Cameron's liver than his own lobe."

"You think he might feel jealous?" Georgiana considered the idea. "It hadn't occurred to me. How...intriguing."

"Georgie," she said, summoning her Don't-Get-Any-Impetuous-Ideas voice.

Her sister waved off the warning. "I was just teasing. As if I would do anything to upset Anthony."

"That's the first sensible thing you've said tonight," quipped Sophie. She plumped her remaining pillow. "Now if you don't mind..."

"Getting back to Cameron's story," continued her sister. "After returning from his mysterious travels, he somehow encountered Lord Haddan and Lord Killingworth and forged a strong friendship. Aunt Hermione says the gossip columns referred to them as 'close comrades,' but unfortunately, she doesn't remember any of the details."

Thank God, thought Sophie. Georgiana's imagination was heated enough without any more fuel to feed the fire.

"Ah, well." A shrug, and then a smile as her sister went on, "Oh, I know—perhaps it will turn out that he's secretly been made a prince in India and is fabulously wealthy. He'll ride into Terrington on a white tiger and carry you to a castle made of rubies and emeralds."

Sophie surrendered a gurgled laugh.

"Or would you prefer a white elephant?"

"I appreciate the sentiment, Georgie, but you are trying to fabricate an enchanted fairytale out of very ordinary cloth. Neither Cameron nor I are fanciful storybook heroes. We are flesh-and-blood people who must do our best to navigate the ups and down of everyday life."

The teasing light in her sister's eye softened to a more serious hue. "You deserve a happily ever after."

Clearing her throat, Sophie took a moment to compose her emotions. "I am so glad that you have found your perfect Prince, my dear. But just because I don't have white tigers or white knights in my life doesn't mean that I won't be happy. I have you and Pen."

"I wish—"

"If wishes were pennies, we would all be rich as Croesus." She made a face. "Now go to bed, Georgie. And in the morning, please forget about fairytales. On the journey home, let us spin plans for your real-life wedding.

There are flowers to choose, patterns to peruse, guest lists to draw up, and a myriad of other details to decide."

Smothering a yawn, Georgiana slid down from her perch. "I suppose you are right."

"Of course I'm right. Age and wisdom go hand in hand."

"Good night," said her sister as she turned for the door. Under her breath she added, "But if you think that I shall forget about fairytales, you are sadly mistaken. It's not necessary to use ink and paper to write a happy ending. If one is creative, why, anything can happen."

Chapter Eight

$\mathcal{A}$ gusty breeze, sharp with the salt-edged chill of the nearby sea, tugged at the collar of Cameron's riding coat, stirring a prickling of unease. Reining his horse to a halt, he slanted a long look around the small clearing and then slowly dismounted.

The long grass swooshed against his boots as he approached the small stone hut. *Was its whisper a warning that walking back into the past was a grave mistake?*

"A grave mistake," he said aloud, the sudden sound startling a grouse from the tangled gorse.

Wings whirred—*fly, fly away!*

"Coward," he muttered. "I'm naught but a callow, craven coward if I can't confront my youthful demons and kick them to Hades."

The cackle of a crow was not the most reassuring of answers.

Stepping over a patch of thorns, Cameron grasped the rusty latch and gave it a shove. Hinges groaning, the weathered door swung open.

Dust motes danced in the hazy light. Poking his head inside, he saw that the lone window still had most of its panes intact, though the cracks in the glass threw strange, shifting patterns on the far wall. The air was heavy with neglect—and old memories. A remote gamekeeper's shelter, the place had already been abandoned for years when he had stumbled upon it as a boy. It had become his refuge, his sanctuary when he needed to escape and think.

But clearly, I made a hash of thinking back then, he thought wryly, looking around at the earthen floor, and the few sticks of furniture. He drew a finger through the layers of sooty specks covering the small table. *I may be older, but God only knows if I've become any wiser.*

He stood very still, soaking in the silence for a moment longer, before turning abruptly and hurrying back out into the sunlight.

Dark and light—a fitting metaphor for his own conflicted existence.

After stabling his horse in the outer shed, Cameron carried his supplies into the hut and set to making the place habitable. He didn't intend to be staying for long, but given the unexpected twists that his life had taken lately, it was best to be prepared.

Shaking the dust from his caped coat, he hung it on a peg and quickly changed into the roughspun country garb he had brought in his satchel. In the past, Sophie had been wont to walk through the rugged hills at this time of the day, taking an hour or two of solitary respite from the duties of caring for her family. Did she still like to wander the same footpaths?

Or had she chosen a new direction?

He would soon find out. Following a narrow footpath up through the wind-carved rocks, he climbed to the crest of the knoll and surveyed the surroundings.

Sloping meadows, the grasses shimmering gold and green in the afternoon light, gave way to darker copses of distant trees. Two hawks floated high overhead, black specks against the scudding white clouds. A fox darted out from its den and disappeared in the tall fescue. A moment later, Cameron spotted a figure coming around a turn in the path.

He smiled. The face was still too far away to see clearly, but he recognized that stride, that tilt of the shoulders in an instant.

"Sophie," he whispered. *Always a beacon of light in the gloom.*

Scrambling over the loose stones, Cameron dropped down to the path. "Sophie," he called in a louder voice.

Her head jerked up and she stumbled, oversetting the herb basket in her hand.

"Sorry to startle you." He leaned down and gathered up the long-stemmed bulbs of wild garlic.

"C-Cameron," she stammered, still a little off-balance.

Her troubled expression betrayed more than a momentary surprise at his appearance. "What's wrong?" he demanded.

She didn't answer right away.

Rising, he took a steadying grip on her arm. "Have you received some new threat from Dudley?"

"Yes," conceded Sophie after another long moment. "A letter arrived this morning. If I don't give him what he wants by the local Hunt Ball, he and his friend Mr. Morton will make an announcement there, in front of Anthony and his parents, of my father's embezzlement scheme. With the two of them corroborating the facts, my family will be ruined, and Georgiana's happiness will be destroyed." She looked down at her dust-covered half boots. "I can't give him what he is asking for."

"When is the ball?" asked Cameron.

Sophie named a date.

"That gives us a month to put an end to these machinations," he mused. "We must end their power over you once and for all."

Hope chased the look of fear from her face, but only for a brief instant. "I—I don't see how."

"That's why you need a ruthless rogue like me to help," he replied. "Tell me again what they want."

"An old church document," she replied slowly. "Which may or may not even exist. I know nothing about it, and Papa is certainly in no condition to remember."

"What document?" demanded Cameron.

Sophie shook her head, refusing to meet his gaze. "Oh, please. Do not ask me that. What matters is that I cannot prove we don't have it."

Seeing her agitation, he decided not to press her for the moment. "Then it's a good thing that I've come along because it's time to change tactics and go on the attack."

His words stirred a new swirl of misgiving in her eyes. "Speaking of which, what on earth are you doing here?"

"Our recent encounter got me to thinking that it was time to revisit the scene of my rebellious youth."

The remark, though said lightly, only deepened her dismay. "You shouldn't have come here. It's too dangerous." She drew in a quick, uneasy breath. "Lord Wolcott still wields enormous power in this shire, and as we discussed, he won't have forgotten his grudge. If you are spotted, he'll have you arrested."

How like Sophie, thought Cameron, to be so protective of others when she herself was in peril.

"First of all, Sunbeam…" The old endearment sent a spasm of emotion skittering across her face. "…my sources assure me that Wolcott is leaving tomorrow morning for a pleasure trip on his yacht. Secondly, I am very skilled at eluding detection. Trust me, the marquess won't be aware of my presence here in Norfolk unless I want him to know of it."

She snagged an errant strand of hair from her cheek and carefully tucked it behind her ear. "But why take the risk?"

"Because." There were a myriad of reasons, a myriad of longings. "Because you need me." *And against all reason I need you.*

Sunlight beaded on her downcast lashes, glistening like tiny drops of amber honey.

"Because," Cameron added, "you know that risk seems to kindle a strange spark in my blood. I can't help it—fire boils and bubbles through my veins, setting off all sorts of reckless urges."

Sophie shivered as he skimmed a palm along the line of her jaw.

"Like this one." Tipping up her chin, he kissed her.

Her lips trembled beneath his mouth, and then parted with a ragged moan. For a dizzying instant her need seemed as searing as his own.

But all too swiftly, the sweetness was gone.

"Dear God." She broke free from his embrace. "We must be careful. You cannot be spotted."

"Don't worry about me," he rasped. "But you are right about being careful. I mustn't savage your reputation."

She looked away quickly, masking her reaction with a flick of her shawl. Smoothing out the folds, she replied, "I can't help but worry, when you take such awful chances, Cam. Where are you lodging? The inns along the shore road are not safe. Someone is bound to recognize you."

"I've altered a great deal over the last ten years, Sophie. And while many of the changes are not for the better, my physical appearance now bears little resemblance to the skinny, smooth-faced stripling who absconded with Wolcott's money box."

That finally drew a tiny smile. "True. You've grown at least eight inches in height and have more sculpted muscle than Lord Elgin's Greek statues at the British Museum." Her brows drew together. "Still, it's asking for trouble."

"Put your mind at ease on that," said Cameron. "I've settled into the old stone gamekeeper's hut where we used to meet and spin fanciful dreams about the future."

A pink-tinged flush stole over her cheeks.

Cameron couldn't hold back a low chuckle. "As I recall, we also indulged in some terribly wicked behavior there. Do you remember the time I nipped a bottle of brandy from Wolcott's garden party?"

"Oh, please!" Sophie pulled a face. "You and your devilish ideas. I was sick as a dog the next day."

"I was an awful little fiend," agreed Cameron. His laughter died away. "However, I intend to make it up to you now."

"How—"

"Don't ask me that right now," he cut in, touching a finger to her lips. "I've an idea or two. But before I say anything more, I wish to have a look around in Wolcott's study."

A hiss of breath. "You mean to break into Wolcott Manor?"

"My dear Sunbeam, I'm never clumsy enough to *break* anything. Indeed, my skills at gaining access to a place, no matter how well guarded, are rather well honed."

"But since you left, the marquess has installed the latest puzzle locks from Prussia."

"Pffft." Cameron snapped his fingers.

"The servants—"

"Sleep like logs," he finished. "Besides, I never make a sound."

Sophie refused to give up. "There's a dog—a huge, hairy mastiff that prowls the grounds at night."

"A dog?" Cameron tapped at his chin. "Hmmm. I may have to purchase a vial of laudanum to dose a ball of chopped meat."

"No, I won't let you drug poor Rufus. He's really quite sweet when you get to know him." She set a hand on her hip. The wind had loosened her hair, and with her bright curls dancing in martial splendor around her scowling face, she was the spitting image of Boadicea, the mythical Warrior Queen. In that she hadn't changed. Always fighting to protect others, leaving herself unguarded.

"He won't bark at me, so I had better come with you."

"Sophie, I applaud your spirit, but I won't allow you to take that risk. I've a great deal of experience in this sort of thing, and you do not."

"On the contrary, I've trained Rufus to be docile as a dormouse around me, which was no small feat. He eats out of the palm of my hand, so I could be a big help in keeping him quiet." A pause. "He has a very loud bark."

Loath as he was to admit it, she had a good argument. *But not quite good enough.* Even hardbitten scoundrels had certain moral scruples.

"Look, you may be able to silence the shaggy beast, but it would be reckless of me to allow you anywhere near the manor."

"And why is that? Because it might be *dangerous*?" she said with more than a tinge of sarcasm.

"Yes," he replied, trying not to feel like a hypocrite. How the devil had she managed to put him on the defensive?

"As I recall, I faced more than my share of dangers with you in the past, and never quailed. Remember Squire Allen's gun room? And Mr. Kensington's painted pony?"

"Child's play," he replied through gritted teeth.

"Why, you odious, insufferable man!" Fire sparked in her eyes. "Don't talk to me in that condescending way, as if I were still a ink-smudged schoolgirl. You have grown out of adolescence, and so have I."

Bloody hell—since when had Sunbeam learned to turn her light into such a thunderbolt? Cameron quickly regrouped and tried another argument. "Be reasonable, Sophie. You don't know the first thing about manipulating locks or scaling walls."

Her mouth quirked up at the corners. "So teach me."

"I beg your pardon?"

"So teach me," repeated Sophie. "Nowadays, I am

tired of feeling that I have no control over my own destiny. In the past, I wasn't afraid to take risks—and you have to admit that I was good at it."

"These aren't youthful pranks anymore, Sophie."

"As if I don't know that," she retorted. "It's me who is being threatened by a powerful enemy. I want to learn how to fight back."

"A frightening thought," quipped Cameron. "One angry female is more terrifying than a horde of whirling, knife-wielding dervishes."

The shock of seeing him had her nerves tied in a tangle, and his tone tugged the knots tighter. To her, this wasn't remotely amusing. "Don't you *dare* laugh at me, Cameron Daggett!" she exclaimed.

His lips thinned, his gaze shuttered.

"It is unfair of you to make light of my wish to be a little bold, a little daring. Oh yes, I know you think I've become a staid, cautious mouse, too timid to throw caution to the wind."

"Sophie—"

"Let me finish!" she demanded, feeling her eyes suddenly prickle with hot anger. "But unlike you, I wasn't free to follow my own heart. That does not mean I have no backbone."

"Sophie." She tried to dodge his grab, but Cameron was too quick. Catching her up in his arms, he crushed her to his chest with a fierce hug. The heat of his body through the rough wool sent daggerpoints of fire dancing willy-nilly across her flesh.

"I'm all too aware that you have a backbone, Sunbeam." His fingers slowly teased down the length of her spine. "Along with a number of other equally impressive body parts," he whispered as he gave a little nibble to the sensitive shell of her ear.

"You—you are trying to distract me," protested Sophie, trying to keep her ire from melting into a very different emotion. He had always had a maddening, mercurial effect on the sensible part of her mind. At times, she wasn't sure whether to laugh or cry.

"Ah, but of course," drawled Cameron. "I've told you before that I'm an unscrupulous rogue who will use all manner of underhanded tricks to get what I want."

"Yes, I consider myself forewarned." Still, it took a great deal of mental discipline to shake off the delightful sensations tickling down her neck. "Getting back to the dog…"

"Weren't we just discussing the Hellhound?"

A little shove sent him reeling back a step. "Be serious, Cam. I refuse to be patted on the head as if I'm naught but a toy spaniel and sent off to curl up on a spot by the hearth." Sophie forced herself to focus on the tiny turquoise stud in his earlobe, rather than the subtle shades of green rippling in his eyes. "I demand to be part of whatever you have planned. I won't be a hindrance."

No answer.

Her heart thumped against her ribs, once, twice, three times in succession, forcing her to draw a shallow breath. More silence, and disappointment hit again, leaving her feeling a little bruised.

Rejection, however oblique, hurt like the devil.

Fisting her hands, Sophie fought to compose her conflicting feelings. On one hand, she wished to hit back. A foolish notion, of course. It would be like velvet striking against stone. And yet…

"Very well."

At first, she thought it might only have been a whisper of the wind, but he said it again, louder, and with more force.

"Very well, if you truly wish to come along, I have no right to say no. However, I ask that you think long and hard about your final decision. Make no mistake—there are grave risks involved, and I cannot answer for the consequences."

Sophie nodded, not trusting her voice.

"No matter how carefully plans like these are made, they can—and do—often go awry," he went on.

"I understand."

"Do you?"

Silence shivered between them, but she stood firm.

"There will be rules," he warned. "And the one promise I demand from you is that you'll obey them without question."

"You hate rules," she pointed out.

"Not the ones that ensure survival." Cameron ran a hand through his windsnarled hair, looking for a brief instant like the hunted instead of the hunter. And then his gaze hardened, turning impenetrable as the weathered granite around them. "Yes, I take chances, but not foolhardy ones. There are times when it's best to cut my losses and run."

This was becoming more and more intriguing. "All this sounds very professional on your part. Do you do this sort of thing often?"

"Taking chances?" Distraction, again. He did it well.

"No, stealing into private places. Searching for secrets while leaving no trace of yourself."

"Often enough that it's become second nature," Cameron answered. "And the more closely guarded the place, the more of an interesting challenge it is. Not long ago, I heard through my informants in the docklands that there was an undergovernor of the East India Company who was falsifying records on the diamond shipments coming from Golconda. I also learned—never mind how—that he was using a small building on a side street east of St. Paul's as a private office for his side business. So I slipped inside one night during a heavy rain, knowing the Sikh guards were unused to the sounds of a London storm. From his papers I discovered the location of the warehouse where he was hiding his ill-gotten gains until a gem merchant from Antwerp arrived buy them." He smiled. "I confess, there is a rather sweet satisfaction in outwitting another thief."

Intrigued, she asked, "What are some other of your exploits?"

"You don't want to know every sordid detail about my life, Sunbeam. There are dark crevasses there where even your light cannot penetrate."

"Yes, I do." *I want to wrap myself in the knowing, rubbing its hard and soft textures over every inch of my skin.* "I want to know everything."

"Not now," he growled. "There are things I must do to get ready for the visit to Wolcott's inner sanctum."

"Like what?" pressed Sophie.

"Supplies, reconnaissance," answered Cameron after a long moment. "All the little things that tilt the odds in my favor."

The boy she remembered had worn his passions— every hurt, every triumph, every defiance—writ plain on his face. This man had learned wariness. It was impossible to know what he was really thinking.

"You may be very good at these games, Cam, but you may bet on one thing," she said slowly. "If you change your plans and go on without me, I shall make a number of new holes in your flesh—and they won't be located in your earlobe."

His gaze danced and darted around hers, refusing to reveal more than a flicker of beautiful green. "You don't trust me?"

She lifted a brow. "Should I?"

At that, he gave a sardonic laugh, but his eyes, however evasive, betrayed its lie. Cameron Daggett might be a master of manipulation, but some things he could not hide. "No, not for an instant. That way, you won't be disappointed." He shifted his stance. "Again."

The wind rose in a sudden gust, its low, keening whistle echoing off the stones.

"Let's just be sure we understand each other, Sophie," he added, his voice almost too low to be heard.

I have always understood you, Cam. More than you think.

"As I said before, Sophie, I have my own selfish reasons for pursuing these men, so don't make the mistake of thinking me motivated purely by noble altruism."

"You may have a clear conscience on that," she replied. "You've taken great pains to disabuse me of any girlish illusions."

He appeared to be studying the lone hawk floating high in the sky. A hunter, spinning its predatory circles. *Always alert, always watching.*

"But as I said, I'm not a girl any longer, so the terms

of your offer are perfectly acceptable." She reached down for her herb basket. It had fallen and now lay on the hard-scrabble ground, its greenery powdered with a gritty dust. "Where shall we meet? And when?"

Cameron crouched down and began helping her gather up the herbs. "At the north gate of the gardens, the one by the orchards." He had very deft hands, with long, tapered fingers that skimmed over the pebbles with a lithe grace. Held by some shadowy spell, her gaze remained mesmerized by his movements. Gentle, caring—in contrast to his jaded words.

"Let us say at midnight," he went on. "The witching hour when darkness will cover our evil deeds."

A smile found its way to her lips. "Georgie would like that. It sounds like something out of the latest novel she purchased in London. Which, by the by, is called *Lady Avery's Awful Secret.*"

He softly blew on a clump of purple-flowered borage, stirring a pale puff of sandy grains. *A laugh?* The *whoosh* seemed to ease the tension between them. "Georgiana," he said, "has grown into a very interesting young lady. It isn't often that one encounters..." The dark strands of his hair caught in the breeze, revealing a peek of amusement in his eyes. "...such enthusiasm and exuberance for life."

"You haven't met Penelope," murmured Sophie.

A chuckle, dry as dust. "That roly-poly little pixie?"

"Is now nearly as tall as Georgie. And nearly as vexing." She sighed. "I am surprised my hair hasn't turned gray."

Swiftly, silently, Cameron gathered the rest of the meadow herbs and placed them in the basket. "Think on it, Sophie, and whether you wish to take such a dangerous gamble."

Dangerous. That word again.

"If you use your usual good sense, you won't show up tomorrow night." He rose. "I'll keep my promise and be there tomorrow at midnight. But if you are a moment late, I'll go on without you."

"I'll be there," she assured him. "You don't frighten me."

His look turned even more inscrutable than before. "Oh, but I should."

Chapter Nine

The next day seemed to pass slower than a turtle crawling through treacle. Her nerves wound tight as a watchspring by Cameron's appearance and Dudley's new threat, Sophie made herself stay busy, inventing chores to keep from glancing at the clock every quarter hour. The pewter was burnished to silvery brightness, the pantry shelves were spotless, the stove swept free of ash.

"Good Lord, you are jumpy as a cat on a hot griddle," said Penelope, the youngest of the Lawrance sisters, as she looked up from her mending. "This is the second time this afternoon that you've dusted the mantel. Are you expecting to entertain company tonight?"

"No, of course not," she mumbled. The Staffordshire figurines seemed to roll their ceramic eyes as she wiped a rag over the painted wood one last time, while the ticking of the small silver-plated clock added an audible reproach. "Things always need an extra measure of attention after I've been away for a while."

"Mrs. Hodges would not be happy to hear you say so," quipped Penelope. "Oh, a pox on Lucifer and his legions," she added, seeing that she had dropped a stitch.

"A young lady should not use such salty language," scolded Sophie, happy for the distraction from her own wayward thoughts. "Especially if she is only thirteen."

"Yes, and furthermore, a young lady should not read private letters where she might acquire such salty language," piped up Georgiana from the far corner of the parlor. "Especially if she is only thirteen."

"You left Anthony's latest missive lying open on the desk," protested Penelope. With a theatrical swish of the old sock in her hands, she heaved a swooning sigh. "La, he uses *far* more interesting phrases than that. Especially at the end, where he declares—"

Georgiana cut her off with a word that would have put a Death's Head Hussar to blush.

"If I *ever* hear you repeat that, Pen," cautioned Sophie. "You will be emptying the chamberpots for a month." A pause. "Or worse still, I shall put all the novels in this house under lock and key."

Penelope quickly rethreaded her needle and went back to work.

Leaving her sisters to their sulks, Sophie slipped away and sought refuge in tidying up the henhouse.

At last the supper hour arrived, though the meal seemed to drag on interminably. Too on edge to eat a bite, Sophie made mincemeat of her pork and simply pushed it around on her plate. Thankfully, her father seemed more lost than usual in his own thoughts, and her sisters were too busy discussing the latest London fashions to notice.

Somehow, she managed to sit still until the pudding plates were cleared, and their father's chair scraped back. Offering up a silent prayer of thanks, she quickly rose as well.

"Sophie, we are going to read the next chapter of *Lady Avery's Awful Secret*," murmured Georgiana as Mr. Lawrance drifted off toward his study. "Would you care to join us in the parlor? It's really quite entertaining."

"Alas, I think I will forgo the pleasures of Lady Avery's perils," replied Sophie. *I am facing enough of my own.* "I'm tired, and feel a beastly headache coming on. So if you will excuse me, I am going to retire early."

"Sorry. I know you dislike shopping, so London was a tax on your patience. Do you wish for me to make you a tisane?" asked Georgiana in concern. "There is a fresh batch of chamomile in the stillroom."

"No, no. I assure you, a night of uninterrupted peace and quiet will be remedy enough."

"Sleep well," said Penelope. She crinkled her nose. "You do look a little frayed around the edges."

"No doubt my advanced age is beginning to show," replied Sophie dryly. "Enjoy your heroine's adventures."

Chuffing a sigh, Penelope fingered her braid. "Nothing adventurous ever happens to any of us. I wish..."

Repressing an inward wince, Sophie started up the stairs. *Oh, be careful what you wish for, Pen.*

Rope, grappling hooks, an assortment of thin steel probes, tiny wood wedges to keep doors and drawers open...Cameron rechecked the items in his leather rucksack one last time before extinguishing the candle and easing open the hut's planked door.

Wispy swirls of sea-damp mist ghosted through the trees. The air was heavy with moisture, muffling the riffle of the breeze through the long grasses. He stood very still, letting his all senses readjust to the textured nuances of a country night. The slums of London were not exactly rife with the twitter of nightingales or the scent of heather. Its symphony of sounds and smells were sharp and piercing as knives—they lanced right through a man's gut.

Here the dangers were more subtle.

Clouds scudded through the skies, playing a rag-tag game of hide and seek with the starlight. The shadows deepened as Cameron started off down the path, but despite the gloom, he moved swiftly, surely over the loose stones.

"I am a creature of Darkness," he murmured, feeling the cool fingers of night nymphs tickle his cheeks and thread through his hair. A man whose heart was now carved out of coal. *Black, oh-so black, and cold to the touch.* "Connor and Gryff may be Lords of the Land, but I am a Wraith of Midnight." A specter whose place in the world was here, moving through the realm of the Moon.

The Moon and not the Sun.

That he was letting Sophie set foot into this murky netherworld was wrong. Selfish. *And yet, I've made it clear to her that I'm not a saint*, he told himself.

But somehow that didn't absolve him of guilt.

A flitting movement up ahead drew his attention. There within the dark, leafy branches was a figure, tugging at the folds of her cloak.

How like Sophie to be early for the rendezvous.

He wasn't sure whether to laugh or groan.

Coming up behind her, Cameron tapped her lightly on the shoulder. At least she had thought to wear dark clothing.

"Mmmph!"

His hand quickly, clapped over her mouth, muffled her cry. "Shhhhh, it's me."

"You nearly scared me out of my skin," muttered Sophie, once he had released her.

"Would that I had startled some sense *into* your head," he retorted. The scent of verbena, warm with her heat, tickled at his nostrils. Its sweetness made him even more ill tempered. "You need to be more observant. The next time it might be a foe, not a friend, creeping through the trees and you'll find your lovely throat cut."

"Thank you for the first lesson in skullduggery. I shall make careful note of it."

"You had better pray that you are a quick learner." His tone was deliberately rough. Allowing her to come, he decided, had been an error on his part. A weakness. And survival, he repeated to himself, depended on unyielding strength in this dog-eat-dog world. "Sophie, on further reflection, I—"

It was her turn to cut off a sound. "Don't waste your breath. I'm not going home. So you can either continue on with me, or scuttle your plans. I have an even louder howl than Rufus, and I vow, I'll wake the entire shire if you try to leave me in the dust."

"When did you turn so devious?" muttered Cameron.

"That is rather like the pot calling the kettle black," she replied. A rustle of wool, and a small package appeared from her cloak pocket.

An odd odor wafted up from the oiled paper. "What's that?"

"Raw chicken and anchovies. Rufus adores the combination."

A fish-and-fowl-loving hound, a doggedly determined young lady—the foray was fast descending into farce.

Ah, but I have always been the Devil's own fool.

The forces of Nature seemed aligned against him, and so with an ungracious sigh, he surrendered to the inevitable. "Where are we likely to find this epicurean beast?"

"Under the archway leading into the walled rose garden," said Sophie. "It's the one to the left of the swan fountain, tucked behind the privet hedge."

"I know the spot," said Cameron curtly. He took her hand. "Come along, before I change my mind."

Beneath the hood of her cloak, her face was naught but a blur of pearl and charcoal shades. But the hiss and crackle of sparks in her hidden eyes was almost audible.

Sophie's inner fire, fighting to break free?

Grass flattened under her half boot as she swung into a long-limbed stride. "What are we waiting for?"

"Not so fast." Holding her back, he edged forward to take the lead. "Follow my lead and try to stay light on your feet. From here on in, you must be silent as the grave."

"You might choose a less grim metaphor," she murmured.

"I believe in calling a spade a spade." The gate latch of the perimeter released with a rusty *snick*. "Let us hope it is not going to end up digging us into a very deep and dirty hole."

On that note, all talk ceased. They crossed the lawns, keeping low and hugging close to the slanting shadows of the shrubbery. At the far end of the formal gardens, the imposing manor house rose from a sea of silvery mist, its jagged black silhouette of turrets and towers looking slightly menacing against the night sky. A sleeping monster, ready to devour anyone who dared to trespass on its hallowed turf.

For an instant, Cameron felt his chest tighten. He was a boy again, torn between fear and loathing.

Grrrrrrr. The cavernous rumble seemed to be emanating from the very bowels of the earth.

He took shelter behind a decorative urn, flattening Sophie against the smooth marble. "A friend of yours, I trust?" The shaggy shape padding toward them was big as a bear.

"Yes," she hissed. The dog—at least he assumed it was a dog, and not some hairy Nordic Viking come back to life from one of the nearby ancient burial mounds—was favored with a far nicer tone. "Rufus. Come here, sweetheart, and let me scratch all the little spots that you love to have touched."

Until that moment Cameron had never imagined he could be jealous of a four-footed beast. "If I get down on my hands and knees and lick your hand, do I get the same offer?" he asked.

She darted him a quelling look. "Ignore him, Rufus," she whispered, fondling the dog's drooping ears. "I brought you a little treat."

The growl was now more of a purr.

"Here you are, darling."

The massive jaws opened, revealing a peek of gleaming dragon-sized teeth. A snorty little snuffle was quickly followed by a soft *whoof* of contentment.

"Now lie down. And stay." That was directed at Rufus. To him she said, "It's safe to approach the house. Have you decided where you are going to seek entrance?"

Cameron squinted at the façade. No lights were visible in any of the windows. *So far, so good.* He would continue according to his primary plan. "There is a side door that opens into the foyer adjoining the Gun Room," he answered. "It's set in a corner of the East Wing, and sheltered by a slate portico, so I'll be well hidden from view."

Sophie turned abruptly and moved to block his way. Her hand grasped his coat collar, light against dark in the mizzled moonlight. "Are you sure about this, Cam? The local blacksmith—you remember Neddy Wadsworth, don't you—helped install the new locks. He said he had never seen such baffling mechanisms."

"Clearly Neddy is not nearly as well traveled as I am." Seeing her troubled expression, he smiled. "I told you, don't worry. Now that that I've slipped past the Guardian of Thunder..." Rufus was now snoring. "...the rest will be child's play."

A poor choice of words, for her face tightened, the pale skin stretching taut over her delicate cheekbones. "Wolcott hates you, Cam. He'll squash you like a bug if you're caught."

"I'm not a bug to him. I'm a stinking piece of pond scum, a much lower form of life. But the thing about scum is, it's slippery stuff, and surprisingly adept at survival. Not easy to kill a squiggle of slime."

His sarcasm made her flinch.

Good. Maybe he could chip away at her trusting resolve. Make her see him as he was, uncolored by her illusions of the past.

"Well, I'd rather not test that assumption by provoking His Lordship's servants into shooting at you," replied Sophie.

"If you would keep your voice down, I might have a chance at avoiding a hail of bullets."

She scowled, but answered in a low whisper. "Perhaps we should withdraw and reconsider our plans."

"According to you, time is now of the essence. We can't afford to waste a single moment."

This time she had no retort.

"Stay here and keep rubbing Rufus." He uncurled her hold on his coat. "I will be back shortly."

"Damnation." Rufus twitched beneath her stroking fingers but did not waken. "Damn, damn, damn." Sitting back on her knees, Sophie watched for any sign of life within the manor. *Nothing.* There was nothing but a brooding blackness that matched the darkening of her mood.

Why? Why was Cameron hellbent on taking such cursed risks?

A stupid question. She knew what fire burned in his belly. Oh, yes, he hid it well these days, deep down inside a shell of laugh-at-Lucifer cynicism. His face and his voice told the same carefully controlled lie. Only the heat of his skin betrayed the burning coals within, hot as hellfire, sizzling, smoldering just beneath the surface.

The Marquess of Wolcott had been Cameron's nemesis for as long as she had known him.

Wolcott. Lord of the manor. He was a cold-hearted aristocrat who refused to acknowledge that he shared any of his precious, privileged blood with a bastard brat.

In the past, youthful passion had driven Cameron to poke a red-hot pitchfork in the Devil's eye. His attack was far more adroit now, his weapons far more sophisticated.

Which didn't make the danger any less frightening.

"If your master catches Cam, he will kill him," she murmured to Rufus.

The dog snuffled in response, utterly lacking in canine sympathy.

She had never imagined that accepting Cameron's help would draw him back into the perils of his own personal past.

Woof.

"Yes, I know. I've been a weak-willed widgeon." She rose to a half crouch. "He has to leave. Flee. Never come back here."

At that, Rufus lifted his huge head.

"Not you. Stay."

Sophie moved, quickly and quietly, cutting around the graveled walkway and creeping past the stone balusters lining the music room terrace. An open archway allowed her to cross a small cobbled courtyard. Ivy vines hung heavy on the high walls, the echoing murmur of the leaves amplified by the ancient limestone.

A turn brought her to the corner of the East Wing.

Sophie paused and held her breath in her lungs, straining to hear a telltale sound. He was good—very good. There wasn't the slightest whisper to betray his presence.

Drawing her cloak and skirts tight to her body, she tiptoed over the soft grass.

"I told you to stay with the dog." Cameron's disembodied whisper floated out from the murky alcove. It was only when she moved under the jut of roof that she could make out his broad shoulders hunched in front of the door. He didn't turn around.

A tentative step brought her a little closer. "Unlike Rufus, I'm not trained to obey orders."

"Perhaps I should have fed you raw chicken and stinky fish."

"That's not funny."

"Forgive me—my sense of humor is not always at its best when I'm trying to concentrate." He shifted ever so slightly. "Kindly move—preferably all the way back to your cottage. You are blocking what little light there is."

She came and knelt down beside him. It was black as Hades in the recessed doorway, and aside from a faint rasping—a sound like the scratch of a demon's claws against unseen metal—a heavy silence hung in the air.

Sophie made herself breathe, half expecting to find her lungs fill with the choking smell of brimstone. As her eyes adjusted to the darkness, she saw that he had two thin steel rods inserted in the lock, and was working them ever so carefully.

"What—" she began.

"Shhhh. I need to listen for the clicks."

Cocking an ear, she held herself very still. A minute passed, then another. She could sense that his lean, lithe body was on full alert, every muscle and sinew like a coiled spring, ready to react in an instant. And yet, there was also an air of cool calmness about him. The hot-headed youth had learned to temper fire with ice.

"Ah."

She heard it, too. A tiny *ping*, which signaled the tumblers of the mechanism springing open.

The bolt released and the door moved perhaps a quarter inch out from the stone molding.

Against her better judgment, Sophie was duly impressed. At the time of their installation, Neddy the blacksmith had explained in excruciating detail why the marquess's new locks were impregnable.

"How did you do that?" she whispered.

"Years of practice."

Clearly her Pirate had sailed through oceans of intriguing adventure since hoisting anchor from Terrington. Curiosity prickled along her spine. "Where?" Sophie asked.

"In too many hellholes to recount, Sunbeam."

"Was it difficult to learn?" she pressed.

He eased the door open a touch wider before answering. "I seem to have a knack for this sort of thing. Perhaps my hands were made for sin."

The prickling turned to a more needle-sharp sensation as she watched him slip a finger inside to test the latch.

Along with all his other plunder, how many hearts had he stolen along the way?

Sophie shoved the unsettling thought back into the iron-banded storage box of her brain and quickly turned the mental key. He had warned her that his growth into manhood had left him without a noble bone in his body. So she must take him at his word. But that did not alter her own sense of right and wrong. A sudden twinge of guilt tugged at her heart.

Rising, she folded her arms across her chest. Looking down on him gave the illusion of taking some control of the situation.

"Your prowess is extraordinary. But be that as it may, I can't let you go on with this."

He turned, a small upward curl tugging at one side of his mouth. "Interesting. And just how do you intend to stop me?"

"I'll scream."

"No you won't, Sunbeam. You are far too loyal and stalwart to betray a friend."

Curse the plaguey pirate for knowing me so well.

Her resolve, which just an instant ago had felt as solid as the granite slab beneath her feet, suddenly splintered into a jumble of sharp-edged shards. "Blast it all, Cameron Fanning-Daggett. You make me feel so confused." It felt as if she were walking on knives. "I can't seem to decide whether I find your bravado alluring or appalling."

"If it's any consolation, my friends often express the same exasperation." Cameron slid the steel probes back into his boot. "I am often deliberately difficult and disagreeable. And I don't really give a damn about it."

Sophie couldn't help but recall one of her uncle's favorite lines from *Hamlet*—*The lady doth protest too much, methinks.*

"It's one of the reasons I choose to live alone," he went on. "That way I answer only to myself."

"Your domestic arrangements are no concern of mine," she replied tartly. "But as for business—tonight, you are going to have company." She lifted her skirts, gathering a tight ball of fabric in one fist to keep them off the ground. "If you insist on breaching Wolcott's bailiwick, I'm coming with you."

The pale point of her chin rising in defiance was all Cameron could make out in the gloom.

"Sophie, you are still as stubborn as old Mr. Lawrie's black-and-tan sow. The one who would break down the sty fence a half-dozen times every autumn so that she could feast on fallen apples."

"Isabelle," she replied. "Her name was Isabelle, and she should be applauded for not letting any obstacle stand in the way of her reaching her goal." A pause. "Though

I daresay you did not mean it as a compliment. But then again, many men now refer to me as an apeleader, so perhaps being compared to a pig is an improvement."

"*Who* calls you an apeleader?" he asked softly. The fellow would soon be whistling his words through a gap of missing front teeth.

"It doesn't matter," she replied. He heard another rustle of cloth. *Good God, ladies were encumbered with enough fabric to make sails for a forty-gun frigate.* "We haven't got all night."

"A point I was about to make." The fact that this wing of the manor house was deserted was the only reason he was allowing this prolonged discussion. Normally, he didn't waste a blink of an eye in completing an intrusion. *The key was to get in and out.* Dallying was dangerous.

"Sophie…" How to appeal to logic? "Sophie, be practical. You will raise holy hell trying to sneak through a strange house wearing those flapping skirts. Tables falling, china shattering… and God perish the thought if you truly had to move quickly."

"For next time, I will have to obtain a pair of boy's breeches and some shirts," she muttered, smoothing the dark cloth over her hips.

The mental image of Sophie clad in skintight male clothing stirred his privy parts to attention. The trouble was, from there it took only a tiny leap of imagination to picture her in nothing at all.

Stay focused. A man who thinks with his cock will end up with his neck in a noose.

"There won't be a next time for you, Sunbeam. I was a fool to let you come along on this foray. It won't happen again."

"Ha." The sound was like a sharp slap of leather. A glove to the face, a gauntlet brandished in challenge.

"Hand me that sack," he said, refusing to cross verbal swords. "And then, I really must insist that you return home. I'm not jesting—this isn't a game, and your continued presence puts me in jeopardy."

It was a low blow, hitting her where she was most vulnerable. However it had the desired effect.

"I—I see your point." Her voice was low and tight. It took her a fraction longer to add, "And so I'll go. But only as far as the orchards. There's no danger in waiting there."

"Don't delude yourself, Sophie. Danger lurks everywhere, especially at night, when the black velvet of midnight covers a multitude of sins." Cameron pulled a mask from his pocket and knotted it over his eyes.

"And you think a thin strip of silk makes you any less vulnerable to its jaws?"

"I've no time to argue," he snapped. "I ask you again— go home. If you insist on an update, I'll meet you at the stone hut an hour after noon."

"You promise?"

"Yes. I promise." He hoped she didn't hear the tiny hitch in his exhale. Lies usually slid smooth as satin from his lips.

Sophie retreated to the edge of the portico. Out of the gloomy darkness and into drizzle of moonlight. He wished he could send her off in a gleaming chariot, drawn by golden bumblebees—high, high, to honeysweet skies ablaze with sunlight.

A place that was always warm, always bright. Always safe.

Damnation. He couldn't allow such weak-willed thoughts. There was no place in his life for them.

She hesitated, and then melted into the shadows.

Cameron quickly forced his gaze back to the darkness...and his own devil-cursed demons.

"Wolcott, Dudley, Morton," he whispered. "Time to see how my high-and-mighty half brother fits into this puzzle."

Chapter Ten

$\mathcal{W}$here are you off to?" Georgiana eyed the fresh-baked sultana muffins with curiosity.

"Neddy is very fond of Mrs. Hodges's baking," murmured Sophie as she covered the still-steaming pastries in her basket with a checkered cloth. "I thought it would be neighborly of me to drop some off on my way into town."

"Rekindling a romance?" teased her sister.

"Don't be absurd," she muttered. "Trust me, I have no amorous intentions in mind."

Penelope, who was developing an unsettling habit of lurking near doorways, poked her head into the room. "Oh? So you don't intend to steal Neddy Wadsworth's heart?"

Sophie swallowed a snort. *No—actually I intend to purloin a far more interesting mechanism from his shop.* "Is that Lady Avery's Awful Secret? The fact that she cuts out the vital organs of unsuspecting males and sells them to the turnip vendor?"

Penelope responded with a rude noise.

"It's a little early for paying visits, isn't it?" Georgiana stole a quick look at the clock.

"Oh, Neddy rises at dawn, and a big man is always hungry. Besides," she said casually, "I feel the urge to stretch my legs, so I plan on taking the roundabout way into town."

"Really?" The arch of Georgiana's brow did not quite rise to the height of suspicion, but it was uncomfortably close. "In London, you were complaining about having to traverse the short stretch of Bond Street."

"That was on account of the crush of people and the clatter of all the fancy carriages. A long walk through the peaceful hills and vales will afford a welcome change of scenery."

"Ah. And here I was under the impression that you found some of the scenery in London much to your liking."

Sophie narrowed her eyes in warning. By unspoken agreement, the subject of Cameron Daggett had not been mentioned since they had arrived home. God forbid if Penelope got wind of the Green Park groping.

However, the youngest Lawrance seemed to sense when intrigue was in the air. Like a bird dog sniffing the scent of its prey, Penelope lifted her nose. "*What* scenery?"

For all of her sly teasing, Georgiana didn't have a malicious bone in her body. "Vauxhall Gardens," she answered quickly. "We both enjoyed strolling the lanternlit paths."

"I wish *I* could explore a pleasure garden," groused Penelope. "I would *love* to wander down the Dark Walk."

"You wouldn't sound so enthusiastic if a white slaver were to snatch you from the shadows and ship you off to some exotic harem."

"Oh, pish. That's just a silly rumor." Penelope brushed a crease from her skirts. "Isn't it?"

Looking a little smug, Georgiana tossed her a basket. "It's your turn to gather the eggs from the henhouse."

"I'll be on my way, too," announced Sophie, watching her youngest sister stomp off. "I've a number of errands to run, so I will probably be gone for most of the day."

"Enjoy your scenic stroll." Georgiana plucked a copper pot from the hanging rack, and took a canister of sugar from the cupboard. "I'm going to help Mrs. Hodges make strawberry jam."

"My favorite," murmured Sophie.

"Speaking of favorites, if you pass by Mrs. Turner's shop, will you buy me a length of her scarlet ribbon? It will make a perfect match for the cherries on my new chip straw bonnet."

"Of course." Eager to escape any further demands, she hurried out the front door and skirted around the barnyard to where a white-painted gate opened onto a winding country lane. A half-mile walk brought her to a slate-roofed cottage with several large outbuildings set around a large clearing. The rhythmic clang of metal hitting metal drifted up in the air, twining with a curl of iron-gray smoke.

"Sophie!" Looking up from his anvil, the blacksmith set down his hammer and wiped the sweat from his brow. "I haven't seen you in a dog's age!"

The mention of canines was another little nip at her conscience. Not a pleasant sensation, seeing as thoughts of a certain hound from Hell had been gnawing at it all night long.

"Halloo, Neddy," she replied, forcing a weak smile.

"How was London?" he asked.

"Hot." She slapped at a tiny red ember that had landed on her sleeve. "Crowded."

Neddy dampened a rag in his water barrel and carefully dabbed at the speck of soot. "Here, let me make sure that it's out. You can't be too careful around fire. Sparks may seem harmless, but *Whoosh!*..." He flapped his large, coal-smudged hands. "...I've seen them flare up in flames just like that."

"*Whoosh*," she echoed. "Well, seeing as I'd rather not play a part in any Guy Fawkes celebration, I am grateful for your caution.

"Guy Fawkes..." Neddy frowned for a moment. "Oh." His dark face was suddenly split by a pearly grin. "Oh-ho—Guy Fawkes! Ha, that's very clever, Sophie. You always have something bright to say."

His guileless good cheer made her stomach clench, as if she had swallowed a lump of molten iron. "I brought you some of Mrs. Hodges's sultana muffins. They are still warm."

"That's very sweet of you."

No, I'm not sweet. I'm sneaky.

"You should put the others away in your kitchen," she suggested, after watching him down two of the pastries in quick succession.

"Oh, they will just be fine here." He set them on the workbench near the blazing forge. "Keep them warm, you know, ha, ha, ha."

"No, no," she protested. "Soot and grit will quite ruin them. They must be tucked away in your larder, where they will be safe. I insist!"

Neddy fixed her with a bemused look. "You may put

down that poker. I shall do as you ask without any further prodding."

"Just a little jest." Sophie hung the pointed piece of iron back on its hook. "Ha, ha, ha."

The tongues of fire licking up from the burning coals wagged a hissing reproach.

He gathered up the napkin. "I'll only be minute. May I bring you some lemonade?"

"Thank you but no. I really can't stay long." *Just long enough to take advantage of your friendship.* Averting her gaze, she feigned a sudden interest in the set of horseshoes he had just finished. *Hell's bells—Cameron Daggett is a bad, bad influence on me. Already his to-the-devil-with-caution nature is rubbing off on me.*

That couldn't be good.

As Neddy's steps faded, Sophie sidled over to the large storage cabinet where he kept his supplies. A twist of the handle, a snatch from the top shelf . . . it took only a moment to secret the oilskin-wrapped object into her basket.

"So sorry, Neddy. But this is all for the Higher Good," she muttered, concealing her misdeed within the folds of the remaining napkin. "I'm likely heading straight down the primrose path to perdition, and yet there's no turning back."

Not with the Threat of Ruin snapping at my heels.

"There." Neddy's big bulk cast a sudden shadow over the forge. "Satisfied?"

"Oh, yes, quite." Sophie made herself smile. "Well, I really must be running along."

His face fell. "Why the rush? The shops won't be opening for a while."

"Oh, er, I plan on taking the roundabout route into town. I—I've missed walking in the hills."

"Aye, like you, I, too, prefer simple country pleasures." An awkward silence, which Sophie pretended not to notice. Shifting his hobnailed boots, Neddy dispelled the moment by cracking his knuckles. "We have a lot in common, you know."

Swallowing the sour taste of deception, she forced a cheerful laugh. "Yes! Like you, I'm very fond of sultana muffins."

"I was speaking of—"

"And strawberry jam," Sophie quickly added, hoping to keep the conversation from taking a personal turn. Neddy still seemed to harbor a tendre for her, despite all her attempts to gently discourage him. "Georgie is helping to make up a fresh batch. I'll make sure she drops off several jars." She began edging toward the doorway. "It was lovely chatting, but I mustn't keep you from your work."

A shadow flickered over Neddy's face but he made no further effort to detain her. "Have a care up on Hawthorne ridge. I heard the path is a trifle dangerous near the ledge on account of a recent rockfall."

"You know me—I'm always cautious."

"Not a soul more sensible than you," agreed Neddy. "Enjoy your walk. And please give Mrs. Hodges my thanks for the muffins. Tell her I shall hammer out a new set of kitchen hooks for her."

"She'll be delighted to hear it."

"You may soon be privy to some good news, too, Sophie," he blurted out, just as she turned to go. "I've contracted for a very lucrative job. One that will, God willing, pay me enough to provide a comfortable living for a wife."

"That's lovely news," she mumbled. "What sort of work?"

"I can't say. I'm sworn to secrecy," he replied.

"It sounds... very important."

"Oh; it is."

"Again, congratulations on your good fortune." Fluttering a faint wave, she ducked outside, drawing in a great gulp of the fresh air to clear her lungs. The Devil's own brimstone was swirling around her conscience, sour and acrid, making it difficult to breathe.

Guilt was an uncomfortable companion as she hurried through the steep sloping meadow. It clung hot and heavy to her shoulders, and soon a beading of sweat was teasing down her spine. By the time she had climbed through the winding turns and crested the windswept ridge, her dress was damp, and her mood was foul.

If she had guessed right...

Squeezing through a gap in the stones, she entered the small clearing. "Where the devil do you think you are going?"

Cameron finished tying the satchel to his saddle before turning around. "To London," he replied calmly.

"We had an agreement." Anger started to bubble up inside her. "You promised. And yet here you are, sneaking away hours before our appointed rendezvous."

His sardonic smile made her itch to slap his face. "My dear Sunbeam, I told you not to trust in anything I say."

Two swift strides brought her close. Close enough to thump the basket hard against his chest.

"Ouch." His lips twitched. "What have you got in there? Rocks?"

"No." Sophie thumped him again. "It's my second lesson in fighting Evil with Evil, and you—you devious, double-crossing serpent of sin—are not going to slither away without teaching me what I want to know."

"Are you always this grumpy early in the morning?"

Her temper, already dangerously frayed, snapped. Dropping the basket—squarely on his foot—Sophie drew back her arm and swung as hard as she could.

"If you are going to hit a man where it hurts…" Cameron caught her wrist in mid-flight, as if it were naught but a gossamer butterfly fluttering on spun silk wings. "…you need to know several things."

Hot with humiliation, she lashed out again, determined to break free.

"That's much better," he murmured, deflecting her knee from his crotch. "But do it with a real vengeance."

Swearing, Sophie took another wild swing at his face.

"That's more like it, however don't go for the jaw—you'll only hurt your hand." Cameron carefully uncurled her fingers. "Strike at the eyes, and claw like a fiend." He let her go and stepped back, folding his arms across his chest. "Go ahead, give it a try."

She didn't move. "It's not a fair fight if you won't defend yourself."

"Lesson Number Three—never, ever fight fair."

"You are, without question, the most awful, aggravating man in all of Christendom." Sophie kicked at the ground, sending a spray of pebbles ricocheting against the rocks. "I should pound your thick skull to smithereens. But I can't quite bring myself to do it."

"Sweetheart—"

"Oh, don't try to sweeten the truth. I'm a fool." The scattered *pings* had dissipated her flush of fury into something far more nebulous. Anger was easy to understand. This—this hot and cold surge of emotion—was horribly confusing. "A dim-witted, addlepated fool to have thought this could ever work."

Turning on her heel, so he wouldn't see the quivering of her lips, Sophie hitched up her skirts. "So go ahead—disappear! And never come back. It's for the best. I've precious little time to come up with a plan to defeat Dudley and his friend Morton—and defeat him I will! So I can't afford any distractions."

Which way, which way? She couldn't see through the sting of salt, but all that mattered was getting away from this cursed spot. Slipping, sliding on the stone shards, she scrambled around the granite outcropping. There was no sound of steps behind her.

Damn those beautiful sea-green eyes. Damn that terrible, taunting mouth.

"The wretch," she muttered, head down, gaze glued to the uneven ground. A hard kick sent more pebbles skittering in all directions. No wonder men were so fond of fisticuffs. There was something supremely satisfying about hitting something, even if it was only a tiny inanimate object.

"The rapscallion, the—"

"Reptile," finished Cameron, as she collided headlong into his chest.

He must be a *djinn*, or a puff of smoke. Surely no flesh-and-blood creature could slither so swiftly, so stealthily.

"I was going to say 'rogue.'" Her voice was a bit muffled by folds of soft linen. For someone who had slept rough, he smelled surprisingly nice. Earthy. Masculine. Wood and leather spiced with a hint of bay rum. "Why are you here, and not on your horse?"

"You forgot this." Cameron held up her basket. "You may need to crush a few more toes on the way home."

Sophie bit back a reluctant laugh. "Be grateful I didn't crush your skull."

"Yes, and I'm exceedingly grateful that you didn't angle it at a far more sensitive part of my anatomy."

"I considered it."

"Thank God for small favors."

"You ought to count your blessings." She grasped the basket's handle. "I had better return its contents to the rightful owner."

"Purloined property?" His grip tightened on the woven willow. "What risks have you been running?"

"Never mind. I was going to ask your advice, but seeing as you are so hellfire anxious to head back to London, I'll handle it on my own."

"Oh, very neatly done, Sophie." He leaned in closer. "You are getting awfully good at the art of manipulation."

"I'm learning."

A wry chuckle, low and a little rumbled, set off a strange thumping inside her ribcage. His jaw was peppered with an intriguing texture of short, dark bristles. The perfect image of a pirate—slightly wild, slightly menacing.

Alluring as sin.

"I'm not sure whether to laugh or gnash my teeth over the fact that you are such a gifted student. The trouble is, a little knowledge can be more dangerous than none at

all," murmured Cameron. "So you had best come along
with me. I can't in good conscience leave you in the middle of a lesson."

"You don't have a conscience," pointed out Sophie.
"Or so you said."

"On rare occasions, it rears its ugly head."

*Wind-tangled hair, sun-bronzed skin, a dark-edged
smile . . . beauty was in the eye of the beholder.*

"W-what do you have in mind?" she asked, finding her
throat had gone dry as dust.

"Hard to say. First of all, let's see what you have
wrapped in that dainty little napkin."

After setting the basket on the table inside the hut, Sophie
carefully peeled back the folds of calico. "It's a lock."

"Yes, I can see that." Cameron rubbed at his chin.
*Would that the female mind's intricate intertwining maze
of gears and tumblers were as easy to comprehend.*
"What's not nearly as clear is *why* you have it, and *what*
you intend to do with it."

Her eyes darkened several shades—never a good sign
with Sophie. Squalls rarely stirred her steady demeanor.
When clouds rolled in, they usually presaged a full-blown
storm.

"I should think those answers are obvious," she
replied. Edging forward in her chair, she braced her palms
on the rough-hewn wood. "It's a puzzle lock, like the ones
guarding Wolcott Manor, and I borrowed it from Neddy
Wadsworth."

"Borrowed?"

"In a manner of speaking," she replied.

"Ah."

"I want to learn how to open it. And since you showed some skill in the subject last night, I thought you would be the best person to teach me."

"No," he said flatly.

"Fine." She smoothed the napkin back in place.

Damnation, there was a new depth to her resolve that he couldn't quite fathom. She was the same Sophie, and yet different. Shaped by forces he knew naught of.

"Would you care to elaborate on that?" he asked.

"No."

Their eyes locked with an almost audible click. For someone new at the game of opening impregnable defensive mechanisms, she was proving awfully skilled at choosing all the right little levers to push.

"Click," he muttered, shrugging his shoulders in reluctant surrender. "You appear to have a God-given natural talent for manipulation. You've turned the right key this time. But only because if I left you to your own devices, you might get yourself in deep trouble."

The shadows softened, allowing a glimmer of light to brighten her gaze. *Sunbeam.* A spun-sugar flicker of gold, dancing like a dragonfly through the air. How was it that something so delicate could penetrate his Hellhound hide and fill his chest with warmth?

It was a question that he didn't care to face at that moment. *Damnation, I should have slipped away when I had the chance.* For a lone predator, cold logic and icy cynicism were essential for survival. The longer he stayed near Sophie, the more dangerous it became. For both of them.

"Thank you, Cam," replied Sophie. "If I am to defend myself, I need to know how to attack an opponent's weakness."

Ominous as that sounded, he decided to let it pass. "A wise strategy, in theory. However, if I am to help you put it into practice, I need to know a little more about what you have in mind."

The wariness was back in her eyes. "There may come a time when I want to have a look around somewhere that is under lock and key."

"Look, I applaud your spirit. But listen to reason—"

"Damn you, Cameron Daggett. Has it ever occurred to you that I am sick of being reasonable?" Her voice was perilously close to a shout, ragged and raw with emotion. "For most of my adult life, I have worn Reason like a corset, its unyielding stays and constricting laces pinching so tight that at times I could barely breathe."

He watched her chest rise and fall.

"And yet," she continued, "an ailing father and two high-spirited sisters depended on me to be sensible. Sensible! And so, every time a crisis loomed, I erred on the side of prudence." She expelled a sharp sigh. "While look at you—you were never afraid to meet adversity head on, and haven't altered a whit."

"Good God, Sophie, don't hold me up as a shining example of how to deal with trouble. I am hardly a patterncard of wisdom when it comes to making the right decisions in life."

"But it seems to me that one is more apt to regret the things one hasn't done," she said. "Rather than the other way around."

"Does it? Right and wrong is never black and white. We can't always control the consequences of our actions." Cameron turned back her cuff and gently traced a tiny scar cutting across the top of her wrist. "You have only to look here. I thought it a great lark to sneak into Squire Stoneleigh's orchard and steal his prized apples. I was ready to suffer any consequences, but when I tripped and his mastiff came at my throat, it was you who fended him off."

Sophie freed her hand and hastily hid it under the fringes of her shawl. "You cannot deny that there is risk in doing nothing as well. I—I don't know how to explain it, but I feel I need…" She rose abruptly and began pacing the perimeter of narrow space. "…action."

Watching the willowy grace of her body in motion, Cameron found himself distracted by the sway of her slim hips and the subtle rise and fall of her perfectly shaped breasts.

Lust pooled in his belly and spiraled to his privy parts. *So much for the resolve to respond to her arguments with reason.*

It took a moment of iron-willed resolve to bring his rebellious body back under control.

"My mind has been tied in such terrible knots these last few months," she went on. "I've been so confused, and unable to think clearly… And then, your first mad midnight kiss seemed to tug a strand loose. And…" In a frothing of skirts Sophie spun around. "And I'm not making any sense, am I?" She made a face. "I'm babbling."

"I like the sound of your voice," he murmured.

Sophie stopped, and all at once it was very quiet in the hut.

"I like the tilt of your chin, and the way you bite your lower lip when you are puzzling out a problem."

Her lashes flicked up slowly, uncertainly.

"Sit down, Sunbeam. Life is a terrible tangle of spiders

and serpents, and I, of all people, can give little guidance on how to untwine them." He tapped a finger to the lock. "However, I can be of help in solving the secrets of this particular puzzle."

She hesitated before resuming her spot in the facing chair.

"*If* I so choose." Cameron held up a hand to cut off the protest he saw about to fly from her lips. "Against my better judgment, I shall. But in return you will have to promise me one thing. Before you put your new skills into action, you will have to tell me what you are planning."

"Will you share your plans with me?" countered Sophie. "It seems only fair."

"Hmmm."

She frowned. "Which means?"

"Which means that I am thinking."

"While you do so, I have another question. What were you looking for in Lord Wolcott's study?"

Truth or lies?

"I was looking for any correspondence between Wolcott and Dudley or Morton," he replied, choosing for the moment to answer honestly. "It's important to understand the connection between them." He steepled his fingers. "Much as I dislike Wolcott, I find it hard to see why he would involve himself in petty blackmail. He has no need of money, and why would he care about an old church mistake made by your father?'

"I—I don't know." Sophie shifted her eyes, just enough to catch his attention.

Truth or lies?

"I think," said Cameron slowly, "that you are not

telling me everything about Lord Dudley and the threat that he and his friend Morton are holding over you."

"W-what makes you say that?"

"The fact that I've spent most of my life dealing with cutthroat criminals and conniving cheats. Sensing the slightest whisper of a false note is key to surviving in the stews."

"I see that I have much to learn about the underworld of intrigue," said Sophie softly.

A growl formed deep in his throat.

"It's true, I haven't given you all the details. But I didn't want to draw you any deeper into my affairs, Cam," she went on in a rush. "Good Lord, if I had thought Wolcott was involved in this sordid scheme, I never would have let you become involved in the first place. If not for me, you wouldn't have come back here to Terrington, and put yourself in danger."

"I have a nose for trouble," he quipped. "A whiff of danger is perfume to my nostrils."

Her expression grew even more pinched. "What Dudley wants from me isn't important. If I get the wretched document back from him, he has to leave my family alone."

"You underestimate evil. If a man like Dudley wants something badly enough, he won't stop, Sophie. He'll simply find another weakness, another target. Georgiana or Penelope, perhaps."

All the color leached from her face.

Taking ruthless advantage of her fear, he pressed on. "So you had best trust me to be the judge of what is important."

"Trust," repeated Sophie. "You keep sending me conflicting messages. One moment you ask me to have faith in you and then in the next breath you warn me not to believe a thing you say. Which Cameron should I listen to?"

A good question. "That depends on how much you are willing to risk, Sunbeam," he said softly.

Curling her fingers in strings of her bonnet, she slowly untied the bow beneath her chin. "Very well—I might as well throw caution to the wind." A flick sent the chip-straw headcovering fluttering to the earthen floor. "Let's get down to business, shall we?"

Chapter Eleven

Sophie loosened a few hairpins, allowing a twist of curls to fall free. "I think better without all these cursed constrictions."

"Far be it from me to object," murmured Cameron.

Was he amused? It was impossible to tell what emotions were hiding behind the half-mocking specter of a smile.

"Now that you've shed those strictures, why not untighten your tongue as well? I want to know what you've been holding back."

She made a face. "You ought to bare a few things, too."

"Strip away all of our secrets?" He waggled a brow. "We'll discuss that later. First, tell me about Dudley."

A gust rattled the window casement and a hiss of air slipped in through a crack in the glass.

Trust, trust, it taunted.

"As I told you before, he and Morton are looking for some sort of church document. They think my father might know something about it."

"So you've said. Go on."

"I've also told you Papa's memory is so foggy that

even if the paper ever existed—which I think is doubt-ful—he couldn't tell them about it." Sophie watched the dust motes dancing in the air, rather than meet Cameron's gaze. "I've finally convinced them that his mind is not all there. However, they refuse to believe that I know nothing about it."

"What makes them think you would have any knowl-edge about it?"

She hesitated.

"Sophie?"

"Because of you," she admitted. "They seem to know that we were friends growing up."

His expression remained inscrutable. Like the Sphinx, a half man, half beast carved out of solid stone.

"What sort of document?" pressed Cameron.

"They didn't say, but along with some probing in-quiries about you and your background, their questions concerned church marriage records. I pretended to have no clue as to what they were talking about."

"Ah."

The small sound could have meant anything. Silence followed, but with every nerve in her body on edge, she could almost hear the gears spinning inside his head.

"Cam..." They had only spoken of the subject once, when Lord Wolcott's refusal to pay for a London doctor to treat Cameron's mother had left him feeling utterly helpless. Furious at Fate's cruelty, he had confided a fam-ily secret...

"This certainly casts a different light on things, Sun-beam," he mused. "There was a letter mentioning Morton in Wolcott's desk, but the implication seemed meaning-less until now." He didn't explain. "Given what you've just told me, it's even more imperative that I return to London and begin making some inquiries."

"You think the proof of your mother's marriage to Wolcott's father, the old marquess, actually exists?" she whispered.

"To her dying day, she insisted that she was, in fact, his wife," he replied. "But my half brother claims there was no such record in my father's papers, making me naught but a bastard by-blow. I've always suspected that he destroyed the proof to protect his precious pedigree from mongrel blood."

Sophie knew that the old marquess's first wife, the mother of the present Lord Wolcott, was a highborn lady. While Cameron's mother was an obscure governess who had met his father on sea voyage returning from Italy, where he had sought a warmer winter clime for his ailing health.

"What puzzles me," she said slowly, "is how my father's name has come to be involved in this. He could not possible have performed the ceremony, as it took place abroad."

"There are a great many mysteries," replied Cameron tersely. "None of which we will solve right now." He picked up the lock and turned it over in his hands. "The thing about puzzle locks is, they may look horridly complicated, but as soon as one understands where the few key levers are located, they open quite easily."

"Show me." The words slipped out of their own accord.

Cameron didn't react for a moment. He sat very still, the dark fringe of his lashes accentuating the black, brooding shadows beneath his eyes. "Mistakes can be costly. A slip sometimes triggers a hidden danger. I once encountered an Italian lock that spit a burning acid if the wrong tumbler moved. And then, there are clever Swiss models that set off a warning within the house, so the owner is waiting to welcome you with a brace of pistols."

"I'm willing to take the risk," answered Sophie.

"Are you?"

A question? *No, a challenge.*

She made a show of dusting her hands, feeling a tingling in her flesh as her palms touched together. "I'm ready to go *mano a mano*, Cameron. In the past, I could hold my own against you in any game we played." *Almost every game, that is.* "So let the tumblers fall where they may."

Her bravado provoked a twitch of his lips. Setting the lock down, he slowly removed his coat. "Very well." His cravat fell in a lazy, looping twist and hooked over the back of his chair. "Like you, I like work best when I am free of sartorial restraint." Slowly, slowly, he rolled up his shirtsleeves, revealing a bronzed pair of muscled forearms.

In response, Sophie unfastened the top two tiny buttons of her bodice and fanned her cheeks. "Is it me, or it is warm in here?"

His throaty chuckle set a lick of heat teasing between her legs. Clenching her knees together, she shifted her legs a fraction and gave her skirts a small shake.

"Pay attention, Sunbeam. The lesson is about to commence." A dangerous glitter kindled in his eyes. "A lock is like a virtuous lady." He circled a fingertip around the keyhole. "There is a special little opening which allows you to delve inside her and learn her intimate secrets, but

to gain entrance requires a carefully choreographed seduction. She doesn't yield to just anyone. You must have
a skillful touch to coax her into opening up. One clumsy
slip can ruin all your hopes."

Sophie felt herself blush.

Cameron chuckled again, and her cheeks were aflame.
"Shall I go on?"

"I am all ears," she said, trying to match his silky tone.

"Sorry, but I must ask you to use other bodily parts in
this exercise."

"I..." To her dismay, her voice seemed to catch in her
throat.

"Your *hand*, Sophie." A devilish grin. "Give me your
hand, palm up if you please."

His long, lithe fingers encircled her wrist. "Relax," he
murmured. "Tension makes it hard to perform delicate
maneuvers."

"You are certainly an expert in this subject," she said a
little testily. "Can we get on with it?"

"Alas, you are right. A lock, unlike a lady, needs to be
opened as quickly as possible. Still, its seduction is about
more than mechanics." Drawing a slim shaft of steel from
his boot, Cameron carefully positioned it in her hand.
"It's about feel."

The steel was sleek and cool against her skin.

He guided the probe to the keyhole and dipped the tip
inside. "Close your eyes, circle the metal, and tell me
what you feel."

She did as he asked. "It's smooth... and hard."

"Come, you can do better than that."

Frowning, she tried again. "There are two ridges—no,
three."

"That's better." Cameron pushed the shaft in a little deeper. "What about now?"

"A series of indentations."

"Press each one very gently. Do you feel any movement?"

Sophie was surprised at how subtle a shift the steel could detect. "I—I think so."

"Excellent. These locks are tricky, for they have a few additional elements. But it's good practice. Now, give a little jiggle here..."

For the next hour, Cameron led her through the basics of how a lock worked. It was difficult, demanding training, requiring great patience and concentration. And Sophie found it exhilarating. She liked solving problems, and here, her efforts were rewarded with a supremely satisfying *snick* when she got it right.

"Not bad, Sunbeam," he said, once she could spring the catch all on her own. "I know a number of cracksmen in London would be happy to engage your services, should you ever decide to seek employment."

"I daresay it would be far more interesting than serving as a governess to a pack of unruly children." Sophie blotted her brow. "Admit it—I do have a knack for this."

"Pride goeth before a fall." Cameron took a pocketwatch from his coat pocket and snapped open the case. "It's all very well to master a mechanism when there is no pressure to perform. But when it's dark, and time is of the essence, the task becomes a good deal tougher."

He propped up the timepiece against an earthenware jug and angled the white porcelain dial her way. It was a beautiful object, elegant in its simplicity and exquisitely made. *Expensive*, she guessed, noting the finely crafted engraving and rich patina of the two-tone gold.

"Where did you get that?" she asked.

"Geneva," he replied casually. "The citizens there are renowned for their watchmaking skills."

"It must have cost a fortune."

His lips twitched. "The asking amount was indeed quite high. However I was able to negotiate my own price."

The ticking seemed to change to a deeper, darker tone. *Danger, danger.*

Ignoring the warning, she pressed on. "What do your friends think of your illegal activities?"

Cameron shrugged. "As friends do, Connor and Gryff tolerate my faults. And while they don't condone some of my more outrageous exploits, they do concede that I have some redeeming qualities. My skills have on occasion proved useful in helping Good triumph over Evil."

Black and white. As shadows scudded across his angled face, Sophie studied his profile. How strange—even though he had changed in a myriad of ways over the years, he was still essentially the same. *Cameron. Mercurial and mysterious.*

Her opposite, and yet a kindred spirit.

Sensing her scrutiny, he turned abruptly and gave a quick tap to the watch's crystal. "Back to our lesson, Sunbeam. Try to open the lock in, say, two minutes."

Sophie watched several seconds tick away. "That's an awfully short allotment."

"You have no business attempting a real job until you can do it in half that time."

Taking up the probe, she set to work. *Tick, tick, tick.*

"Drat." A rushed flick had jigged one of the wrong levers, freezing the gears in place.

Cameron looked a little smug as he released the catch on the inside of the lock. *Too smug.*

"Let's see you do it in under a minute."

He proceeded to do so with maddening ease. "Forty-one seconds, to be precise."

"I'll bet you can't do it in thirty seconds," retorted Sophie.

A pause. "How much?"

The butcher's bill was due on the morrow...Reluctantly, she shook her head. "I'm not plump in the pocket. I can't wager money."

"Fine." He regarded her with a lazy, lidded gaze. "I'll accept a different forfeit."

"Like what? I left all of the sultana muffins with Neddy Wadsworth, and I doubt that you would care for hairpins."

"You may keep the pins," agreed Cameron. "I'll take an item of clothing instead. I get to choose."

"You are incorrigible," she exclaimed.

"Impossibly so," he drawled. "Dangerously so." He shifted slightly, a subtle move, and yet Sophie was intimately aware of the ripple of masculine muscle, the powerful primal grace.

Dangerous, indeed.

"That's enough of a foray to the dark side of propriety for today. You are smart to refuse the wager." His expression didn't alter, but she could sense that his mood had suddenly changed again, like quicksilver presaging a coming storm. She hated it when he retreated into himself, leaving only the shell of a stranger.

"Return to the light, Sunbeam," he said, leaning back in his chair. "It's too risky for you to stay here with me."

Sophie watched the ornate steel hands of the pocket-watch sweep through another moment. "On second thought, I'll accept your terms."

I ought to make her go. Cameron sucked in a shallow breath. *Make her flee before she's drawn deeper into my netherworld of darkness and demons.* The risks were too great. It wasn't just the physical threat, though God knows that was terrifying enough. Worse was the knowledge that to let her be part of his shadowy life was to draw her closer to the abyss of ruin. He still couldn't offer her a respectable life, so it was wrong to relive their youthful camaraderie, when together they laughed in the face of any danger.

His heart shuddered against his ribs. Cameron reached across the table. The pocketwatch was mere inches away. Click the case shut and the game was over.

But I am an evil devil, who cares for naught but my own selfish desires.

His fingers pinched . . . and picked up the probe.

"Tell me when to start," he said, turning a deaf ear to the chiding voices in the back of his head.

"Now," called Sophie, her eyes intent on the dial.

Tick. The catch popped open.

"Drat."

"The higher the stakes, the faster my fingers," he murmured, savoring the sudden flush of color that suffused her flesh. A soft pink-gold, the exact shade of a ripe, sun-warmed peach. "Hmmm, let me consider the choices. What item should I pick? A stocking, perhaps?"

She shot a reproachful look at the pocketwatch.

"A gentleman would let you off lightly. The Devil, however, might choose your dress."

The pulsepoint on her throat gave a little jump. "You *wouldn't.*"

"That," drawled Cameron, "is exactly the wrong tumbler to press when playing with man who does not wear a stitch of honor." He gave a flick of his arm, which was bare to the elbow. "Off with the gown. Unless, of course, you wish to renege on the bet."

"And concede that at heart, I'm a craven coward?" Sophie scowled. "Ha! Let the Devil have his due."

A few hurried tugs released the tabs at her shoulders. A shrug, a wiggle, and the garment slithered over her head and fell to the floor, forming a soft pool of muslin at the foot of her chair.

"There." A prickling of gooseflesh pebbled her arms as the air stirred and tickled against skin. "In gambling, a loser is always allowed a chance to recoup his losses, correct?"

Turn away from temptation. "Yes," he replied. "But most often the sensible decision is to cut your losses and quit."

"If I wished to be sensible, I wouldn't have come here in the first place," retorted Sophie. "Twenty-five. You have twenty-five seconds. If you fail, you lose a piece of clothing."

"I accept—with one small alteration. As the previous winner, I reserve the right to decide which garment to shed."

"As you wish."

At her signal, Cameron once again attacked the lock.

"Oh, fie!" she cried, watching him fumble away the seconds. "You failed on purpose!"

"I do have a shred of decency left," he replied, removing his shirt. "I couldn't allow you to sit there and shiver on your own."

Sophie swallowed hard, her eyes widening slightly as she stared at his chest. "I—I've seen Lord Elgin's marbles, but somehow a man's naked torso looks different in the flesh."

"Everything—and I mean everything—about them is smaller, for one thing," he said slowly.

Her face flamed.

"They are pretty, in a very abstract way," went on Cameron. "However, something gets lost in translation from flesh to stone."

"A different language completely," she agreed with a worldly nod. But a tiny tremor inflected her voice. Unlike the smooth, solid Greek sculptures, her composure appeared on the verge of cracking into a thousand tiny shards.

"Shall we call it a draw?" The fire had now reached her eyes, provoking his deliberately risqué comment. "Another loss and you'll lose your shift," went on Cameron. "Clad only in a tissue-thin corset, your lovely nipples might tighten and pucker from the cold."

"Without your breeches, your intimate parts might also suffer shrinkage," countered Sophie.

Cameron let out a bark of laughter. "How do you know such shocking details about male anatomy?"

"You snuck a swim in the sea when you were twelve, and left me to hold your clothes."

He had forgotten about that long-ago interlude until

now. But then, they had shared many adventures over the years. "Good God, how extremely embarrassing."

"Extremely."

Her grin, sparkling with suppressed mirth, suddenly silenced the warning voices in his head. "So, I take it you wish to go another round?"

She nodded.

"Let's make it a little more interesting." He pulled a different tool from his boot. "You'll get a second try at one minute with the thin probe. But I shall have to work with a hook, which is designed for a different type of mechanism. That should even the odds."

"Do you always carry such an interesting assortment of implements in your footwear?" asked Sophie.

"It's best to be prepared for the unexpected. So yes, I always have a number of intriguing items hidden within my clothing."

"Interesting." Her gaze lingered on his leg for a moment, and then she leaned forward to readjust the pocketwatch, giving him a tantalizing peek at her rounded breasts and valley between them. It was dark and inviting—just wide enough for a tongue to dip in and taste a trace of salt and spice.

A strange, sweet music began echoing in his ears. *Sophie the Siren.* Luring a man to break himself on the rocks of forbidden desire.

Don't. Cameron closed his eyes for an instant. *Don't go there. She is a Sunbeam and I am the Devil's own Darkness*—a bastard in the eyes of the world, which was the only truth that mattered.

He hadn't been able to offer her a decent life in the past. And after ten years, the only thing that had changed was now he was even more dangerous, more disreputable. Sophie deserved better. He knew that. Oh, yes, he knew that.

"Are we ready?" she asked.

"But of course." Shutting his ears to the whisper of his conscience, he pressed his palms together. "In this round we will simplify the rules. If you open the lock in the allotted time, you are the winner and get to name the article of clothing that I must forfeit. Fail, and it is the other way around."

"Perhaps I'll ask for your snake when I win," she murmured. Her gaze slid to the small gold hoop dangling from his earlobe. It was, in fact, a tiny hooded cobra holding its tail in its mouth.

What goes around comes around?

"Another word of warning, Sophie. Don't make assumptions or think ahead. Concentrate on naught but the present moment when you are in the midst of a perilous job. Otherwise you are apt to make mental mistakes."

Chapter Twelve

*N*o mistakes. Concentration is key." Sophie rubbed her hands together. "I vow, this time I shall do better." Closing her eyes for an instant, she imagined that the blue-black steel lock was more than a lifeless mechanism, and that if she wielded her touch skillfully enough, she could release more than a clever array of levers and gears.

"Time," called Cameron.

The probe seemed to move of its own accord. *Trust.* She decided to let go of conscious thought and to trust her instincts.

"Well, well, well." He sounded a little surprised as the lock signaled its surrender just before the final seconds ticked away.

"A boot," she announced.

"A lowly boot?"

"I plan on fine-tuning my timing," she replied. "And I don't want your most delicate parts to take a chill."

"Careful, Sunbeam. Remember what I told you about overconfidence," said Cameron over the thud of leather hitting the earthen floor. "The gods love nothing better than to humble a mortal who shows hubris." He took up the hook. "Twenty-five seconds?"

"Yes," replied Sophie, sure that in half a minute all of his toes would be clad in naught but stockings. The allotted time was impossible.

Snick, snick, SNICK.

The rapidfire metallic sounds proved her woefully wrong.

"Ha! Now we shall see who will be shivering."

"Drat." She made a face. "Last time, it looked as if you were working as fast as you could."

"It's wise to hide both your weaknesses and your strengths, Sophie. It keeps an opponent off-balance and always guessing."

"A painful lesson to learn," she responded, obeying his hand signal to strip off her shift.

Gooseflesh pebbled her arms as the lawn cotton grazed against her skin. It wasn't, however, the tickle of the fabric or the breeze that stirred the reaction. His lidded gaze was like a physical caress, stroking along the ridge of her collarbones before dipping down in a lazy, lingering path to her half-bared breasts.

The corset lacing suddenly seemed to tighten, squeezing the air from her lungs.

"Painful, indeed." Silent laughter quivered at the corners of his mouth. "I imagine that the chair's seat is prickly with splinters that may prove deucedly uncomfortable on a naked bum."

Sophie glanced down at her drawers, which offered scant protection from rough planks or roving eyes. "I shall just have to see that I don't lose."

"That may delay the inevitable," said Cameron. "But

you don't control your own destiny. I have only to win..."
He paused to carefully count what little she had left on.
"...six times and you will be entirely naked."

A shiver collided with a curl of heat licking up from
her core.

"Twenty-five times six equals one hundred and fifty
seconds—exactly two-and-a-half minutes." A snap of his
fingers made her jump. "It will be gone just like that."

"That's assuming you won't make a careless slip," she
said. "You have little left to sacrifice, and if I take away
all your garments first, the game will be over."

Cameron leaned across the table, the rippling sunlight
making his smoothly sculpted muscles glow like burnished bronze. "Actually, we never defined what would
bring play to an end. We have been making up the rules
as we go along."

A cat-like stretch and he touched the hook to the top
row of her corset's lacing. "The lock has become awfully
familiar. What if I changed the challenge to a new puzzle?"

His teasing smile belied the coiled tension of his body.
The air between them crackled with temptation.

Sophie had only to say no in a myriad of subtle ways—
pull back, shake her head, whisper a word. She had done
it before, choosing rules over recklessness. At the time, it
had been the right decision, no matter how much it had
hurt. They had both been too young, and her family had
been too much in need of her.

And now?

A flick of her lashes and he would ride off—perhaps
forever—leaving her to face yet another interminable
stretch of gray days. A lifetime leached of all color and fire.

The rules, of course, left no doubt as to what her choice should be. But rules did not understand regret. Rules did not lock out uncertainties. Rules did not keep longing at bay.

A split second. Cameron had warned that in the heat of danger, one could not hesitate in making a decision.

No. No, no, no. This time, she was older and wiser. In her heart she now knew that any life worth living entailed risks.

And suddenly the sliver of space separating their lips was gone.

"Sophie," he rasped against her mouth. "Think—"

"Oh, please, Cam. Let us let go of the past and the future and seize the present moment."

"If you are sure."

"Yes." She had never been more sure of anything in her life. "Yes."

"Then God help me, I shall be selfish enough to accept your decision without argument." Framing her face between his hands, he possessed her in a hard, hungry embrace. "Though a true gentleman ought to be more honorable."

"I don't want you to be honorable." Her hands skimmed over the taut chiseling of ribs, drawing a muffled groan. "I want you to be to mine." *If only for a fleeting interlude.*

His restraint, held hard in check, suddenly snapped. A deft few tugs of the clever little hook and the knotted bow of her corset strings came undone. Sophie felt his hands unloop the laces and strip away the fabric. Rising, she twined her arms around his neck as he shoved the table aside and pulled her close. The thud of its fall was echoed by her half boots. Freed by two wiggled kicks, they landed atop her crumpled skirts.

Cameron spun around, their mouths still joined in a deep embrace, and in two swift strides carried her to the makeshift bed. He had left a thin bedroll of blankets spread over the wooden frame.

"You deserve silk and champagne, candlelight and crystal," he whispered, breaking off the kiss to feather his lips along the arch of her neck. "Not a primitive hovel."

In answer, Sophie found the flap of his breeches and worked the fastenings free. "I care naught for fancy frills, Cam. I am no highborn London lady, no glittering Diamond of the First Water. A simple setting is perfect, for I am...simply me."

"And your pure, sparkling light, Sunbeam, puts all the London belles to the blush."

I should be suffused with shame, thought Sophie, peeling the buckskins down from his thighs. Held in check by only the thin scrim of his cotton drawers, his arousal was rampantly apparent.

But I am not.

She undid the ties and boldly pressed her hand to its ridged length, reveling in the sensation of liquid heat pulsing against her palm.

Cameron inhaled a ragged breath and held himself very still as she explored its contours. Steel sheathed in velvet. Alluring, mysterious, a conundrum of contrasts— like Cameron himself.

"The Devil take me," he finally gasped, catching her wrist and easing her down onto the bed.

That she could stir such a swirl of molten color in his eyes sent a trill of excitement thrumming through her body. Gold-flecked fire, smoke-tinged jade—a sensuous sea. Dark, alluring. Daring her to dive into its depths.

He kicked away his fallen breeches and wrenched off his remaining boot. His drawers followed, slithering to the ground with a sinuous whisper. And then he was gloriously naked, all taut muscle and primal male, limned in the honeyed morning light.

"Think one last time about whether you want to do this," he murmured, dropping to his knees and tugging off her garters and stockings. "For in another instant, Lust will be deaf to Reason."

"I don't want to think," said Sophie, remembering his words from their rainy night London tryst. "I just want to *feel*." Her fingers twined in his long, silky hair.

I want the texture of your skin, the chiseling of your muscles, the shape of your manhood forever imprinted on my body.

"Touch me, Cam. Let us hold onto this moment, come what may." Her mind was made up—she intended to hold on to it now and forever. Love was too precious to let slip through her fingers again. Win or lose against Dudley and Morton, she would be free to follow her own heart. Either Georgie and Anthony would provide a stable, secure home for the family...or they would all be ruined, so it would hardly matter if she chose to partner with a pirate.

That realization was incredibly liberating.

"Sophie." Cameron's sigh was soft as satin as he slid his hands up her legs and gently parted her thighs. "It was only by keeping a grip on the sweet memory of you that I managed to survive the bleak, black twists my life has taken since leaving Terrington."

She arched up to meet him, wrapping her arms around his neck. Shadows danced over his skin, the scent of him now an earthier musk that left her a little dizzy. The stubbling of whiskers on his jaw was rough against her cheek, his mouth was now hard and demanding.

Cameron claimed that he did not want to share his solitary life with anyone, but she meant to challenge him on that. Surely love was stronger than cynicism.

Surrendering to his need—and her own—Sophie eagerly opened herself to his embrace. Their tongues twined, the slow, sensuous play of flesh teasing a sudden surge of heat at her very core.

Oh, this is wicked...and wonderful.

A purr of pleasure slipped from her lips as Cameron settled his body atop hers, melting, molding flesh to flesh. His cock nudged between her thighs, grazing the honey-slick flesh nestled within their "V."

"I shall try to go slow, Sunbeam." His voice was low and rumbled. "There may be a pinch of pain, but I promise you it will quickly pass."

An exquisite ache was already building inside her. Sophie lifted her hips in wordless urging.

He responded with a ragged groan. His fingers—those oh-so-skilled fingers—delved into her feminine folds and found her hidden pearl.

A moan caught her throat as he stroked and stroked the sensitive spot. Fire swirled beneath his touch, the heat growing unbearable.

"Hush, sweetheart." Cameron muffled her cries with a kiss.

"I want...I want..."

"I know what you what." The head of his cock was

now pressing against the opening of her passage. "And God knows, I want it, too." He eased forward a fraction. "Desperately," he added through clenched teeth. Sweat sheened his forehead, the tiny beads of moisture dampening his tangled hair.

So good, so good.

A fierce need, too new to have a name, was cresting inside her. Hands clutching the broad slope of his shoulders, Sophie could bear it no longer. With an upward thrust of her hips, she drove him deep inside her. The momentary stab gave way to a surge of far sweeter sensations. She felt herself clench around him, and for an instant it was as if two had become one. He was part of her—and always had been.

She could, at that instant, have wept for joy.

Sucking in a breath, Cameron slowly rocked back.

"No—" she cried, only to be filled again with his sleek heat.

Another thrust, another withdrawal. Urged on by some elemental intuition, Sophie matched his rhythm, slowly at first, but the friction sent a thrumming through her limbs. Her breathing quickened, as did his.

Cameron's thrusts were now coming harder, faster.

With a moan, she rose to meet him, again and again and again.

Higher, higher. The sun in all its blazing white-hot glory seemed to be floating just overhead. And then in a blazing, brilliant burst of light, it seemed to shatter into a shower of golden sparks.

By sheer force of will, Cameron held himself together as Sophie came undone in his arms.

Oh-so many dark, devilish nights, his dreams had taunted him with this moment. He hardly dared to believe that the sound of her voice, the scent of her skin, the heat of her passion was real.

Sophie. She was now his, body and soul.

With the cries of her climax still swirling in the air, he gave one last shuddering thrust, his own hoarse growl of exultation breaking free, and then withdrew, just in time to spill his seed safely.

"Sunbeam." Her face was wreathed in a beatific glow. And for an instant, his own inner darkness was banished by its sweet, sweet light.

Utterly spent, he collapsed beside her and gently gathered her in his arms. Of all the dangerous, demented risks he had taken in his life, this was perhaps the most foolhardy.

A man like me must be heartless. And yet the rapidfire thud in his chest warned that his vital organ had come back to life...

Passion. Peril. Somehow he would keep Sophie safe. As for himself...

She stirred, and murmured a sound against his shoulder.

"Sunbeam," repeated Cameron, stroking a hand over her tumbled curls. "Forgive me for behaving like a randy schoolboy. Lovemaking is more than a frenzied coupling," he murmured. "It should be done slowly, savoring the sensations like a fine wine."

"Mmmm, no wonder ladies are warned to keep their lips far, far away from the glass of passion," she replied in a muzzy murmur. "This first sip was intoxicating." A feline stretch twined her legs with his. "A fizzy bubbling through the blood, potent as sin."

Cameron felt himself start to harden at the touch of her flesh. Quelling the fresh rush of lust, he shifted and pressed a light kiss to her forehead. *I have sinned enough for one morning.*

"Whatever the strictures say, you've done nothing evil, Sophie. That said, we must be careful..."

A soft snuffle, and Cameron realized that she had drifted into a doze.

"I'll not have your reputation shredded," he went on, making the vow to himself. "For all my past failings, I will guard you from danger."

Sophie woke, and for a moment lay hovering in a cloud-like haze, wondering whether the enchantment that had wrapped around her body was some otherworldly spell.

Black magic. Wielded by a dark-haired pirate...

Cameron shifted, his long lean body brushing against hers.

No, not magic. Something infinitely more powerful.

Love. Through half-opened eyes, she watched winks of sunlight steal through the weathered thatching. Bird-song—a linnet?—rose above the murmur of the long grasses swaying in the breeze. *Love.* She had loved Cameron for as long as she could remember.

A smile played on her lips. *I suppose I am now a strumpet, a shameless wagtail, for surrendering my virtue.* There were strict rules about that—unyielding, unbending rules—and she had broken them all to flinders.

"To the Devil with rules," she whispered. *Right and wrong.* They were not simply black-and-white concepts but possessed a far more subtle range of shades. In her heart she knew she would have no regrets, whatever the future might bring.

Closing her eyes, Sophie let her thoughts drift. Cameron's beautiful face, his jade-green eyes, his gold hoop earring...strangely blurring with images of locks and keys and needle-thin shafts of glittering steel.

Locks. A hazy picture flitted up from out of nowhere and floated around the edges of her consciousness. *A cabinet with an ornate wrought iron keyhole?* Something about it seemed oddly familiar, but try as she might, she couldn't bring it into focus...

Cameron stirred again and lifted a lid. "You've a pensive look on your face. What are you thinking about?"

"You," she replied truthfully.

"Good." A lazy smile stretched his sensuous mouth.

Vague thoughts of a musty old cabinet gave way to a more enticing subject. On impulse, she leaned over and flicked her tongue along its sinuous curl. "You taste better than champagne."

"And you—you are learning far too many dangerous skills this morning." Cameron rolled over onto his back. "I can think of a number of delicious ways to keep your mind filled with naught but thoughts of me. But however much I would love to lie here and spend the day and night teaching you more about pleasure, it's too dangerous for us to linger here any longer."

Sitting up, he angled a glance through the window. "Secluded as this spot is, there is a chance that a shepherd or hunter might pass this way."

His words reminded her that the interlude, however idyllic, could not last forever.

"Yes, of course." Suddenly a little shy about her nakedness, Sophie scooted to the edge of the bed and grabbed up his shirt from the floor. Clutching it to her breasts, she went on, "I've an excuse for the hours of my absence, but I dare not stretch it too far."

With lordly grace, Cameron rose and flexed his muscles, clearly comfortable in his own skin.

She couldn't help but stare at the dark hair dancing along the sloping ridge of his shoulders. Half wild, half civilized—wholly male. How else to describe the aura of raw vitality radiating from every pore? Her gaze slid down through the coarse curls peppering his sculpted chest to the lean, tapered waist... and then lower still.

Her scrutiny stirred a lift of his brow. "Shocked?"

No, intrigued.

She matched his teasing smile. "Hardly. If you recall, I saw you bare-arsed when you were twelve."

He gave a mock grimace. "How very lowering. Has the view not changed?"

"Hmmm. Hard to tell. My memory has grown a little fuzzy."

"Minx."

As he began to gather up their clothing, Sophie suddenly caught sight of a scar on his left thigh. Eyes widening, she asked, "Is that a..."

"Bullet wound?" he finished for her. "Yes."

"So your nocturnal forays are, in fact, not quite so safe as you led me to believe."

"As it so happens, it was acquired in a more noble pursuit than my usual endeavors. Connor's new bride had been abducted, and I was helping him rescue her."

"Abducted!"

"It is a long story," replied Cameron. "Suffice it to say

that Lady K possesses the same stalwart courage as you do. When an unknown enemy tried to kill Connor, she insisted on doing some sleuthing..." A pause. "Actually, never mind about the details." Placing her garments down beside her, he quickly changed the subject. "Come, we ought not tarry any longer. I'll step outside so that you may have a bit of privacy."

As his shadow slipped away, Sophie began to dress, a little surprised that the familiar items still fit. Her body felt completely altered.

"I am a different person," she mused, tightening the laces of her corset. "But at least I haven't sprouted horns or cloven hoofs." She studied her hands, which still tingled with the memory of Cameron's body. There might be no outward signs of her surrender to sin, but the feel of him would be forever imprinted on her palms.

A few quick twists of her hairpins secured the worst of the errant curls. Thank God that the wind and prickly gorse would serve as a plausible excuse for her disheveled appearance.

As for her kiss-swollen lips...

She tied her bonnet strings and ducked through the narrow doorway. *One challenge at a time.* Her own tumble down the Path to Perdition was of less concern at the moment than Cameron's scrapes with deadly peril. Her troubles had drawn Cameron back into conflict with the Marquess of Wolcott—and back into mortal danger.

So regardless of how dexterous his cunning hands were, she was not going to let him pick her up and shift her to some out-of-the-way shelf, far from the action, while he took all the risks.

Chapter Thirteen

$\mathcal{T}$hank you," said Cameron, as she crossed the clearing and handed over his shirt. "My sartorial eccentricities are well known in London, but I have yet to ride down Piccadilly Street bare-chested."

The thought of all the sophisticated Town beauties ogling his body momentarily diverted her attention. Her stomach clenched, but she made herself laugh. "No doubt the ladies wouldn't mind."

Turning away with a wordless shrug, he tucked the shirttails into his breeches and pulled on his coat.

All at once, the magic of just moments ago gave way to embarrassment. Awkward and unsure of how to go on, she looked down at her rumpled skirts, suddenly feeling like a naïve country chit. *Was there a protocol for taking leave of an illicit lover?*

"Sophie?"

She looked up to find that he had moved close—close enough for her to see that his eyes had clouded.

"I regret—"

"Oh, please, Cam," she interrupted. "If you start to

apologize, I swear I shall stick your steel lock probe right through your liver."

"My liver?" He waggled a brow. "How kind of you to spare a more vital organ."

"Don't press your luck," muttered Sophie.

Despite the quip of humor, his expression remained guarded. "What I was going to say was that I regret having to take my leave so quickly. A real gentleman would not…ah, well, never mind. A real gentleman would not be in this position." He touched a fingertip to her face and slowly traced the line of her jaw. "I've taken shameless advantage of your trust—and I'm enough of a cad that I won't say that I'm sorry about it. Be that as it may, there are pressing reasons for me to return to London. The information I saw in Wolcott's study may give me a weapon to wield against Dudley and Morton. But it's imperative that I move quickly, for as we both know, the clock is ticking and until I make some inquiries, I won't know for sure."

"You need not worry that I expect you to be tied to my skirts on account of what happened. Nothing has changed between us." Sophie gave a rueful smile. "Save for the fact that I'm no longer a virgin."

A shiver of silence stirred the air. And then…

"Virginity is vastly overrated," replied Cameron lightly. "I am glad to hear that you hold no girlish illusions over our interlude."

A little nettled by his casual tone, Sophie quickly replied, "At my advanced age, *girlish* illusions have long since been buried in the attic, along with my old jam-streaked pinafores."

"It was meant as a jest, Sunbeam," he murmured. "I…" There was a hitch of hesitation. "I did warn you that

I don't take anything seriously, a fact that annoys even my closest friends." With a careless flourish, he pulled on a pair of York tan gloves. "So once again, don't take it amiss, but I really must be off. As I said, there may be a key clue in Town, and if I am to help you, I need to uncover it without delay."

"You'll hear no argument from me. There is just one thing before you ride off." Sophie moved to stand between Cameron and his horse. "I've been thinking it over, and seeing as we are, for better or for worse, partners in this affair, I've decided it's only fair that we pool all our information. So I really must insist that you tell me what clue you are seeking."

The demand provoked a frown. "There are certain things you do not need to know."

"That," she said slowly, "is perhaps the most odious, insufferable, condescending remark you have ever made to me."

"I'm simply trying to protect you from the sordid details—"

"*Protect* me from the sordid details?" Her voice rose of its own accord. "That's a little like trying to close the barn door after the horses have galloped away. Have you forgotten that I'm already so deeply submerged in this muck that it's nearly clogging my nostrils?"

The furrow between his brows deepened.

Sensing his indecision, Sophie went on, "I want to be more than . . . a pleasure partner in your bed, Cam. A fleeting dalliance to be tucked away on a shelf whenever it suits your purposes."

He shifted his stance, his boots scraping against the rocks.

"I don't expect you to recite sentimental poetry or declare your undying love," she said. "But I do expect you to treat me as an equal." Her gaze locked with his. "And a comrade-in-adventure. After all, we've been through some horrible scrapes together, and I think I deserve that respect. Haven't I proved my mettle?"

His lashes lowered, hiding his eyes from scrutiny. Evasive and elusive, Cameron was like a spectral Underworld wraith, a quicksilver shadow, always twisting and turning away from the light.

For a long, long moment, the morning sounds of the breeze and the birdsong fluttered in cheerful oblivion to the tension between them. Sophie held her breath, waiting, waiting. A look, a gesture might break the one bond between them that truly mattered.

Yes or no. She was either a true friend or passing fancy.

A grunt—or perhaps it was a growl—finally rose in his throat. "Here I thought myself the master of manipulation. And yet, your tongue is far more clever than my fingers." Cameron didn't appear happy about having to make the admission. "I fear I am making a mistake. But then, my life has been ruled by so many lapses in judgment that I suppose it's only fitting."

"Hardly a vote of confidence, but thank you nonetheless," murmured Sophie. "Now, seeing as time is of the essence, go ahead and tell me about the clue without further ado."

He blew out a harsh breath. "I wish to find out more about the line of succession regarding Wolcott's title. The present marquess has no brothers—no legitimate brothers—and his only son is but a lad of seven."

"How does that relate to Dudley's blackmail?" she asked.

"I don't know that it does," Cameron admitted. "But there were several letters on Wolcott's desk from Frederick Morton, which raised some interesting questions. The connection between them appears to be closer than I thought."

Wolcott and Morton.

Was it merely the rustling of the leaves that gave the words a sinister sound?

Sophie was quick to understand the implications of his words. "If Morton were next in line for the title after Lord Wolcott and any male offspring he might have," she asked, "then you think that they might conspire to ensure that the boy they know as Cameron Fanning can never step in with proof that he supersedes Morton's claim."

"Wolcott considers me a pollution of his precious lordly blood, and Morton is not the sort of man who would yield the chance of inheriting a title and a fortune with good grace." The serpent earring in Cameron's ear seemed to spark as it twisted in the breeze. "They are, by your account, on cordial enough terms that Morton is invited to visit the manor. Just how deep the friendship goes is worth investigating."

"Do be careful, Cam." A platitude, she knew, yet it slipped out before she could think better of it.

The cynical curl of his mouth grew more pronounced. "I'm always careful, Sunbeam. That does not mean I don't take risks—rewards are rarely won without them. However, the Hellhounds are known for having a knack of turning the odds in their favor."

"Would that you didn't have to take such a terrible gamble," Sophie whispered.

"In a few short weeks, your father will be accused

of embezzling from the Church," he replied bluntly. "A charge that will ruin your family's reputation and destroy any chance of your sisters making a good marriage. So erring on the side of prudence is not a choice."

"I know." Her throat was dry as the dead leaves underfoot. "I know."

Moving around her, Cameron untied his horse's reins from a low-hanging tree branch. "All of life is a gamble, Sophie. The game calls for sharp wits and canny wiles." The leather suddenly looped around her waist and drew her close. "And a sweet embrace from Lady Luck."

"I hope you don't kiss *Her* with such ardor," she said, a little breathless when finally he released her lips.

"You need not fear that another might steal my heart. If I had one, it would be yours." The slivered shadows of the leaves made his expression even more inscrutable than ever.

Yet another warning, an oblique reminder that danger was not just physical.

"In other words, a pirate cannot afford to be weighed down with tender sentiment," she said evenly.

"Precisely," said Cameron softly. "You've always understood me, Sophie."

Better than you think.

He hooked his boot in the stirrup, and then paused with his hand on the saddle's pommel. "You'll see me again soon. But if for some pressing reason you need to contact me, send a letter addressed to Lady Haddan on Grosvenor Square. Writing to another woman will draw no undue attention, and Gryff will make sure I receive any missive."

"A prudent suggestion," she responded. "I won't pester you unless it's truly important."

He looked about to speak, but then merely touched a hand to his hat brim in silent salute.

Sophie watched him ride away, waiting until his dark shape was naught but a distant speck among the stones before turning away. She, too, should be hurrying away, but rather than return to the footpath, she slipped back inside the hut and took a seat on the bed.

Cameron had left his roughspun country clothing folded neatly on shelf above the pillows. Reaching up, Sophie took down the shirt and clasped it to her chest. The linen still held a trace of his cologne, and the rumpling of the fabric released a faint swirl of scent. She drew in a deep, deep breath and held in it her lungs, hoping to quiet her topsy-turvy emotions.

A big mistake.

The perfume of their passion lingered in the air, its musk teasing her insides into a slow, spiraling somersault.

Blinking back tears, Sophie stared down at the faint scuffs left by his boots on the earthen floor. Had she made a big mistake? She had grown accustomed to life without Cameron. It was steady. Solid.

And now?

Love was so confusing and conflicting. Sophie touched her fingertips to her lips. It was maddening and mystifying. Shifting slightly, she felt a tiny pinch between her legs. It could hurt. *And perhaps it could heal.*

At that, she couldn't help but let out a wry laugh. "Oh, fie, Cameron Fanning-Daggett-Hellhound. I swear, I should feed your mangy hide to the ravenous little imps of Satan. You make me so angry—but you also make me feel so alive."

In the shaded quiet of the hut, the surrounding stone

seemed to amplify the tiny *thump* within her ribcage. Like a bird beating its wings to break free.

Another sniff of the shirt and Sophie sighed. How was she going to untangle all the conundrums? *Villains. Lovers. Duty. Family.* She wasn't sure she could trust her judgment anymore.

A linnet's song drifted in through a crack in the windowglass, its trilling notes sweet and clear as opposed to her own muddled murmurs.

"So perhaps I should just trust my heart."

Guiding his mount down through the spiky green gorse to the winding country lane, Cameron spurred the big stallion to a canter. "Come, Lucifer," he murmured after tightening his grip on the reins. "Let us outride any demons who seek to follow."

The horse gave a foam-flecked snort and lengthened its stride, hooves kicking up clouds of pale dust. Cameron leaned low in the saddle, urging him to greater speed, hoping the drumming would drown out the voices of his inner devils.

Cad! Coward! The jeers were too loud to ignore.

I was selfish, he confessed to himself, squinting against the slap of the wind. *Weak. Foolish.* Discipline and detachment were the keys to survival. And yet he let every god-benighted lesson he had learned over the past ten years fall to the wayside every time Sophie was near him.

Damn, damn, damn.

The drumming hoofbeats seemed to echo his inward oaths.

The Inner Voices refused to be silenced. *Admit it! You are bedeviled—besotted—by love!*

"Bloody hell." Slowing his lathered stallion to a sedate trot, Cameron straightened in the saddle. "Laugh all you want," he called out loudly, startling two grouse from a nearby thicket. "Yes, I am in love with Sophie Lawrance! I shouldn't be, but I am." Oh, how his fellow Hellhounds would laugh themselves sick to hear him howling at the heavens. "I daresay I shall have to crawl into the Lair with my tail between my legs," he added in a lower voice. "And Cupid's arrow protruding from my bum."

Cameron winced, thinking of all the barbed teasing he would take. But fair was fair, he conceded. He had taken ruthless delight in nipping at their flanks. He could hardly complain if the teeth were now turned on him.

Lapsing into a pensive silence, he rode on, his thoughts turning from his friends to Sophie—a much more complex and confusing topic. There was no denying the physical chemistry between them. Like oil ignited by sparks, flames licked up at the first touch. As for her deeper emotions...

Expelling a harried sigh, he looked up at the scudding clouds playing hide and seek with the sun. Sophie did not wear her heart on her sleeve. Like him, she had taught herself to keep her true feelings well hidden. And yet, and yet—beneath the careful show of logic, a glimmer of her innermost thoughts had shone through.

A glorious, gleaming flicker of sunshine, which had warmed him to the very core.

Love. It should be simple. But what kind of life could he offer her? He was a bastard who made a living in the netherworld of clandestine crime, slithering through shadows and secrets. *How can I ask her to dwell in such darkness?* Sophie was a creature of light and sun. She would deny it, but after a time—a month? a year?—she would start to wither away.

As if influenced by his own stormy mood, the skies chose to unleash a sudden rainsquall. Throwing up the collar of his coat, Cameron forged on through the lashing drops and whipping winds. It soon stilled to a sullen gray fog and intermittent showers. By the time he reached London, he was wet, cold, and bone tired.

Mist swirled over the cobblestones, a silvery sea of moon-dappled haze lapping against his mud-spattered boots. He paused on the corner, about to hail a passing hackney to take him across the river, when a sudden change of heart turned his steps southward.

The mizzled chill grew sharper with every stride through the unlit alleyways. As did the fetid smells of the stews, an acrid reminder that he and Sophie lived in different worlds. He rubbed at his bristled jaw, all at once feeling weary beyond words.

"Well, well, look what the cat dragged it," quipped Sara as he entered her private office and flung off his oilskin cape. "Ye look like Hell. Have ye been on one of your little adventures?"

"You could call it that," he grunted, massaging at the crick in his neck. "If you don't mind, I'm going to help myself to the rest of your Scottish whisky. Put the bottle on Haddan's bill."

"It's in the cabinet. Oh, and before I forget, a package arrived for ye yesterday." With a flick of her pen, Sara indicated the sideboard by the entrance. "It's over there."

The item was wrapped in plain brown paper and bound with a twist of ordinary twine. Hardly the sort of thing that should strike terror in the heart of a hardbitten adventurer. And yet, Cameron felt a frisson of fear as he picked it up and caught sight of the spidery script.

It had been a long time—longer than he could remember—since he had received any communication from *that* person. Along with all the other trappings of his former life, the acquaintance had been left in the dust of the twisting Norfolk roads.

But apparently the past has once again caught up with me. First Sophie, and now...

From across the small office, Sara looked up from a stack of ledgers. Suddenly aware that he had stopped dead in his tracks, Cameron angled his eyes to the looking glass and made an exaggerated adjustment to his sodden shirtpoints before taking a seat by the fire, the whisky forgotten.

The scratch of a pen picked up again as she went back to checking the monthly accounts.

Taking up the fancy silver letter opener—Connor had gifted Sara his Andalusian dagger as well as The Wolf's Lair—Cameron cut the twine. Several documents spilled out, the sheets of folded paper dominated by a square of thick white parchment sealed with a blood red wafer. He stared at the crest and felt the color drain from his face.

Lucifer be damned. For an instant he was tempted to consign it—unopened, unread—to the coals of the fire. The blaze would bring some temporary warmth, perhaps. But the truth would only rise again, phoenix-like from the ashes, to hunt him down.

Best to get it over with, he decided.

The wax cracked with an audible snap. His composure proved nearly as brittle—it was only with great effort that he bit back a sound on skimming the first few lines. He hadn't been sure what to expect. But never in his wildest dreams had he imagined...

"Daggett, are you unwell?" Sara set aside the columns of numbers, a shadow of concern shading her features. "Good God, I haven't seen ye looking so pale since the night when that hulking, hairy cove from the East India docks barged in here and threatened to cut off your testicles and fry them in olive oil and paprika."

"Oregano," said Cameron softly, trying to muster a show of his usual sardonic humor. "It was oregano. De Cecci was from Sicily." But for once, his rapier wit failed to hold its edge.

She rose and quickly poured a glass of her expensive malt. "Here—drink this. You look dreadful...as if you had seen a ghost."

Haunting specters, sinister shadows. He suddenly felt a little ill.

"Daggett?" She touched his shoulder.

By God, if only that were true.

"Ghosts...demons..." He finally looked up. "I take it Gryff has been lending you his collection of Mrs. Radcliffe's novels." His tone had regained a measure of steadiness, but as he reached for the letters his hands betrayed a slight tremor. Tucking them into his coat pocket, he picked up the brandy glass and took a small sip. "Surely you are far too sensible to take those silly, supernatural scenes seriously."

"Actually, I find them quite entertaining."

"Just as long as you don't confuse fact with fiction."

She raised a brow. "Are ye trying to tell me something?"

"Never mind—it's not important." Cameron set aside his drink. "I must be going."

"But ye just got here!"

"Ah, but you know that I rarely stay in one place for very long," replied Cameron.

Sara looked loath to let him slip away. She drew in a sharp breath, only to let it out in a sigh. "Be off with ye, then." A brusque wave shooed him on his way. "But I hope you know you can always confide in me. We have weathered some rough seas together, and without your help in the first few months of trying te run this business on my own, I should never have managed to keep my head above water. I should like to return the favor."

"I…" Cameron fingered his gold earring, wishing that the tiny serpent might sprout dragon wings and carry him away to the exotic East, far, far from England.

But then again, that would mean abandoning Sophie and her family to Dudley and Morton's filthy scheme.

"I am grateful, Sara. And I shall endeavor to explain things more fully soon. But for now, I must sink or swim on my own."

Chapter Fourteen

"You…"

Sophie nearly jumped out of her skin.

"…are beginning to worry me," said Georgiana, carefully closing the study door behind her.

"I—I don't see why," she replied, picking up her feather duster and setting back to work on the bookcases by the hearth.

"You are not usually forgetful," said her sister.

"What have I forgotten?"

"My point exactly. I was hoping to trim my new bonnet with the red ribbon from Mrs. Turner's shop, remember?"

Sophie bit her lip. "Oh, Georgie, I'm sorry. It slipped my mind."

"As did a number of other things. Mrs. Hodges asked you pick up some powders at the apothecary, as well as some thread and buttons for Papa's Sunday coat."

"Sorry," she intoned again.

"I didn't want to say anything in front of Pen, but I

happened to peek in your basket and it was empty," went on Georgiana. "That was an awfully long walk to come home empty-handed."

Sophie felt a flush of color stain her cheeks. "My mind was woolgathering."

"And what," asked her sister, "was your body doing while your thoughts were off chasing the sheep? Dallying with the wolf?"

Setting down the duster, Sophie slumped into her father's desk chair and pressed her palms to her brow. "Yes." Georgiana was too sharp by half to swallow a lie. And she could be trusted to keep a secret. "Cameron was here for a few days, but nobody must know. Lord Wolcott has a terrible grudge against him. If it ever gets out that he is alive and living in London, the authorities will arrest him and see him hung for theft."

"Is that why he left Norfolk?"

"Yes," she answered.

Georgiana tapped the tip of her nose.

"Partly yes," amended Sophie.

"This is all very dark and mysterious, just like *Lady Avery's Awful Secret*."

Sophie cringed, wondering whether the book's Secret was the fact that Lady Avery had surrendered her virtue to a rakish lover in a wild, passionate sexual tryst.

"Knowing the danger, why did Cameron return here?" pressed Georgiana.

The room was suddenly very still, as if all the leather-bound books and dog-eared papers were holding their collective breath. Even the Staffordshire spaniel on the mantel seemed to cock a curious ear.

Still she hesitated, trying to convince herself that ignorance was bliss. However the rebellious voices in her head were quick to counter.

Hypocrite! Hadn't she raked Cameron over the coals for just such an insufferable attitude?

Conceding defeat with a slow exhale, Sophie replied, "Because—"

Peltering footsteps in the corridor cut her off. A thump and the door flew open.

"Oh fie, Pen—you are supposed to knock before you burst into a room like a rag-mannered hoyden," scolded Georgiana. After eyeing Penelope's disheveled clothing and half-wild braids, she added, "Lud, you look as if you've run backwards through a briar patch."

Chest heaving, her face beet red, Penelope needed several gulps of air before she could reply. "Ivejustrunfromthevillageand—"

"Slow down," counseled Sophie, feeling a clench of fear seize her chest as she shot up from her chair. "Is it Papa?"

Penelope shook her head. "No, no." Another wheeze. "It's Lord Wolcott!"

"What about him," demanded Georgiana.

"He's dead!"

Sophie felt the blood drain from her cheeks. "Dead?" she repeated.

"Drowned." Penelope had now recovered enough to explain more fully. "I met Squire Ashmun on the road and he told me the news. Wolcott's pleasure yacht sank in a storm. And that's not all..."

A dramatic pause had Sophie vowing to curtail her youngest sister's reading of horrid novels.

"The marquess's wife and son went down with him,"

announced Penelope. "The village is all at sixes and sevens—nobody knows for sure who will be the next marquess."

Her legs went suddenly limp. *Dear God.* Sitting down abruptly, Sophie needed a moment to master her emotions. "How is Squire Ashmun so certain?" she demanded. "The sea is a vast place, and if there were witnesses, surely they would have made an attempt to save the people on board."

"It appears that there is no doubt," answered Penelope. "A naval frigate found a lone survivor of the crew clinging to a broken mast shortly after the accident. The crewman said the rudder pins snapped off during a squall, taking with them a large chunk of planking below the waterline. The yacht quickly filled with water and capsized. It sank like a stone within minutes."

"Dear God." This time Sophie said it aloud.

"The marquess and his family were belowdecks. What with the chaos of crashing rigging and sweeping seas, there was no chance for them to escape from the cabin."

"Even if they did manage to break free of the hatches, the North Sea waters are too cold for anyone to survive for more than a short while," said Georgiana quietly.

"The frigate searched, but found nothing, save for a few more bits of the yacht's wreckage," added Penelope.

Dead—the marquess was dead. A wave of dizziness washed over her.

"Sophie? Sophie?" said Georgiana. "Are you all right? You look pale as ashes."

Quelling the swirl of nausea, Sophie nodded. "Yes. I'm just a little shocked, that's all. This is all...so sudden." Her stomach gave another lurch. Good God, there was no denying the momentous implications for Cameron, but at the moment, trying to sort them all out was a little overwhelming.

"Lord Wolcott won't be sorely missed," murmured Penelope. "He wasn't a very nice man."

Georgiana frowned. "Hush, Pen."

"Well, it's true."

Intent on getting her own churning emotions under control, Sophie said nothing.

"True or not, one shouldn't speak ill of the dead," replied Georgiana. "As penance, go finish your chores."

Penelope made a face, but seemed to decide that argument was futile. "You *could* say thank you for rushing helter-pelter to give you the news," she grumbled. "Next time I have a momentous announcement, I'll tell it to the chickens first."

Georgiana waited until the door slammed shut before heaving a sigh. "Pen is right. Few people will mourn Wolcott's passing. He was an arrogant, clutchfisted master of the manor. Let us hope the new marquess will treat his tenants better."

"Yes," said Sophie faintly. "Let us hope."

Her sister reacted with a quizzical frown. "You sound, well, strange."

I feel strange. Her mind was still a little numb from shock. Hard as it was to imagine, the possibility might exist…

"I would think that if anything, you would feel some relief at the news." Georgiana lowered her voice to a whisper. "With the marquess's demise, Cameron will be out of danger."

Danger.

"Oh, Lord, Georgie, it's imperative that I get word of this to Cam right away."

"Do you have a way of sending him a letter?"

A reasonable question, but Sophie wasn't feeling reasonable. "Yes, but the message can't be conveyed by ink and paper." She needed to touch him, to feel his blood thrumming beneath his skin.

"Sophie, won't you please explain to me what's going on?" said her sister.

"I was about to, before Pen burst in with the news. Or at least, as much I can at the moment about why Cameron is here in Terrington." Some secrets were not hers to reveal.

Georgiana leaned forward, bracing her elbows on the desk.

"He came back to see if he could learn more about a possible connection between Wolcott and...two other men. One that could result in a great evil being done."

"And did he succeed?" asked Georgiana.

"Yes and no," answered Sophie. "Yes, there is a connection. But he needed to return to London to follow up on the clue. That's why I need to inform him of Wolcott's death without delay."

"You mean to say, he might be in danger."

Thinking of Dudley and Morton, Sophie gave a wordless nod.

"Am I correct in assuming that this danger you speak of has something to do with you and whatever Awful Secret you are hiding from me?"

Her lips twitched up in an involuntary smile. "I'm afraid so." She held up a hand to forestall further questions. "Georgie, I can't explain more than that, save to say, someone is threatening to ruin Papa's reputation—

and with it, all of us. Cameron is trying to help me keep that from happening."

Georgiana paled, understanding the implications, but did not flinch.

Thank God for her sister's quick wits and stalwart courage.

"What can I do to help?" asked Georgiana stoutly.

"I've a plan," responded Sophie quickly. "I need to get to London without stirring any gossip." Reputations could be ruined in Terrington as well as Town. "It's against the rules for me to travel by coach on my own. However, if we say that I was meeting Aunt Hermione's carriage in Walton, then that will raise no eyebrows. And from there I can catch the express mail coach without anyone being the wiser. Plus my absence won't be questioned."

Before Georgiana could open her mouth, she went on, "However, I need you to stay here and look after Pen and Papa." *If a novelist is allowed to embellish the dangers, why can't I?* She dropped her voice a notch. "I don't expect trouble, but if it strikes, someone must be here to defend them."

Georgiana swallowed her protest. "You can count on me." Her eyes narrowed in thought, only to fly open an instant later. "I could send for Anthony. He would happily lop off a few limbs if need be."

"No, no, it's best to keep Anthony out of this," said Sophie. "Cameron is very good with a sword." She felt her face grow a little warm and quickly added, "And with solving conundrums. We must let him handle it."

"Very well." Reluctance resonated in Georgiana's voice but she didn't try to argue further for her fiancé's presence. "Have you money for the trip?"

"Aunt Hermione and Uncle Edward gave me some funds, to be used for an emergency," said Sophie. "I'll travel overnight in the mail coach, so I won't need to spend anything on accommodations. I shall of course stay with them once I reach Town, and they will send me home. So there is little cost—and little risk to my reputation, once we reach Walton."

"You go pack a valise while I tell Mrs. Hodges that we are walking into town. We had best be gone before Pen returns," advised her sister. "From there we'll have Mr. Stellings drive us to Walton and drop you at The Grapes Inn—with me along, it's all very respectable. Once we've left, you can sneak away to The Brass Spyglass, where the mail coach makes its stop."

"You seem very conversant with intrigue," observed Sophie.

Georgiana flashed a grin. "Reading is very educational."

"Thank you for coming." The elderly solicitor reshuffled the stack of papers, his words barely louder than the whisper of foolscap. "I don't imagine that you would wish me to offer condolences, so I won't...Lord Wolcott."

Cameron's head jerked up. He fully expected to see his half brother come striding through the double doors, shouting in that imperious baritone, or slapping that infernal silver-tipped walking stick against his polished boot. A figure who saw himself as larger than life, the marquess liked to make his presence felt. Even halfway around the world, there were times Cameron had awoken in a cold sweat with the roar of remembered ire reverberating in his head...

He found himself staring at a silent swath of paneled oak.

That marquess was dead. Along with his only son.

"You can't call me that. There's no proof," said Cameron tightly. "And if there was, Wolcott would have destroyed it long ago."

"Your father assured me on his death bed that you were his legitimate son, and as the old marquess was nothing but truthful with me for the forty years I knew him, I believe it," said the solicitor. "Unfortunately, he shuffled off his mortal coil just as he was starting to tell me about his marriage to your mother. He feared his elder son would not be pleased. And so he had taken precautions."

"Which did precious little good," muttered Cameron.

"I don't disagree. I did what I could to look after you and your mother. I wish I could have done more."

Cameron was aware of how much Griggs had done for them over the years. The solicitor had forced Wolcott to provide a modest cottage and stipend for them, as well as to publicly acknowledge Cameron and his mother as poor relations—though in private his half brother always referred to them as "the whore" and "the bastard."

"I am very grateful for your kindness, Griggs," said Cameron through clenched teeth. "I know that my mother would have been turned away without a penny if you had not threatened my half brother with stirring up a scandal by publicly announcing that you intended to look for records."

"He knew that it was for the most part an empty threat—even your mother had no idea where the papers might be. But being a high stickler, he didn't want any hint of impropriety attached to the Wolcott name." Griggs steepled his bony fingers and bowed his head. "Your half brother was a very hard, stubborn man. Knowing him as I did, I am sure he battled the elements right down to his very last breath."

Cameron heaved a sigh. Hell hath no fury like agitated Augustus Aiden George Rowland. No doubt the marquess had thundered at the heavens as the pleasure yacht sank beneath the waves. But in the end, neither pride nor privilege nor pedigree had been worth a spit in the eye of the elements. He wondered whether Wolcott had soaked in the irony of it as a watery grave had swallowed him up.

He rather doubted it. Introspection was not a quality much admired by his late half brother.

Shifting in his seat, Cameron pursed his lips. "You are quite sure the marquess's son was aboard, Griggs?"

"Absolutely sure. I should not have sent off the packet if there had been the slightest doubt," intoned the solicitor. "A lone crewman was rescued by a passing naval frigate. He confirmed that the boy and his mother went down with the marquess."

"Bloody hell," muttered Cameron. It was one thing to want his rightful heritage acknowledged. It was quite another to find himself faced with its unexpected ramifications. "I did not like or respect my half brother, but I never would have wished for him and his family to perish in such a horrible fashion. Drowning is not a pleasant death."

"Horrible, indeed." Griggs coughed. "Especially in light of some unsettling information that has just surfaced."

A serpentine chill uncoiled in his gut. "What information?"

"We will get to that matter in moment. But first I think

it important for us to discuss the subject of your position."

"Which is a damnably awkward one."

Griggs acknowledged the sarcasm with a small shrug. "For the moment, yes. But I would like to move quickly to change that."

"Why the damnable rush?" demanded Cameron. "I—"

"Please hear me out, sir," interrupted Griggs. "I'll explain that shortly. However, you need to make some important decisions first and I should like them to come from the heart."

Biting back an acid retort, he nodded for the solicitor to go on.

"With the marquess—the previous marquess—gone to his Maker, I can be, shall we say, a bit more forceful in establishing your rights," explained Griggs. "Even without the marriage lines, I can swear that your father made an oath to me of its veracity. It will take some fancy legal arguing and maneuvering. However, I have reason to think we have a good chance of prevailing."

Cameron responded with a rather churlish reply.

"I cannot claim to have ever understood your actions over the last decade. Nonetheless, I adhered to the bargain we made, both in letter and in spirit."

Early on in his flight from Wolcott, Cameron had made contact with the solicitor to make sure his mother would not suffer any consequences. Griggs had promised to see that she was cared for, in return for an address where contact could be made.

"For which I am thankful," he murmured.

"Never once did I let on to your mother that you occasionally kept me informed of your travels," went on the solicitor.

She understood why I went away, thought Cameron to himself. *She knew that my youthful anger and pride would have ended up destroying me.* And while he hadn't written letters, he had sent other tokens that let her know he was alive.

"Furthermore, as you asked, never once did I contact you, save for the direst of emergencies." The solicitor cleared his throat. "I had thought your mother's illness qualified as such."

"I did see her, Griggs," whispered Cameron. "The night before she died."

"But—"

"I am very adept at slipping in and out of places unnoticed."

Their eyes locked. "As the new Marquess of Wolcott, you will likely find such anonymity impossible in the future. People will tend to scrutinize your every move."

Assuming I agree to step out of the shadows.

"I need you to sign several documents, my lord." A sheaf of papers slid across the leather blotter. "A mere formality for the moment, sir, but in the event that our suit is accepted, the rules must be followed."

The looping of the elegant copperplate script looked to his eye like the twist of a hangman's noose.

James Cameron Fanning Rowland.

The devil-may-care Cameron Daggett was about to meet an untimely end. In his place was an utter stranger, a starchy-sounding aristocrat who bore no resemblance to the rascally rogue who was more at home in a Southwark gin house than a Mayfair drawing room.

"What if I refuse?" Cameron paused, pen in hand. "Why the devil should I give up my freedom for fetters?"

"There are two reasons why you should you return to Wolcott Manor," said the solicitor. "First and foremost, because I watched you grow up on its lands. You fished its rivers, hunted its hills, rode hell-for-leather over its pastures. I daresay you stole your first kiss somewhere within its woods."

"It was never my home," said Cameron.

"You loved it more than your half brother ever did. It *is* your home, and it needs your stewardship." The soft snap of papers added a wordless rebuke. "Don't you think it is time to stop running from whatever youthful folly—"

"Damn you, I wasn't running away from anything, save my half brother's hateful pride," snarled Cameron. A thump of his fist punctuated his words. "The day I rode out through the manor's south gates was the happiest day of my life."

"Ah. And are you happy now?"

"Exceedingly."

The solicitor's silvery brows shot up in skepticism.

Cameron looked away to the mullioned windows. Respectability might mean he could offer Sophie...No, he dare not think about that. "Your second reason had better be more compelling than the first."

"Oh, it is. After you, the next in succession is your second cousin, Frederick Morton."

Ah, finally some welcome information.

"I was just going to ask about the succession." Curious as to the solicitor's opinion of Morton, Cameron said, "Perhaps he would make a better marquess. Since leaving the manor, I have acquired expertise in a great many professions—most of which you would not care to know about. Suffice it to say that being a pompous prig of a peer was not among them. I never paid any attention to the nuances of being a marquess. I don't know a bloody thing about the job."

"Trust me, sir, whatever your perceived faults, you are by far the lesser of two evils," replied Griggs. "The consequences of turning the title over to Morton are decidedly grim. He paid me a visit yesterday to submit his family papers and make a formal request that proceedings begin to confirm him as the new marquess. He also informed me that he means to turn half the tenants off their farms and sell the land. Most of the families have been there for generations."

"But the entail—"

"There is a coda in the original grant that allows for the entail to be broken. All of the previous lords have felt honorbound to abide by the traditions of Wolcott Manor."

"And my relative was fox enough to discover the loophole?"

"Morton is not a fox," sniffed Griggs. "He is a weasel. And that is maligning a whole species of vermin." The solicitor fixed him with an owlish squint. "Bear in mind, the Marquess of Wolcott has the power to affect a great many lives."

"Are you appealing to my vanity?" asked Cameron.

"No, I am appealing to your conscience."

"Most of my current acquaintances would assure you I have none."

"But I know you better than they do." Griggs merely nudged the documents a touch closer. "I have every confidence you will make the right choice, my lord."

"Bloody hell, stop addressing me by that pompous

title," he muttered. "I am not yet puffed up with a sense of my own consequence."

"I am afraid you will have to get used to it." Was it his imagination, or did Griggs allow a twitch of his lips? "Might I remind you that words do not make the man, sir."

"Spare me any more platitudes. You and your misguided moralizing have done enough damage for the day." Drawing a deep breath, Cameron scrawled his signature across the pristine paper. "There, it's done." The force of his hand had sent up a spattering of ink. "A blot on the family copybook, as my half brother was so fond of saying."

Griggs sprinkled a bit of sand on the document.

Ashes to ashes. Dust to dust. It was, after all, a funeral of sorts.

After checking that all was in order, the solicitor looked up. "I think you may surprise a great many people."

"That is a bloody understatement," muttered Cameron.

This time, there was no mistaking the smile. But it lingered for only a heartbeat before thinning to a grim line. "And now that you've made your decision, let us turn back to the subject of the late marquess's untimely death." A tiny pause. "As I mentioned, some unsettling information has just surfaced which may or may not be meaningful. Be that as it may, I cannot let it go unsaid."

"What information?"

Griggs steepled his fingers. "The rescued crewman swears that your half brother's yacht was always kept in perfect repair. He is of the opinion that the only way the rudder and planking could come loose was by an act of deliberate sabotage."

"Wolcott murdered?" mused Cameron. *Yet another treacherous current to navigate.*

"A possibility," said the solicitor. Light winked off his spectacles. "There is no proof, but I thought you ought to know."

"Indeed."

"Do be careful, my lord. As I said, Morton is a cunning weasel."

Cameron rose. "Then it's a good thing that I'm experienced in dealing with vermin."

Chapter Fifteen

*M*iss *Lawrance*?" The scratch of the pen stopped. "This is a surprise—and to be honest, not an overly welcome one."

"Forgive me, Miss Hawkins," said Sophie, quietly closing the door to Sara's private office behind her. "I know I should not be trespassing on your goodwill again, but it's very urgent that I speak with a...a mutual acquaintance."

The request elicited a basilisk stare.

"Mr. Daggett," went on Sophie, refusing to be intimidated. "I'm not here to cause any trouble, truly I'm not. I need to warn him of something."

"What makes ye think Mr. Daggett might be here?"

Sara was clearly a shrewd woman—no surprise given her line of work—but that she was also fiercely protective of her friends made Sophie like her even more. "Because he mentioned that he considers you a friend," she replied.

"Did he now?" Sara studied her for a long moment, her expression unreadable in the low lamplight. "Well, well, ain't that interesting. Yer saying that the two of you are acquainted? How?"

Seeing as Cameron's fellow Hellhounds now knew about his childhood, she decided that she wasn't betraying a confidence. "Actually we grew up together. He is helping me with a family problem, and I've discovered some new information that may..." Her hesitation was for naught but a heartbeat. "...keep him out of danger."

"Ha." Sara let out a dry laugh. "No offense, Miss Lawrance, but it would take an act of the Almighty to perform *that* miracle."

"Perhaps. But I can at least try."

"Ye got spirit. And courage, I'll give ye that." Sara rose and circled around from her behind her desk. "Mr. Daggett is indeed here, but he's holed up with some very havey-cavey fellows, and last time I looked, they were deep in conversation. When ye've been working at a place like the Lair for as long as I have, ye just know when it's not a good time te interrupt."

"May I wait?" asked Sophie.

A frown pinched at Sara's mouth.

"Please. It's very important." She set down her valise, and nudged it out of sight behind the curio cabinet. "Once I go on to my uncle and aunt's residence, it will be a great deal more difficult to get away."

"Yer stubborn, ain't ye?"

"Exceedingly," murmured Sophie.

That earned a grudging smile. "The trouble is, too many people come in and out of here. And the parlors are all in use. However, there is the small back office at the end of the corridor..." Sara tapped at the tip of her chin. "Put up yer hood—at least ye were smart enough to wear a dark cloak. We'll have to be quick about it."

"Thank you. I—"

"Shhhh." A hiss warned her to silence. Opening the door a crack, Sara peered up and down the corridor before signaling Sophie to follow.

Muted murmurs drifted out from behind the closed doors, the sound swirling with the haze of cigar smoke and the red-gold flicker of the lamp flames. An air of the unknown seemed to hover in the narrow space. *Dark, forbidding.*

Sophie felt her pulse kick up a notch as she plunged deeper into the shifting shadows. The chocolate-colored paneling accentuated the murky shades of midnight. Clinging close to the walls, she hurried to keep pace with Sara's stealthy steps.

A sudden wink of light up ahead drew a whispered oath.

"Damn." Sara spun around and grabbed her arm. "This way." A quick push popped open a door hidden in the carved wood.

Sophie was propelled into the pitch-black space. She heard the latch snick softly into place.

"Have a care," whispered Sara. "There is a flight of stairs that twists tightly to the right. For God's sake, try not to take a tumble."

Up they climbed, skirts brushing against the passageway. At the top, Sara eased open yet another door. "Quickly, quickly!"

This corridor was far more elegant than the one below—Sophie caught a blur of burgundy reds before being shoved inside the room facing the secret stairwell.

"I swear, I am getting too old for intrigue," muttered Sara, drawing a packet of lucifer matches from a pocket hidden in her sleeve. A flare of phosphorus hissed to life and she lit a branch of candles on the sidetable. "Mr. Daggett owes me a debt of thanks—not that he ever pays his tab."

Sophie's gaze widened as her eyes adjusted to the light.

"But he's a rather engaging rogue, despite his many faults," added Sara. She turned and on catching sight of Sophie's face gave a grimace. "Sorry for sticking ye here in a Chamber of Sin, but as we can't get to the more respectable back office, it's the only place where ye won't be seen. I hope ye ain't shocked out of yer stockings."

"I'm afraid my sensibilities are not as tender as they ought to be," answered Sophie. "It's actually rather... fascinating. I've never been in a brothel bedchamber before."

"Lud, I should hope not," replied Sara, looking a little harried. "I vow, I shall ring a peal over Mr. Daggett's head for exposing ye to such wantonness."

"He's not to blame. I made the decision to come here on my own."

"Hmmm." Sara shot her an appraising glance, then turned and began to fiddle with the ornate door latches. "Everything appears to be in good working order here. I've got to return to my patrons. I will send up Mr. Daggett just as soon as I can, but in the meantime, you must promise me to stay in here with the door locked." Metal clicked against metal as she tested the knobs. "And ye got te stay quiet as a crypt."

Sophie swallowed hard. Her nerves were already on edge, and the metaphor did not exactly inspire confidence. "I do hope that deaths don't occur with any frequency here at The Wolf's Lair."

Sara quirked a wry grin. "Well, ye know, the Frenchies call a female's climax '*la petite morte,*' so—" She stopped in mid-sentence. "Oops. Sorry, I forgot you are an Innocent."

Actually, I'm not, thought Sophie to herself. *Though I haven't much experience in Sin.*

Uncertain of how to reply, she remained silent. But something in her expression must have hinted at the truth, for Sara's smile gave way to a frown and a searching stare. "Oh, tell me that rascal didn't..."

Sophie felt her cheeks begin to burn.

"Now I'm not just going to ring a peal over Mr. Daggett's handsome head—I'm going to whack his skull with a big brass bell," said Sara darkly. "He's a bloody good thief, but he knows better than to steal a lady's virtue."

Oh, he didn't steal it. She looked away. *I handed it to him on a platter.*

"Hmmph." Sara let out a low snort. "Well, we'll have to sort all that out later. Right now I must be off." *Click.* "Remember, lock the door, and don't let anyone in save for me or that Hellhound."

Click, click, click. Sophie dutifully twisted the keys, and then turned to survey her surroundings.

Good God, it's as if I have stepped into an exotic fairy tale.

Stepping to the center of the room, she turned in a slow circle. *Aladdin's treasure cave.* Exotic, yes. *And erotic.* Large star-shaped lanterns, the polished brass incised with intricate patterns, hung over a huge four-poster bed. A profusion of richly embroidered pillows lay piled against a colorful headboard, the designs depicting...

"Oh." Sophie blinked and then leaned in for a closer look. "Ummm." Surely one would have to be an acrobat from Astley's Circus to bend the human body into *that* position.

Trailing a hand along the plush plum-colored velvet coverlet, she moved to the foot of the bed. Its ornate brasswork was crafted in the shape of two sinuous snakes intertwined in looping curlicues. The metal was smooth and cool to the touch.

"My, it's awfully warm in here," she murmured, untying the fastenings of her cloak. The fire in the hearth had burned down to red-orange coals, softly crackling with gold sparks. "Though I suppose it's quite comfortable if one isn't wearing any clothing." She shrugged the felted wool from her shoulders and tossed the garment onto the dressing table.

Circling back to the door, she pressed her ear to the paneling. A loud laugh reverberated through the thick wood, too close for comfort. Sophie retreated back to the bedside, and began to pace up and down the thick Turkey carpet.

Up and back, up and back. "What the devil is keeping Cameron?" As the minutes stretched on, her stride began to falter. The arduous hours of travel had left her tired, tense...

On impulse, Sophie climbed onto the thick mattress. Spotting a glass container of lucifers on the bedside table, she lit the overhead lanterns and lay back to watch the fanciful winks of light undulate across the ceiling.

Her eyes followed the burnished glow back down to the table where it dipped and danced over the cut-crystal facets of a fancy perfume vial.

Wriggling to the edge of the bed, she picked it up and pulled out the glass stopper.

A cloud of lush scent filled her nostrils. *Slightly sweet. Slightly musky. Slightly naughty.* Inhaling deeply, she held it in her lungs for a long moment, savoring the tickle of spice inside her.

"Well, I can't claim anymore that nothing adventurous has happened to me lately," she whispered after letting out a perfumed sigh. "The Sophie of just a few weeks ago would have found that thought frightening, but since then, I...I seem to have become a different person." She sniffed again. "A more daring person. Like in the past."

Stirred by the breath of air, the lanterns swayed slightly, dappling her face with tiny swirls of light.

"I'm rather like that lamp in Aladdin's tale—rubbing my body seems to have released some mysterious force of nature from within."

A serpentine curl of fragrance rose from the vial.

Unfastening the top two buttons of her high-necked dress, Sophie dabbed a generous splash of scent on her throat, and then on her wrists.

As she set the vial down, she noticed two small porcelain pots and a silver looking glass on the far corner of the ebony tabletop. Curious, she peeked under the lids.

Midnight dark kohl and a luscious red lip color.

"Oh, fie—when will I ever have a chance to explore a brothel again?" *A smudge of black, a touch of carmine.* "I look like a bold-as-brass hussy," Sophie murmured, after regarding her reflection from several different angles. "Perhaps some of that devil-may-care spirit will rub off on me." She loosened another button. The last item on the table was a decanter filled with a dark amber liquid. In the flickers of hide and seek candlelight, it looked like liquid fire.

Brandy? Or port? There was only one way to tell.

"I promise you, Daggett, you shall have your money soon—and with a generous bonus if you will agree to be patient," said Dudley. The rattle of dice and slur of shouts from the gaming tables was muted by the half-drawn drapery that separated the alcove from the main saloon. Still, his voice was hard to hear clearly. "Just for a little while longer."

"How long?" asked Cameron, deliberately ignoring Morton, who was seated beside the viscount. The man didn't recognize him, which, given the past, stirred an inward smile.

"A month at most." Dudley shot a quick look as his friend, who appeared to confirm it with a flick of his lashes.

"Patience is not one of my virtues," drawled Cameron. "Nor is trust. I've made some inquiries about your finances, and the answers aren't overly encouraging. Why should I think your circumstances will alter?"

Dudley wet his lips. "Because…" Another sidelong look.

"Because," answered Morton, "I have expectations of a rather substantial change in fortune, and I'm willing to guarantee my friend's debt."

"Indeed?" Cameron curled a mocking smile. "I find that a surprise. No title. No lands, no inherited wealth…according to my sources, your expectations are modest at best."

Anger tightened the muscles of Morton's jaw, but he

managed a low laugh. "Your sources are wrong." Edging his chair a little closer to the table, he added. "Perhaps they haven't heard that the Marquess of Wolcott and his son met with an unfortunate boating accident."

"I'm aware of Wolcott's demise." Cameron took a lazy sip of his brandy, savoring the cat-and-mouse game he was playing. *No matter the piles of money being wagered nearby, these stakes are higher by far.* "But I don't see how that affects you."

"No?" The single candle flame caught the gleam of Morton's scimitar smile. "Then perhaps you are not as well informed as you think, Daggett. A closer look at the family bloodlines will show that I may be a mere 'mister' at the moment, but with Wolcott's son dead, I am the next in line."

Cameron lifted a brow. "On the contrary, I keep *very* well informed. So I'm aware that your claim to the title might not be quite so certain as you say. There are rumors that the recently departed marquess has a younger brother."

"How the devil do you know that?" gasped Dudley. "I—"

Morton speared him to silence with a scowl. Turning back to Cameron, he answered, "The brat—assuming he ever existed—is a bastard. So it's hardly a matter of concern."

"That's not what I hear." Time to start luring the two men toward a trap. *And away from Sophie.* "I've heard whispers that a document exists that might alter that."

"Satan's ballocks!" rasped Dudley. "How..."

"I make it my business to know all the sordid little secrets of the *ton*," interrupted Cameron. A pause as he watched Morton begin to drum his fingers on the table. "I find it pays to be informed."

Dudley refilled his glass with brandy and swallowed it in one gulp.

Morton was not so rattled. "Yes," he said slowly, "I've heard you make a living profiting from the weaknesses of others, Daggett."

A smirking laugh. "That's rather the pot calling the kettle black, isn't it?"

Ignoring the barb, Morton regarded him with a flat-eyed gaze. Like a snake watching, waiting for a prey to come within striking distance. "Perhaps. But it occurs to me that by pooling our talents, so to speak, we might both come away with a handsome reward."

"I've already got a pretty penny in my possession." Cameron held up the promissory note. "Why should I expend any effort on getting what is already mine?"

"Because I'll double the amount."

He pretended to consider the offer. "Triple it," he said after a long moment.

"Why, you conniving bastard," growled Dudley.

"Bastard?" repeated Cameron softly. "Be advised, I don't take kindly to insults from scum."

The viscount started to rise from his chair. Morton reached out a restraining hand, but Cameron had already kicked Dudley's legs out from under him, knocking him to the floor.

"Challenging me to a fight would be a grave mistake," he murmured as the viscount picked himself up.

"Get hold of yourself, Dudley. Daggett is right—let us use our brains rather than our fists," snarled Morton. Pursing his lips, he said, "I'll agree to your demand, Daggett, assuming you can make the question of a brother...go away." His tone dropped to taut whisper. "I've reason to believe that a local spinster by the name of Lawrance knows something about a document that could upset our plans. Her father is half-mad, but she—"

"Forget the Lawrance family," cut in Cameron. "I happen to know for sure that it's not with them."

"I think you're wrong," countered Dudley. "Miss Lawrance is hiding something. I feel it in my gut."

"Maybe you've simply eaten a piece of putrid fish," mocked Cameron. He looked at Morton. "I don't intend to waste any more of my breath on this." A sliver of silence. "So make up your mind about who you think is clever enough at clandestine activities to entrust with your future—me or Dudley."

The twitch of Morton's throat told him that the bait had been swallowed.

"Very well, Daggett, I agree to your terms. Sit down, and let us negotiate the details..."

The taste of brandy was a little disappointing. Its burn left her mouth feeling scorched, but on the other hand, it did give a pleasant, pooling warmth in her belly. Sophie took a few more small sips, before setting the decanter and glass back in its place.

"Penelope would be in awe—that is, if I dared to tell her," she said to the brass lanterns.

The red-gold patterns of light shimmied with silent laughter.

"I've painted my face, I've tippled strong spirits, I've lain on a bed of forbidden pleasures..."

A sharp rapping suddenly roused her from her reveries.

"Oh, blast." It took a moment to untangle herself from the velvet coverlet. Her stocking-clad feet finally found the carpet—she had kicked off her half boots some time ago—and she hurried to the door.

"Damnation." It was Cameron, his voice sounding taut as a bowstring. "Open the door."

Sophie fumbled with the latches, finally releasing the lock.

He cracked the door just wide enough to slip inside and quickly kicked it closed. "Good God, Sophie, why would you risk coming—" His words trailed off as he looked up.

"Good God," he repeated.

It was only now that she caught a glance of herself in the large cheval glass set by the dressing table. *Hair spilling over her shoulders, bodice hanging open, face painted to rival Jezebel...*

"Good God," she echoed.

"What has happened to you?" he demanded. "Have you lost every last whit of sense that you ever possessed?"

YOU are what has happened to me. You have come back and stirred wild longings to life.

"I saw no harm in experimenting a little," she said defensively. "You kept me waiting forever."

"Had I known you were here," he growled, "I would have had Sara order you to leave. This isn't a damn game, Sophie."

"I know that. I may look like an utter fool right now, but I haven't completely lost my wits. There was a very important reason for me to come here," she replied. "Lord Wolcott is dead. You needed to know that before you delved too deeply into danger."

The scrim of shadows made it hard to be sure, but his expression seemed to soften.

"You were concerned about my safety?"

"Yes, you big lummox! I couldn't be sure the news would reach you," replied Sophie hotly.

"Actually, I learned of it last night," he said.

She now felt a little ridiculous. "Forgive me for rushing helter-pelter to save your ornery hide," she muttered.

Cameron took a step into the room. "How did you get here?"

"By mail coach." She retreated toward the bed, unsure of the strange glitter in his eyes. "And then by hired hackney. I was carefully cloaked and veiled, so don't you dare accuse me of being a featherbrained female." A glance in the cheval glass made her add, "Though I look like a hen-witted strumpet."

His boots slid noiselessly across the carpet. "That is not precisely the description I would use."

Sophie felt her flesh begin to tingle with heat as Cameron came closer. It must be the brandy that was making her so lightheaded. Or perhaps the potent perfume.

"You—"

Whatever he was about to say was cut off by a jarring *thump* on the bedchamber door.

Cameron spun around.

The *thump* came again, followed by a jiggling of the latch. "Damn room is supposed to be unoccupied," exclaimed a drunken voice. "Sally checked her ledger earlier."

To her horror, Sophie realized the lock had been left open.

Thump.

In one swift, spinning motion, she was lifted off her feet and shoved against the wall.

"Don't," warned Cameron, "breathe a word." And then covered her mouth with a bruising kiss.

Chapter Sixteen

Thump. The door finally gave way to a hard shoulder butt.

"Ought to oil the hinges," groused an aggrieved male voice.

A high-pitched titter sounded in answer. "Oh, don't worry, duckie. We keep all the *really* important working parts well lubricated here at the Lair."

"Ha, ha, ha…" The laugh died away. "Er, what's this? I don't remember contracting for a ménage à four…er, not that I'm opposed to trying something new, but I imagine it costs a pretty penny extra."

"No, no, it's not on the slate," said the lightskirt, sounding somewhat bemused. "Ye must be the new girl, dearie," she trilled to the shadows on the wall. "Yer supposed te make sure that Sal assigns ye a chamber, so there ain't any awkward encounters."

Keeping his back to the intruders, Cameron waved them away with a wordless snarl.

"See, some gents prefer privacy," explained the lightskirt. "Ye'll learn that soon enough." There was a scuff of steps as she turned her inebriated client around. "Come along, duckie. We'll find a nice, quiet spot of our own."

With that the door clicked shut.

Sophie wriggled her lips free of the embrace. "I—I think they've gone," she whispered.

Cameron kept his weight against her for a moment longer, wanting to be sure. *One little mistake—one small slip.* He had let himself be distracted by devil-dark eyes and Lucifer lips. Next time, it could mean more than an embarrassing encounter. It could mean the difference between life and death.

Fear adding an edge to his movements, he pulled away and hurried to twist the lock's bolts into place.

"Well, no harm done," murmured Sophie, sounding far too cheerful for the situation.

"Only by the skin of our teeth," he replied.

"Mmmm, you have nice teeth, and nice skin," she murmured. "And I like the way your mouth tastes of smoke and fire. It makes me feel deliciously warm all over."

Hell and damnation. An unwilling, unwanted heat suddenly pooled in his privy parts.

Cameron touched his tongue to the inside of his cheek. "You've been drinking brandy," he murmured, realizing with a jolt why the sweetness of her spice was a little different.

The low, velvety laugh was a very un-Sophie-like sound. "Just a little," she admitted. "It's a little raw, but perhaps it's an acquired taste."

"Not by you," he rasped, trying to quell his rising response. Good God—this new Nymph of Pleasure side of Sophie was a little alarming. Not to speak of arousing.

Steady now, he cautioned himself. Only a beast of the

lowest order would be thinking impure thoughts of an Innocent within the walls of a brothel.

But she is no Innocent, thanks to you, jeered an inner demon.

Which was all the more reason to keep a grip on his emotions.

"Come along, Sophie," he said a little roughly. "I need to get you out of here as quickly as possible." Two swift strides and he was back at her side. "Where's your cloak?"

She gave a vague wave at the bed. "I left it over there."

Averting his eyes from the temptingly plump pillows, he took her hand. "Well. Let. Us. Find. It." he said through gritted teeth.

"I know, I know." With a sigh, Sophie slumped against his side. "I look absurd. Me, a Damsel of Desire?" Her lust-red lips pursed. "Ha—and pigs might fly."

"You don't look absurd," growled Cameron. "If you must know it, you look ravishing."

"I—I do?" Her lashes fluttered. "I rather like the way my eyes appear when they're all smudgy."

"Yes," he agreed. "They are as...seductive as sin." A loud commotion in the corridor outside the door drew his attention from the intriguingly dark, dappled shadings. Wrenching his head around, he listened for a moment before letting out a low oath. "Damn, we had better wait for a bit before trying to leave."

Several distinctly off-key male voices were raised in a bawdy song, their efforts encouraged by the titter of female laughter and demands for another chorus. By the sound of it, the performance might go on for a while.

Sophie leaned back against the velvet-draped mattress

and looked up at the gently swaying brass lanterns. "It's really quite pleasant in here."

"Yes, well, it's meant to be."

"And the bed is exceedingly comfortable." She bounced her bum against its side. "Have you tried it?"

Coming from anyone else but Sophie, the comment would be a flagrant come-hither invitation. She, however, was blithely unaware of what she was saying.

Or was she?

Fanning a hand over the deep "V" of flesh exposed by her unbuttoned bodice, she gave a cat-like stretch. "Aren't you warm in that coat? Why not take it off?"

"Because," answered Cameron, trying not to watch the slide of patterned muslin pull taut over her breasts, "we are going to be leaving here in another moment." He crossed the carpet and took hold of her arm.

"What's the rush?" she asked, shaking off his grip. "I have been thinking it over, and appearing on my uncle's doorstep at this late hour might provoke too many unwanted questions. Perhaps we should stay here for the night and then I will go on in the morning."

God must be punishing me for my many misdeeds.

"Sophie, this isn't a inn, it's a bordello."

Her hands set on his shoulders and slowly slid inward. "Yes, and if truth be told, I find that rather exciting." A sigh tickled his neck. "I've so rarely done anything reckless, anything naughty."

Cameron drew in a ragged breath as she twined her slim fingers in his hair. His self-control was hanging on by a mere thread. "While I, on the other hand, have spent my life breaking most every rule in Creation."

"So break another," whispered Sophie.

He met her gaze and saw longing ripple the blue of her eyes, its hue deepened by some other emotion he couldn't put a name to.

"Please. I'll soon be returning to my life as sober, safe Sophie, so I'd like to have a few memories to keep me warm." A tentative smile. "You did, after all, say that you should make love to me on a real bed, with our bodies bathed in candlelight. I—I doubt we shall ever have a more perfect opportunity than this one."

The patterned flames, amber-gold from the color of the burnished brass, played across her upturned face in a sensuous, seductive dance.

"Sophie..." A plume of perfume, lush and liquid with desire, tickled his nostrils.

Lucifer, throw me into the fire. The thread unraveled in a swirl of sparks.

"God help me, I should be stronger," he rasped, touching his lips to her brow. "But I am a selfish, snabbering, weak-willed Hellhound."

"Mmmm." Sophie tilted her head back and slowly slid her mouth from the tip of his chin to the swell of his lower lip. "Then it's a good thing..." Nibble, nibble. "...that I have a fondness for canines."

"I think I've unleashed your inner devil," murmured Cameron. A flick of his tongue tickled a tiny laugh from her. "Yet another black-as-Hades sin on my soul."

Dropping her hands to the knot of his cravat, she began loosening the linen. "Let's not talk of darkness, Cam. I would rather fill this fleeting interlude with naught but shimmering light."

Dark and Light. He had dwelled so long in the shadows that the temptation was too great to pass up.

"Very well, then, Sunbeam. Let us throw ourselves into the flames."

Sophie shivered as Cameron teased his tongue along the line of her jaw. Strange, she hadn't thought of her chin as a particularly sensitive spot, but his touch seemed to make even the most mundane bit of her body feel erotic.

Her fingertips tugged at his cravat, acutely aware of the finespun fabric giving way to the lightly stubbled skin of his throat. Eager to explore his intriguing male textures, she hurriedly unfastened his shirt and slipped her hands inside.

Sleek muscle, coarse curls of hair...

"Easy, sweetheart," he murmured. "This time, we'll not rush things. Rather than drink our pleasure in one great gulp, let us savor each sip, like the finest wine."

The idea was...intoxicating.

"First of all, I did promise you champagne, didn't I?"

"Alas, there is only a tiny tipple of brandy on the drinks tray—"

A laugh bubbled up in Cameron's throat. "Never fear. These pleasure rooms very rarely run dry." Shucking off his shirt, he moved to a low lacquered cabinet set in the far corner and opened the cinnamon-colored door.

"Ah, excellent." Turning, he held aloft a wrought silver cooler. The glow from the lanterns showed the slender neck of a dark-green bottle emerging from a twinkling of ice. "Sara serves her French champagne *à la russe*. Cold as the Siberian tundra."

A fizzy pop punctuated his words.

Cameron quickly poured the sparkling wine into a pair of rounded crystal glasses and carried them over. Along with the bottle. "When Dom Pérignon, the monk who discovered the secret of making champagne's bubbles, first tasted his new wine, he supposedly said, 'I think I am drinking the stars.' So, let us raise a toast to both the Sun and the Moon."

She took a long sip, feeling the effervescence dance like daggerpoints along her tongue. The sensation sent shivers skating down her spine.

He edged closer, his bare chest darkening to bronze in the flickering shadows. Licking a tiny shard of ice from his fingers, he slowly refilled his glass and held it up to the light. "The champagne coupe also has an interesting story. It's said that that the shape was molded from the left breast of Diane de Poiters—though some people claim it was Madame Pompadour, Louis XV's mistress, or perhaps Marie Antoinette."

"You appear to be quite an expert on wine."

A gleam of teeth, a pearly flash of an earring. "I'm an expert on a great many subjects, sweetheart."

"Women among them?" she asked, emboldened by the wine.

"I have lived a hellfire life, and don't deny my experiences, Sunbeam. But they were only passing fancies."

As am I. Repressing a twinge of jealousy, Sophie forced a smile. Time enough for maudlin musings in the future. She would not let such thoughts spoil the magic of this moment.

Cameron spun the stem of the glass between his long, lithe fingers. The tiny bubbles were like liquid sparks within the crystal, whispery explosion of white-gold light.

"My guess is that your left breast has a far more pleasing shape to it—slightly plumper, slightly rounder."

Her flesh began to tingle as he reached out and undid the remaining buttons of her bodice. "Shall we put my assumption to the test?"

It was wicked, it was wanton...and yet Sophie felt a frisson of excitement as she wiggled out of her dress.

He drank off his wine and set down the glass. "This," he murmured, "requires a delicate touch. A corset is cursedly complicated." The top lacing slipped free. "Rather like a lock."

A tickle of cool air caressed the valley between her breasts.

"There, you see—when one understands the mechanism, it's easy to make it release."

Sophie felt the stays slide away from her ribs. "Very clever," she quipped, stepping out of the corset.

Cameron kicked it aside. "Oh, I haven't yet begun to be truly clever. That comes a little later." He made a little swirling motion with his forefinger. "Now off with your shift."

Stand naked as a nymph, save for my garters and stockings?

She looked up at the lanterns, wondering if it was just her imagination that was making them start to slowly spin on their chains.

"I can do it for you if you wish. But I'd rather watch you reveal the glorious splendor of your body."

Glorious? Splendor? The words were like honey against her skin, and somehow the thin cotton seemed to come off of its own accord.

A rush of air escaped his lips. "You are so beautiful, Sunbeam. A pure, perfect picture of gilded goodness."

A blush stole over her body, hot and prickling in all

her private places. "Please, I want to see you naked, too."

"Fair is fair." Boots, trousers, drawers, stockings—they all came off in rapidfire order. He turned to face her, stripped to the supremely masculine essence of sleek muscle, corded sinew, curling hair, and...

She couldn't help but stare.

In the glow of the candle flames, his jutting arousal took on a ruddy, reddish glow as it rose from the thatch of coarse curls.

"And you, Cam, are breathtaking to behold. A dazzling, devil-may-care corsair. A Pirate Prince." *Wild, free.* Sailing wherever the Four Winds might blow him.

"I care about some things, sweetheart," he said in a darkly rumbled tone. "Quite passionately."

Sophie wanted to ask what, but in the next moment he reversed his wineglass and the cool, smooth rim was cupping her left breast... and all rational thought just bubbled away.

"Ah, yes, just as I thought." Cameron flashed a devilish grin. "You are far more shapely than any French femme."

A lingering drop of the ice-cold champagne splashed on the tip of her nipple, drawing a gurgled moan.

"Chilly?" He let the glass fall to the carpet. "Here, let me see if I can warm your flesh." Lowering his head, he drew the rosy nub between his teeth, and gently nipped.

"Cam!"

He suckled the sensitive flesh, again and again and again.

Her blood was boiling, bubbling through her body—oh, surely it would melt her skin.

Cameron gave a husky chuckle and reached for the bottle. A small splash of champagne drizzled over her areola, cold yielding to heat as he licked off the pale gold liquid.

Sophie cried out again, her voice sounding very far-away. The sensations—fire and ice, fire and ice—were unbearably sensuous. In another moment, she feared that she would shatter into a thousand crystalline shards.

He lifted his mouth, only to begin anew on her right breast.

Her body was suddenly boneless, and with a breathless gasp, Sophie felt herself slipping, slipping. Cameron caught her, and stepping between her widespread legs, he eased her back against the velvet coverlet.

Hard, soft, rough, smooth—a myriad of different sensations teased against her flesh. His mouth was doing such delightful things, but his cock...

Heat flared in her core as his erection kissed against her folds. Arching up, Sophie opened wider.

"Yes," she cried. "Oh, yes."

"Yes," he echoed, moving closer, so the head of his manhood nudged in a little deeper.

So close, so close. Sophie lifted her hips higher.

And then suddenly his knowing hand was at play, and the swirl of sweet, sweet heat and friction rose like a frothing storm-whipped wave, carrying her to its crest.

With a hoarse cry, Cameron surged forward, thrusting himself deep inside her.

Swirling—her whole being was swirling, swirling. Spinning, spinning as their bodies came together as one.

Thunder—or was it just the pounding of her heart as she felt herself come undone.

His own release splashed on the dark velvet, and then his weight covered her, his sweat-skimmed skin warm, his pulse thudding in skittering harmony with hers.

"That," she mumbled after a number of long, languid moments, "was wonderful—too wonderful for words."

"Then don't speak," murmured Cameron. He shifted, gently adjusting their spent bodies to lie full length on the bed. "Just feel." He gathered her in his arms and drew her close.

Sophie snuggled her head against his shoulder. "Mmmm, next time…" *Oh, please, let there be a next time.* "I would like to feel *you*, explore you, and learn more about your body's secrets."

His lips feathered lightly against the nape of her neck. "There are still several hours until dawn. More than enough time to unlock a few more mysteries of desire."

Cameron lifted an eyelid and drew in a deep, spice-scented breath of air. The perfume of their passion was still thick, lightening the darkness with memories of the night.

A fleeting smile, and then his gut clenched as guilt warred with exultation. *This was too damnably danger-ous…*

Sophie stirred and stretched. "Is it morning?" she asked, sounding muzzy with sleep and sated passion. "It's hard to keep track of time when you can't see a glimmer of the real world."

"That is precisely the point," he drawled. After dropping a kiss to her brow, he untangled his legs and rose. "It's still early," he murmured after consulting the small clock that was discreetly hidden in the dressing table drawer. "But we had best begin getting ready to take our leave."

"Must we?" She yawned and flashed a feline smile.

Oh, do not tempt me.

"I'll have one of the girls bring up your valise," answered Cameron, hurriedly gathering his clothing and dressing. "And ask Sara to arrange for a tub and hot water, if you like."

"A bath would be heavenly," murmured Sophie.

"Very well. I'll leave you to dress at your leisure." He drew the door shut and headed downstairs, where the rose-colored dawn had finally brought the night's revelries to an end. The corridors were quiet as he made his way to Sara's office.

"Perhaps she's retired," he murmured to himself, "and I can deal with McTavish."

No such luck.

As he feared, she was waiting for him, and looking none too pleased about what had transpired.

"You," she said through her teeth, "ought to be ashamed of yerself. Bringing an Innocent here and treating her like a lightskirt."

"I didn't bring her here," he pointed out.

Sara waggled a warning finger. "Don't ye try to make a jest of it or I'll slice off yer... tongue."

"I am not making light of the situation. There was no choice but to spend the night here. In my defense, things were a little raucous upstairs. It would have been very dangerous to try to spirit Miss Lawrance away. If Dudley or Morton had happened to spot her, there would have been hell to pay."

Sara scowled. "That doesn't absolve ye of all guilt.

I've worked at this business long enough to be able to read a girl's face as easily as our friend Haddan reads his fancy books. And written plain on Miss Lawrance's features is the fact that you two are lovers."

Cameron didn't wish to insult their friendship by denying it. Hoping to distract her from the subject of his own shortcomings, he hastened to ask, "Would you be so kind as to send up her clothing and a bath? The sooner she can make her toilette, the sooner I can remove her from the premises."

"Lucy is already arranging it." Sara crossed her arms, unwilling to drop the matter. "And what, may I ask, are your intentions? A gentleman—"

"You are forgetting that I am not a gentleman…" *Damnation, actually I am*, Cameron realized belatedly. "Be that as it may," he hurried on, "you can be assured that I will see that Miss Lawrance does not suffer any damage from this night."

"Are ye going to marry her?"

A heartbeat of silence. "What makes you think she would say yes if I asked her?"

"Ye daft bugger! Because she's in love with ye—though God only knows why. Ye don't need spectacles te see it writ plain on her face."

Cameron refused to meet her gaze.

"And ye—ye ain't so hardbitten as ye wish te seem," went on Sara. "Maybe it's time te let yer better nature come out of hiding."

"Don't be so sure that I have one." Even to his own ears, the cynical quip sounded a little flat.

She made a rude noise. "Bark all ye want, but yer a bloody fool if ye let pride stand in the way of happiness."

Can I make Sophie happy?

Cameron wished he could be sure. But before he could even consider that thorny question, he had to resolve the conundrum of his heritage—and the threat to the Lawrance family.

"It's not a question of pride, Sara. It's far more complicated than that." He blew out his breath. "That's all I can say at the moment."

"Hmmph." Her gimlet gaze softened just a touch. "I'll cease raking ye over the coals. But be advised that if ye don't heed my advice, ye'll find yerself banished from the Lair."

"Ye gods, that would be a fate worse than death. Where else would I drink for free?"

"Out." Sara picked up her letter opener and made a shooing gesture with the razored steel. "Go to the gentlemen's retiring room and make yerself presentable. And I warn ye, I'll have the Wolfhound and Haddan skin ye alive if ye don't do the right thing by Miss Lawrance."

He walked off, happy to escape, and yet unsure whether having to face his own reflection in the looking glass would be an even greater ordeal.

Do the right thing by Miss Lawrance.

Would that he knew what that was. Until recently, it was never a question—his old life would have snuffed all the light out of Sophie.

And now?

He touched his earring, letting his fingers linger on the silky smooth pearl. And now he felt as if he was hovering somewhere between Hades and the Heavens.

Shadowed by both the past and the future.

Could a man change his skin? Cameron stared into the looking glass and studied the hazy reflection for a long moment. "Griggs seems to think I have it in me to be more than...what I am now," he murmured.

So, perhaps the answer is up to me.

Chapter Seventeen

A blissful soak and a cup of hot chocolate had done much to clear the seductive haze of champagne and sex from Sophie's mind. Not that clear-headedness was all that welcome. As she made her way down the back stairs, her hooded cloak drawn close to conceal her identity, she was uncomfortably aware of how far she had strayed past the boundaries of propriety.

"I'm likely halfway to Hell," she quipped to herself. "Maybe three quarters."

Still, Sophie didn't regret her trespassing into the Land of Sin.

"As Cam said, virginity is vastly overrated." She sighed, yet couldn't repress a smile. "I may live the rest of my days in virtuous spinsterhood, so I'm glad I had this night to hug and to hold in my memory."

Cameron was waiting for her in the landing, watched by Sara, who stood framed in the doorway of her private office. The proprietor's expression made Sophie even more uncertain of her position.

I am somewhere between a rock and a stone.

"Th-thank you for you hospitality," she said hesitantly,

suddenly aware of how ridiculous the words must sound.

Sara's mouth tightened to a fleeting semblance of a smile. "Yer a very nice and intrepid young lady, Miss Lawrance. So don't take it amiss when I say that I hope never te entertain ye here again for the night." She shot a daggered look at Cameron. "Some folk ought to have more sense."

He cleared his throat. "Speaking of sense, I have decided on a change of plans, Sophie. On reflection, I think it best that you return directly to Norfolk. There is no reason for your aunt and uncle to know of this visit."

"But..." She bit her lip. Returning home without raising awkward questions would be a difficult endeavor if she did not arrive in her uncle's carriage.

"Sara and I have worked out a plan that should satisfy every stricture of Society. We've hired a reliable coach and driver, and Lucy will accompany you on the journey. You've simply to say that your uncle's carriage cracked an axle, and it was decided that your visit to London should be put off. Seeing as the repair was going to take several days, he sent you home with a local driver and tavern maid."

"Yes, that should work," Sophie conceded, rather relieved that she didn't have to fabricate a story for Aunt Hermione. "But we have not yet talked about..."

Again, Cameron had anticipated her concern. "I will ride with you for a short while so that we may discuss the situation."

Sara made a small noise in her throat.

A warning growl? Whatever the message, Cameron chose to ignore it. "The carriage is waiting outside. Let's be off."

Once she had settled back against the squabs, Sophie carefully pleated the folds of her skirts into place. Lucy had taken a seat on the driver's perch, so privacy was not an issue. Still, she felt a little nervous as she looked across the space separating the facing seats. "I—I suppose we should have dealt with business before anything else last night, but my mind wasn't functioning very well."

"I can't say that I was thinking very clearly, either," he said softly. "Sophie, before we talk about Dudley and Morton and Wolcott, we had better deal with our own personal problem."

"Is that how you see it—a *problem*?" she asked, trying to keep the pinch of dismay from her voice.

"Yes. A grave one," he answered. "We cannot keep having these illicit encounters. It's too risky. I am taking precautions, but there is always a chance for a mistake. And if I plunge you into scandal and disgrace, all our efforts to counter Dudley and Morton will be for naught. I doubt Anthony's parents would allow him to marry Georgiana."

Sophie's throat grew painfully tight. He was right—until her sister's marriage was settled, they must avoid disaster. But after that...In her own mind she had already decided that she was willing to risk everything for love. However, for the moment, with so many things still so unresolved she dared not voice that sentiment aloud. Instead, she replied coolly, "Put that way, I see your point. I shall endeavor to think things through more clearly."

If Cameron noticed the edge in her voice, he gave no sign of it. "It's me who should have being thinking more clearly. From here on in, I shall keep a leash on my lust."

She felt a flutter of disappointment deep down in her chest. "Yes, of course. That would be the wisest thing to do." The window glass rattled as the wheels clattered over the cobblestones, allowing a draft of damp air to sneak in and chill her cheeks. "Well, now that we've settled personal matters, let us move on to the real threat."

In the gloomy half-light, his expression was impossible to read. Only the slight shrug of his shoulders showed any reaction to her words. Even then, there was an interval of silence, as if he was gathering his thoughts.

Or perhaps simply relegating the memory of the night to some far corner of his brain.

Oh, don't be maudlin, she told herself. *He has always been honest about the fleeting nature of his attachments.* Pirates sailed where the tide and wind took them. If she cast off caution and sailed after him, she must be prepared for the fact that her own ship might founder on uncharted rocks.

"As I told you," Cameron murmured, when at last he began to speak, "I knew about Wolcott's demise from a source of my own. I also learned that it is Morton who stands to inherit everything, assuming, of course, that I am either illegitimate or dead."

Sophie couldn't repress a shiver. "Oh, surely he is not so depraved as to ever contemplate murder."

"I have good reason to believe otherwise," answered Cameron. "According to my source, there is compelling evidence to suggest that Wolcott's yacht was sabotaged."

The revelation momentarily robbed her of breath.

"And the more I think about it, the more it makes sense," went on Cameron. "I did a little digging. Morton is, by all accounts, a clever man, who feels that it is an unfair accident of birth that has robbed him of the money and position in Society that goes with the Wolcott title. He devised a clever plan—and then discovered the rumors about me."

He crossed his legs and flicked a speck of mud from his boot. "It was a minor enough detail to leave to his friend Dudley."

"It seems too impossible," she protested. "First of all, Morton would have to know when Wolcott was planning a sailing excursion with his family."

A flash of teeth glimmered in the shadows. "Oh, but he did. Remember the correspondence I saw on Wolcott's desk? Though I didn't see the significance at the time, there were several letters discussing the itinerary. You see, it turns out Morton is an expert sailor, and knows the North Sea coast like the back of his hand. Wolcott asked his advice on anchorages."

"Good God," intoned Sophie as the significance of what he was saying sank in. "You mean that Morton..."

"Would know how to weaken a boat enough to make it founder in rough weather?" finished Cameron. "Yes, without a doubt."

She took a measured breath, trying to control the sudden churning in her stomach. "That means you are in terrible danger."

"Not at all," he responded. "To Morton and Dudley, I am simply Daggett, a Hellhound of highly questionable morals who has a reputation for getting his paws dirty in any number of unsavory ventures. In fact..." A hint of humor shaded his voice. "...I have been hired by the pair to eliminate the pesky problem of Wolcott's long-lost brother."

"Cam—"

He silenced her with a touch to her knee. "Don't worry, Sunbeam. You must trust that I know what I am doing. I've hinted that I know where the elusive marriage document is, which will keep Dudley away from you."

Sophie fisted her hands, squeezing so tightly that her nails dug into her palms.

"Furthermore, I've arranged to rendezvous later this week at Morton's house on the coast near the Fens—and I think it likely I shall find your father's incriminating paper hidden there, and perhaps some proof of their perfidy regarding my late half brother."

"How did all this come about?" she asked.

"I met with them last night at the Lair. It was the reason that I was late in coming to you."

Sophie frowned, trying to find some argument to dissuade him from such a dangerous plan. "You alone with those two miscreants? It's too risky. There must be a better way. Can't you simply sneak inside Morton's residence and steal the evidence against my father?"

"I could," he agreed. "But that does not address their other crime."

"What about going to the authorities?" she pressed.

He lifted a brow. "There is no proof at this point, only conjecture. And be assured that any assertions from me would hold little water with the Powers-That-Be. We are not, to put it mildly, on the friendliest of terms."

"What can I do to help?" asked Sophie, feeling wretched that she had drawn him into a cesspool far worse than anything she had imagined.

He was no longer looking amused. "Promise me that you will stay at home in Norfolk for now. I've a plan in mind, but if I must worry about your safety, it will be a distraction."

Defeated, Sophie leaned back. "How can I argue with that?" she said in a small voice. "You have my word. However, in return, you must vow not to take any undue risks." The thought of losing him squeezed like a vise around her heart. "Nothing—no title, no fortune, no avoidance of family scandal—is worth your life, Cam."

His lashes flickered, stirring a strange spark that was quickly swallowed by shadows. "I've no intention of sticking my spoon in the wall just yet, Sunbeam. I am always careful, so you need not fret."

The assertion did nothing to quell her worries. Biting her lip, she turned away to stare at the fog-misted buildings.

"I must leave you here," he said quietly and rapped a signal on the trap for the driver. "There are things I must do to set the trap."

Sophie nodded, blinking back the sting of salt. "You will keep me apprised?"

"Morton's hideaway is not far from Terrington. I shall come to you after my visit there..."

Assuming you are still alive, she thought.

"...and the danger to your family will be over."

A tear slid down her cheek as he brushed a caress to her rigid spine. "What if...what if..." She could not bring herself to speak her real fear. "What if I have need to send word to you?"

Cameron was silent for a long moment. "If there is something urgent, leave a sign for me at the hut. No note—we can't be too careful. Simply put a stone on the

center of the table. I will check the spot on way to Terrington, and if you need me, I will find you."

"H-how?"

A low laugh. "If you remember, I was always rather
adept at rousing you from sleep to come on some madcap
night adventure."

"Yes, I remember." She dared not turn around. The
blurred reflection of his face would have to be the image
imprinted in her mind's eye. "G-godspeed, Cam."

"Safe journey to you, Sophie." He hesitated. "Don't
worry. I may be a Hellhound, but like a cat, I have nine
lives, and I daresay I have a few of them still left."

A blade of cold air cut across her back and then the
door clicked shut.

It was long past midnight, but a light still glimmered
behind the diamond-paned windows of the third floor library. Easing open the back gate of the walled garden,
Cameron crossed through the ornamental shrubbery and
let himself in through the tradesmen's entrance. The back
stairs by the pantries brought him to the corridor leading
to the library.

"I have a perfectly good front door, you know." Gryff
looked up from his writing in response to the soft greeting. "You might try knocking."

"And wake your butler? He's already miffed at me for
removing some of your rare books," replied Cameron.
"By the by, you really ought to upgrade your locks."

"I would if I thought it would deter you."

He moved to the sideboard and poured a glass of
brandy. But rather than drink, he merely rolled the cut
crystal between his palms. "Why are you back in Town?"

he asked abruptly, putting off the real reason he had come for a little bit longer. Asking a favor did not come easily.

Putting down his pen, Gryff tilted back in his chair. "A few more cursed revisions to the final page proofs, and then the book will finally be ready to go to print."

"Eliza did not come with you?"

"No. She's been feeling a trifle unwell lately, and we decided that it was best for her not to travel."

Cameron regarded his friend for a long moment. "Are you, too, starting your nursery?"

"It's too early to know for sure. But yes, I think so." Gryff's face blossomed with a broad smile. "And if you make another one of your snide remarks about domesticated dogs, you'll be digging glass shards out of your gullet for the next fortnight."

His usual cutting quips seemed to have deserted him, so Cameron merely lifted his glass in salute. "Congratulations."

The chair legs hit the carpet with a soft thud. "Are you, perchance, ill?"

"Simply preoccupied." He fingered his earring. "The truth is, I was hoping you might give me some advice."

Gryff raised a brow. "About what?"

"The Peerage, and all its convoluted rules and regulations," answered Cameron reluctantly.

"That's a rather broad topic. I'm afraid that you'll have to be a little more specific."

Stepping over the hearth, he braced a hand on the mantel and forced out a hurried growl of questions.

"Stop mumbling into the coals," interrupted his friend. "Did you say 'marquess'? If so, I hope it's not some disparaging comment about me. I've been slaving for hours over these essays, and my sense of humor is not at its best."

I feel naked, thought Cameron. It was damnably diffi-cult to shed his lifelong scales and expose the tender new skin beneath them. *And vulnerable.*

Quelling the urge to slither away and seek refuge in solitude, Cameron took a measured breath and managed to get out a terse explanation of his meeting with Griggs and the truth of his heritage.

"Well, well." Gryff pursed his lips, looking pensive. "You a lord? The next thing you'll be telling me is that the moon is made of green cheese." His eyes narrowed. "This isn't some hum, is it? Because at the moment I don't have time for any puerile pranks."

Cameron shook his head. "It's no hum. I've got a number of documents here from my late father's man of affairs." He took out a packet from inside his coat and tossed it onto the desk. "He assures me that he has as-sembled the necessary papers, and even though the actual marriage lines have yet to be found, with his affidavit, he feels that the petition should be confirmed. However, given the circumstances, the process of sorting through the legalities promises to be rather convoluted. To begin with, I haven't a clue as to where to begin. But more im-portantly..."

"Yes?" encouraged his friend as the hesitation stretched out for several seconds.

"More importantly, Sophie—that is, Miss Lawrance—is caught in a nasty bit of blackmail, mostly on account of our childhood friendship. I need to deal with that, and adroit as I am with my fingers, I find that I can't be jug-gling both balls at the same time."

"If I were an arse," said Gryff slowly. "I would make a sarcastic comment about a Hellhound having his own fanged words about love come back to bite him." With a silent waggle of his fingers, Gryff mimed a snapping dog. "However, much as it amuses me to learn you have a soft spot hidden on your mangy hide, I shall refrain from sinking my teeth into it."

Cameron accepted the sharp-tongued teasing with good grace. "I suppose that I deserve to have both you and Connor nipping at my flanks. And you may savage me all you want, once Sophie is safe."

His friend's grin thinned to a grim line. "What would you like for me to do?"

"Help Griggs shepherd this through whatever process is necessary. I'm hoping you have some influence within the House of Lords. Having my title confirmed as quickly as possible is important. But even more important is that rumors should be circulated through all the gentlemen's clubs suggesting that long-lost heir to Wolcott's title has been found and is about to step forward. I want the villains to be nervous when next I meet them—fear often forces a careless mistake."

"I take it that Dudley is the man threatening your Miss Lawrance?" asked Gryff. "And that's why you asked Connor to win at cards and give you the vowel."

Cameron hesitated. In the past, he would have brushed off the question, for no one, not even his closest comrades, was allowed to know his inner thoughts or feelings. But of late, he was coming to realize that trust was not a weakness but a strength.

"Yes," he answered slowly. "Having in him in my debt allowed me to set a plan in motion. But the main culprit is his crony, Frederick Morton. And it turns out that thwarting him will not only save Sophie but will also allow me to settle an old score. Being recognized as the legitimate marquess is an added assurance that they will not have any power to hurt her and her family. If I am respectable..." Cameron couldn't quite bring himself to admit the idea that had been lurking in the back of his head.

I must deal with the present before I can think of the future.

Instead, he finished giving a quick explanation of Dudley and Morton's perfidy. "Don't press me for any further details right now, for I need to be off to Norfolk tonight."

Gryff waved him on his way. "Leave the House of Lords to me. I have a few favors to call in among my fellow peers. And as for gossip, you may be sure that it will spread like fire through the clubs."

"Thank you." Sophie's touch must have deftly released all the locking levers of his inner defenses, for it suddenly didn't feel so bloody hard to express gratitude for his comrade's show of unflinching friendship.

"Good God, I would think you had brain fever if I didn't know you were suffering from a different affliction," quipped Gryff. His amusement, however, was only momentary. "But enough jesting. I take that you are heading off to deal with the culprits alone?"

Cameron nodded. "Morton has a country house on the coast north of Holbeach. I'm meeting with them to plan my own demise. A fact that my cynical sense of humor finds highly amusing."

His friend didn't crack a smile. "If these men have killed once, they won't hesitate to do so again. Are you sure that you wouldn't like some eyes to watch your back? Connor returned to Town this afternoon. We could rendezvous with you near the coast."

"What? And pull the two of you away from your books and your goats?" A brusque wave dismissed the suggestion. "I appreciate the offer. However, I work best alone."

Seeing that Gryff was opening his mouth to argue, Cameron quickly added, "Besides, your lovely bride is still a little ambivalent in her feelings toward me. If I muck up your publishing date, I'll be *persona non grata* forever."

The quip brought a grudging grimace to his friend's face. "I'll back off then. But only because you seem to have a knack for surviving hellish risks that would make the Devil's own hair stand on end."

"Trust me, these two spawns of Satan are going to roast over coals of their own making."

"Just one last thing, Cam."

Pausing in the doorway, he looked back through the flickering of lamplight and shadows.

"Good luck." The flame flared for an instant, gilding Gryff's smile. "And don't look so damned terrified. We old dogs can learn new tricks—like allowing others into our hearts. Being in love is not such a bad thing."

Love?

The whisper of the word, soft as his light-footed step, followed him down the corridor.

"Love," murmured Cameron, taking the darkened treads of the stairs two at a time. Strangely enough, that word was also getting easier and easier to say. And strangely enough, it seemed at long last to silence the hissing and spitting little demons who had inhabited his head for so long.

No jabbing pitchforks, no sulfurous stench, no cynical sneers.

Perhaps Gryff was right. Perhaps it was possible for a Hellhound to acquire a few new moves.

As long as the first one when I confront Morton and Dudley isn't rolling over and playing dead.

Chapter Eighteen

Jhe lock gave a rusty groan as the key turned…"

Supper over, their father tucked away for the night, Penelope opened her book and began reading a new chapter aloud from *Lady Avery's Awful Secret*.

Sophie lingered in the shadows, listening with only half an ear to the gothic tale of subterranean dungeons, nasty secrets, and wicked villains.

A wry grimace pinched at her lips. *At the moment my own life is far more lurid.*

She waited for several more pages and then slipped out of the parlor, anxious to sneak a few moments alone. Cupping her candle flame, she tiptoed down the dark corridor and took sanctuary in her father's deserted study.

The dust had yet to settle on her spinning thoughts. At least the journey home—including an overnight stay at a respectable inn—had passed without incident and her explanation of the change in plans had been accepted without question by her neighbors.

"They are used to me being honest, sensible Sophie Lawrance," she muttered to herself. "I suppose that I should be grateful that the Almighty hasn't tattooed the word 'LIAR' in large red letters on my forehead." A sigh. "There may be no such outward signs that I have changed irreparably. But…"

"Are you talking to yourself?" Georgiana edged into the dimly lit room and looked around. "Or is someone here with you?"

"Just the Devil," quipped Sophie. "But I was about to ask him to leave."

"You are in an odd humor."

Sophie deliberately avoided her sister's gaze. This was the first moment since her arrival earlier in the day that they had found themselves with the opportunity for a private chat. And she was determined to make it as short as possible.

"Did things not go well in London?" asked Georgiana. "Did you not find Cameron?"

"No, we met, and he's been apprised of Wolcott's death. Though I need not have bothered—the dratted man seems to have an unnatural ability to sniff out trouble on his own."

"Is there a reason you are so dreadfully upset about that?"

I'm not dreadfully upset. I'm dreadfully confused— about so many things.

"Not one that I care to talk about," answered Sophie, hoping her tart reply would make Georgiana go away.

Her sister, however, refused to take the hint. Settling into the facing armchair, Georgiana tapped her fingertips together. "That has an ominous ring—rather like the latest chapter of *Lady Avery's Awful Secret*."

Sophie chuffed a harried laugh. "I'm afraid that truth can sometimes be stranger than your horrid novels."

"And more Awful?"

Tears prickled at the corners of her eyes. Squinting into the far shadows, she pretended to be lost in thought. It wasn't hard—all of a sudden the events of the last few weeks seemed to tumbling and twisting inside her head.

"Sophie?" pressed Georgiana after a stretch of silence. "Sophie?"

Her eyes narrowed and her sister's voice faded to naught but a faint buzzing.

"Sophie?"

"Good Lord," intoned Sophie, rising from her chair. "Why didn't I think of that before?"

"*What?*" Looking alarmed, Georgiana grabbed hold of her sleeve. "Sit down. I am going to send for the apothecary."

"No, no, I'm not ill or demented." She gestured at opposite corner of the room where a small age-blackened oak cabinet sat beneath the wall shelves, half hidden by the window draperies. "Papa's heirloom!"

Her sister looked baffled. "The Staffordshire spaniel?"

"No, the cabinet!"

"That musty old thing? Why, it hasn't been opened in years," pointed out Georgiana.

"My point precisely!"

"Let me fix you a tisane," murmured her sister. "Or perhaps a draught for your nerves. I think you are overwrought."

She shook off the restraining hand. "Georgie, there's a chance that cabinet holds a vital document. As you pointed out, it hasn't been opened in years, and this piece

of paper was likely misplaced ages ago, and then its existence was forgotten. It will not only help Cameron counter
the threat to our family, but also reveal a Very Important
Secret that will affect the lives of many in this area."

"Now you are sounding even more histrionic than a
novel."

"I know, I know." Excitement welled up in her chest.
"But I swear, it's true." If she could find proof that
Cameron was the rightful heir to the Wolcott title...

It will, you know, put him far, far above your touch,
whispered a voice in her head.

A pirate could steal an occasional dalliance with a
country spinster. But a titled aristocrat? Cameron would of
course be expected to marry a lady of his own station. A
polished London gem, one of the glittering Diamonds of
the First Water, rather than a roughcut chip of granite...

"But the key has long since disappeared," said Georgiana, her brow furrowing in dismay.

Shaking off her dispiriting thoughts, Sophie flexed her
fingers. "Run to the kitchen and find me some poultry
skewers."

"Why?"

She was already at her father's desk, searching the
drawers for a pen knife. "Please, Georgie, just do it."

A short while later, the implements neatly assembled
on a pewter tray, Sophie knelt down on the carpet and
pulled the draperies away from the iron-banded wood.
She had considered sending Georgiana away but decided
against it. Her sister had proved herself to be a stalwart,
steady ally, and had earned the right to be trusted. True,
there was still a secret that could not be revealed, but only
because it was not hers to share.

"Bring the candle a little closer," she murmured, peering at the lock's keyhole.

Crouching down, Georgiana shifted the flame.

"Hmmm." She took a moment to examine the various widths of steel. Deciding on the narrowest, she carefully inserted it into the opening and gave a small jiggle. *Nothing.* Holding it in place, she took a second skewer and slid it in a touch higher.

This time, the jiggling was rewarded with a small *snick*.

Her sister let out a soft whistle. "Where did you learn to do that?"

"From Cam." Sophie set to work on the second tumbler. "He's awfully clever with his hands."

"I'll bet he is," murmured Georgiana dryly, a spark of mischief lighting her eyes.

"Shhhh—don't distract me." As it was, the thumping of her heart was loud as cannon fire in her ears.

Georgiana leaned in expectantly.

Snick.

"Oh, well done!" exclaimed her sister as Sophie slowly turned the knob and the door sprang open.

Inside were several thick packets of papers, smelling of dust and mold. She carried then to the desk and spread them out on the blotter.

"Do you know what you are looking for?" asked Georgiana.

"Yes." Blowing a cloud of cobwebs and dead spiders from the first folder, Sophie paged through its contents. *Old sermons, choir schedules, lists of rectory books . . .*

She set it aside and started on the next one. But its contents proved just as mundane.

"Blast." Sophie felt a stab of disappointment on seeing

that the top few documents in the last folder were naught but inventories of church linens.

So much for divine inspiration.

Spirits sinking, she paged quickly through the stack, and was about to toss it aside when her fingers touched on a thicker, smoother piece of paper. Holding her breath, she eased it out and held it up to the light.

"Well?" demanded Georgiana. "Is that *The* Secret?"

"Yes." With great care, Sophie set it aside on the edge of the desk. "And for the time being, you must not breathe a word to anyone of what we have discovered. It could be a matter of life and death."

Her sister's eyes widened.

"I am deadly serious, Georgie, not a word." She gathered the folders and carried them back to the cabinet. After relocking the door and drawing the draperies back into place, she picked up the tray. "Please take these back to the kitchen." On impulse, she took the thinnest skewer and slipped it into her apron pocket. "If Pen asks you any questions, tell her that the window latch was jammed, but we managed to fix it."

"You aren't going to tell me what The Secret is?"

"For your own safety, I had better not." Seeing Georgie's scowl, she quickly added, "It's not my secret to share. But I promise that you will learn all about it very soon." She folded the document and tucked it inside her bodice. "Within a week, if all goes well."

If all goes well. Was it just the tautness of her nerves that made the faint crackle of paper sound like mocking laughter?

Picking up her candle, she took several deep gulps of air before following her sister into the corridor.

* * *

Cameron reined to halt on the brow of the hill. Holding his hat firm against the salt-rough gusts, he stared out at the sea. In the fading daylight, the rolling waves were leached of all color, their sullen gray hue accentuated by the dark, brooding clouds hovering on the distant horizon.

Like violent bruises. An apt metaphor, he decided, listening to the dull roar of the surf against the rocky shingle. Death and skullduggery swirled in the currents below. He had no love for his prideful half brother, but no man deserved such a foul fate, sunk along with his family in a watery grave. Whatever Wolcott's sins, Morton and Dudley were a far worse evil.

"And I shall stop them," he vowed. "Though the irony of me—a fellow who has lived most of his years on the dark side of life—as a champion of Good versus Evil is rather ironic."

Shielding his eyes from the sting of the wind, he surveyed the shoreline for a bit longer, and then, as dusk settled over the surroundings, Cameron turned his horse for the trail leading down to the water's edge.

There had been no signal from Sophie at the stone hut. A relief, he admitted, at least for the moment. He had likely made far better time traveling than she had, and so he would try to check back if circumstances allowed. But if she kept her promise—and Sophie was nothing if not honorable—there should be no pressing need for his assistance.

True, they had much to discuss. Much to resolve. But like the ocean waters, so much between them was still just a muddle of grays. Better to wait until certain things sharpened into black and white.

Though his own thoughts were still so unclear.

What if she says no again?

Cameron felt his insides clench. A fancy title wouldn't hide his many faults. Not from Sophie, who knew him far too well. Would she trust that his heart—an organ he had claimed was hard as stone—had come back to life? Would she believe that reckless danger no longer held any allure?

"Let me defeat two cunning, murderous criminals first," he muttered, allowing himself a wry smile. "That may be the easiest of the two challenges."

Up ahead, just visible through the thinning copse of trees, Cameron spotted the dark outlines of a boathouse silhouetted against the rising night mists. Dismounting, he untied a small sack of tools from behind his saddle and approached the building on foot.

There was no glimmer of light within, and the set of double doors was locked. A quick check showed the dock was deserted, save for a tabby cat that darted off into the reeds. Tied to the brass stanchions was a large, graceful yacht, its rigging thrumming in rhythm with the gentle roll of the incoming tide. Next to it was a smaller racing sloop, a sleek vessel designed for speed and maneuverability.

A pretty picture. Frederick Morton's seaside retreat was an idyllic spot. But was it hiding some ugly truths?

"Despite my reckless reputation, I'm really quite a cautious fellow," murmured Cameron as he backtracked to the boathouse and did a slow circuit around the perimeter to ensure that he was alone. Two sheds at the rear of the building sheltered coils of hemp and several rusting anchors, but they, too, were deserted.

Satisfied, he returned to the entrance. The lock was more complicated than expected, but he made quick work of it.

Once inside, Cameron lit a small shuttered lantern and made a quick survey of the cavernous space with its narrow beam. A large wooden cradle dominated the center of the building, its slanted timbers designed to hold a boat hull hauled in for repairs. Nothing out of the ordinary there, he thought, quickly directing his attention to the work benches aligned along the far wall.

His cat-footed steps across the earthen floor stirred a whisper of wood shavings, mingling the scent of oak with the more pungent smells of pine tar and linseed oil. In the flicker of lanternlight, the array of tools hanging above the counters threw menacing silhouettes on the planked wall—clawed hammers, sharp-faced axes, and razored saws looking as large as dragon's teeth.

"The Devil's workshop," Cameron muttered, beginning a methodical search of the crannies and crevices. The odds were against finding any evidence of Morton's involvement in Wolcott's death, but experience had taught him to overlook nothing when seeking to uncover an opponent's weakness.

However cunning, most people were careless enough to leave some telltale clue lying around that could be used against them.

Slowly, slowly, he made his way down the length of the drawers and cubbyholes.

No luck.

Coming to the end of the benches, Cameron paused and made another angled sweep of the beam. A rack of freshly varnished spars and a pile of weathered sails sat in a narrow alcove. Deciding it was worth a look, he ducked inside the cramped space and quickly searched through the heavy canvas.

Naught but gritty streaks of sea salt.

The smooth lengths of spruce yielded nothing, either.

It was only as he rose from his crouch that the light fell on a crumpled piece of paper lying in the sliver of space beneath the spars. Reaching into the shadows, he fished it out and smoothed out the wrinkles.

"Well, well, well." There were two pencil sketches— the top one detailed a boat's rudder and fastenings while the bottom one showed the basic arrangement of bolts holding a lead keel in place.

"Interesting." Not positive proof for a court of law, perhaps. But a telling bit of evidence. Cameron tucked it in his pocket, now sure in his own mind that his half brother had been murdered.

In the morning he would ride on to the meeting with Morton and Dudley, who had taken a deadly gamble and believed they held a winning hand.

But the final cards had yet to be played.

Breakfast over, Sophie hurriedly gathered her cloak and bonnet, grateful that Georgiana had agreed to distract Penelope with a flurry of morning chores. With all that was on her mind, she was glad to avoid awkward questions on why she was taking a walk so early in the morning.

"I won't be gone long," she murmured, ducking into the storage pantry for a last word with her confidant-in-intrigue before leaving.

"You are sure that you don't want me to accompany you?" asked Georgiana.

"No need. I'm simply leaving a signal for Cam at the old shepherd's hut." She had decided to share some of the details of the plan with her sister. It seemed only fair—and in truth, Georgiana had proved herself a stalwart ally.

I shall have to stop thinking of her as a child, thought Sophie. *After all, at her age I had already been forced to make momentous life choices…*

"Be careful." Her sister's sharp caution cut off further musings.

"I walk the hills nearly every day. I know where the crumbling parts of the footpath are."

Georgiana didn't smile. "I'm serious."

"Don't take this skullduggery too much to heart, Georgie," she murmured. "It's Cam who is in danger. I can only twiddle my thumbs and pray that he won't come to any harm."

"I have a feeling that Cam can take care of himself these days," replied Georgiana. A smile twitched on her lips. "No need to rescue him from bat-infested caves or foul bogs."

"Oh, lud, that mud *was* evil-smelling." Sophie allowed a fleeting grin at the memory. "You were right—it took a week to wash away the stink."

"It was more like two." Crinkling her nose, Georgiana gathered up a handful of dusting cloths and a bottle of lemon oil. "I had better go and put Pen to work."

Sophie waited a few moments before heading in the opposite direction and letting herself out through the scullery door. Dewdrops glittered in the morning sun, diamond-bright against the green grass. Squinting against the glare, she hurried across the side lawn and made her way out to the lane, wishing that her spirits could soak up a bit of the sparkle.

If only my thoughts weren't so clouded with misgivings. She couldn't help wondering whether Cameron would consider his new position in Society a blessing or a curse. As a youth, he had seethed with fire over the injustice to his mother. But now? He had carved out a niche for himself—admittedly one filled with dark shadows and twisting passageways, but nonetheless made by his own hand. His own spirit.

Perhaps I am wrong to be interfering with his destiny. There was, after all, an old adage about letting sleeping dogs lie…

A marquess had responsibilities. How would Cameron feel about that? Throwing them to the wind whenever he wished to embark on a Pirate adventure would affect the vast estate lands and the numerous tenants.

Her steps slowed as Sophie wondered whether she should turn back and think things over. But the hesitation lasted for only a moment before her own sense of right and wrong pushed her forward.

Cameron had lived in the netherworld of lies too long. The truth, however challenging, must come to light.

"It is not my decision to make," she assured herself. "Cam must come to grips with the future on his own."

Looking up from rutted lane, Sophie saw that she was already passing by Neddy's cottage. The sight of the smoke rising from his forge sent another twinge tugging at her conscience. She still felt a little guilty for manipulating his goodwill. The puzzle lock had been put back without him knowing of her ruse. However, the fact that she had deceived a friend brought a faintly sour taste in her mouth. Especially as it seemed that he still harbored a tendre for her, despite her gentle efforts to discourage his attentions over the past few years.

Swallowing hard, she picked up her pace. The footpath leading up to the hills was just around the bend...

The thick hedgerow, heavy with hawthorn and vines of pale pink wild roses, stirred in the breeze, the rustle of leaves releasing a sweet scent into the air. Filling her lungs with the fragrance, Sophie sought to calm her jangled nerves, so it took a moment to realize that the sound of the swaying branches was growing louder, louder.

Roused from her reveries, she saw that a coach was rattling down the lane. Shading her eyes, she watched it approach, trying to make out any distinguishing marks. The dark horses and black woodwork were unfamiliar, as was the driver. Hat drawn low, the collar of his caped driving coat turned up despite the mildness of the day, he sat hunched on his perch, giving no sign of greeting.

Sophie stepped onto the grassy verge, giving the vehicle ample room to pass by.

The horses, however, came to an abrupt halt.

"Are you in need of directions?" she asked. The fellow had likely lost his way and that would account for his surly mood.

A brusque flick of the whip snapped in answer, the leather lash motioning to the side of the coach.

How odd. As well as horribly rude. Repressing a tart reply, Sophie made her way around the snorting, stomping team.

The brass latch jiggled and the door opened a crack.

"Are you in need of directions?" she repeated, peering into the gloom.

The draperies were drawn over the windows, making the coach's interior dark as Hades. She could just make out a murky silhouette—Hessian boots, caped coat, high-crown hat.

A gentleman. Though one with shoddy manners, reflected Sophie as he edged closer and spoke in a muffled growl through the scarf wrapped around his lower face.

"I'm sorry, sir, you will have to speak up." Perhaps he was ill with a catarrh in his throat. "If you are looking for the main road to Lynn Regis, you have missed the turn." It was easy to mistake the fork in the road back by the river. "If you return to the mill—"

A sudden movement in the iron-gray shadows squeezed her words to a strangled gasp. Blinking in disbelief, Sophie found herself staring down the snout of a pistol.

"Get in the carriage, Miss Lawrance." The words were no longer soft or blurred. "Now."

"I—I don't understand," she stammered.

"Oh, but I think you do." The scarf slowly unwound, revealing the grim face of Lord Dudley. "You may think yourself very clever, but I saw you with that filthy scoundrel Daggett at The Wolf's Lair." He let out a nasty laugh. "For all your prim and proper façade, it seems that you are simply a common slut."

"But..." With her mind reeling, she could muster no argument.

"Get in," ordered Dudley. "Or would you rather that I go on and ask your sisters to join me? The older one is a pretty little morsel."

Sophie climbed into the coach. Her heart was beating so hard that she feared it might crack a rib. "Leave them alone, or..."

"Or what?" he sneered. A rap on the trap signaled the driver to start moving.

"Or you will be sorry." It was, she admitted, a rather buffle-headed threat, but it helped steady her courage.

"It is you who will be sorry if you don't start talking—and fast. I don't know what game you and Daggett are playing," said Dudley. "But I intend to find out."

"I've nothing new to tell you, sir." Why not try to bluff him, she decided. There seemed little to lose. "I know what you want, but I haven't got it. Nor do I have a clue as to where it might be found."

The pistol was now only inches away from her chest. "Then why were you with Daggett?

"Because he, too, is trying to blackmail me into telling him where the blasted paper is," she exclaimed, quickly spinning a lie. "He saw me with you on my first visit to the Lair, and forced me to tell him why. He seems to think that if he obtains the paper before you do, he can sell it to Mr. Morton for a handsome sum."

"You're lying." But a flicker of doubt rippled through his shadowed gaze.

She remained steadfastly silent. *Don't flinch, don't flinch.* Thinking of Cameron and how coolly he dealt with adversity gave her added strength.

"If you aren't in league with him, how do you explain what the two of you were doing upstairs on the pleasure floor of the Lair several nights ago?"

"Quite easily," answered Sophie with a grim laugh. "Because of you, I have nothing left to pay a black-mailer's demand—save for my body."

Dudley frowned, but before he could respond, the coach lurched to a halt.

"Why are we stopping?" she asked.

"You will see in a moment."

She heard footsteps outside and the thud of a bag being tossed in the luggage compartment. Then the latch clicked and the door swung open.

A gasp slipped from her lips as a slash of sunlight cut across a familiar face.

"Make yourself comfortable, Miss Lawrance," said Dudley. "The three of us are going to be taking a little ride."

Chapter Nineteen

"A glass of brandy, Daggett?" Morton held up a crystal decanter. "Or would you prefer a Scottish malt?"

Cameron watched the sunlight flicker through the amber spirits, setting off tiny red-gold sparks. "Brandy," he answered, fingering his earring. He had chosen the replica of Sophie's teardrop pearl as a symbol of poetic justice. What goes around, comes around. "It's so much more civilized, don't you think?"

Morton eyed the jade-green length of silk styled in a perfect Waterfall knot at Cameron's throat and lifted a brow in disdain. "Pray, what do you know of civilized behavior? My sources tell me you don't move within the circles of Polite Society unless your two titled friends put you on a leash and invite you to pad along at their heels."

Cameron let out a low laugh. "True. I make no pretensions of being a gentleman. I am who I am." He paused to accept his drink. "And unlike you, I do not covet another man's skin enough to kill for it."

A dark flush mottled Morton's cheeks. "What are you implying?"

"*Moi?*" Cameron quaffed a long swallow of the brandy

before giving a careless shrug. "Only that I make it my business to keep my ears open to the whispers floating around Town." He lowered his voice, "And trust me, one hears far more interesting things in the stews than one does in your fancy gentlemen's clubs. That's where the real secrets swirl."

Morton's gaze betrayed a spasm of alarm.

"Not that I give a rat's arse for what you have—or haven't—done. Money is the currency of my morality. We have a deal that promises to pay me handsomely." He cocked a salute. "So let us toast to our business partnership. I look forward to both of us getting our just rewards."

"Indeed." Morton's mask of arrogance was back. "Let us hope your reputation for being skilled at thievery is not overrated, Daggett. I will be sadly disappointed if you come up empty-handed."

"As will I." The reply was deliberately cryptic. Shouldering past his host, Cameron strolled to the terrace railing and perched a hip on the smooth stone. "A lovely view," he said, gazing out over the sea. Today its waters were a sparkling blue with naught but a few lazy whitecaps dotting its surface. "I find the ocean appealing, too. It's so unpredictable, which I find interesting."

The clink of crystal indicated that Morton was refilling his glass.

"Are you familiar with the paintings of Mr. Turner?" continued Cameron, seeing that his nattering was annoying his host. "He's very good at capturing the sea's ever-changing moods."

"I didn't invite you here to discuss art, Daggett," snapped Morton. "There is only one piece of paper that I care about and it isn't splashed with paint." He took another hurried gulp of his drink. "Seeing as you suggested this meeting, I pray that you have something worthwhile to tell me about it. Be assured that I would not be hosting you here otherwise."

Flicking a mote of dust from his sleeve, Cameron curled his mouth upward. True, an overnight stay here at Morton's country residence had been part of his plan—a reckless part, perhaps, he conceded, watching his host stalk to the terrace doors and call an order to one of his servants. As Sophie had suggested, a thorough search of the place would have been easy on his own. *In and out, with her father's incriminating document safely in his pocket.*

However, in this case he wished to wield more than stealth as a weapon. In the Peninsular War, he and his fellow Hellhounds had learned from brutal experience that to eliminate the most dangerous enemies, it was best done *mano a mano.* Hand to hand combat. *Oh, I shall not plunge a dagger into their black hearts, but I shall take a very visceral satisfaction in manipulating them into making a fatal mistake.* Once he had drawn out all the details of how they had sabotaged Wolcott's yacht, he would figure out a way to pass the information on to the authorities.

"But of course I have information," he replied after Morton had returned to the terrace. "There is no profit for me in frittering away time."

Morton looked somewhat mollified. "Good."

"But speaking of profit, I must ask for a token of good faith before I subject myself to the dangers of fulfilling your request. Say, a quarter of the money up front. Not that I don't trust you. But in my world, as opposed to yours where the gentlemanly code of honor rules, we prefer to deal in tangible things rather than abstract promises."

"Damn you!" sputtered Morton. "You made no mention of needing money up front."

"I changed my mind." Cameron held out his empty glass. "By the by, that is excellent brandy."

Hands shaking with rage, Morton poured him another measure. "Don't toy with me, Daggett. You don't know whom you are dealing with."

Oh, yes. I do. But the same cannot be said for you.

"Tut, tut. Is that a threat?" Cameron asked, keeping his voice soft as silk. "You could, of course, refuse my demands. However that would leave you dependent on your friend Dudley's prowess. And so far he hasn't shown himself very adept at finding what you want."

A sharp exhale. "You miserable cur of a Hellhound."

"Yes, but I have a keen nose for sniffing out valuables, while Dudley is barking up the wrong tree."

Turning on his heel, Morton began to pace the perimeter of the terrace.

Cameron coolly sipped his brandy, for the moment content to let the varlet stew in his own juices. Time enough later to bring things to a boil.

"How do you expect me to scrape up funds here in Norfolk?" Morton finally asked. "For that, I shall have to return to London." The scuff of his boots on the slate tiles grew more agitated. "That will take time, and with every delay, we lose the advantage." After another few steps he added, "Just before I left Town, I heard rumors that a rival for Wolcott's title was about to crawl out of the woodwork. I would prefer to crush such a pest before he does any damage."

Ebb and flow—like the sea, subterfuge had a natural rhythm of push and shove.

"Yes, I can see where that would be to our advantage," he agreed. "Perhaps we can work out a barter, rather than an exchange of money."

Morton paused in his pacing. "What do you have in mind?"

"I've learned that Dudley possesses a cache of valuable jewels," replied Cameron. "Which he recently won in a card game." He let the information sink in for a moment before adding another untruth. "The Wolf's Lair isn't his only gambling haunt. Did you not know that he plays for high stakes in Seven Dials, at Satan's Cauldron?"

Morton's jaw tightened in reaction to the lie. "He never said anything to me about that."

"Hardly a surprise," drawled Cameron. "Like most opportunists, he wishes to share in your largesse, but is unwilling to part with his own ill-gotten gains."

A muttered oath.

"Seeing as it's his gaming debt that drew me into this affair, it seems only fair that he pay for the chance to be part of your success." Cameron moved to the wrought iron table and helped himself to an Indian cheroot from the cedarwood cigar box. Now that he had sown the seed of dissension, perhaps he could reap some useful information. "After all, what's he really done so far for you?"

"He's had his uses," growled Morton, sounding somewhat defensive. Nobody liked to look like a fool. "He found a document that allowed him to blackmail the Lawrance family—"

Cameron interrupted with a rude sound. "And what does he have to show for such efforts. A few puny trinkets?"

"He also found a clever fellow to make a few little modifications to Wolcott's yacht," said Morton in a low voice.

"That is, I grant you, a worthwhile contribution." He blew out a perfect ring of smoke and watched it float upward and slowly dissolve in the breeze. "Still, he ought to be willing to invest more than talk in ensuring your plans come to fruition. Why should you take all the risk?"

His host's eyes narrowed in thought.

"You know, if I were you, I would make sure I had proof of Dudley's dealings with the yacht." *Keep talking, keep talking—let your own words coil a hangman's noose around your neck.* "That way, you will always hold the winning hand if he ever seeks to doublecross you."

"I know the name of his co-conspirator. That should ensure Dudley's cooperation."

"Perhaps." Cameron edged his voice with skepticism. "Let us see if it's enough to squeeze any gems out of your clutch-fisted friend."

"Dudley is supposed to arrive here shortly," muttered Morton.

"You know, sharing the fellow's name with me might add just enough pressure to make him crack," he suggested. Given a witness, the authorities would have more than just vague suspicions to go on.

"Yes, I see what you mean." Morton appeared to be thinking it over.

Cameron maintained a casual silence, puffing on his cheroot as he watched the wheeling of the herring gulls high overhead.

"Yes," repeated Morton, and added a humorless laugh. "Let us see how he likes being squeezed in a vise of vice, ha, ha, ha."

"Ha, ha, ha," echoed Cameron, his ear cocked for the critical name.

"The fellow is—"

A knock on the glass-paned door caused Morton to stop short. "What is it?" he called, signaling for the servant to join them.

"Forgive me, sir. Lord Dudley has arrived." The man cleared his throat. "And he is not alone."

As hour after hour rolled by, Sophie sat hunched in a corner of the coach, drifting in and out of a troubled sleep. For the first few miles, Dudley had tried to cajole information out of her, but she had refused to speak. She had a feeling he might have resorted to physical force if the third passenger hadn't murmured a halting plea for restraint.

Let him threaten, bluster, or bludgeon—I won't be intimidated by him any longer, she vowed to herself.

Dudley had finally given up and lapsed into a surly silence, save for an occasional ominous growl and smack of a fist to his palm. His companion had also abandoned his attempt to coax her into conversation, and now lay back against the squabs, snoring softly.

Squeezing her eyes shut, she tried to clear the haze of shock from her brain. *I must think clearly—there has to be a way out of this coil...*

But inspiration refused to budge. With the mocking clatter of the wheels echoing in her ears, she lapsed into a fitful doze.

It was Dudley's curt command that roused her. "Get up. We're here."

Her limbs cramped, her head aching, Sophie stumbled as she descended from the coach.

A hand shot out to steady her. "Have a care, Sophie." As Dudley moved off to confer with his driver, the voice dropped a notch. "Don't make things difficult for yourself or your family. Give him what he wants and—"

"And what, Neddy?" She fixed her old friend with a piercing stare. "He will send me home with a pat on the head and a bag of sugarplums to share with my sisters?"

Neddy had the grace to flush. "Dudley has promised me that if you cooperate, no one else will be harmed in this. He's merely helping a friend make sure that what is rightfully his is not stolen from under his nose."

"Rightfully his?" repeated Sophie, aghast at Neddy's reasoning. "Forgive me for parsing the details, but it seems to me that Lord Wolcott's right to the title was never in question."

At that, Neddy's look hardened. "Wolcott was an arrogant, nasty son of a sow."

"True. But that does not mean we have the right to murder anyone we find unpleasant."

"He was a cheat and a liar," responded her friend. "I worked my fingers to the bone, fitting the manor with expensive, impregnable locks, and do you know what he did?" His voice pinched to a shrill note. "He refused to pay me more than a pittance, saying the merchandise was inferior, no matter that I had all the proper receipts. And it's not only me who will be better off—a great many people in Terrington will have better lives with a new marquess overseeing the lands."

One who is a conniving murderer?

Sophie swallowed a sarcastic retort, deciding it would be better to learn all she could about the sordid scheme. "Tell me," she said softly, "How did you come to be drawn into all this?"

"Dudley and Morton were visiting at the manor while I was working there. They complimented my skills," he said, "and appreciated my talents—far more so than the high and mighty marquess. They even brought me to London, and arranged for me to install locks on the Duke of Linonia's townhouse, for which I was paid quite handsomely."

Sophie heaved a silent sigh, realizing how easy it had been for the two gentlemen of the *ton* to seduce her old friend. He toiled in anonymity, a plain, ordinary fellow with little in the way of looks, charm, or imagination to distinguish himself.

Why, even I have rejected him.

But her twinge of remorse quickly faded on recalling that six people—the marquess and his family along with three of their crew—were buried in a watery grave because Neddy had let himself be manipulated.

"They even took me to the Café Royal, where I sat with the Quality and drank champagne," went on Neddy. "And they are paying me handsomely. Enough to take a bride and live very comfortably."

Equal measures of pity and disgust bubbled up inside her. She had known him all her life, and yet the man before her was a total stranger.

"Sophie…" His voice turned more urgent as the crunch of gravel indicated that Morton was returning. "I can help you, but only if you heed my advice and do as Dudley asks."

"I can't," she whispered, feeling no compunction about lying through her teeth. "Because I don't have what he wants."

Neddy had no chance to answer, for Dudley rounded the rear of the coach, pistol still in hand, and took rough hold of her arm. "Come along. Let us see if Morton can loosen your tongue."

I am at Morton's country house? A chill spiked through her.

A servant led the way through a gloomy entrance hall dominated by dark wood paneling and gold-framed paintings of hunting scenes. Averting her eyes from the bloodied stag, Sophie sought to control her skittering pulse. If Cameron was here...

Then we are in hot water.

Or perhaps boiling oil, she added with an inward grimace. Thank God she had a few moments of warning to think... to think...

"Move." Dudley punctuated his growled order by pressing the steel gun barrel against her spine.

Up ahead, at the end of the corridor, she saw a stirring of sunlight through the half-open French doors. The sound of the sea—or was it just the thrumming of her pulse—rose up in a wave to fill her ears, drowning out all but a faint buzz of voices.

Sophie closed her eyes for an instant, willing herself to stay calm.

"What the devil is this?" An unfamiliar voice, most likely that of Morton. "Damnation, explain yourself, Dudley."

"Actually why don't we let that guttersnipe Daggett and his slut do the talking."

Improvise, improvise. It was important to let Cameron know as much as possible about what Dudley knew.

She turned to face Dudley, needing to draw little on acting ability to appear agitated. "I am not, as you put it, his slut. Yes, I was forced to endure his advances at The Wolf's Lair, but only because he, too, was blackmailing me."

Darting a daggered look at Cameron, who was puffing nonchalantly on a vile-smelling cheroot, she added. "Men! To the Devil with the lot of you! I'm being bullied and threatened for information that I don't possess. Nor, for that matter, is there any certainty that it actually exists."

Neddy was first to speak up. "I believe her!" he said, leaping to her defense. "Sophie is no slut."

"Shut up," snapped Dudley. The pistol pointed for a moment at Neddy's chest before drawing a bead on Cameron. "So, what do you have to say for yourself, Daggett?"

"About what?" drawled Cameron, though his mouth had gone dry as dust on seeing Sophie shoved out onto the terrace.

"They are diddling us, Morton," snarled Dudley. "After you left The Wolf's Lair, I went upstairs for a tup and who did I happen to spot in one of the rooms?" The pistol cut an obscene little gesture. "This Hellhound and his she-bitch engaged in a bit of slap and tickle. So I can't help but wonder—what game are they playing?"

Morton's jaw tightened. "Well, Daggett?"

"Lord Dudley isn't the only one who likes to peep at private encounters in the Lair," he replied. "I spied on an earlier encounter between him and Miss Lawrance, and decided there was money to be made from whatever trouble was afoot." He flicked a bit of ash from the glowing tip of his cheroot. "Alas, Miss Lawrance had nothing of value to trade, save for her rather charming body. And as I am not averse to pleasures of the flesh—especially when they come for free—I took my pound of flesh, so to speak."

A growl rumbled in Neddy's throat.

"I must say there is something rather titillating about deflowering an Innocent in a brothel." Cameron waggled a wolfish grin at Sophie. "And seeing as you appeared to enjoy the experience, perhaps we can do it again—"

Emitting an inarticulate roar, Neddy launched his beefy bulk forward, his huge hands grabbing for Cameron's throat.

Sidestepping the charge with a deft spin, he smashed his knee into Neddy's groin. "It seems that you have another admirer, Miss Lawrance," he remarked as the blacksmith dropped to the slates, his voice now pitched to a whimpering moan. "But apparently he was more of a gentleman than I."

Morton's face relaxed slightly. "You are a right bastard, aren't you, Daggett?"

"A fact that ought to please you," responded Cameron coolly. He offered a hand to the still-groaning Neddy. "No hard feelings, Wadsworth. Had I known you had a tendre for the gel, I would have tempered my tongue."

"Bastard," hissed Neddy through his teeth as he took the proffered help and hauled himself to his feet. Arms locked together, the two of them stood face to face for a long moment.

A tactical mistake, realized Cameron, watching the other man's eyes narrow to a slitted stare.

"Bastard," repeated Neddy, recognition dawning on his blunt-cut features. "Why, it's Cam Fanning—who we all speculated was the old Wolcott's by-blow." Letting out a grim laugh, he turned to Morton and Dudley. "His name isn't Daggett, it's Fanning. He's Sophie's old sweetheart—and the man you are hunting."

Cameron didn't wait for the pair's reaction. Shoving Neddy hard into Dudley, he darted forward and clipped Morton with a solid punch to the jaw.

Seeing the three men down and dazed, he seized Sophie's hand and hustled her to the terrace railing.

"Hold on tight, Sunbeam," he murmured, swinging her up into his arms. "Time to fly."

Chapter Twenty

Sophie clung to Cameron's shoulders, and for a moment, the solid shape and strength of him melted the ice-cold terror from her bones.

He was alive and well—nothing else mattered, she thought as they hit the ground with a jarring thud.

Rolling to his feet, he grabbed her hand and set off at a dead run.

Safety—safety lay just a few swift, sure strides ahead.

But an instant later, that illusion was shattered by the crack of a pistol shot.

"Cam!" Sophie screamed as he stumbled and nearly lost his footing on the steep path leading down the wooded slope. She ducked, branches whipping against her cheeks, and spotted an ugly gash in his right boot just below the knee, the torn leather stained with crimson.

"Cam!"

"It's just a scratch, sweeting," he said through gritted teeth. Keeping hold of her hand, he lurched into the cover of the trees. "This way—if we can make our way over the top of the hill, we can circle back to the stables."

Briars snagged at her skirts, roots tripped up her heavy walking shoes. Gasping for breath, Sophie tried to shake off his grip. She hadn't eaten since dawn and with her limbs still badly cramped from the coach ride, she found that her strength was fast ebbing.

"Go!" she pleaded. "Go on without me."

He answered with an oath.

"Please, Cam. They will kill you if they catch you. But I—I won't come to any harm."

"Leave you to their mercy?" He let out a mirthless laugh as he swung her around a fallen tree. "You've far too sunny a view of human nature, Sophie. These men are utterly ruthless and will stop at nothing—*nothing*—to achieve their goals."

Another shot rang out.

"Keep moving," urged Cameron, slowing his pace to push and pull her through the tangled brush.

Sophie scrambled to keep up with him. Her lungs were burning, her legs were aching.

"Cam…" Try as she might, she couldn't seem to make herself move any faster.

Twisting around, he murmured another encouragement. "That's it, Sunbeam. I've got your hand, and I won't let go."

Her breath now coming in ragged gasps, Sophie looked up to argue.

"*Cam!*"

Her warning scream came a split second too late.

The oak branch smashed into the side of Cameron's head with a sickening thud.

"Serves him bloody right." Neddy dropped the make-shift weapon and stared down in grim satisfaction at

Cameron's crumpled form. "The impudent whelp. Even when we were bantlings, Fanning was always clinging to your skirts, looking to pull himself above his station in life." Lifting his gaze, her erstwhile friend smiled. "Surely you see now that he's naught but a vile weasel. He used you! Ruined you!"

Sinking to her knees, Sophie gently cradled Cameron's head in her lap. "Lord have mercy."

"Oh, don't despair, Sophie—your fall from grace hasn't changed my feelings!" assured Neddy. "I'll have you anyway, and with the money I earn from my work here, we'll have enough for a cozy, comfortable life together."

Had thwarted desire had twisted his mind free from the linchpins of sanity?

"Lord have mercy not on *my* soul, Neddy, but on yours!" she rasped. Tears were trickling down her cheeks. "I thought you were a friend, but in truth, you've turned into a monster."

"Sophie!"

Ignoring the plea, she touched the purpling bruise, and expelled a sigh on feeling Cameron stir beneath her trembling fingertips. "Oh, thank God. He's alive."

"But not for long." Dead leaves crackling under his boots, Morton slithered down the slope from the shortcut trail hidden by the trees. "Well done, Wadsworth. Get him to his feet and drag him back to the house." He twined his fingers roughly in Sophie's loosely coiled hair. "While you—you'll come with me."

"W-what are you planning to do?" asked Neddy.

"Figure out the best way to dispose of these two troublemakers." A sneering smile. "Actually I owe Dudley an apology. It was a brilliant idea to bring Miss Lawrance here. There is an old adage about killing two birds with one stone."

"Just as there is one about he who laughs last laughs best," whispered Sophie.

He tightened his grip and yanked back, sending a jolt of pain through her scalp. "Shut your mouth."

"I won't allow you to hurt Sophie," said Neddy, glowering at Morton. "Lord Dudley promised that she would be safe from harm."

Dudley, who had been trailing the flight from the terrace, pushed through the brush and came to an out-of-breath halt. "So I did, so I did. And be assured that my friend will be bound by my word."

Morton locked eyes with his cohort for a moment and then gave a shrug. "Yes, of course, you're right. A promise is a promise."

Looking mollified, Neddy heaved Cameron to his feet and staggered off.

Promises, promises.

Sophie was not so easily deceived. She had seen the flicker of a smirk tug at Morton's lips just before he had spoken. Well, vipers weren't the only ones who could speak with forked tongues. Cameron claimed that the key to survival was staying alone and aloof. *Every man for himself.* However, she had a different strategy—she was going to fight with every weapon she had in order to keep him alive.

Pray God that my new sleight of hand has rubbed off on my tongue.

"You know, Cameron is not without high-placed friends. Lord Killingworth and Lord Haddan are aware of his plans to come here," she warned. "They will not allow his murder to be swept under the rug, as it were."

Forcing her up, Morton released his hold and stepped back a pace. "They would have to prove it murder," he retorted, but the tiny spasm in his sneer did not echo the same bravado.

"Three bodies will be rather difficult to explain as an accident," she replied, sure that they intended to add Neddy to any unmarked grave. "Especially after what happened to the marquess and his family."

"Perhaps," countered Dudley. "But considering the stakes, it's well worth taking a gamble."

"And yet," said Sophie coolly, "Cameron tells me you aren't very good at playing games of chance."

Dudley raised a hand to strike her, but Morton held him back. "Daggett—or Fanning—hasn't played his cards very well, either. I can't help but wonder why he bothered coming here. The dangers are obvious and I cannot see what he hoped to gain."

"The answer is simple. He came to find the paper you have that implicates my father in a crime," said Sophie.

"You expect us to believe that he's acting out of the goodness of his heart?" exclaimed Dudley. "Ha! You have no money."

"No." She smiled. "But I had a rather valuable paper to offer him in exchange."

Dudley's pistol reappeared from inside his coat pocket. "Where—"

"Don't bother with threats." Sophie took a tiny steadying breath and launched into her bluff. "It's too late for that. I've already given the document to him, and he's passed it to his friend Lord Haddan, to hold for safekeeping until our bargain is complete."

Her claim caused the two men to lock eyes.

"She may be telling the truth," muttered Dudley. "Rumors were floating around the clubs that Wolcott's heir was about to step forward."

Sophie hurried to press her advantage. "You're a clever man, Morton—surely you see that you can't win," she said. "Why not cut your losses and save your skin? Let us go, and flee to the Continent before any questions can be raised about Wolcott's death. Given the lack of evidence, you'll likely get away with that crime." She paused to let the suggestion sink in. "However, if the new marquess is found dead, too, do you really think you will escape justice?"

She saw Dudley's brows momentarily pinch together. "Perhaps—"

"Quiet!" Morton's face tightened, his cheekbones looking sharp as knifeblades beneath the pale skin.

Sophie waited, feeling the tension crackling through the air.

"Move," he said abruptly, giving her a hard shove. To Dudley he added, "They have been clever. But all is not lost. I've got an idea."

"Ouch." Cameron winced as Sophie dabbed the wet scrap of fabric to his lacerated temple.

"Lie still. This cut has to be cleaned." She tore another strip from her skirts. "Then I must tend to your leg. Thank God it's only a nick. Once it's bandaged, you should feel better."

"Yes, well, why don't we order up some lobster patties

and champagne so we can be truly comfortable," he quipped.

She looked down at his iron-shackled wrists and chuffed a sigh. "At least I convinced them not to put manacles on your ankles."

"You were," he conceded, "very persuasive."

"Would that I could have persuaded *you* to do my bidding. You should have run when you had the chance."

"And leave a damsel to the mercy of vile villains and their clanking chains and dark dungeons?" They were, in fact, locked in a dank cellar room with only a single guttering lantern for light. "God forbid. Georgiana and Penelope would never have let me hear the last of it." He winced again. "Not that my attempt at nobility did much good. Neddy Wadsworth always was a hulking brute, but he's now even more like a Highland bull—a flea-sized brain and a elephant-sized wallop."

"This is no jesting matter, Cam," said Sophie.

"I know, Sunbeam." His gut had been twisted in knots since seeing her in Dudley's clutches. "But as soon as you reach in my boot and retrieve my lockpick, I'll have myself out of these irons and our prison door open."

She felt gingerly at the torn leather. "It's not here—it must have fallen out during the chase."

"Damn." His gaze skimmed over the stone floor and walls. Nothing, save for the puddles of brackish water left by the constant *drip, drip, drip* from the ceiling.

"But no harm done." Flipping up her skirts, Sophie began to feel along one of the seams. "I brought along a spare."

Torn between amusement and guilt, Cameron watched as she started to ease a slim length of steel from the hidden pocket. "I've introduced you to a number of shockingly evil habits."

"Indeed. You've been a *very* bad influence on me," answered Sophie, not looking up from the task. "Just a few months ago, I would never have dreamed of kissing a mysterious pirate, or breaking into a lordly estate, or drinking fire-kissed brandy."

He wished he could see her eyes.

"And I never, *ever* would have made wild, passionate love in an exotic pleasure room of London's most notorious brothel."

Yet another sin on my slate. Cameron gave an inward wince. The Almighty must be running out of room to record the litany of his misdeeds.

"This is no jesting matter, Sophie." He found himself throwing her earlier reproof back at her. "Not only have I corrupted you, but I've put your life in danger." His voice tightened in self-disgust "If I were truly a gentleman—"

"Actually, you are."

"I beg your pardon?" The wet stone and uneven angles of the roughhewn space were beginning to impart an oddly distorted echo to their words.

"Actually you are," repeated Sophie. "A gentleman, that is." Shadows yawed and pitched over the rough stone. "I found the proof."

Cameron opened his mouth, but found he couldn't think of anything suitably sardonic to say. "Oh" seemed to be the only sound he could muster.

Struggling up to a sitting position, he tried to discern her expression through the harshly drawn patterns of murk and glare.

"It was in an old cabinet in Papa's study," she went

on. "One that hadn't been opened in years because the key had been lost. I suppose it was the lesson on locks that stirred a vague memory, and then the other evening, I happened to be in the room..." The corners of her mouth tweaked up. "So my recently acquired bad habits have actually resulted in some good."

He still could not find his voice. Strange, but having lived his whole life in doubt, the sudden certainty felt oddly unreal.

"There was a rather rambling note from your father to mine attached to the document." Sophie paused to rinse her rag in the small bowl that their captors had provided. "It wasn't very clear in explaining the details of his marriage to your mother, save to say it took place on the isle of Madeira."

"You actually found the proof?" Cameron was feeling a little stunned by the revelation.

"Yes. Ironically enough, I was going to place a signal at the hut that I needed to see you when Dudley abducted me."

"Irony seems to have played a great role in my life." He drew in a harsh breath. "Or perhaps I should call it farce."

Sophie shook her head. "It was an unfortunate twist of fate that had such an important exchange take place between two men whose minds were not quite razor-sharp." She exhaled a sigh. "I remember my mother saying that father's attention was already wandering in those days—he was always unworldly and never remembered the important things. And the letter that your father wrote makes it clear that illness had fuzzed his thoughts. Apparently, he was concerned about your half brother's reaction to the marriage, and worried about your mother's reception. But I wonder why he did not send the document to Mr. Griggs."

"I don't know," said Cameron softly. "Griggs was equally puzzled as to why he never had any word from my father. He did say he always wondered whether your father had received any missive. It seems they were friends and met often to talk about Greek art and philosophy." He made a wry face. "If only they had both not become lost in abstraction."

"If only my mother had come across the correspondence, she would have known to forward it on to the marquess's man of affairs," mused Sophie. "But instead, Papa put it away in his cabinet, along with a stack of mundane bookkeeping records—and there it lay forgotten."

"There are so many 'if only' moments in this whole cursed affair," said Cameron. "If only my father had not been so ill. If only my half brother had not been so proud. If only my mother had not been so timid..."

"I confess, I have always wondered why your mother did not speak out and demand that you be acknowledged as the old marquess's rightful child."

"You remember Mama—she was exceedingly sweet, but she was afraid of her own shadow." A grimace pulled at his lips. "I sometimes wonder if that is why I was born with enough recklessness for two people."

Sophie allowed a fleeting smile.

"It was partly her background, I suppose. She was from a poor family," Cameron went on, the explanation seeming to be as much for himself as for her. "And she feared that she would never have been believed by highborn Society. They had left the ship in Madeira and had taken up residence there, for my father had found the climate eased the inflammation in his lungs. His death was rather sudden, and so when Mama first returned to England, alone and pregnant, she went to live with her uncle, who warned her she might be prosecuted for false claims if she raised a ruckus. So she lived quietly as a widow with an infant son, content with a modest life until her uncle passed away, leaving us penniless."

Cameron's lips thinned to a momentary pinch. "It's then, when I was seven, that we moved to Terrington, where she threw herself on my half brother's mercy. It seems he wanted to send her away with a flea in her ear, but Griggs intervened and forced him to provide a cottage and a small stipend. Word was put out that we were poor relations—which is what I, too, believed." A quiver of a pause. "As you know, it wasn't until I was fifteen that she let slip the truth. If only she had…"

"Let us not dwell on all the past mistakes," said Sophie decisively. "Whatever the old wrongs, you can make them right." The lantern's lone flame caught a momentary flutter of emotion beneath her downcast lashes. "Better late than never."

Could that possibly be an oblique hint that not all was lost between them? He dared not let hope flare to life. A sidelong glance at the present surroundings was enough to dampen any romantic notions.

At least there were no rats…so far.

"Speaking of timing, once we remove the manacles from your wrists and open this dreadful door, have you a plan for escape?"

Wrenched back from his musings, Cameron flexed his shoulders. "In situations like this, it's a waste of time to bother making much of a plan. Things never go as you expect, so it's best to simply improvise."

"Improvise," said Sophie. "I'm becoming rather familiar with that word."

"Sorry," he muttered. "I've turned your whole steady, sensible world on its ear."

"Or some other, more intimate part of my anatomy," she responded, a sweetly pink blush suffusing her cheeks. "Don't say you are sorry, Cam—I'm not. Yes, my life has been tumbling in topsy-turvy somersaults of late. But it's been exhilarating. I feel so . . . alive."

"I'd like to keep it that way," he said, feeling his chest clench as he watched the oily flame illuminate her smile. *Sophie—she had always been the light of his life.* "Forget about my leg and let's get to work on the dratted manacles. This particular model requires a hard push upward once you insert the tip of the picklock between the first two levers."

She inserted the steel tip into the keyhole and gave a little jiggle. "You appear awfully familiar with metal restraints."

"Having escaped from the gaols of six different European principalities, I consider myself somewhat of an authority on the subject . . . Yes, yes, that's the spot, Sunbeam, but you have to press down harder." Cameron cocked an ear. "Harder."

The manacle finally released with a reluctant rasp.

"Hand me the picklock."

Sophie passed it over, but rather than remove the other iron bracelet, he tucked the tool into his undamaged boot.

"Why?" she asked.

"Options, Sunbeam, it gives us options. There is a

crafty Chinese fellow who has written a book on the art of warfare, and in it, he stresses that the element of surprise is a very effective weapon."

The echo of the assertion was suddenly amplified by the tramp of footsteps descending the spiraling cellar stairs.

Cameron quickly eased the manacle back in place around his wrist as a key rattled in the door's lock.

"Stand back," ordered Morton, before kicking the portal open. He entered the space, a pistol in each hand, followed by Dudley and Neddy.

Three opponents, two weapons, and little room to maneuver. He decided to wait and see what his captors had in mind. A slight shift of his body allowed him to press his knee to Sophie's thigh.

She gave a tiny nod, acknowledging the subtle signal.

"What a touching tableau," sneered Dudley. "The loyal maiden comforting her lover's last hours of life." Darting a malicious glance at Neddy, he let out a nasty cackle. "See, what did I tell you, Wadsworth? Women aren't worth mooning over. At heart they are naught but sluts."

Neddy wheeled around, his big head down and swinging from side to side as if he were a bull who had just been prodded with a red-hot iron. "Sophie isn't a slut."

"Of course she is," taunted Dudley. "Slut. Wagtail. Slattern. Ha, ha, ha."

"Quiet—both of you!" ordered Morton.

Seeing the cooperation between the co-conspirators was beginning to unravel, Cameron was quick to add his own razored words. "You don't really think that these two toffs ever intended for you to live happily ever after with Sophie, do you, Neddy? More likely they're setting up a scenario where you will take the blame for their crimes."

"Shut your mouth, Daggett!" cried Morton, his voice perilously close to a shout. "Get up." The dual shadows of the pistols shimmied across the waterstained wall. "You, too, Miss Lawrance."

"Actually, I'm quite comfortable where I am," drawled Cameron. "Though an extra blanket or two would be welcome. And perhaps a bottle of champagne, seeing as the water tastes a trifle foul."

"Let us shoot him now," growled Dudley, shifting his hand to his coat pocket. "And be done with it."

"Silence!" roared Morton as he cocked both of his weapons. "The next one to make a sound will get a bullet in the brain."

Seeing the wavering of the gun barrels was growing even more erratic, Cameron decided that he had pushed his captors far enough. Bowing his head in submission, he kept quiet.

To her credit, Sophie had not panicked during the exchange. No tears, no wailing. Just like their childhood adventures, where she had always been brave, resourceful. Intrepid to the bone.

I will get her out of this mortal peril, he promised himself.

And then…

"Get up, Daggett." Satisfied that he had reasserted his command over the situation, Morton relaxed his grip on the pistols. "Slowly. Any trouble and Miss Lawrance will be the one to suffer."

Levering to his feet, Cameron nodded in submission. "Meek as a mouse, that's me."

"Now you, too, Miss Lawrance."

"I still say we should put a bullet in his mangy hide," muttered Dudley. "The sea swallows a body without leaving a trace."

"That is why you should leave the thinking to me," snapped Morton. "It does no good for him to simply disappear—the Wolcott title and fortune could be wrapped up in legalities for years." His pale lips stretched to a humorless smile. "No, no, I've got a better plan."

"Do you?" murmured Cameron, as he slowly limped past him. "You had better pray so. For so far, your efforts haven't been overly impressive."

A shove propelled him through the doorway. "Keep moving," snarled Dudley.

"Take them to the coach, Wadsworth," ordered Morton. "Dudley and I will be along in a moment."

"So this is where our fellow Hellhound cut his teeth?" Shading his eyes from the bright sun, Connor reined his mount to a halt and slowly surveyed the craggy hills and wind-ruffled meadows that tumbled down to the sea.

"Yes, the town of Terrington lies over the next rise," replied Gryff.

"I confess, I'm a bit disappointed. I rather liked thinking of Cam as some exotic changeling, a puff of colorful smoke rather than an ordinary flesh-and-blood member of the human race."

"Ha, ha, ha," chuckled Gryff. "I daresay that he'll be forced to make a great many transformations in the coming days, though it's highly doubtful that he'll ever turn into a bland, boring shade of gray."

"Cam a lord? It still boggles the mind," said Connor. "God help the peerage."

"It's survived us, so I imagine that it can tolerate Cam's eccentricities. Besides, I think Miss Lawrance will be a steadying influence on him."

"It's hard to picture him putting his paw in the parson's mousetrap."

Another chuckle. "Stranger things have happened."

Connor allowed a small smile. "Actually, I take umbrage at that. Cam's foibles are far stranger than mine."

"Let's just say that none of us can claim to be a paragon of propriety."

Gryff shifted in his saddle. "According to the innkeeper at our last stop, the Lawrance cottage is nestled in a small hamlet about a half mile ahead. Let's pay a call and see if there is any word of what our friend is up to."

A short ride brought them to a narrow road, its high hedgerows twined with wild roses. Taking a turn down its winding way, they continued on at a leisurely trot until they spotted a rambling whitewashed cottage tucked behind a stand of apple trees.

"Good day, Miss Georgiana," called Gryff, immediately recognizing the willowy young lady who had just come through the garden gate and was hurrying toward the lane. "We were passing through the area . . ."

She was now close enough for him to see her face.

"Is something amiss?" he asked tersely.

"I . . . I . . ." She hesitated, her eyes clouding with confusion. "I am not certain that I should say anything until my uncle and aunt arrive, milord." Her lips trembled. "God willing, they should be arriving this afternoon."

Her words drew a frown to Gryff's face. "I applaud your caution, Miss Georgiana. But if there is any sort of trouble, you must trust that we can help."

"The fact is," added Connor, "we are in the area because we think Mr. Daggett may have got himself in a dangerous situation. If perchance, your sister has also become involved—"

At the mention of Sophie, her resolve suddenly crumbled. "Shesbeenabducted."

"Slow down, Miss Georgiana," counseled Connor, "Take a deep breath and start from the beginning."

Several quick inhales seemed to calm her nerves. "Sophie has been abducted."

"When?" demanded Connor.

"Y-yesterday."

"Did you see who did it?" asked Gryff quickly.

Georgiana bit her lip. "Not precisely. That is, I saw a large traveling coach stop—it was mostly black, with claret-colored wheels and trim—and a man with a pistol ordered her to get inside." Another ragged breath. "I had followed her because I knew she was going to leave a signal for Cam—we had discovered something important—"

"Miss Georgiana," began Gryff.

"But that's not all," she peltered on. "The coach then stopped at Neddy Wadsworth's cottage and Neddy got in, too."

Connor frowned. "Who, pray tell, is Neddy?"

"He's the local blacksmith and...and he's been sweet on Sophie for years, though she turned down his proposal of marriage."

"I think," said Gryff to his friend, "that we had better ride like the wind to Holbeach. I know—"

The thud of fast-approaching hoofbeats caused him to cut off. Easing a hand to the satchel tied at the back of his saddle, he drew a cavalry pistol and slipped it inside his coat.

Connor did the same.

"Aunt Hermione! Uncle Edward!" Georgiana let out a sigh of relief as a carriage rumbled into view. "I sent immediate word to my aunt and uncle of what happened," she explained. "But until they arrived, I thought it best not to tell anyone else. Sophie warned me to be careful."

"That was very sensible, Miss Georgiana," said Gryff. He and Connor remained silent while Georgiana rushed through a tearful greeting and a more detailed account of all that had happened. It was only when her uncle looked around, face grim with worry, that he introduced himself and offered his own explanation.

"We're here because we have reason to suspect that our friend Daggett may be in trouble, too."

"And we've an idea of where to look—for both him and your niece," added Connor. "Never fear, we shall find them and bring them back unharmed."

"While you wait here, we will head to the Wash," began Gryff.

"With all due respect, milord, we're coming with you," interrupted Hermione. "And that's flat."

"Indeed," echoed her husband.

Gryff frowned. "But..."

"Really, sir. You might have need of a traveling coach," argued Georgiana. "Or someone to coordinate messages, or to handle...any number of useful tasks."

"We shall not get in your way," promised Edward. "Sophie and her sisters are as dear to us as daughters. Surely you must understand why we feel compelled to be close to the action."

"There is an inn near Holbeach," murmured Connor. "Spotted Dick and his ring of smugglers have used it on occasion."

"Ah well—the more, the merrier, I suppose," quipped Gryff, giving in with a wry grimace. "I can see that arguing will only waste precious time. We'll ride on ahead, and rendezvous with you at the inn after we have had a chance to look around. With luck, we shall be returning with Miss Lawrance."

Gathering his reins, he turned his stallion to the road. "Come, Connor. Let us show these miscreants that the Hellhounds still have some teeth."

Chapter Twenty-One

Sophie gratefully accepted a slab of bread and cheese from Neddy as they waited inside the coach.

"I ought to let *you* starve, you miserable bastard," he muttered before grudgingly handing Cameron a share.

"I shall remember your kindness when I am lord of the manor," replied Cameron cheerfully. "That is, if Morton lets you live." Metal rasped against metal as he lifted his manacled hands to take a bite of cheddar. "Which is highly doubtful. Now that you've helped them with their dirty deeds, you are of no further use to them."

"Cam is right," said Sophie. "These men have used you cruelly, Neddy, and made you carry out a horrible act." Seeing his face pinch, she pressed on. "An innocent woman and innocent child were on that yacht."

"I—I didn't know that," he whispered. "I swear."

"When the authorities hear of how you have been manipulated, they will show some leniency," she replied. "Won't they, Cam?"

"I will do what I can for you, Wadsworth," he answered. "I have some influential friends who will help as well." He swallowed the last bite of his food. "And unlike your present cohorts, I honor my promises."

The coach gave a slight lurch as the driver climbed up to his perch.

"Think about it," murmured Cameron, amid the creak of harness leather and stomping of hooves.

A moment later, Morton and Dudley climbed inside. Shoving Cameron to the middle of the seat, they each took a place on either side of him.

"You can sit next to your slut," said Dudley to Neddy.

Glowering, the blacksmith did as he was told.

"Well, well, isn't this a jolly little group," remarked Cameron as a crack of the whip set the team in motion. "Perhaps we can stop and enjoy a picnic overlooking the sea?"

"Only if I can serve your head on a platter," retorted Dudley.

Sophie tried to catch Cameron's eye, worried that his sarcasm might push one of their captors over the edge. As it was, he was dancing on a razorblade. One small slip and he might find himself sliced into mincemeat.

Her gaze could not penetrate the deep gloom. All she could see was the dark tangle of his hair and a tiny glimmer of pearl-white light. He was wearing the replica of her mother's earring, she realized. *A talisman?* A beacon of hope, even though things looked awfully black?

Clinging to the remembered warmth of Cameron's smile when he called her "Sunbeam," Sophie leaned back against the squabs. *Patience, patience.* And perseverance. Cameron would likely leap into action when she least expected it, and she must be ready to move with him.

The rocking motion of the coach, however, made it

difficult to stay alert. She found herself drifting in and out of fitful dreams... *Georgiana and Penelope frantic with worry... Sara Hawkins of The Wolf's Lair wagging a chiding finger... the Devil chortling and beckoning her to join him in eternal hellfire...*

She awoke with a start as the coach jolted to a halt.

"Keep watch on the prisoners," said Morton to Dudley and Neddy. "We won't be stopping long. I need to retrieve something from the boathouse, then we'll be on our way."

She saw Cameron crane his neck to dart a look through the narrow gap in the window draperies.

"By the by," Morton added as he reached for the door latch. "Do you wish to know how you are going to meet your demise?"

Dudley gave a nasty laugh.

"Let us just say that carriage accidents are not uncommon on the steep northern roads heading to Scotland."

"Good drivers are rare as hen's teeth," said Cameron. "That is why I prefer other modes of transportation."

"What a pity for you that the choice is not yours to make." With that parting shot, Morton climbed out and let the door fall shut behind him.

Cameron waited a few long moments before half-turning in his seat. "Actually, I've decided that it is." A quick flick freed his wrist from the unlocked manacle. A second swift motion of his other hand whipped the dangling iron hard into Dudley's forehead. Stunned, he slumped back on his spine, his pistol slipping away and falling to the floorboards.

Sophie kicked it out of Neddy's reach.

"Come, Sunbeam. It's time to take our leave." He looked at Neddy, who had not yet moved a muscle.

"Don't make me fight you, too, Wadsworth. I'll crack your skull, but I would rather not have to waste the time."

Neddy dropped his gaze to the floorboards.

"Thank you—I won't forget it."

"Nor will I," added Sophie, pausing for a last look at her old friend's downcast face before following Cameron out the door.

"I don't think that we can outrun them," she warned, stumbling over the rocky ground.

"Agreed." He ducked low and took shelter behind one of the storage sheds. "Follow me."

Sophie sucked in a sharp breath as he set off in the direction of the sea. "I hope you aren't planning for us to *swim*," she muttered. "My blood still runs cold thinking of the time you had us dive into the River Ouse to escape Squire Coxe's wrath."

"The stolen apples were well worth it." Cameron paused for a peek around the corner of the building.

"Speak for yourself," she muttered.

"Swimming won't be necessary—save as a last resort." He gestured at the dock. "We're simply going to sail out of trouble."

Two dauntingly tall masts were silhouetted against the gray-clouded sky. "You know how to handle such a large vessel?" she asked, thinking of the small rowing skiffs they had rigged with old sheets when they were children.

Cameron winked. "But of course. I'm a pirate, remember?" Taking her hand, he zigzagged through the trees and cut across to the salt-streaked pilings. "And you, my love, are a hard-won treasure I don't intend to part with."

Love? Screeching gulls, thrumming rigging, gusting wind—the sound had surely not come from Cameron's lips, thought Sophie as he lowered her into the cockpit of the racing sloop. *Love?* Love was too soft a sentiment for a swashbuckling pirate. He had most likely dallied with exotic princesses, danced with alluring beauties, dined with luscious courtesans.

How could she hold a candle to such excitement? *I am simply Sophie.*

"Sophie!" A heavy manila rope, slimy with smelly seaweed, landed in her lap. "Stop woolgathering and untie the stern line!" called Cameron. "And be ready to hoist the mainsail when I give the word." After swearing like a stevedore as the swinging manacle clipped his jaw, he added, "I'll take the tiller once I push us free of the dock."

The sharp *crack* of a gunshot scattered the flock of seabirds. Sophie cringed, but kept working at the knotted lines. "Please hurry," she called to Cameron, fearful that in the next instant a pelter of footsteps would come pounding along the slatted walkway.

Barnacles scraped against the sloop's side as he maneuvered the bow out into the ebbing tide. A last mighty push, and he leapt onto the stern, just as the vessel floated away from the pilings.

Grasping the tiller, he gave a jaunty salute. "Haul up the sail, Sunbeam and let us set a course for wherever the wind will take us."

With the waves rising and the gusts growing stronger, Sophie had no time for reflection as she scrambled to carry out Cameron's barked order. An ominous line of stormclouds was hovering on the horizon, their dark, pewter-gray color smothering the slanting light of the setting sun.

"It looks like a squall is heading this way," she called, feeling the salt spray sting her face as she turned.

Cameron nodded grimly. "Worse than a squall, I fear." He, too, cast a glance over his shoulder. "But don't worry. I wasn't jesting when I said I was a pirate. After leaving Terrington, I spent quite a bit of time sailing the seven seas with a band of smugglers, so I know how to handle a ship in a storm."

Grasping the shrouds for support, Sophie stood for a moment and squinted into the gloom. Fog was drifting in wispy tendrils over the white-capped waters, blurring the fast-receding shoreline. At least the only enemy they faced now was the weather, she mused. "We are safe from pursuit..." A pale flicker in the scudding shadows made her pause. "Aren't we?"

He didn't answer.

"Cam?"

"Go below," he said calmly, "and see if you can find the sloop's charts. They will likely be stowed near the binnacled table."

Sophie hurried to do his bidding. Locating the oilskin bag, she quickly returned to the cockpit.

"Can you find one with the town 'Wrangle' marked on it and spread it out on the bench?" Cameron had to raise his voice to be heard over the whistle of the wind through the rigging.

"Here." Sophie smoothed out the chart. Venturing a look past him, she saw the unmistakable shape of a sail looming out of the fog.

"Is it them?" she asked.

He nodded. "The chase is on." As he lifted his arm, the iron manacle swung in a wild circle. "Help me get rid of this. Then I shall show you that a pirate always has a few tricks up his sleeve."

"Will he live?" asked Connor, turning from his surveillance as Gryff came out of the boathouse shed.

"No. The bullet was lodged too close to his heart. He's already stuck his spoon in the wall." Wiping the blood from his hands with an old piece of sailcloth, Gryff swiveled his gaze to the angry sea. "Mr. Wadsworth remained conscious long enough to confess his role in sinking Wolcott's yacht, and finger Morton and Dudley as the masterminds of the crime."

"No great revelation," muttered Connor.

"Agreed. However he did pass on some useful information. Cameron and Miss Lawrance apparently slipped away from their captors and fled in one of Morton's sailboats."

"Cam knows how to sail?" asked Connor.

"Our friend could most likely steer Charon's ferry across the River Styx if need be," answered Gryff dryly. "God only knows where he acquired such a skill, but I hope it was somewhere other than a duck pond. Dirty weather is coming on, and my guess is that it will get even dirtier as the night goes on."

"Damnation," swore Connor.

"Bloody hell is more like it," replied Gryff, "for Morton and Dudley set off in pursuit."

"Now what?"

"It appears that Miss Georgiana was right in suggesting that we might have need of a traveling coach. The wind is blowing like a banshee, so with these rough seas, they can't be headed in any other direction but north."

Raindrops began to patter on the overhanging leaves. "So, I suggest that we should ride to the inn, and prepare to follow the same course along the coast."

In the hide-and-seek moonlight, Cameron studied the chart. In his experience, knowing the lay of the land—or sea—was always an advantage in battle. For now, the tide and wind would not allow them to seek refuge in one of the harbors that dotted the coastline. But the sleek design of the racing sloop should allow him to pull away from their pursuers. *As long as the weather didn't get much worse.* In rough seas, the bigger, heavier yacht would gain the advantage.

He glanced up at the scudding clouds and felt the first spit of rain.

"I found some oilskin coats below," said Sophie, coming up through the hatchway and handing him one of the hooded garments. She crouched down in the shelter of the cockpit. "Is it my imagination, or are they getting closer?"

"They are gaining on us," confirmed Cameron. He edged the tiller over a touch. "We are the lighter and faster vessel, but in a storm, the advantage shifts to the yacht. Because of its weight, it can cut through the waves better than we can."

"What will they do if they catch us? They aren't carrying cannons, are they?"

"No, they'll not be firing a broadside at us, but most likely they will have muskets or hunting rifles," he replied. "My guess is that they mean to board us."

"Won't that be difficult in this storm?"

"Morton is an expert sailor."

Sophie lowered her rain-spattered lashes, trying to hide the worry in her eyes.

"But so am I, Sunbeam."

"You need not try to cast a bright light on a dark situation," she replied with a watery smile. "I can see that our situation is not good."

"Trust me, I've been in far worse." He tapped at his chin. "There was the time off the coast of Tripoli that my friends and I ran into a pair of heavily armed corsair ships cruising for plunder. We were carrying a cargo of smuggled silks, spices, and oils from Venice to the English coast."

"Good heavens, what did you do?"

"We used our wits as weapons. With our load, we couldn't outsail them, and as they came closer, their cannon fire began to hit home."

Her eyes widened. "*And?*"

"And then, I thought of emptying all of the oil we were carrying onto the water."

"In hoping of slowing them down?"

"No, in hoping of blowing them to Kingdom Come." Cameron grinned, deliberately distracting her from their own dire troubles. "We waited until they were smack in the middle of the slick and then Jem, our bosun from Yorkshire and a former poacher, took his bow and with a few well-aimed flaming arrows set the oil ablaze. Whoosh—their sails caught fire, and several of their cannons exploded."

"You," she said, "are exceedingly resourceful. Not to speak of exceedingly mad."

"I am," he agreed, gratified to see that she was no longer looking so deathly pale. "This is just another one of our daring little adventures. And I must say, I much prefer it to the bats."

Her laugh stirred a swirl of warmth in his chest.

"I daresay that Georgiana and Penelope will find this story far more thrilling," said Sophie. "Perhaps you can convince your friend Lord Haddan to write a horrid novel, once he's done with his essays."

"Perhaps. Gryff is a very imaginative fellow." As a shaft of moonlight cut through the clouds, Cameron took another peek at the chart and then at the compass set in the middle of the cockpit. "Interesting," he murmured after a moment of gauging the wind and the currents.

Sophie scooted a little closer. "What?"

"See this?" He pointed to a line of black dots curling up toward the town of Skegness. "It's a reef, located some distance offshore. According to the notation here, at high tide, it's well under water. But with the sea ebbing, as it is now, the rocks are a hazard to some larger vessels."

She frowned. "Are we in danger?"

Cameron looked back at the yacht. It was now close enough that he could make out several figures on the bow, working to raise another sail. *Damnation.* Some members of Morton's crew must have been working in the boathouse, for the boat looked to be well manned.

"No, not us. We've a shallow keel, but our pursuers do not." He altered course. "Can you hold the tiller steady while I tighten the mainsail sheets? We need go a few knots faster..."

Dark water foamed over the rail as the sloop heeled over and picked up speed. Wind whipped through the rigging, spray whirled in the chill air, the salt and rain stinging his face.

"They are still gaining," called Sophie.

"All we have to do is cross the reef ahead of them. Unless they are utter fools, they will have to come about, and in this wind, it will take them quite a while to tack around the danger. By the time they do, we will be well away and can lose ourselves in the storm."

A gust buffeted her sideways, but she clung resolutely to the tiller.

Do I dare trim the sail any more? Cameron slanted a look upward. Already the mast was bowing from the strain. "In for a penny, in for a pound," he muttered, hauling in another half turn of the manila rope. The varnished wood groaned but held firm.

Scrambling back to the stern, he took over the steering.

Through the swirling fog, he could just make out a riffling line of white-capped water up ahead. "We must head for the center," he muttered through clenched teeth. Praying that his pirate instincts were still sharp, he angled their vessel for the gap in the surf.

Kicked up by the crosscurrents, the waves steepened and slapped against the hull. The sloop shuddered and he saw Sophie hunch down inside her hooded coat, like a turtle withdrawing into its shell.

Despite his own inner turmoil, he managed an encouraging smile. "Remind me to tell you about the chase off the isle of Madagascar."

"Can it wait until we are back on dry land?" she called back. "I would rather—"

The rest of her words were drowned in a clap of thunder.

A brilliant burst of lightning slashed across the sky, and for an instant the two sailing ships racing across the churning sea were brightly illuminated. As Cameron came back to take over handling the tiller, he caught sight of Morton on the bucking deck of the yacht, trying to take aim with a hunting rifle before darkness once again swallowed them up.

His arms were aching like the devil from fighting the currents, but somehow he held his course. Catching the crest of a wave, the sloop shot forward and skimmed through the opening in the treacherous rocks. *A scrape, a bounce, a shudder.* And then suddenly they were past the danger and back in the open sea.

Sophie expelled a whoop of excitement. "Oh, you did it, Cam! You are the very Prince of Pirates."

"Just a marquess," he called dryly.

With the prevailing winds forcing him out to sea, Cameron had to tack before venturing a look back.

"Bloody hell, even *I* wouldn't be that reckless," he muttered.

Sails drumming in the wind, hull surging through the eddying waters, the yacht was following in the sloop's wake. Its long, dark bowsprit was cutting wildly through the mists, like a saber seeking to strike a mortal blow to an enemy.

For a moment, Cameron thought that his dare had failed. Outgunned and outmanned, he and Sophie had little hope of fighting off an attack at close quarters.

And then...

And then with a shuddering crack, the yacht's mainmast snapped. In a tangle of canvas and ropes, it plunged into the sea, spinning the yacht in a yawing circle. Out of control, the hull smashed against a submerged rock, splintering the mizzen mast. It, too, fell in a jumble of cordage just as a large wave rose up and broke over the deck.

Foam flew through the air, streaking the darkness with a ghostly spray. A moment later, what remained of the battered yacht capsized.

"Good God." Sophie let out a horrified gurgle as the wreckage sank beneath the swirling waters.

"Poetic justice, I suppose," murmured Cameron as he stared into the darkness. "I wasn't lying when I said that I had personal reasons for wishing to help you fight these men," he added after a long moment. "This was the second time that Morton tried to destroy me. He was the blackguard who was beating the tavern girl—the smarmy weasel whose purse I took, and who then ran to Wolcott proclaiming me a thief." The vortex of ink-black water spun round and round and round. "If you navigate through life using greed and evil as your compass, you deserve to founder on unseen shoals."

Sophie nodded. "I cannot mourn Dudley and Morton," she said in a tight voice. "But still, we should search for survivors."

"I would if I could, Sunbeam. But it's simply not possible to sail into the teeth of this storm," replied Cameron. "Already the wind has risen to gale force. We must go with it and even then, we'll be hard-pressed to keep ourselves afloat." Seeing her stricken expression, he added, "The chances of finding anyone alive in that maelstrom are virtually nil."

"Poor Neddy," she murmured softly.

Cameron did not feel quite so charitable. "We must all live—or die—with the choices we make. Wadsworth knew right from wrong. So he must accept the consequences for his actions." He shook a hank of sopping hair from his brow. "As I said, if you live by the proverbial sword, choosing to take by violence that which is not rightfully yours, you must be prepared to die by the sword."

"You know, for all your devil-may-care bluster, you are the very soul of honor." She turned and slid her arms around him in a fierce hug. "A hero in every sense of the word."

"Don't exaggerate my nobility, Sophie." And yet, for all his carefully calculated detachment, he found her words lit an odd warmth in a certain region of his chest.

You are becoming a soft-hearted sentimentalist, scoffed one of the demons in his head.

Yes, and what is so wrong with that? he asked wryly.

Somewhat to his surprise, the demons and devils had no answer. Slinking away, their red-hot pitchforks melting into limp little twists of metal, they disappeared into the darkest crevasses of his brain.

"You *are* noble," she said, pressing her lips to his stubbled cheek, "And I have the paper to prove it."

"I never thought I would live to see the day..." The waves surged and tiller smacked into his side, nearly knocking them both overboard. "And I may not yet if we don't keep our minds on the challenge at hand." Cameron brushed a kiss to her brow, and then reluctantly released her. "I fear the blow is going to be a bad one. We will have to use every ounce of effort to keep ourselves afloat."

Muttering under his breath, Gryff crunched his way over the piles of broken oyster shells and hurried back to the coach.

"No luck here, either?" asked Sophie's uncle, trying to keep the disappointment from his voice.

"The fishermen of Lincolnshire and Yorkshire all seem to take fiendish delight in telling me that no vessel could make it to land in this storm," grumbled Gryff. All of them were tired and testy. They had been traveling hard for nearly two days, following the coast road with precious few stops for rest or sustenance. "According to the fellows of this harbor, anyone caught out on the water when the gale started will likely end up in the Shetland Islands—or the arctic port of Spitzbergen."

"We just have to keep going north," said Georgiana stoutly. "The storm has to blow itself out sometime, and when it does, Sophie and Cameron will find a safe harbor."

Hermione tried to smile, but worry was etched around her eyes.

Gryff and Connor exchanged glances, neither one giving voice to the increasingly obvious fact that the continuing violence of the ocean was fast sinking any chance of survival.

"Er, is Mr. Daggett an expert sailor?" asked Edward.

"He excels in any number of different skills," replied Connor tersely.

A silence. "You did not say that sailing is one of them," pointed out Georgiana.

Gryff cleared his throat with a cough. "Let us take some refreshment at the local inn while we arrange for a fresh team of horses. Then, if I may be so bold as to make a suggestion..."

"Please do, milord," said Edward.

"Here is what I propose." He slanted a look up at

the leaden clouds, which showed no sign of lightening. "We all continue on to the Scottish border together. If we still haven't found Miss Lawrance and Daggett by then, you three should return to Terrington to await word while Connor and I continue the search into the Highlands on horseback. The roads there are barely more than cart tracks and your coach would soon come to grief."

Edward gave a reluctant nod. "That is a sensible plan, milord, and much as it hurts me to abandon the effort, I can't argue that we would be more of a hindrance than a help."

Hermione blew out a sigh.

"It can't be helped, my dear," said her husband.

"Well, I, for one, haven't given up hope," announced Georgiana. "If you knew some of the scrapes that Sophie and Cam have survived in the past, you might have a little more faith in their chances."

At that, Gryff chuckled, the first show of amusement since the journey had begun. "Quite right, Miss Georgiana. Being intimately acquainted with Daggett's uncanny knack of staying a hairsbreadth ahead of disaster, I shall, like you, remain optimistic."

To Cameron's dismay, his prediction regarding the storm's strength proved all too true. For the next day and night he and Sophie battled the relentless elements, the rain, wind, and the surging seas all swirling together in an iron-gray blur. Wet, cold, exhausted, they stumbled through the arduous task of trimming the sails to keep the sloop from being broached by the waves, subsisting on old biscuits, moldy cheese, and a keg of cider that Sophie had found in one of the lockers.

Gray, gray, and more gray—there seemed to be no end to the raging storm in sight.

Muzzy from lack of sleep, Cameron had no idea where they were, save for the fact that the needle of the compass kept pointing relentlessly north. Rubbing his salt-reddened eyes, he felt himself drifting into a daze, despite the thrumming of the gusts against the taut canvas.

"Go below for a nap," insisted Sophie. "I can handle the steering for a bit."

"Maybe just for a short while," he mumbled.

"Go!" she ordered, and this time he didn't argue. Nodding off at the helm could spell disaster.

Cameron wasn't sure how long he had been asleep, but he suddenly awoke with a start, aware that the motion of the sloop had changed dramatically. Scrambling up the hatchway, he found himself blinking into a blaze of diamond-bright sunlight. The wind had dropped to a gentle breeze and the water shimmered with shades of celestial blue.

"Look—oh, look!" Sophie was pointing to a faint line of gray cliffs just visible in the distance. "Land!"

Terra firma.

The sight of earth and stone, however hardscrabble, had never looked more divine.

"Let us haul these sails around one last time and head for shore." Rubbing his chafed hands together, he moved to the tiller and altered course. "I don't know about you, but for me a pot of coffee, hot and strong as the fires of Hell, would be nothing short of heavenly."

Chapter Twenty-Two

I look like a drowned muskrat." Sophie looked down at her tattered dress and grimaced as the sloop glided into the calm waters of the cove. The salt-crusted muslin was liberally streaked with pine tar and pitch from the rigging. "And my hair must be more hideous than a tangle of smelly seaweed."

Cameron scratched at his bristly chin. "Honesty compels me to admit that you are not shining with your usual light, Sunbeam."

He wasn't exactly a paragon of perfection, either, she observed. And yet somehow his disheveled appearance—scruffy beard, ripped shirt, windsnarled locks, raffish earring—looked sinfully dashing rather than woefully drab.

"I hope we do not frighten the locals," she murmured. "They may think we are dreadful sea demons, spit up from Neptune's underwater kingdom to wreak mischief here on land."

"I'm sure they have seen much worse," he quipped. "Like hairy horned Vikings in monstrous dragon ships."

"I suppose we are not quite as threatening as that." She patted back a yawn. "Any idea where we are?"

"Not a clue," responded Cameron. The sloop nudged up against a weathered wharf piled high with fishing nets and eel traps. "And at the moment, the question is not of paramount importance. As long as there is a bed and blankets—preferably free of fleas—we could be in Xanadu or Hyderabad for all I care."

"A bed," repeated Sophie with a wistful sigh. "I am so fatigued that I may simply curl up on those burlap sacks and sleep for a day . . . or maybe a week." The mention of time suddenly snapped her thoughts into sharper focus. "Oh, Lord. But the first thing I must do is send word to Georgie—"

"Rest assured that I'll have a message sent, but not until I get you tucked between the sheets," said Cameron, lifting her unresisting body up to the slatted walkway.

"Oh, I can't think of a more blissful suggestion." Even if she had wanted to, Sophie was too tired to protest.

"No?" His brows gave a suggestive waggle. "I may have to refresh your memory. But that, too, can wait until later." He finished snugging the mooring lines to a set of brass cleats and then took her hand. "Come, there looks to be an inn across the way."

Happy to cede all decisions to him, Sophie floated along in a fog of fatigue, oblivious to the curious stares from townsfolk gathered around the harbor market stalls. Cameron's negotiations with the innkeeper were naught but a vague buzz . . . and she wasn't quite sure how she managed to move her feet on the stairs. All she knew was that somehow her half boots came off with a plop and a soft woolen blanket dropped over her shoulders.

And then sleep—blessed, blessed sleep—wrapped itself around her weary body.

How long she lingered in sweet oblivion was impossible to gauge. All she knew was that the room was dappled in pale morning sunshine when she awoke.

"Ah, back from the world of Morpheus?" murmured Cameron, drawing her into his arms.

"Mmmm." She gave a little stretch. "Yes, but I was having such delightful dreams."

"Oh?" He nibbled at the shell of her ear. "Of what?"

"Shirred eggs, a rasher of bacon, hot scones slathered with butter and jam," she murmured. "And an ocean of steaming hot tea...though to be honest, if I never see an ocean again, I shall not be disappointed."

"And here I was hoping that your fantasies were straying to other appetites."

Sophie felt a blush steal over her face, suddenly conscious of the fact that he was in bed with her, and wearing only his drawers. "Now that you mention it..." she began.

"Hush." He silenced her with a light touch of his lips. "Much as I would like to tempt you into sin, I have an even more sensuous treat in store for you. Wait here." He rose and moved to the washstand set in the shadow of the painted armoire.

Crockery clinked, releasing a wafting of heavenly aromas. A moment later he returned to the bed bearing a large tray heaped with food and drink.

"Cam!" The word was slightly muffled by a mouthful of muffin. "Your friends are right—you are a creature with unearthly powers. Who else but a magician could conjure a feast from a pitcher of cold water?"

"There's a far more mundane explanation. The innkeeper's wife took pity on us poor, lost bairns." He passed her a plate of eggs and toast. "By the by, I also ordered up a bath. I assume you would like to wash the salt and sea grit from your skin."

"You are *truly* a magician." Sophie blew out a sigh after sipping her tea. "Now, if only you could wave a wand and make a freshly laundered gown appear out of thin air."

"Sorry. That's beyond my repertoire of skills," replied Cameron. "But would you settle for a new garment? The selection was rather limited at the local shops, but I found a shade of dusky blue that will look quite lovely with your eyes." He pulled a paper-wrapped parcel from beneath the bed. "I've also added a few other essentials. I made an educated guess as to size."

A roguish smile. Which she covered with a cinnamon-dusted kiss. "I'm not sure which is more delicious," she murmured. "You or this spiced fruit shortbread."

"I'll be around long after you've swallowed the last sultana."

Oh, how I wish that you would be by my side... forever.

A lump formed in her throat, turning the taste of sweetness to ashes. Cameron made her laugh. And all too soon he would make her cry. She would return to her family cottage and he would head off to... wherever a Pirate Prince called home.

Forcing herself to swallow her heartache, she looked up. "Thank you for the clothing."

A questioning pinch pulled his brows together, but before he could respond, a knock thumped on the door.

Donning trousers and shirt—he, too, had acquired new clothing—Cameron went to open the door.

Two young serving maids lugged in buckets of hot water, and after several trips back and forth from the kitchens, the copper tub behind the bathing screen was filled. They flounced away in a flutter of blushes and giggles brought on by Cameron's dark-lashed wink, leaving a cloud of sweet-scented steam rising up to the ceiling.

"I swear, you could seduce the Devil's Serpent out of his scaly skin," said Sophie, watching the swish of skirts disappear and the door fall shut.

"I would much rather convince you to shed that salt-stiff rag you are wearing. It must be dreadfully itchy."

Her skin began to prickle under his lazy, lidded gaze. She drew in a lungful of the moist air, savoring the subtle perfume of rosemary and heather. "You won't have to twist my arm."

"What a pity. I was looking forward to manipulating your lovely limbs."

"I doubt that it would be very amorous wrestling with a bedraggled sea-witch." Feeling a little shy, Sophie scooted out of bed, grasping the blanket to her chest. "The odor of brine and fishscales does not strike me as an aphrodisiac."

"I purchased some soap made with wild Highland heather and honey," murmured Cameron. "Along with a soft sponge. It's all there by the tub."

A gurgle of longing escaped from her lips.

"If it feels too wantonly wild to disrobe in front of me, you may do so behind the screen. I won't look." He paused. "Well, maybe just a peek."

Sophie was already scurrying to the shelter of the screen. "How on earth did you manage such luxuries?" she called as she tugged the remains of her gown over her head and kicked it into the corner. "I left my reticule in Morton's coach and your purse was lost overboard."

Her shift followed. "Aside from the lone farthing that you found in your pocket, we haven't any money."

"I am a very persuasive fellow," answered Cameron. "And I've a good deal of experience in making up stories. There was a time when I was penniless in the port of Genoa and managed to convince one of the wealthy merchants there that I was the son of a Hapsburg prince, kidnapped in childhood by Barbary pirates. Enthralled by the detailed description of my escape from a desert palace and subsequent commandeering of a corsair ship, in which I outfought my pursuers before finally sinking within sight of the Italian coast, he lent me a King's ransom so that I could continue my journey home to Vienna."

"It appears that your tongue is as skilled as your fingers at pressing all the right little levers and gears," she said dryly.

"With all due modesty, I can spin a yarn of dastardly villains, a perilous adventure, and a long-lost heir that rivals those of Mrs. Radcliffe."

"A pity you did not write it down. Given their current taste in reading, Georgie and Pen would be enthralled by such a story." Sophie let out a little purr of pleasure as she eased her now-naked body into the steamy water. "Oh, dear. Speaking of my sisters—"

"A message has been dispatched to Terrington."

"Thank you, Cam." Picking up the sponge and soap, Sophie lathered up a froth of sweet-smelling bubbles and squeezed, letting a drizzle run down between her breasts. *Oh, bliss.* "What would I ever do without you?" she murmured, trailing the sponge down the arch of her neck. "This is heavenly—I may be here for hours, for I intend to scrub every last inch of my skin."

"Hmmm, then I may need to offer my services." He stepped behind the screen. "You can't reach that spot on the very center of your back."

She sank beneath the bubbles. "What a naughty suggestion," she scolded. "You know, you really ought not come in here. We are back in the real world now and must have a care about shamelessly flouting the rules of Society."

"I ought not do a lot of things, Sunbeam. But by now you know that I am incorrigible."

"Wickedly so," said Sophie. And then, seeing the glint in his eye as he stared at the swirls of water, she suddenly felt a little wicked herself. *To the Devil with propriety. The rules could wait until her return home.* For the moment, she would pretend they were in an exotic land, where the customs and strictures were different from those in England.

Lifting a leg high in the air, she slowly drew the sponge down its length.

"You," he said in a softly smoky voice, "are inviting Trouble to take over your toilette."

Yes, and Trouble had never sounded so alluring. "Well, in that case, can Trouble reach that pesky place on my back?" she asked. "It's beginning to itch."

"Hmmm." Cameron shucked off his new shirt. "That may take a bit of maneuvering." He moved behind her and Sophie heard the sound of his trousers slithering down over his thighs.

I am bad. Very bad.

"Hand me the sponge, Sunbeam."

She passed it back, her flesh already tingling in anticipation.

The sudsing of the soap set off a gossamer gurgle.

"You will have to sit up and bend forward," said Cameron, perching a hip on the edge of the tub.

Feeling deliciously decadent, Sophie did as she was told. She knew—oh, yes, she knew—that it was sinful to savor such intimacies. But...

But I don't regret it. Not for an instant.

"Is the itch here?" asked Cameron, massaging the sponge along her left shoulderblade. "Or here?" His touch teased down her spine.

"Mmmm." Her body was humming with pleasure. "I can't remember."

"Then I had better be sure to scratch every spot." His lips, warm and wet with the swirling steam, pressed against the nape of her neck. "You had better shift just a little so I can reach..."

Sophie sucked in her breath as he slid his hands down the soap-slickened slope of her shoulders and drew her closer. They lingered for a moment on her arms before tickling across her ribs to cup her breasts.

"We ought not neglect the front of your person," he murmured. "And then, ministering to every speck of skin means I might have to suckle your toes."

The sound in her throat deepened to a moan.

Cameron chuckled. "But the toes can wait." He released her just long enough to find the bar of herb-flecked soap. *Rough and smooth.* The texture teased against her nipple, sending shivers of fire coursing to her core. Switching to her other breast, he repeated the slow, circling rub.

"No more seaweed and salt," he whispered. "You are perfumed with heather and honey." Inhaling deeply, he added, "It makes me think of sunlight dancing through wild meadow grasses."

Pale plumes of steam twined with the curling strands of his hair. "And you," she replied, "are scented with bay rum and...is that brandy on your breath?"

"The local whisky," corrected Cameron with a husky chuckle. "The innkeeper insisted I join him in a glass of his special malt as he listened to the story of our travails. As for the bay rum cologne—which by the by is from Floris, the famous scentmaker in London—it was forgotten by a previous guest. Mr. McGregor insisted I avail myself of it when he arranged a bath for me earlier in one of the unused inn rooms. I didn't wish to wake you."

"Is there anyone you can't charm with your silver tongue?" asked Sophie, tilting back her head to inhale another whiff of his beguiling fragrance.

Cameron captured her mouth in a long, lush kiss. "My tongue," he said after a lengthy interlude, "is only interested in charming one person in particular. Is it having any luck?"

Sophie touched her lips to his. "Ask me later."

After a rather lengthy interlude, the water stirred in a shimmering vortex as she twisted around in the copper tub, drawing her knees beneath her so she could face him. His chest was glistening with moisture, the droplets clinging to the peppering of dark curls looking like tiny pearls in the silvery haze of light. Pressing her palms to the chiseled contours of his ribs, Sophie leaned in and licked a bead of water from his sun-bronzed skin.

A deeply masculine sound rumbled in his chest. "I like your growls," she said, licking again.

"Sophie." Cameron caught her face between his lithe hands. "I'll soon be howling to the heavens if you continue that."

"I like your howls, too," she answered. The heat of him felt so good. *So good.* Trailing a hand down his flat belly, she dipped a finger into his navel. "Even your barks."

His inhale was more like a groan.

With a throaty laugh, Sophie tickled her touch lower.

"Don't. Tempt. Me." He rose, pulling her up with him in a froth of splashing water and rainbow bubbles.

"Why not?" she asked, knowing full well that this enchanted interlude would soon be over and Sophie the Sea Siren would return to being Sophie the Spinster.

"Because," he rasped. Grabbing up a towel, he began to dry her dripping shoulders. "Because we are scheduled to meet with someone. And if we don't hurry and dress, we will be late."

An appointment? That did not bode well. A magistrate, perhaps? Or a mail coach heading home? That thought ought to be a welcome one, but instead it had her insides twisting into a tight knot.

"B-but we don't know a soul here in...in..." Sophie realized that she still had no idea where they were. "In this unknown place."

"We are in Scotland, Sophie," he answered.

Scotland? Of all the ironies! She gave an unsteady laugh, thinking of the history. "Imagine that! I never would have guessed we had traveled as far as the northern border."

"Yes, the prevailing winds of the storm were quite powerful." His voice was oddly flat as he set to drying her back. "But the local fishermen said that's not uncommon at this time of year."

"Indeed?" Talking about the weather was at least delaying the scheduled meeting. "It must have been one of those North Sea gales that starts off the coast of Denmark. I think there is a name for the phenomenon, but I can't seem to recall it." She knew she was babbling but didn't care. Anything to put off stepping back into the real world. "Whatever the name, it has certainly carried us a great distance out of our way."

"On the contrary," said Cameron softly. "I would say that Fate has blown us to exactly where we ought to be."

Strange sparks of light were dipping and dancing in his gaze. "Have you perchance imbibed one too many drams of the innkeeper's whisky?" asked Sophie. "You aren't making any sense."

His mouth twitched with silent laughter. "I think that I'm making perfect sense, Sophie." The towel dropped to the floor as he hugged her close. "I asked you to elope with me to Scotland once before—and you were right to refuse. But now, I hope you will reconsider. I am older, and while I can't claim to be much wiser, I have at least learned from the impetuous mistakes of my youth."

He is asking me to marry him for a second time?

"I spoke to the local curate first thing this morning. As you know, we don't need a clergyman to marry in Scotland, or need to post the banns. All we have to do is proclaim our intentions before two witnesses and the act is done. But I assumed that a Church certificate would be more welcome to your family."

The ground suddenly seemed to be rolling like the deck of their storm-tossed sloop.

"He's waiting in the little church beyond the village green. Mr. McGregor and his wife have kindly consented to act as our witnesses. Within the half hour we can be man and wife."

Her heart began to sing. But only for an instant. A deeper, darker sound rose up, clouding her initial joy. "You can't marry me, Cam. You are a fine lord now and must choose someone of your own station. A lady who knows how to be a marchioness."

"Ah, but since when I have ever bowed to convention?" replied Cameron with a wry smile. The quip quickly gave way to a more serious expression. "The new life I am facing is frightening enough. I can't imagine facing it with a pasteboard marchioness—someone who has been carefully groomed for the position and knows how to go through the motions, but who has no real heart or substance."

He reached up to frame her face between his palms. "We are kindred souls, Sophie, and we've dared to take a number of madcap adventures together in the past. I hope you will be by my side for the future ones."

Oh, how she longed to say yes. *And yet . . .*

"I've no more experience than you do in being an aristocrat," he went on. "You have all the perfect qualifications—you are kind, caring, compassionate, Not to speak of sensible and practical."

Sophie's throat tightened. They were, to be sure, all very nice compliments. But none was the word she longed to hear.

He hesitated, using the sliver of silence to draw in a lungful of air. And through the dark fringe of his lashes, she saw a flicker of vulnerability. "But most of all, I love you, Sophie. I've been wandering in a world of shadows since I left you, too foolish, too proud . . . too frightened of failure to make another try at winning your heart. And then, Chance brought us together."

"It wasn't Chance," she whispered. "It wasn't Fate, it wasn't Luck."

"I know, I know. It's hard for a jaded cynic to admit it aloud," he replied. "But you are right—it was Love all the while, guiding me through the labyrinth of darkness."

A rueful grimace tugged at his lips. "So I shall get used to saying it, Sunbeam, no matter that my fellow Hellhounds will laugh themselves sick when they hear me. Not that I don't deserve it, for all the needling I've given them over the years."

"Love," repeated Sophie, savoring the sound of it echoing off the walls.

"Love." Cameron slowly unfastened the gold and pearl earring dangling from his lobe and held it out on his palm. "I haven't a proper wedding ring, so we'll have to use this as a token of my pledge. I hope you don't mind. We'll pick something more fitting once we return to London."

She watched sunlight flicker off the piece of jewelry. *Pirate gold.* A treasure beyond measure.

"It will be a very simple service." A pause. "I hope you didn't have your heart set on a fashionable ceremony at St. George's in Hanover Square, with all of Society invited."

"Good heavens, no! Such elaborate extravaganzas are not my style. I'm simply—"

"Simply Sophie," said Cameron, silencing her with a brush of his lips. "The light of my life. A Sunbeam who is perfect exactly the way she is."

A new wave of salty drops splashed on her cheeks.

"Now, please say yes, Sophie. Or do I have to sail off with you to some deserted Pirate island and hold you captive until you relent?"

"Oh, please, no more sea journeys. So much as a deserted island sounds alluring, I had better say yes," she murmured. *Yes. Yes. Yes.*

"A very wise decision," said Cameron. "Confinement in a haunted Italian villa, with a mad monk as your jailer, was next on my list of threats."

"Georgie and Pen will probably never forgive me for passing up such an adventure."

"I'll make it up to them by buying every horrid novel the shelves of Hatchards." His smile turned a trifle more tentative. "You aren't teasing me, are you, Sunbeam? Your answer truly is yes?"

"Yes," said Sophie. "The truth is, I've loved you ever since you rescued my pet hedgehog from the jaws of Squire Mather's mastiff."

"Ouch." He grimaced. "I still have those scars on my knuckles."

"Which only goes to show that despite your assertions to the contrary, you have always been noble at heart."

"You give me far too much credit." Another kiss. "But I shall try not to disappoint you."

"Never, Cam." She brushed a lock of damp, curling hair from his brow. "Never."

For the next little interlude, the only sound in the room was the flutter of birdsong outside the window and the *drip, drip, drip* of water from Sophie's still-wet body.

"Much as I love the feel of your naked limbs pressed to mine," Cameron murmured after tracing the arch of her throat with a kiss, "you are shivering—and we are late. We really must dress." He handed her a fresh towel. "It would be very remiss of us to keep them all waiting at our own wedding. But rest assured that we will resume this delightful tête-à-tête when we return."

Our own wedding. Sophie floated through the rest of her ablutions in a silvery fog.

"Ready?" called Cameron, smoothing the knot of his red and white striped neckerchief. Somehow, despite the limited choices offered by a small village, he had managed to add a touch of his usual outrageous style.

Sophie took his proffered hand and smiled. "I won't wait for you to ask twice."

"Wait here for a moment." Ignoring Sophie's bemused look, Cameron veered off the footpath and rounded a patch of prickly gorse.

"I thought you were worried about being late," she called.

"This will just take a tic." Returning to where she was standing, he bowed low and with a flourish presented her with a bouquet of wildflowers. "Every bride ought to have a posy, right?"

"Oh, they are beautiful!" she exclaimed.

His breath caught in his throat as she held the unruly blooms up to the light and smiled. The pale pink climbing roses matched the color of her cheeks, and the cornflowers were the same shade of blue as her sapphirine eyes.

"Their beauty wilts in comparison to your natural splendor, Sophie," he murmured.

A dappling of sun heightened the rosy blush stealing across her face. "Perhaps you should take up writing poetry as well as tales of dangerous adventures."

"I wouldn't want to steal Gryff's thunder—he is the lyrical, literary Hellhound." He pursed his lips as they resumed walking. "Hmmm, Connor has become a goat farmer...I suppose that I, too, shall have to choose some respectable profession to occupy my time. Which is a pity. I rather enjoy my covert activities."

He had said it in jest, but Sophie's expression turned pensive. "And you are very good at what you do. Perhaps there is a way to put your prodigious talents to work for a Higher Good."

"Higher Good? You haven't seen my private art collection yet," he quipped. "Before you say a word, I am *not* going to return any of the items."

"That wasn't what I had in mind."

Cameron could almost see the mental gears spinning inside her head. He loved that she found cerebral conundrums an intriguing challenge.

"I was thinking," she said slowly, "that the Crown might find your services useful."

"You mean...work hand in glove with the government?" The idea was interesting, and one that had never occurred to him.

"Given your military background—at least, I am assuming you were not just jesting about your prowess with a cavalry saber—it seems a logical connection."

"I have a feeling," mused Cameron, "that we are going to have some very fascinating adventures ahead of us."

"Now that I've mastered locks, I would like to learn how to scale a manor wall."

"We will discuss it..." Looking up, he saw the small stone church just ahead, nestled among a stand of towering oak trees. "But enough talk of clandestine activities. It's not exactly the sort of discussion a lady wants on her wedding day."

"As you pointed out, we are not a conventional couple," said Sophie.

"Amen to that."

Stepping off the footpath, they started to hurry across a freshly mown swath of grass. "The curate looks to be waiting by the door," she said in some concern. "I hope we aren't too tardy."

Cameron took her hand and as he quickened his pace, he turned his head and winked. "Better late than never, Sunbeam."

Chapter Twenty-Three

Man and wife. The words of the curate were still ringing in her ears, the official paper was peeking out of Cameron's coat pocket, and yet, it all still felt a little unreal. Perhaps, thought Sophie ruefully, because she wasn't quite sure of her new name. There was now not a shadow of a doubt that Cameron was a legitimate Rowland. However, the legalities had yet to be confirmed. Cameron had hesitated just a fraction before signing the certificate.

His scrawl had been hard to decipher...

"What moniker am I to give when asked who I am?" she murmured as they strolled back to the inn.

"Lady Wolcott," he answered decisively.

"Oh, but I feel like an imposter."

"You are not," assured Cameron. "And besides, the tavern girls would be horribly disappointed if they can't curtsey and say 'milady.' I have been regaling them with the perils you have passed through before Love conquered all, and they wish to share in the celebration."

"I shudder to think of what you have told them."

He grinned. "I may have embellished things a bit, but you have to admit, the truth is quite a yarn in itself."

"Perhaps even more suspenseful than *Lady Avery's Awful Secret*." Sophie hugged his arm a little tighter, savoring his closeness. "Though I must say, I have just realized that both stories have a key element in common."

"Which is?"

"They both have a dashing storybook hero," replied Sophie with a grin.

"How can you be sure? You've not heard the end of Georgiana's book," said Cameron.

"We all know it must end with a Happily Ever After, so there has to be a hero." She allowed a mischievous pause. "Even though we both know a heroine is perfectly capable of saving herself, it's nice to see a knight in shining armor riding to the rescue."

He gave a martyred sigh. "Why is it that ladies find a suit of steel attractive? It makes a man look...chunky. And it creaks worse than the Prince Regent's corset."

"Very well, you may continue to wear Pirate garb," said Sophie. "After all, a helm would hide your earring." She held up her hand, feeling a flutter of joy on seeing the flash of gold and pearl clasped between her fingers. "And it was that glint of precious metal which first caught my eye when you found me in the dark alley."

"And here I thought it was my scintillating wit and flashy smile that captured your fancy."

"Those, too," conceded Sophie. "In fact, I adore most everything about you, Cam." She eyed his shirtpoints. "Save for that garish neckerchief."

"You don't like it? The alternative was a ghastly shade of puce. And white seemed far too ordinary a choice." His lazy grin sent slow, spiraling shivers through her body. "However, I am more than willing to take it off."

As he opened the door to the inn and led the way up the stairs, Sophie heard titters of laughter, followed by the hurried swish of skirts turning the corner of the hallway. But before she could voice any question, Cameron swept her up into his arms and shouldered open the door to their room.

Sophie blinked, and found herself bereft of speech. They had been talking about fanciful stories. But this—this was a fairytale! Dozens of honey-colored candles blazed merrily in every corner of the room, their undulating flames bathing the pine paneling in a golden glow. A trail of pale pink rose petals led from the threshold to the bed, where two cut-glass goblets were filled with sparkling champagne.

"I see that the girls took my request for a romantic setting to heart," he observed, setting her down.

"It's..." Sophie eyed the sprigs of fresh-cut heather and holly decorating the windowsill. "It's the most beautiful setting I've ever seen. I feel like a princess."

"Let us hope that when you kiss me I don't turn into a frog."

"We will just have to take that risk," she said, throwing her arms around him and pressing her lips to his.

His croaking quickly dissolved into soft laughter. And then into no sound at all. Touching, teasing, tasting—that was all the language they needed. His hands and his tongue were doing delightfully naughty things to her body.

"Come, let's not wrinkle your new gown." The ties loosened, the tiny buttons slipped free of the fabric. "I've convinced the shopkeeper to give me these garments on credit, but I don't wish to press my luck."

"Indeed, not. We mustn't..." Sophie wriggled out of the muslin. "...take advantage of his kindness." She unknotted Cameron's neckerchief and undid the fastening of his shirt.

He managed to hang the clothing neatly over the single chair in the room as he spun her around to the bed.

"*Sláinte*." He handed her one of the goblets. "That is a traditional Gaelic toast, which roughly translates as 'may your cup bubble over with happiness, now and always.'"

"*Sláinte*," repeated Sophie. Was it possible to be any happier? She wondered, savoring the effervescence of the wine as it danced down her tongue.

Her answer came a moment later.

Smiling, Cameron took a long swallow of his drink, and then with his mouth still sweet with the pale gold liquid, he lowered his head and possessed her chemise-clad nipple.

Oh. A wave of dizzying pleasure washed over her. *Oh, oh, oh.*

The friction of the cotton and the coolness of the champagne ignited a tingling fire. "Is it," she gasped, "too terribly wicked and wanton to want you to keep kissing me like that in the middle of the day?"

"Oh, trust me, Sunbeam, there are far more wicked and wanton things for us to do together." Her body tumbled back against the down pillows and his warm, muscled weight kissed up against her flesh. "Like this."

A flare of fire ignited at the apex of her legs.

"And this."

Heat sizzled down the insides of her thighs.

"Or we could try..."

Sophie squeezed back a cry of delight as his fingers

traced a spiraling trail of sparks as they delved down to her innermost desire. "Don't. Stop."

"Your wish is my command. For be it day or be it night, I can now, in good conscience, make mad, passionate love to my wife."

Dusk was turning the moors a hazy purple when Cameron woke from a blissful sleep. Carefully slipping out from under Sophie's outflung arm, he turned on his back and found himself smiling as he watched the flitting shadows play across the whitewashed plaster ceiling.

He smiled—at nothing and everything at the same time.

The faraway trilling of a nightingale, the lazy flutter of the drapery in the breeze, the faint laughter from the taproom below—at this moment, mused Cameron, the world seemed in perfect harmony with his mood of profound peace.

Oatcakes drizzled in wildflower honey. He would order up something sweet for Sophie to nibble on when she awoke. For himself, port and Stilton. Perhaps some pears and walnuts—

A clattering in the stableyard suddenly intruded on his lazy reveries. Other travelers arriving in this out-of-the-way coastal village? "Of all the cursed luck," he muttered, not overly happy at having their private interlude interrupted by strangers. "But mayhap they are simply seeking directions." he added hopefully.

Heaving a reluctant sigh, Cameron rose and went to the window for a cursory peek.

"Damnation. How the devil…" His mouth pinched, hovering somewhere between a grin and a grimace as he watched the occupants of a large traveling coach climb down to the rutted ground. "I was hoping that my message would reach them quickly, but the Royal mail coach must be using winged unicorns on their Southern routes."

"Did you say something?" Sophie, looking wonderfully rumpled, lifted her head from the pillow.

"Yes." Cameron turned. "You had better put on some clothes."

She sat up in alarm.

"We are about to have visitors," he added, reaching for his shirt.

"Dear God, don't tell me that Morton and Dudley survived—"

"No, no." He pulled a wry grimace. "It's not any enemy." A quick toss landed Sophie's gown in her lap. "You had best hurry."

Without further ado, Cameron tugged on his trousers and with another rueful oath began looking for his boots. The words, however, turned into a chuckle.

Friends and family—I am used to living as naught but a solitary specter but I now must step out of the shadows. In the past, the idea had been unthinkable. But now...

Thump, thump.

His warning had come none too soon, for a fist began hammering on the door.

Seeing Sophie spear her last hairpin into place, Cameron unlatched the lock and let it swing open.

"I'll have you know that we've been searching over half of England for you," announced Gryff. "However I will refrain from ringing a peal over your head as we are deucedly glad to find the two of you alive." He tipped his hat to Sophie. "Especially you, Miss Lawrance."

"Sophie!" cried Georgiana, Hermione, and Edward in unison.

Nudging Connor, Gryff discreetly moved to block the view into the bedchamber from Sophie's family. "You know, Cam," he said under his breath, "if I might make a suggestion, you really ought to do the right thing—"

"Save your breath. Things are not quite as scandalous as they look," interrupted Cameron with a grin. In a louder voice he added, "How lovely to see you all. Had we known you were coming, we would have delayed the wedding ceremony. But be that as it may, allow me to present my wife, Lady Wolcott—the soon-to-be Lady Wolcott, that is."

Hermione and her husband exchanged looks of mingled elation and relief.

Georgiana was a bit more vocal in expressing her feelings. "Huzzah! It's about time you came to your senses, Cam."

Sophie ducked her head to hide her blushes.

"Excellent, excellent," said Gryff. "We must celebrate! I'll order up a few bottles of champagne from the cellar, along with a repast from the kitchen and a private parlor, so we may have a jolly little wedding supper."

"I did have other plans for the evening…" drawled Cameron.

Sophie's color deepened to beet red.

"But since you are all here," he went on, "a celebration is a splendid suggestion."

They all trooped downstairs, and in short order, wine and laughter were flowing with equal exuberance.

Sophie sat at the head of the table, blinking back tears as she soaked in the surrounding good cheer.

Cameron leaned in to brush a lock of hair from her cheek. "Happy?" he asked.

"Beyond words."

"I have just one complaint to voice," announced Georgiana loudly, having just finished her second glass of champagne. "I am disappointed that Anthony missed all the excitement and didn't get to display what a dashing hero he is."

"Oh, don't worry," called Cameron. "I have a feeling the poor fellow will have plenty of harrowing adventures of his own."

Much merriment greeted the quip, and after a fleeting scowl, Georgiana allowed a reluctant grin. "Am I that terrible?"

"Some things are too dangerous to desire," answered Sophie as she slanted a look at her husband. "But if you throw caution to the wind and dare to do so, the reward is well worth the risk."

Ha—I told you so, mouthed her sister.

And you were oh-so right, thought Sophie.

After a whispered exchange with Connor, Gryff rose and raised his glass. "Allow me to make a belated wedding toast."

She saw Cameron was regarding his friends with a look of guarded bemusement. They were, she suspected, too gentlemanly to say something truly evil. But a little barbed teasing was to be expected.

Catching her glance, he responded with a little shrug. "Ah, well," he whispered, just loud enough for her to hear, "if you wield a verbal sword, you must expect that once in a while the blade will swing around and stick you in the arse."

"Quiet," chided Connor.

"My apologies," murmured Cameron. "Do go on."

"To friends. To family," called Gryff.

Glasses clinked.

"To Hellhounds..." There was a pause as he inclined a courtly bow to Sophie. "And, most especially, to the lovely ladies who have brought out their better nature."

Georgiana let out a fluttery sigh as Hermione dabbed a handkerchief to her eyes.

"I confess I never thought to see the elusive Cameron Daggett tamed by love," continued Gryff. "Of the three of us, he is perhaps, the most hardbitten cynic. But luckily for him, an intrepid young lady was more than a match for his snaps and snarls."

"She is, without doubt, brave and resourceful," murmured Connor. "But there is a slight question as to her judgment in men."

"Ha, ha, ha," said Cameron. "I shall reserve my retorts until the next time I meet with Lady K."

Gryff quieted the laughter with a *tap, tap* to his glass. "I trust that our friend knows that he is a very lucky dog. But all jesting aside, let us raise a heartfelt toast—To Sophie! To Cameron!"

Sophie smiled, watching the candlelight dance in her husband's eyes. *No more shadows, no more darkness.*

Rising, she lifted her own goblet of sparkling wine.

"And to Love. That wondrous, magical force which binds us all—husbands and wives, families and friends—together."

"To love," echoed Georgiana, who came over to enfold her in a sisterly hug. "Didn't I tell you that Cam would turn out to be a titled nabob and carry you away?" she added in a whisper quivering with mirth. "But where is he hiding the white tiger?"

There was no white tiger, no exotic elephant, no castle made of rubies and emeralds.

There was just Cameron. Dangerous, dashing Cameron... which was all that her heart had ever desired.

Alexa Hendrie is happiest in the quiet of the country. But when her brother's recklessness forces her to London, a chance encounter with the *ton*'s most wicked rake—and his searing kiss—awaken a longing for adventure...

Please turn this page for an excerpt from

Too Wicked to Wed.

Prologue

So *this* is what a brothel looks like. It is not at all what I expected."

"Good Lord in Heaven," muttered Captain Harley Stiles as he blotted the sheen of sweat from his brow. "I would hope that you haven't given the matter a great deal of thought."

"Not a great deal," replied Lady Alexa Hendrie. She turned for a closer look at the colored etching hung above the curio cabinet. "But one can't help being mildly curious, seeing as you gentlemen take great delight in discussing such places among yourselves."

Her brother's friend quickly edged himself between her and the offending print. "How the devil do *you* know *that*?" he demanded.

Despite the gravity of their mission, Alexa felt her mouth twitch in momentary amusement. "I take it you don't have any sisters, Captain Stiles. Otherwise you would not be asking such a naive question."

"No, by the grace of God, I do not." Though a decorated veteran of the Peninsular Wars, he was still looking a little shell-shocked over the fact that she had outmaneuvered his objections to her accompanying him into the stews of Southwark. "Otherwise, I might have known better than to offer my help to Sebastian, no matter how dire the threat to his family."

Alexa bit her lip...

"I, too, am curious." A deep growl, dark and smoky as the dimly lit corridor, broke the awkward silence. "Just what *did* you expect?"

She spun around. Within an instant of entering The Wolf's Lair, she and Stiles had been sequestered in a small side parlor to await an answer to the captain's whispered message. The door had now reopened, and though shadows obscured the figure who was leaning against its molding, the flickering wall sconce illuminated the highlights in his carelessly curling hair.

Steel on steel.

Alexa froze as a prickling, sharp as daggerpoints, danced down her spine. "Oh, something a bit less...subtle," she replied, somehow mustering a show of outward composure. She would not—could not—allow herself to be intimidated. After taking a moment to study the muted colors and rather tasteful furnishings of the room, she returned her gaze to the lewd etching on the wall. "By the by, is this a Frangelli?"

"Yes." Straightening from his slouch, the man slowly sauntered into the room. "Do you find his style to your liking?"

She leaned in closer. "His technique is flawless." After regarding the graphic twining of naked bodies and oversized erections for another few heartbeats, she lifted her chin. "But as for the subject matter, it's a trifle repetitive, don't you think?"

A low bark of laughter sounded, and then tightened to a gruff snarl as the man turned to her companion. "Are your brains in your bum, Stiles? What the devil do you mean by bringing a respectable young lady here? Your message mentioned Becton, not—"

"It's not the captain's fault. I gave him no choice," she interrupted. "I am Alexa Hendrie, Lord Becton's sister. And you are?"

"This isn't a damn dowager's drawing room, Lady Alexa Hendrie. We don't observe the formalities of polite introductions here." The sardonic sneer grew more pronounced. "Most of our patrons would rather remain anonymous. But if you wish a name, I am called the Irish Wolfhound."

"Ah." Alexa refused to be cowed by his deliberate rudeness. "And this is your Lair?"

"You could say that."

"Excellent. Then I imagine you can tell me straight off whether Sebastian is here. It is very important that I find him."

"I can." His lip curled up to bare a flash of teeth. "But whether I will is quite another matter. The place would not remain in business very long were I to freely dispense such information to every outraged wife or sister who happens to barge through the door."

"Is it profitable?" she asked after a fraction of a pause.

"The business?" The question seemed to take him aback, but only for an instant. "I manage to...make ends meet. So to speak."

"Now see here, Wolf—" sputtered Stiles.

"How very clever of you," went on Alexa, ignoring her companion's effort to cut off any more risqué innuendoes. Smiling sweetly, she shot a long, lingering glance at the Wolfhound's gray-flecked hair. "I do hope the effort isn't too taxing on your stamina."

"I assure you," he replied softly, "I am quite up to the task."

"Bloody hell." Stiles added another oath through his gritted teeth. "Need I remind you that the lady is a gently bred female?"

The quicksilver eyes swung around and fixed him with an unblinking stare. "Need I remind you that *I* am not the arse who brought her here?"

"Would that I could forget this whole cursed nightmare of an evening." The captain grimaced. "Trust me, neither of us would be trespassing on your hospitality if it were not a matter of the utmost urgency to find Becton—"

"Our younger brother is in grave danger," interrupted Alexa. "I *must* find Sebastian."

"We have reason to think he might be coming to see you," continued Stiles. "Is he here?"

The Wolfhound merely shrugged.

Alexa refused to accept the beastly man's silence. Not with her younger brother's life hanging in the balance. "You heard what the Wolfhound said, Captain Stiles. He is running a business and doesn't give away his precious information for free."

Sensing that neither tears nor appeals to his better nature—if he had one—would have any effect, she took pains to match his sarcasm. "So, how much will the information cost me?" she went on. "And be forewarned that I don't have much blunt, so don't bother trying to claw an exorbitant sum out of me."

"I am willing to negotiate the price." Despite the drawl, a tiny tic of his jaw marred his mask of jaded cynicism. "Kindly step outside, Stiles, so that the lady and I may have some privacy in which to strike a deal."

"I'm not sure, er, that is..."

"What do you think? That I intend to toss up her skirts and feast on her virginity?" The Wolfhound looked back at her with a sardonic smile. "You are, I presume, a virgin?"

"Presume whatever you wish," she replied evenly. "I don't give a damn what some flea-bitten cur chooses to think, as long as I get the information I need."

"Ye gods, Lady Alexa, bite your tongue," warned Stiles in a low whisper. "You are not dealing with some lapdog. It's dangerous to goad the Irish Wolfhound into baring his fangs."

Dangerous. Another touch of ice-cold steel tickled against her flesh. Or was it fire? Something about the lean, lithe Wolfhound had her feeling both hot and cold.

Stiles tried to take her arm, but she slipped out of reach.

"I really must insist—" began the captain.

"Out, Stiles," ordered the Wolfhound as he moved a step closer to her.

Alexa stood firm in the face of his approach. Oh, yes, beneath the finely tailored evening clothes was a dangerous predator, all sleek muscle and coiled power. And ready to pounce. But she was not afraid.

"You may do as he says, Captain. I am quite capable of fending for myself."

Stiles hesitated, and then reluctantly turned for the hallway. "Very well. But I will be right outside, in case you need me," he muttered. "You have five minutes. Then, come hell or high water, we are leaving."

"Do you always ignore sensible advice, Lady Alexa?" asked the Wolfhound, once the latch had clicked shut.

"I often ignore what *men* consider to be sensible advice." The gray-flecked hair was deceiving, she decided. Up close, it was plain that the Wolfhound was a man not much above thirty. "There is a difference between the two, though someone as arrogant as you would undoubtedly fail to recognize it."

"I may be arrogant but I'm not a naive little fool," he retorted with a menacing snarl. "At the risk of further offending your maidenly sensibilities, allow me to point out that when trying to strike a bargain with someone, it is not overly wise to begin by hurling insults at his head."

Alexa felt a flush of heat creep across her cheekbones. "Actually, I am well aware of that. Just as I am well aware that any attempt at negotiations with you is probably a waste of breath. It is quite clear you have a low opinion of females and aren't going to consider my request seriously."

Beneath his obvious irritation, Alexa detected a glimmer of curiosity. "Then why did you agree to see me alone?" he asked.

"To show you not everyone turns tail and runs whenever you flash your fangs." She squared her shoulders. "By the by, why is everyone so afraid of your bark?"

"Because I am reputed to be a vicious, unpredictable beast," he replied. "You see, I tend to bite when I get annoyed. And my teeth are sharper than most."

Lamplight played over the erotic etching, its flickering gleam mirroring the devilish spark in his quicksilver eyes. It seemed to tease her. *Taunt her.*

Alexa wasn't about to back away from the challenge. "Do you chew up the unfortunate young women who work here, then spit them out when they are no longer of any use to you?"

For an instant, it appeared she had gone a step too far in baiting him. His jaw tightened and as the Wolfhound leaned forward, anger bristled from every pore of his long, lean face.

But just as quickly, he seemed to get a leash on his emotions and replied with a cynical sneer. "You know nothing of real life, so do not presume to think you understand what goes on under my roof," he snapped.

"Perhaps you would care to explain it to me."

The Wolfhound gave a harsh laugh. "Nosy little kitten, aren't you? Seb ought to lock you in your room, before you stray into real trouble."

Alexa fisted her hands and set them on her hips. "Ha! Let him try."

"You have spirit, I'll grant you that." He paused for a moment. "Still interested in making a deal?"

"What is your price?"

"A kiss."

Her face must have betrayed her surprise, for he flashed a rakish smile. "Haven't you ever been kissed before?"

She sucked in a sharp breath. "O-of course I have."

"Oh, I think not," drawled the Wolfhound. "I'd be willing to wager a fortune that no man has ever slid his tongue deep into your mouth and made you moan with pleasure."

"Why, you impudent whelp—"

Her words were cut off by the ruthless press of his mouth. He tasted of smoke and spirits—and a raw, randy need that singed her to her very core. She swayed and suddenly the Wolfhound swept her into his arms. With several swift strides, he crossed the carpet and pinned her up against the wall, setting off a wicked whisper of crushed silk and flame-kissed flesh.

Alexa meant to cry out, but as he urged her lips apart and delved inside her, outrage gave way to a strange, shivering heat. Her protest melted, turning to naught but a whispered sigh. As did her body. Against all reason, it yielded to his touch, molding to every contour of his muscled frame. Broad shoulders, lean waist, corded thighs—Alexa was acutely aware of his overpowering masculinity. The scent of brandy and bay rum filled her lungs, and the rasp of his stubbled jaw was like a lick of fire against her cheek.

She knew that she should push him away. Bite, scratch, scream for help.

And yet. And yet...

And yet, as his hands moved boldly over her bodice and cupped her breasts, she could not resist threading her fingers through his silky gray-threaded hair. Like the rest of him, the sensation was sinfully sensuous.

A moment later—or was it far, far longer?—the Wolfhound finally ceased his shameless embrace and leaned back.

"A man could do far worse on the Marriage Mart than to choose you," he said softly. "For at least he will likely not be bored in bed. Indeed, I might even be tempted to swive you myself, if innocence was at all to my taste."

The crude comment finally roused Alexa from the seductive spell that had held her in thrall. Gasping through kiss-swollen lips, she jerked free of his hold and all of her wordless, nameless, girlish longings took force in a lashing slap.

It connected with a resounding crack.

His head snapped back, the angry red imprint of her palm quickly darkening his cheek.

"*That* was for such an unspeakably rude insult." She raised her hand again. "And *this*, you arrogant hellhound, is for—"

He caught her wrist. "Is for what? The fact that for the first—and likely only—time in your life, you have tasted a bit of real passion?"

She went very still. "Do you really take pleasure in causing pain?"

The Wolfhound allowed her hand to fall away, then turned from the light, his austere profile unreadable in the flicker of the oil lamps. "Most people think so," he said evenly as he moved noiselessly to the sideboard.

"I—I don't understand," she began.

"Don't bother trying," he snapped. "All that should matter to you is the fact that I am a man of my word. You paid your forfeit, so in answer to your other question, your brother is not at present in The Wolf's Lair. And if he were, it would not be for the usual reasons that gentlemen come here." Glass clinked against glass. "Like you, he is seeking information and I've heard word that he thinks I may be able to help him. Should he come by tonight, I will inform him of your quest, and how desperate you are to find him."

Alexa turned for the door, yet hesitated, awkward, unsure.

Taking up one of the bottles, the Wolfhound poured himself some brandy and tossed it back in one gulp.

"Now get out of here, before one of my patrons recognizes you. Trust me, the tabbies of this Town are quick to pounce on any transgression. And their claws are far sharper than mine."

"Th-thank you," she said, hoping to show that her pride, if not her dignity, was still intact. "For showing a shred of decency in honoring our bargain."

"Don't wager on it happening again."

Alexa stiffened her spine. "I am not afraid to take a gamble when the stakes are high." She could not resist a parting shot. "And I'll have you know, I am *very* good at cards."

"Here at The Wolf's Lair, we play a far different game than drawing room whist. You have tempted the odds once—I would advise you not to do it again."

"How very kind of you to offer more counsel."

The Wolfhound's laugh was a brandy-roughened growl. "You mistake my sentiments, Lady Alexa. I am not being kind. I am simply trying to stack the deck in my favor. If I am lucky, the cards will fall in a way to ensure that our paths never cross again."

THE DISH

Where authors give you the inside scoop!

From the desk of Kate Brady

Dear Reader,

People always ask: "Where do you get your ideas for books?" Usually I don't have a clue. But in the case of WHERE ANGELS REST, I actually recall the two seedlings of ideas that ultimately grew into this story. The first was a trailer on TV for an upcoming talk show. The interview was to be with a mother who had chased her child's rapist from state to state for years, basically raising hell wherever he tried to surface.

I never saw the show, but I remember thinking, *That would make a great heroine:* a woman who has dedicated her life to exposing someone she knows is dangerous.

Dr. Erin Sims was born.

The second idea evolved more gradually, but I can still name it: It's the town where I grew up. You see, I'm from Hopewell, Ohio. Well, not really, because there is no "Hopewell" in Ohio—at least not one I could find on a map. But I grew up in *a* Hopewell. Towns like my fictitious Hopewell are scattered all over the Midwest and, for that matter, the whole country. They're chock-full of sleepy charm, and they provide the perfect haven for someone battered and beaten by the evils of the larger world.

Sheriff Nick Mann was born.

When the two ideas merged—a man protecting the

sanctity of a town that appears peaceful, and a woman who knows that appearances can be deceiving—I knew I had the makings for a story.

In WHERE ANGELS REST, Erin Sims takes her hunt for a demented serial killer to a quaint town that couldn't possibly harbor such evil. There she unearths secrets Nick Mann refuses to believe—after he's spent years working to make Hopewell his refuge from a tortured past and a safe haven for his daughter's future. Eventually he can't deny the truth, no more than he can deny that the fire in Erin Sims has reignited not only his long-buried passion for police work but also his long-denied desire for love.

I hope you'll enjoy the ride as Erin and Nick set out to unravel a demented villain's compulsion to silence the angels who are privy to horrific, long-hidden truths. And while you're at it, catch a glimpse of my next hero, Nick's brother, who will hopefully whet your appetite for the second book in the series, coming soon!

Happy Reading!

Kate Brady

www.katebrady.net

♥ ♥ ♥ ♥ ♥ ♥ ♥ ♥ ♥ ♥ ♥ ♥ ♥ ♥ ♥

From the desk of Laurel McKee

Dear Reader,

For as long as I can remember I've been a "theater geek"!
My parents took me to see a production of *A Midsummer
Night's Dream* when I was about six, and I loved everything about it—the costumes, the music, the way it felt
like an escape from the real world into Shakespeare's
fairy-tale woods. I decided right then that I wanted to
be an actress. I put on productions at home (recruiting
my little brother and our family dog to be the other per-
formers) and made my parents buy tickets. (Until I got in
trouble for using my mom's antique lace tablecloth for a
costume.)

Then I got older, did some community theater, and
found out I was lacking one essential element for being
an actress—talent! But I've never lost my love of going
to the theater. There is just something about settling into
one of those velvet seats, reading the glossy program,
waiting for the curtain to go up and a whole new world to
be revealed. I was so happy to "meet" the St. Claire family
and have the chance to live in their world for a while, to
vicariously be part of the theater all over again.

The Victorian age was a great era for the theater. The
enthusiastic patronage of Queen Victoria meant that the
theater was becoming more respectable, and actors and
actresses were more accepted in society. People like Ellen
Terry and Henry Irving at the Lyceum Theater were
celebrities and artists, and a new style of theatergoing

was taking hold. The audience actually sat and watched the play in silence instead of having supper and gossiping with their friends! Our modern idea of theater was born in this time period.

I loved seeing my own St. Claire family in the very thick of this exciting period, on the cusp between scandal and respectability! But with them, I think they will tend more toward the scandal side of things...

I'm thrilled with how TWO SINFUL SECRETS turned out, and hope that you all enjoy it!

Happy Reading!

Laurel Mckee

www.LaurelMckee.net
Facebook.com
Twitter, @AmandaLaurel1

♥ ♥ ♥ ♥ ♥ ♥ ♥ ♥ ♥ ♥ ♥ ♥ ♥ ♥ ♥ ♥

From the desk of Cara Elliott

Dear Reader,

For those of you who have been asking me about the maddeningly mysterious Cameron Daggett, well, the wait is over! Connor and Gryff—those two other devilishly dashing Lords of Midnight—have been tamed by love, and now, in TOO DANGEROUS TO DESIRE, it's Cameron's turn to meet his match. But trust me, it wasn't easy to find a way to unlock his heart.

The most cynical of the three friends, he had good reason to keep his feelings well guarded, for he had been hurt in the past. Luckily I knew just the right lady to turn the key. (Be advised that opening locks is not as easy as it might seem. Sometimes it takes some very deft and clever manipulations to release all the little levers—as several scenes in the book will show!) But of course, as this is a romance, Cameron finds his happily-ever-after with Sophie Lawrance.

I, however, must confess to shedding a few tears on having my Lords of Midnight trilogy come to an end. All of the characters have become such dear friends, so it's hard not to feel very sad as they move away from the cozy little neighborhood of my desk to live in far-flung places all around the world. I'll miss their wonderful company—we had coffee together most every day for so long! However, it's time to let them go off and have their own future adventures, so I'm looking forward to making new friends who will share my morning jolts of caffeine (along with those afternoon nibbles of chocolate).

And speaking of new friends, I've already met a delightfully unconventional trio of sisters with a passion for writing. Olivia, the eldest, pens fiery political essays; Anna, middle sister, writes racy romance novels; and Caro, who is not quite out of the schoolroom, is a budding poet. Of course, proper young Regency ladies of the *ton*—especially ones who have very small dowries—are not encouraged to have an interest in intellectual pursuits. Indeed, the only thing they are encouraged to pursue is an eligible bachelor. Preferably one with both a title and a fortune. So the headstrong, opinionated Sloane sisters must keep their passions a secret.

Ah, but we all know that secret passions are wont to lead a lady into trouble…

Alas, I can already report that Olivia has set off sparks with the Earl of Wrexham, a paragon of propriety, who—

Oh, but that would be spoiling all the fun! I'll let you read all about it for yourself. All I'll say is that I'm so excited about starting my new series! Please be sure to check out my website www.caraelliott.com for more updates on the Hellions of Half Moon Street!

Cara Elliott

Find out more about Forever Romance!

Visit us at
www.hachettebookgroup.com/publishing_forever.aspx

Find us on Facebook
http://www.facebook.com/ForeverRomance

Follow us on Twitter
http://twitter.com/ForeverRomance

NEW AND UPCOMING TITLES

Each month we feature our new titles
and reader favorites.

CONTESTS AND GIVEAWAYS

We give away galleys, autographed copies,
and all kinds of exclusive items.

AUTHOR INFO

You'll find bios, articles, and links to personal websites
for all your favorite authors—and so much more.

GET SOCIAL

Connect with your favorite authors, editors, and
other Forever fans, and share what's important to you.

THE BUZZ

Sign up for our monthly romance newsletter,
and be the first to read all about it.

VISIT US ONLINE AT

WWW.HACHETTEBOOKGROUP.COM

FEATURES:

OPENBOOK BROWSE AND SEARCH EXCERPTS

•

AUDIOBOOK EXCERPTS AND PODCASTS

•

AUTHOR ARTICLES AND INTERVIEWS

•

BESTSELLER AND PUBLISHING GROUP NEWS

•

SIGN UP FOR E-NEWSLETTERS

•

AUTHOR APPEARANCES AND TOUR INFORMATION

•

SOCIAL MEDIA FEEDS AND WIDGETS

•

DOWNLOAD FREE APPS

BOOKMARK HACHETTE BOOK GROUP
@ WWW.HACHETTEBOOKGROUP.COM